UNDER THE SURFACE

Under the Surface

Copyright ©2023 Madison Stafford

First Edition
Printed in the United States of America

979-8-218-29680-3 – Paperback
979-8-218-29681-0 – Ebook Epub

Dedication

For my husband and all the friends and teachers who supported me along the way. For all the kids who still believe in mermaids.

PART ONE

"Whoever wishes to keep a secret must hide the fact that he possesses one."

~ Johann Wolfgang von Goethe

MORRIS

1994

My shoes squeaked on the bloody floor. The monster in front of me cowered, holding her hands against her bleeding abdomen.

"Please, don't do this," she begged.

"You lied to me," I seethed.

"I had to. Please. We can still get past this." Wailing erupted from another room. My blood ran cold. A ghost of a smile passed over the creature's face.

"He's yours. His name is Oliver," she whispered. I shook my head, my pistol shaking in my grip.

"That *thing* isn't mine!" I spat. I stomped past her, ignoring her pleas, and shoved my way into the nursery. The infant lay in an Ikea crib, waving his chubby fists in the air. Blue swirls stained his delicate skin.

"Please, Morris, don't!" the monster screamed from the other room. "Don't hurt him, he hasn't done anything! He's *yours!*" The baby screeched more at the sound of his mother's voice. I backed away from the crib, shaking.

That thing isn't mine. It's one of them. And it needs to be stopped before it hurts someone. I raised the gun. The monster's shrieks matched the sound of the shot.

She pawed at my ankles as I walked back out of the room. One more bullet silenced her. I washed my hands in the sink and wiped my gun off my shirt.

It's over. My father was right.

AMY

2014

"Happy Birthday dear Amyyyyy!" I grinned and blew out the birthday candles, sending smoke flying across the room. The small group surrounding the table cheered and scrambled for cake as my mom cut pieces. We rushed back outside to eat on the dock. A seagull snapped at my best friend's plate, and she squealed, shying away from it.

"Get back, scoundrel!" I shouted, kicking the gull. It squawked in indignation but retreated with his friends, still eying us with its beady black eyes.

"Thanks!" Cindy said. We walked arm in arm with the other kids, who had already claimed a place on the old dock and were scarfing down their cake. Little toes hung off the edge, straining for the sea. Saltwater dripped down from my hair, making my cake salty, but I didn't mind. I loved the ocean.

"This is really good cake," Markus said through a mouthful of icing.

"Thanks! My mom made it herself!" I said. Across the dock, a white boy with dark brown hair scoffed.

"No, she didn't. I saw the Walmart box on the counter." I narrowed my eyes at him.

"Did too," I shot back. He smirked.

"Did *not!*" Cindy rolled her eyes.

"Stop trying to ruin the party, Tom," she complained. I took another bite, resisting the urge to walk over and kick him like I had the seagull. I hadn't wanted to invite him to my party, but my mom insisted. She said something about how *he's a sweet boy, he just needs a good friend like you to show him how to be sweet.* As if I cared. It's not like Tom had ever invited me to one of *his* birthday parties.

Tom stuck his tongue out at Cindy, which I could not tolerate with Cindy being my best friend. I balled up my plate and chucked it at his stupid face, bursting into laughter as it hit the target. Tom swatted it into the water and jumped to his feet, hands balled into fists. Markus tugged on his swim trunks.

"Dude, you can't just throw trash into the ocean like that!" he protested.

"I'm about to throw more trash into the ocean!" he shouted. I stood up and brushed the crumbs off my bathing suit.

"Oh yeah? Not if I throw it in first!" Cindy and Markus exchanged concerned glances, but neither moved to stop us.

"I'll make you a bet!" Tom said. He pointed out to sea, to a cluster of big black rocks that sprung up from the waves as if the beach had fingers. "Whoever gets to that rock first wins, and the other person has to go home!"

"Deal!" We shook on it. Cindy raised her hand like we were in school.

"Amy," she whispered. "You're not allowed to swim past the dock. You got in trouble for that yesterday, remember?" I ignored her. That rule was as dumb as Tom Falcon was. I was a plenty good enough swimmer to make it to the boulders and back. I had never seen a shark out there - and besides - sharks were more likely to hang around docks anyway. If anything - it was safer out there in the deep. I was ten years old for crying out loud - it was time my parents started trusting me.

"On my mark . . . Ready, set, go!" I pushed Tom backward as I dove off the dock, paddling frantically towards the boulders. I heard him splash down behind me, shouting. I tuned him out and focused on my strokes, closing my eyes against the sting of the salt.

It was farther out than I had ever gone before. I could feel my arms and legs getting rubbery, but I forced myself to continue. There was no way Tom was beating me.

I grappled for a handhold on the boulders and pulled myself up to the top. I squinted back out to the dock to see Cindy and Markus waving and jumping. A soggy Tom pulled himself back up on the beach, apparently having given up.

"I win, I win!" I chanted, unsure if they could hear me. The small group looked like ants in the distance. "Go home, Tom!" I turned back the other way and gazed out at the ocean. More black outcroppings dotted the water. *One day I'm going to explore all those caves*, I thought.

I sat down on the rocks and looked down, trying to catch my breath. There was an opening in the cave that looked like a skylight. The sunlight filtered bleakly into the hole, trying to illuminate the inside. I debated briefly before hanging over the edge and dropping into the darkness. My parents were always nagging me to be a little less curious, but right now, they weren't here to stop me. I wanted to see what was down there.

It was a farther fall than I had anticipated. I landed hard on the rocks, yelping as they pierced my bare feet. I winced in pain, looking for damage. Blood oozed from several cuts, and I had lost a decent amount of skin. *Oh well*, I thought. I squinted and looked around the cave. Various pieces of trash had washed inside somehow. Twisted pieces of strange metal traps dotted the rocks, rusting in the water.

I got to my feet, wincing as the salty rocks burned my cuts. Using the wall to help me balance, I hobbled up to one that looked like an ordinary box. Wondering what could be inside, I nudged it with my toe, and it suddenly flipped inside out, clamping down on my foot like a shark. I shrieked and sat down hard, eying my foot in the trap. I frantically grabbed it and fiddled with it, trying to get it loose. I doubted I could swim back, let alone climb out of the cave with a metal box stuck on my foot.

After a few minutes of flinging my foot against the rocks, it popped back open. I winced as I looked at my ankle, now punctured by angry little teeth marks. Blood trickled down into the sand. *My parents are going to kill me,* I thought. *I'm going to have to wear shoes with socks for forever until this heals up.*

I stood up, testing my weight. It either wasn't as bad as it looked, or I was still in shock. That was a word my parents - both police officers - used a lot. They said people who got shot or really injured on the job usually went into shock - where they didn't feel pain until later.

I decided to take advantage of not feeling any pain while I still had it, and crawled out of the cave, earning more scrapes and cuts as I clamored out. I dove back into the water and started paddling back to shore, taking my time. I was definitely not in a hurry for the lecture in my future if my parents spied the wounds. *How many times have we told you not to swim past the docks? You are so careless! You're going to get yourself hurt one day.*

The more I swam, the heavier my foot got. I slowed down and paused to gasp for breath more and more. My legs felt like concrete. I slipped beneath the water and barely had the strength to pull myself back up. The ocean felt like a vacuum sucking me back down. I waved my arms above my head, my vision beginning to spin. If I had the energy, I would've yelled at the sea for dragging me down. Swimming was my thing; didn't the ocean know that?

"Help!" I shouted feebly, before slipping down again. I sank listlessly through the water, my ankle tingling and getting heavier. Skinny arms wrapped themselves around me and yanked me up to the surface. I squinted at the bright light and coughed, trying to suck oxygen into my lungs.

The arms dragged me onto the beach, where my parents threw their arms around me, crying. Tom stood above me, gasping for breath. *It must've been him that swam out to get me*, I thought hazily. *Gross.*

My other classmates watched on in horror as my parents hovered over me.

"Amy, are you okay? Can you breathe?" my mom demanded. I nodded as I coughed up water, wobbling as I tried to stand.

"My god, it looks like something bit her," my dad muttered.

"We need to get her to a hospital," my mom insisted. Tom's dad marched over from their trawler docked a few rows over.

"What's going on here? I saw her go into that cave," he said.

"Just a stupid game the kids were playing. I think a shark nibbled her ankle," my dad said, hoisting me into his arms. Tom's dad glared down at him.

"I told you to stay away from those rocks," he seethed, grabbing Tom by his hair and yanking him back towards the boat. I was too woozy to protest that Tom hadn't even made it out there. And why was everyone talking about a shark? I wasn't attacked by a shark.

I tried to speak but my tongue felt just as heavy as my leg. I was carried to the car, and my dad sped to the hospital. My mom held me in the backseat, muttering something about shock as she tied a bandage around my ankle.

A weird nurse took care of me at the hospital. She smelled funny - like salt - but I was still too out of it to comment. She smiled and assured my parents she would take good care of me before getting the doctor.

The doctor looked familiar. He had the same dark skin and locs Markus had. I vaguely remembered Markus bragging that his dad was a doctor. The nurse whispered something in his ear, and his eyes went wide. He nodded stiffly as he examined my foot.

"No way to reverse it?" he asked. The nurse shook her head.

"It's too late."

"Stupid kid."

"I'm not stupid . . ." I slurred. They both ignored me as they gave me a shot and wrapped my ankle up.

"Why aren't you putting stitches in?" I asked.

"Stitches can't help you anymore, kid. Just rest."

Usually, when my parents told me to rest, they said it like they were worried about me. He said it like he just wanted to get rid of me. He injected something else into my IV bag, and my vision went dark.

. . .

The lights were blinding when I woke up. Everything around me felt too sharp and real. The machines around me seemed to beep as loud as they could. I groaned, and the weird nurse immediately walked in. I shielded my eyes but didn't have a chance to say anything before she turned the lights off. I could instantly see better and sighed in relief, although everything else still felt too much.

"Did you guys cut off my foot?" I asked groggily. Even as I asked the question, I knew it wasn't true. My legs - both of them now - felt like cinder blocks. As I tried to move, the cinder blocks sparked in pain, and I winced.

"Don't move yet, baby. Do you know what happened to you?"

"I got my foot stuck in some stupid trap out by the rocks," I said. She shook her head.

"That's a no. How are you feeling?" I shifted my body around, trying not to move my legs.

"Heavy."

"The doctor will be in to talk to you in a minute. Just relax. You'll feel better soon." Even though her voice sounded nice, I had a gut feeling she was angry.

"Why are you mad at me?" I asked. She ignored me.

. . .

Markus' dad came in about an hour later, looking very stressed. And angry. *Why are they so mad?* I thought. *Is it because my parents yelled at them? Where are my parents? Don't they want to visit me?*

He dragged up a chair and sat down heavily, resting his head in his hands.

"What do I smell like?" he asked. I wrinkled my nose.

"That's a weird question."

"Just answer it." I sniffed the air, surprised at how many things I picked up.

"You smell like rubbing alcohol. And bleach. And . . . salt. Just like the nurse. Plus – you're pissed." I immediately clamped my hand over my mouth. My parents would kill me if they heard me say that out loud – even though I heard them saying way worse things. He nodded, ignoring my swear.

"Amy . . . do you believe in mermaids?" I laughed out loud.

"Um, no? Mermaids aren't real. I've never seen one and I swim a lot." He sighed.

"Well, um . . . to break it to you quickly. They are real. I am one of them. And so are you." I blinked, confused. He rambled on. "I know you must be confused, but I am telling the truth. You should be able to tell if I'm lying or not." I crossed my arms.

"If you're a mermaid, then prove it!" I challenged. Without a word, blue vine-like markings spread out across the doctor's face. They framed his cheeks and curled around his eyes, slightly shimmery even in the low light. I shrugged.

"Since when do mermaids have stripes?" He fished his phone out of his pocket and held the camera up to me.

"You have them too." I gasped as I looked at my face. I too had blue markings, but mine looked nothing like his. They only covered the left side of my face, and they weren't curly. They looked spiky like someone had let a two-year-old scribble with a Sharpie. Or like a cat had swiped their paws across my face.

I reached up and touched them. They blended right into my skin; I couldn't even feel them. *Okay, these look cool, I guess*, I thought.

"They go down your whole body." I looked at my arm to see that the markings were there as well.

"Don't worry, you can make them go away," he said, making his vanish without a trace. I held my arms to my chest.

"How do blue marks on my face make me a mermaid exactly?" He stood up.

"Let me show you." He helped me to my feet, and I shuffled towards the bathroom. My legs wobbled beneath me, and I had to cling to the doctor's arm to stay upright.

Someone had placed a kiddie pool full of water in the bathroom. *This has to be a joke*, I thought. Tom had sworn he'd seen mermaids his entire life – but I had never seen them. Why would mermaids have stripes anyway? What on Earth would make me turn into one?

"I want my mom," I said. "Where are my parents?"

"I've told them you're still unconscious and can't receive any visitors. I can't let them see you until you know what's going on." With that, he scooped me up and lowered me into the pool. He clamped his hand over my mouth as I started to scream.

My body felt like it was being torn in two. I watched helplessly as my skin and muscles dissolved in the water before condensing back together. Shiny blue scales grew from my skin. My bones stretched and snapped themselves into new formations. Dr. Mercer slowly removed his hand from my mouth.

"Believe me now?" he asked. I tried moving the new appendage attached to my waist, surprised when it obeyed my command. My tail lifted out of the water and curved above my head.

"Wow," I whispered. Dr. Mercer pulled a little mirror out of his pocket and handed it to me. For the first time, I noticed my hands were webbed. I fumbled the mirror several times before figuring out how to hold it with the tips of my fingers.

I didn't look like Ariel, that was for sure. My entire eyeball was the same blue as my tail. My skin was tinged blue and surprisingly rough – like petting a dolphin or a snake. No scales or clamshells covered my chest. My ears were long with little frills hanging off the end. I grinned as I realized I could move them.

"This is so cool," I said. "Wait, is it going to hurt like that every time I get in the water? Can I still take showers? What about baths?"

"The pain should go away once you get used to phasing. And yes, you can still take showers. You won't phase unless most of your body is covered by water. Baths are more risky."

"This is so cool!" I giggled, curving my tail and running my webbed hands over my skin. "I can't believe mermaids are real! When did this happen to you?"

"We don't call ourselves mermaids. We are merfolk," Dr. Mercer said, crossing his arms. "And I was born this way. My entire family was.

We're Natural merfolk. We call merfolk like you Cursed." I pictured Dr. Mercer wiggling his fingers at me like the witches from Hocus Pocus.

"You put a spell on me?"

"It's not a literal curse. Humans can become merfolk after being exposed to our blood. That trap you got your foot stuck in must have had merfolk blood on it. When it stabbed you, the blood on the trap got into your system."

"Like vampires?" I asked. He blinked.

"Sorry?"

"Like how vampires bite humans to turn them into vampires? Like that? Except with blood?" He scowled.

"Sure. Like vampires."

"Do we have any cool powers?" I asked.

"No. Well, probably not the kind you're thinking about. We don't have magical voices or anything like that, but we do have enhanced senses. You'll be able to see better, hear better, all of that. You'll have much faster reflexes. We are also empaths. We can easily tell what other people are feeling, especially if we touch them." He placed his hand on my arm. "Pay attention. What am I feeling?"

I instinctively smelled the air. Dr. Mercer smelled like sweat and something else more acidic. His feelings flooded into me, and for a moment, I felt like I was inside his brain.

"You're stressed. And worried." He nodded.

"Listen, I know that you think all of this is cool, but there are some things you have to promise me." He narrowed his eyes.

"You can never tell anyone what you are. Ever. Especially not that you used to be a human. Especially not how this happened to you. Understand?" I crossed my arms.

"Why?"

"Humans are dangerous. They like to put sea creatures in aquariums to go look at whenever they want. They dump trash in our oceans. If they ever found out we existed, they would dissect us, they would put us in aquariums, they would *use* us."

I thought of my parents and friends. Tom would maybe want to stick me in an aquarium, but there was no way my best friend would do anything to hurt me.

"How do you know humans would do that?" I asked. "My parents and friends love me. They wouldn't let anything like that happen." Dr. Mercer's eye twitched.

"You ever heard of Frankenstein? Vampire slayers? What happens when humans find anything out of the ordinary? They either kill it or use it to their advantage." He poked me in the chest. "Believe me. It doesn't matter how much you think your parents or friends care about you. The minute they find out what you've become – everything will change. You must promise not to tell."

I squirmed under his finger. I didn't want to believe him, but he seemed serious. And scared.

"Okay. I won't tell."

"If you break your promise, you not only put yourself in danger. You put my family in danger. Our entire species."

"How many of us are there?" He shrugged.

"Here? A few families – mostly adults and older kids. In general? Maybe a few thousand. But you are the only Cursed."

"Really? The only one?"

"Only one I know of. It's hard to inject merfolk blood into a human on accident." He plucked the mirror from my hand and put it back in his pocket.

"I have other patients to go see. I'm going to keep telling your parents you need privacy to rest until you get your new body under control. You're going to sleep in here tonight. You need to lock the door behind me so no one comes in here on accident. When I come back, I'll knock three times so you know it's me."

"Why do I have to sleep here?" I complained. The new tail was cool, but I doubted it would be super comfortable sleeping in a hard plastic kiddie pool.

"Merfolk must swim at least a few hours a day to stay hydrated. Most go swim in the ocean at night so they can sleep and still go about their days on land like normal." He left, and I almost fell out of the pool trying to reach the lock on the door.

I curled up in a circle, toying with my tail fins with my webbed fingers, my mind spinning. I lived close to the ocean, but surely my parents would notice me sneaking out at night to go swim. After I got out of the hospital, they were definitely going to ground me for swimming where I wasn't supposed to be.

Dr. Mercer's words repeated in my head. *Humans are dangerous.* Were they really? I was a human a few hours ago, and I didn't think I was dangerous. I didn't throw trash in the ocean. I wouldn't have kidnapped a mermaid and put them in an aquarium. Would I have? I curled up into a tighter ball.

Cindy's dad owned the aquarium. What would she say if she knew her best friend was a mermaid? Would she tell her dad? Would her dad tell my parents? They were strict, but only because they were police officers. It's not like they would go crazy and make me into a science experiment.

As much as I wanted to believe it, the worry in Dr. Mercer's eyes was enough to make me second-guess myself. I didn't want to put anyone else in danger.

As I tried to sleep, a million other questions plagued my head. How long would it take me to get used to phasing back and forth? If mermaids couldn't sing – why did all the legends say we could? How on Earth did mermaids give birth?

After hours of sleep evaded me, I decided to get a head start on my first question. I took a deep breath and ungracefully pulled my body out of the pool, landing in an awkward heap on the cold tile. I grit my teeth, bracing myself through the pain I knew was coming.

Turning back hurt almost as much as growing my tail. I bit down hard on my hand to muffle my screams and lay panting on the floor after it was over. Thankfully, my clothes had returned. The only thing that remained was my markings.

I grabbed the edge of the sink and pulled myself up. I leaned against the porcelain until my legs stopped shaking. I walked several laps until I felt confident and sat on the toilet to give myself a break. As I examined my legs, I noticed the marks from my foot getting stuck in the trap were mostly gone. *Do mermaids heal faster than humans?* I wondered. I added my question to my list as I looked at myself in the mirror.

Dr. Mercer said I could hide my markings if I wanted to. I narrowed my eyes at the girl in the mirror and concentrated. *Go away. Hide. Make me look normal.* To my surprise, they vanished right away. I felt my face, surprised at how easy it had been.

I got up and braced myself. *I can do this,* I thought. *The sooner I can master changing back and forth, the sooner I can get out of here. I don't want to keep my parents waiting any longer than they have to.*

Dr. Mercer looked surprised to see me sitting on the toilet the next morning, markings hidden. I jumped up to my feet, stumbling only a little bit.

"I figured out how to hide my markings! And I practiced phasing all night. It still hurts, but not nearly as much. I've got a lot more questions, but I'm really hungry. Can I eat something?"

A few moments later, I was sitting back in the hospital bed with an enormous plate of breakfast food in front of me. It wasn't the best food I had ever had – but I was too hungry to care. Dr. Mercer watched me eat with a perplexed look on his face.

"Surprised I got used to it so easily?" I asked, reading his emotions. He scowled.

"Frankly, yes."

"I want to go home as soon as possible. I don't want my parents to be worried about me. But I have more questions." He sighed.

"Ask away."

"Can we heal faster than humans?" I asked, holding up my ankle. He nodded.

"For the most part – yes. You won't get sick very often either." I grinned as I thought of all the caves and places I could go exploring if my body healed from cuts and scrapes before my parents could tell what was going on. Dr. Mercer narrowed his eyes at me.

"*However*, if you were ever to get severely injured – you'll be stuck in whatever body you're injured in. So don't try anything risky." I frowned.

"Fine. How do mermaids have kids?" He pressed his lips in a thin line.

"*Merfolk* have kids just like humans do. But *only* with other merfolk." He ground out the words as if he was afraid I would try to argue with him. In reality, it sounded easier to marry another mermaid – sorry *merfolk* – than a human if I had to keep all these secrets anyway.

"What about the legends? Why do all the legends about us say that we can sing and do all these things if they're not true?"

"Merfolk themselves made up those legends to keep humans away from our ancient homes in the ocean," he said. "Our ancestors believed if humans were afraid of us, they would leave us alone. Those who still dared to get too close were attacked." *Seems paranoid*, I thought.

"Can I go home now?" I asked.

"Maybe." He motioned towards the bathroom. We walked in, and I stepped into the lukewarm water. I winced as I submerged myself but didn't scream. What had previously felt like my skin being ripped apart now felt like my body was woken up after being asleep for too long – tingly and sensitive. Surprise flitted across his face as I popped back above the water, a big smile on my face. I climbed back out of the pool and phased back without incident, bowing on my legs. Dr. Mercer crossed his arms.

"What are the three secrets you must keep?"

"Don't tell anyone you're a mermaid. Sorry – merfolk. Don't tell anyone you used to be human. And don't tell anyone how you turned into merfolk," I said, counting down on my fingers. He nodded.

"Are you sure you're ready for this?" he asked, smelling like doubt. I resisted the urge to roll my eyes. I knew I was little, but I was a strong kid. And I was excited to get out of the hospital and explore the ocean in my new body.

"I'm sure."

. . .

My parents were so relieved to be allowed to visit me. I assured them I was fine and endured their lecture about not swimming where I wasn't supposed to. I had to bite my lip to keep from smiling. Little did they know, I would be sneaking out of the house that very night to go swimming where I wasn't supposed to.

I snuck out around two in the morning. Dr. Mercer had given me directions to a cave where his family normally hung out to sleep in case I wanted to join them.

I had no intention of sleeping. I dove into the water and spun with excitement as I melted into my new body. My tail propelled me so much faster than my old legs. I could stay under as long as I wanted, and the salt no longer stung my eyes. Getting my foot stuck in that trap was the best thing that had ever happened to me.

I looped and twirled in the water, taking my time getting to the caves in the distance. I chased fish and braided strands of kelp. My parents said I had always been athletic - I had tried almost every sport under the sun - but my body felt even more powerful now. If only I could join a swim team.

I paused as a shadow passed over me. I looked up and saw a small boat trailing above. Little feet hung off the side, splashing in the water. I sniffed and grinned to myself. Those were Tom's feet. Looked like I wasn't the only one sneaking out to swim at night. How hilarious would it be if I swam up and grabbed Tom's ankle? His scream could be heard for miles!

One quick prank, and then I'll go to the cave, I thought. I swam upwards and was inches away from his ankle when something else grabbed me. I shrieked, although the water turned my sound into bubbles.

I was dragged down until I was looking down into the glowing eyes of Dr. Mercer. This time, my gut told me he was mad. He dragged me towards a cave and practically threw me onto the rocky ledge once we surfaced.

"What were you thinking?" he shouted. I sprawled uncomfortably as I phased back into my human form.

"Chill out! It was just a joke. I wasn't actually going to show myself to him!" I protested.

"Did you forget everything I told you in the hospital?" he snarled. "How could you be so selfish?" I wanted to cry, but no tears came. My hands started to shake.

"I-I'm sorry, okay? I won't do that again."

"I sure hope you won't! This is why I hate Cursed." I blinked.

"What?"

"You Cursed are always such a liability. You don't truly get what it means to be merfolk because your brains are still just as human on the inside! And your ignorance puts the rest of us in danger!" I backed away, hands shaking even worse.

"I-I'm sorry."

"If you are sorry, then you'll never tell anyone! Humans are dangerous, no matter how much you think you can trust them. Do you understand me?" he yelled. I nodded. He let out a breath and slid back into the water.

"Stay away from my family. If you expose yourself, you're not dragging us down with you." He disappeared under the water, leaving me cold and shivering.

I returned home but no matter how much I snuggled under the covers, I couldn't get warm. I had known in the hospital I had to keep hidden, but now, the true weight of those secrets came crashing down on me. Cindy was my best friend; we told each other everything! How could I lie to her – to my parents – for the rest of my life?

Humans are dangerous.

I shivered. *The doctor is right, I thought. I need to keep this to myself. I can't risk the others getting hurt. It'll be fine. It's not like being merfolk changes my whole life - right?*

I was wrong.

AMY

2020

There are a million different ways to lie about who you really are.

Humans like to think they're so above other animals - but they copy them all the time. Surely I can't be the only one who noticed the similarities between a brightly colored frog pretending he's poisonous and that blonde girl who pretends to be stupid even though she's really smart? Or the camouflaged stick insect and that really quiet girl who ends up becoming a famous pop star?

The most startling thing about morphing into a mythical creature was the sudden emotional clarity. Superheroes all talk about their special abilities - enhanced eyesight, flight, teleportation, whatever, but never anything animalistic like this. Wolves can smell fear, but merpeople can smell everything. Your fear, your lust, your love, your anger, especially your lies.

I wasn't supposed to be curious about who I was. Merfolk weren't supposed to ask questions, just keep secrets, so I never Googled pheromones or how it would be possible for an animal to literally *feel* an emotion coming off another animal. It's not important in the grand scheme of things. Merfolk were all about the *bigger picture* – which didn't care about individual Amy Wilson at all.

So, I picked a course of lying like a good little merfolk and perfected it. No one knew, and no one would dare suspect because I picked the smartest path. Ever heard of tuna? Duh, of course you have. Everyone knows what tuna is. There is nothing special, remarkable, or vaguely interesting about tuna. They're a dime a dozen.

Just like me. Average, unremarkable, *she-would-never-be-one-of-those-things*, Amy Wilson.

And it worked.

Before, I was loud and as my parents would have put it, a little *strong-headed*. Someone who wouldn't get called into the principal's office for drugs but someone who would get called in for finishing a fight. Maybe for starting one.

Now, I was your perfectly average white high school girl. I faded into the background like beige paint. I would never get called to the principal's office, but I would get a few silent lunches for forgetting to bring a binder to class or something innocent like that.

My grades were average enough to keep teachers from contacting home but not good enough that anyone asked me to tutor them. I wore the same leggings and hoodies that every high school girl wore - which as an added bonus - made me look more feminine than I otherwise would.

Merfolk typically looked human enough that no one would ever second guess you were anything different - but guessing gender was a little more complicated. We looked pretty androgynous, especially underwater. I had never gotten a period before, which worried me, but not enough to ask anyone.

Once upon a time, I had tried asking Markus questions about being merfolk. We had been friends before, so I figured we would stay friends after my unfortunate incident. He was the only other merfolk kid I knew, and I was desperate for company.

But his father would have none of it. We pretended to be buddies like normal in front of our human friends, but he sighed like my entire existence was an inconvenience every time I tried to ask him about merfolk stuff. I eventually stopped trying and did my best to figure out my problems on my own.

I had to fake puberty by stuffing bras and asking for period products every so often. I had to pretend to cry at appropriate times because merfolk *never* cried. When I was upset, my hands shook instead, which was admittedly easier to hide.

I had my character crafted to perfection. No one ever suspected a thing. And at night, for a few select hours, I was allowed to be my other self, hidden away from all the other merfolk who wanted nothing to do with a Cursed.

. . .

I met Cindy by our lockers like normal. She stared at a math review sheet, practically sweating as I unloaded my bookbag.

"Dude, chill out. You look like you're about to pass out." She bonked me over my head with the paper.

"Shut up, you're the one who's good at math."

"I'm average at math."

"*Average* is better than below average." I rolled my eyes. A subtle brush of her arm told me exactly what was actually stressing her - the swim meet tonight. The fear of her best friend almost drowning all those years ago stuck with her enough to transform her into the best female swimmer on our high school team. Even though we were barely juniors, scouts already had their eyes on her. She pretended it didn't stress her out, but it did. I patted her arm as the bell rang.

"You'll do fine." We walked into math class to see the student teacher, Mr. Johns, tapping his watch impatiently.

"This test will take you most of the - hey, I'm talking here! This test will take you most of the period, so you need to get started now!" I slid into my seat as he passed out the copies. He sighed as Tom came stumbling through the door.

"This test is more important than your girlfriend," he said. Tom grinned before sliding into his seat.

"Doubt that, boss."

"You can have detention for that." Tom shrugged as Mr. Johns handed me my test. Like the other members of my species, he ignored me completely.

I knew Mr. Johns knew what I was, even though we had never met underwater. Merfolk had a certain salty smell to them, and it was pretty obvious unless you doused yourself with perfume. He had started student teaching at the beginning of the year and made a point to get to know all the other students except for me.

I had no clue why a merfolk would want to be a teacher. It was hard enough dealing with feeling the emotions of the random passersby in the hallway, but teaching a hundred of them every day? No, thank you.

I got a better grade than I normally let myself just to show the stupid merfolk teacher I wasn't a total waste of space. The rest of the day consisted of me convincing Cindy she would do just fine at her swim meet.

I hated her swim meets. Not only was there the irrational fear that some stranger would push me into the pool, but the smell of chlorine was enough to make my nose burn. But I went anyway because I was her best friend, and that's what best friends do.

After my *accident*, I milked my fear of sharks to stay away from the ocean, but I still needed an excuse to avoid swimming pools - so I suddenly developed an allergy to chlorine. Which - technically wasn't a lie.

I sat high up on the bleachers and cheered when appropriate. Below on the first row, her father shouted his encouragement, waving around a tacky foam finger.

Cindy placed first in the 500-meter freestyle, guaranteeing she would make it to district. The small crowd in the bleachers swarmed to congratulate her - which meant I was obligated to join. I cheered along with the rest of them - ignoring the burn from the very wet hug I got.

Her father invited me to tag along to a celebratory dinner that night. He took us to a fancy hibachi restaurant, where he proudly announced he was going to take Cindy on a surprise trip to the mountains that weekend. She grinned and hugged him, which made a repressed part of me a little jealous.

My parents were fine - but not the type for celebratory dinners or surprise trips. Cindy's mom had died in childbirth - which I think traumatized her dad into being the best mom and dad for her. He had never missed a swim meet or award ceremony despite his busy job of running the town aquarium.

I told Cindy to have fun as they dropped me back off at my parent's house by the docks. I yawned, the thought of having to be up in a few hours already making me tired. At least I could sleep in on the weekends.

. . .

Sunday morning, my phone startled me awake before my alarm went off. I haphazardly swiped it, fully intending to decline the call but accidentally hitting the accept button.

"Hello?" I muttered, rubbing the sleep out of my eyes. *If this is a robocall, I swear.*

"Amy? It's me. I need you to come over here, now." I blinked several times, my brain struggling to catch up.

"Is this Cindy's dad?"

"Please, it's urgent. Cindy is back." *Back?* I thought. *What do you mean back?*

"She's back?"

"Please hurry." He hung up, leaving me with no choice but to struggle out of bed and walk over at . . . one-thirty in the morning? At least we were neighbors.

I started walking faster once I saw the flashing lights of the police cars surrounding their house.

I burst in the front door, where at least half a dozen cops turned their steely gazes on me. I waved awkwardly as Cindy's dad strode in, sighing in relief as he saw me.

"Amy! Thank god, I need you to talk to Cindy. She's very frightened. She's been asking for you. She won't talk to anyone else."

"What is going on? I don't understand - I thought you guys were gone on vacation or something?" He shook his head. My heart sank as horrible possibilities flew through my head. Had they gotten in an accident? Did they get mugged?

34

"We were supposed to, but we never left. When I woke up yesterday morning, she was gone without a note or anything. Couldn't get a hold of her. She just showed up here an hour ago, soaking wet and delirious. She's been asking for you."

My blood ran cold as I saw her sitting on the couch, shivering into a pile of towels. Her clothes were still dripping and crusted over with salt. I jogged up and knelt before her, taking her hand in mine. Cindy's wave of fear that washed over me was almost enough to make me drop it, but I made myself hold on. She trained her watery eyes on me, shivering. Her lips were blue.

"Dude, what happened?" I whispered. She eyes her father and the other cops around nervously.

"They won't believe me," she whispered urgently. "But I know what I saw. I knew you would believe me." I nodded. She leaned in close to my ear.

"I snuck out Saturday morning to go swimming before our trip, and this . . . thing." She broke down in another round of sobbing before she continued. "This *thing*. It grabbed me and dragged me under to this cave. It said it was going to drown me. But I escaped. I swam back to shore before it came back to finish me off." She collapsed into my arms. I awkwardly patted her back, my mind racing. *What kind of psycho swims out in the ocean to drown some stranger?* I thought.

"Hey, it's okay. That guy is gone now, you're safe," I crooned. She shook her head.

"It wasn't a guy. It was a mermaid." I stopped patting her back. The world slowed down. I leaned back and looked into her tear-streaked face, desperately searching for a lie or some possible drug-induced hallucination but found nothing. Cindy was telling the truth.

"What did she look like?" I whispered. *Please be crazy, please be crazy.* Maybe she just *thought* she saw a mermaid. Plenty of people have mistaken other things for us before – right?

"It had these weird glowing blue eyes and blue markings all over its body. I couldn't tell if it was supposed to be male or female . . . it just looked weird." Damn it, she was describing the real thing - right down to the androgynous nature.

"So not like the Little Mermaid, huh?" I asked, trying for a joke. She hiccupped as she tried to laugh.

"No. You believe me, right? I know it sounds crazy, but I *know* what I saw." Feeling her panic rising, I knew I had to make a decision. Some psychopath merfolk had decided to drown my best friend for kicks - risking our secret for some twisted fairy-tale fantasy.

I knew no one else would believe her - at least no one worth caring about - but what did I, the best friend say, to make her feel better? I squeezed her hand and offered a sympathetic smile.

"I know something attacked you, and that it was very traumatic and scary. But Cindy . . . mermaids aren't real."

. . .

I was a terrible friend. Once news got out around school about what had happened, the mermaid jokes started flying. People jeered and left pictures of cute clip-art mermaids on Cindy's locker, which she hatefully ripped off. When I relayed her story to her dad and the police, he demanded they drug test her. It came back clean - of course it did. A merfolk had actually attacked her, but I couldn't tell her she wasn't crazy because my secret was more important than her trauma.

The guilt tore at my insides, but I knew what the consequences would be if I had said anything else. The other merfolk would get mad at me even though *I* wasn't the one who attacked her. Why didn't they go track down that merfolk and give *them* a lecture for being selfish and putting the rest of us in danger?

What kind of merfolk would attack a random human? Who would risk revealing themselves for such a thing? Cindy didn't have any enemies that I knew of.

Markus and Tom joined in on the teasing, which I found ironic because Tom had insisted mermaids were real way before I was ever Cursed. It was why Markus chose to be his friend. His big lie was that you kept your friends close and your enemies closer - and Tom being a mermaid-believing fisherman like his father counted enough to be an enemy. I doubted Tom still believed in mermaids, but he was having a great time pretending to drown in front of Cindy.

There was an investigation since the police did admit it was weird that a clean girl like Cindy would randomly go off and make up a story like that. They did find a small great white shark lurking in the area and conveniently blamed the whole thing on him. Cindy must've confused a giant pale fish as a mermaid with glowing blue eyes and lived to tell her brain's twisted version of the tale.

Cindy wasn't buying it. After a few days of trying to convince me she wasn't crazy, she quietly and suddenly gave up. I could feel deep down she was angry with me for not believing her, but she knew no amount of begging would convince me or anyone else otherwise. She pretended like she believed the shark theory on the surface, but it was a lie. A lie I tried to convince myself would be better for her and me and everyone in the long run. *Bigger picture,* I chanted. A whole species' protection is worth more than one human's traumatic incident. Even if that human was your best friend.

I too knew, deep down, that I wasn't a good enough liar to convince myself.

. . .

After a few days of driving myself mad with questions, I pulled Markus aside in the hallway at school.

"What kind of merfolk would try to kill a random human?" I whispered. He shoved me away, clenching his jaw before stomping down the hallway. I resisted the urge to call him some colorful words. Why was I the bad guy when I wasn't the one risking our secret?

I simmered in my anger and confusion as I sat beside Cindy on the fountain outside of her dad's aquarium after school. She muttered about her dramatic morning, picking at her ice cream cone. Despite insisting she was fine, she refused to go swimming, whether it was in the pool or the ocean. Earlier that morning, her swim coach had lost her patience after waiting an entire week *for you to get over this little freak incident* and yelled at her for refusing to participate in that Friday's swim meet.

Cindy met her lecture with a cold and stubborn stare until her dad came and picked us both up from school. I could feel the frustration oozing from his pores, but he smiled through clenched teeth. He bought us ice cream on the way to work at the aquarium and told us to *relax by the fountain. It's been a stressful week.*

So we licked our cones and sat, listening to the bubbling water as children dragged their tired parents towards the aquarium doors.

"I'm such a loser. I should've just swum. I know there's nothing in there," she said, letting ice cream drip down her fingers.

"If you're not ready yet, it's okay. I know it was really scary. Our brains don't let go of that stuff very easily." She sighed.

"I know. The whole thing is so stupid." I licked the last of the ice cream. For the first time, I felt her resolve flicker into doubt. I cheered silently, then hated myself for it.

"Does my stupid best friend want my cone?" I teased. She rolled her eyes.

"No one likes the cone, idiot. Go throw it away. Or give it to a seagull." Several strutting around the concrete looked up at that exact moment as if they knew we were talking about them.

"You're not supposed to give them human food. It's why they never leave you alone." I stood up and walked over to the trash can beside the doors. By the time I turned around, Cindy was letting a seagull finish the rest of her ice cream and there was a woman in dark sunglasses standing by the opposite side of the fountain. She wore a brown jacket too thick for heat, and a stony expression.

No one else noticed her as she reached inside her coat and brought out a gun. I bolted toward my friend, thankful for the first time ever I had faster reflexes than most people. Cindy stared at me, confused, as I yanked her down towards the ground. The gun cracked and the bullet flew over us, disappearing into the crowd. More people screamed.

Cindy gawked at me as we lay still on the asphalt, our hearts beating in our ears. I listened carefully and heard footsteps coming from our left. I motioned for Cindy to be quiet and crawled in the opposite direction, keeping my head below the fountain wall.

I stopped when I noticed Cindy was no longer right behind me. I turned and saw that she had crumpled to the ground, crying silently into the dirt. I turned back around and tried to drag her, but she had turned into dead weight.

The attacker turned the corner, gun held loosely by her side. Her makeup was done. She stared at us for a moment and trained her sunglasses on me.

Traitor, she mouthed, before aiming the gun at my friend.

"HELP!" I screamed. I did the only thing I could think of and threw a loose stone at her face. It pinged off her glasses but distracted her enough that the next bullet hit the concrete instead of my friend.

I jumped to my feet to see police lights flashing in the distance. The merfolk grinned at me. I could feel the excitement radiating off of her. I desperately wanted everyone else to vanish so I could have a moment to talk some sense into her. Why was she looking at me like that when she was the one risking our secret out in the open like this? Oh sure, *I'm* the crazy one.

"Get away from us!" I tried to sound intimidating, but my voice came out in a petrified shriek. She sniggered. She still had the gun trained on my trembling friend.

"Move," she warned. I gritted my teeth and refused - like the idiot who gets killed in horror movies. I was a good enough merfolk to lie to my best friend, but I wasn't a good enough one to let her die.

Police swarmed the scene. They shouted at her to put her gun down. Her eyes flicked to the side for a split second, giving me an opportunity. I rushed her, slamming my body into hers. We flailed, grappling for each other's arms. The gun fell and skittered to the ground. The cops screamed at us to let go of each other. She shoved me away from her, and I fell hard on my butt. She seethed at me, her excitement turned to disdain. *Likewise!* I thought, glaring back at her. She stalked towards me again. Why were the officers waiting so long to shoot her?

When she was close enough to me, I kicked her as hard as I could in her stomach. She stumbled backward with a heave. The momentum of my kick was enough to keep her moving backward until the back of her legs hit the fountain.

And then my world fell apart.

She continued to fall. Her head made a spectacular ringing noise as it collided with the metal statue spitting water. The rest of her body fell inside the fountain, motionless. The cops ran up to the fountain as I stood there, frozen. I found myself praying that she had knocked her head straight into the afterlife.

Die, I pleaded silently. *Die before you phase. Die before you kill us all.*

One of the officers lifted Cindy off the ground and delivered her into the arms of her father, who was pale as the concrete. His eyes were fixed on the fountain.

I turned and covered my mouth with my hands. The cops exchanged shocked and confused glances as they stared down at her body. Her glassy blue eyes stared up at the sky. Her tail hung awkwardly off the ledge, almost touching the ground.

Cindy turned and smiled through her tears.

"I told you I wasn't lying," she said.

．．．

My parents demanded I go to the hospital to get checked out when they arrived on the scene. I was too numb to protest. They chalked it up to shock - which was accurate. Just not shocked by what they thought I should be shocked about.

Cindy was too busy insisting to the news cameras that she was right all along to be whisked off to the hospital. The merfolk's body was removed from the fountain and transported twenty yards to the aquarium for safekeeping. Cindy's dad hovered over it like a fly over rotting meat.

A few of the news stories mentioned my heroic actions, but for the most part, it was all swallowed up in the breaking news: Mermaid Discovered.

My parents shook their heads at the TV in the ER room as a merfolk nurse went through the motions of checking my body. She was doing a much better job of concealing her emotions than I was.

"This is crazy," my dad muttered for the millionth time. "I can't believe it."

"Looks like the legends are true. Hopefully, they can figure out why it went after Cindy of all people," my mom said.

"Maybe she was in its territory," my dad mused. I swallowed the urge to get up and protest that merfolk didn't have territories and the vast majority of them certainly didn't drown humans for kicks and giggles.

Except one did. *Why on Earth would she have been so stupid? You don't hide pretending to be the very monster people think you are. Were we all monsters? Was I the only one not allowed to participate in the drowning because I was Cursed? Not that I wanted to drown people. I wasn't crazy!* I made desperate eye contact with the nurse, asking her the questions with my eyes. She ignored me.

The news switched to Cindy's dad. He was still about as pale as the concrete, clenching his hands together.

"Rest assured, my team of scientists will be conducting extensive research on this creature. We will not let another human be attacked again." I shivered. The nurse draped a blanket around my shoulders and told my parents I was fine - just needed some rest and recovery time.

We rode home in silence. My parents offered me ice cream for being so brave. I declined it.

. . .

The movie my parents forced me to watch *to relax* was interrupted by breaking news. Cindy's dad's face popped up. He was in a white lab coat, the sleeves slightly stained pink. He folded his hands and addressed whoever was holding the camera.

"Good evening, my name is Arthur Johnson. I am the current owner of Arthur's Aquarium. As many of you know already, following today's shooting, the creature was brought into my lab. The creature lived for several hours before succumbing to its injuries." I let out a little breath of relief.

"In the meantime, I and my team of marine biologists have tested the creature's DNA and have concluded that it is a previously unknown species. This creature was capable of switching between a human-like form and an aquatic form. The aquatic form consists of a tail, stripe-like markings along its body, and webbed hands. Although we do not yet have an official name - the creature's description fits what humans have historically attributed to mermaids." *Merfolk*, I corrected silently.

"Based on today's incident, this mermaid's behavior matches what has commonly been passed down in so-called myths and legends for hundreds of years. For reasons not yet understood, this creature decided to hunt and kill my daughter. This creature was dangerous, and others of its kind are to be treated likewise." *Not all of us are dangerous,* I protested weakly.

"More research needs to be done, which is why I am offering a reward for any other mermaid-like creatures caught and delivered to my lab. It is my full intention that I and my team of marine biologists will study these creatures until we understand their biology and their motives. Until then, I advise my fellow humans to be very careful swimming out in the ocean. We do not yet know what all these creatures are capable of. It would be reasonable to assume these creatures are capable of manipulating humans' emotions or thoughts based on the legends about them." *What on Earth?* I thought. *He just admitted that he didn't know what we were capable of, but he's just going to assume we have these freaky brainwashing powers?*

"The reward for the capture and delivery of a live mermaid will be one million dollars." My world fell out from beneath me. I vaguely remembered excusing myself to the bathroom, where I curled up on the floor and tried not to scream.

A million dollars.

Team of marine biologists.

Dangerous creatures.

Dr. Mercer was right. The humans hadn't reacted well, and now there was a million-dollar incentive for someone to take me to a lab so I could be dissected.

I wanted to rewind. I wanted to go back in time and tell Cindy what I was before a rouge merfolk attacked her. I wanted to go back to my birthday party and stay on the dock.

A million dollars.

What would my parents do for a million dollars? What would a homeless person do? It was a little late to try to convince anyone I was one of the good merfolk after years and years of lying to their faces. I was screwed. I had no choice but to keep lying if I wanted to stay off an operating table.

TOM

Everyone was losing their shit over this whole mermaid thing. It was almost enough to make me feel bad for making fun of Cindy. I could barely get my trawler out on the water because of all the boats choking the shore. Everyone and their mom were trying to catch one.

If I were a mermaid, I wouldn't dare go swimming right now. Then again, who was to say where they spent most of their time? Maybe they lived in the ocean and only came up on land to chase after their escaped victims? One thing was for sure - I'd never go swimming at night again.

"This stuff is crazy, right?" My dad only had three empty beer bottles on the coffee table, which meant it was still safe to have a conversation with him. He scratched his crotch as he watched the news.

"Can't even get the boat out of the dock," I muttered. He didn't respond. I sighed and started to walk away when he finally spoke.

"These idiots'll never catch one like this. Mermaids aren't dumb enough to hang out in the open ocean." I resisted the urge to laugh. Sure, my dad had told me made-up stories when I was little about mermaids, but he was talking about them as if he knew their habits. Maybe he was drunker than I thought.

"Oh yeah, where do they hang out?"

"Caves," he muttered. I nodded slowly, although the idea made sense. They had to have hiding places, right? They had stayed hidden for this long.

"Well, maybe you can go to the caves and catch some for us, huh?" He surprised me by getting off the couch. I winced as he grabbed my arm and yanked me to his bedroom closet. He flung open the door and pointed to an old cardboard box on the top shelf.

"Grab that." I brought it down and opened it to reveal rusty bits of metal.

"What the hell is this?" He smacked the side of my head.

"Don't sass me, boy! Those traps were my daddy's. You want to catch yourself a mermaid - there's where you start." I stared up at him.

"You're telling me grandpa was a mermaid hunter?"

"Damn good one too." *Obviously not that good since they were only discovered a few weeks ago,* I thought. I kept that thought to myself. What would grandpa have even done with a mermaid if he ever caught one?

"Okay, thanks, Dad." He shuffled back to his couch. I hefted the box out to my boat, fully intending to shove it in the spare closet and forget about it. After waiting a half hour to get out of the docks, I gave up, got bored, and went rummaging.

These traps were designed to hurt. Half of them included long spikes. Then again, if they were meant to hunt mermaids, I guessed they would have to hurt to work. Surely mermaids would be smart enough to see and dismantle an average trap.

I spent the next few hours tinkering until I finally had a chance to move my boat out of the docks. I chugged past the other hopeful mermaid hunters. If I was one of those freaks, where would I hide?

My eyes narrowed on a small outcropping in the distance. If I remembered correctly - the same one my idiot neighbor had swum to when she got attacked by that shark. She had never told me thank you for rescuing her ass.

I sailed to the outcropping and killed the power. I lowered the contraptions into the safety boat and carefully paddled to a small opening in the rocks. I set the trap and covered it with whatever slimy stuff was growing on the rocks to hide it.

Alright, let's see how crazy Grandpa was, I thought.

AMY

Cindy and I came back to school the same day. We were both treated like heroes, her more so than me, but I was fine with that because it took most of my energy to not start screaming in panic. Cindy took the fame like she deserved it, and people gave it to her. No more mermaid stickers were put on her locker. She started swimming again.

No one would shut up about it. It was the topic of discussion in science, social studies, language arts, and even math. In gym, comments and rumors were passed with the ball. I almost got creamed in the face twice because I couldn't focus. Everyone chalked it up to our traumatic experience. After all - I was the heroine who saved her best friend from being murdered by a monster. Or was it murder? Do tigers murder or do they just kill? Mermaids were just animals - right? That's what Arthur said.

Surely mermaids must have a reason for killing - just like any other species. Theories flew, and they were all wrong.

Every mermaid thing ever seemed to be canceled overnight. *The Little Mermaid?* Pulled from Disney Plus. Spartina - that brand of mermaid-inspired purses and notebooks? Closed all their doors for *remodeling*. Those people who made the replica (hardly replica) mermaid fins for people to swim in for fun? Etsy accounts deleted.

At home, I had no escape either. My parents had the news turned on 24/7. Reporters showed up at my house on occasion, begging me to make a statement. My parents refused on my behalf, saying I had already been through too much, which I was grateful for because I didn't trust myself to not fall apart on live TV.

The first night I was brave (read: dehydrated and desperate) enough to go swimming, I froze at the corner of the house because dozens of boats peppered the water, searchlights blazing as they combed the darkness for million-dollar checks. I turned back inside and prayed my parents wouldn't wake up as I filled the bathtub up and let myself soak. It was uncomfortable, but I would rather my parents catch me than a total stranger.

What would my parents do if they found me like this? What would Cindy do? Horrible scenarios ran through my head until dawn, when I had to phase back and go through the day all over again.

While Cindy babbled away with her new adoring fan club, I noticed Markus across the hall - also looking dehydrated. He was listening to Tom blab about something with feigned interest, but I knew he was watching me out of the corner of his eye.

Later in the day, I caught up to him in the busy hallway, desperate for some fellow-species reassurance.

"Have you been able to swim?" I whispered. He glared at me and yanked me over to the alcove by the water fountain.

"Of course not!" he hissed. "What are you thinking, bringing this up at school?"

I wanted to point out that he was making our conversation more public by attempting to make it private, but I kept my mouth shut. I shrugged, looking down at my shoes.

"Just wondering. What . . . what are we going to do?" I asked. He laughed.

"What are *we* going to do? I don't know what *you're* going to do. I am going to keep my family safe by keeping my mouth shut. And you better do the same if you don't want to make this situation even worse than it already is!" he said. I bristled, returning his glare.

"How is this my fault?" I demanded.

"You pushed her in that fountain!" Markus seethed. I swallowed.

"She was trying to kill Cindy!" I protested. Markus clenched the strap of his book bag.

"Then you should've let her get shot." He dove back into the current of the hallway, leaving me speechless and cold.

That night in the bathtub, I let my body succumb to the trembling it had been wanting to do the past few days. Dread curled up cold and heavy in my gut.

Markus was right. I was still certain I shouldn't have had to let my friend die to keep the secret, but I didn't have to kick the merfolk back either. I should've just shielded Cindy and let the cops do their jobs. If the merfolk had died on the concrete, none of this would have ever happened.

This was my fault.

TOM

Going to the house today was a mistake.

"Oh, now you decide to show up here?" A beer bottle flew past my head, shattering on the wall. My dad staggered towards me, eyes rimmed red.

"Where have you been?" he bellowed. I would be wasting my breath if I tried to explain to him that I had just gotten back from school. I quickly slipped out the door and slammed it shut behind me. If I was lucky, he would be too drunk to open it and follow me. I walked out onto the docks and sighed in irritation as I heard banging and cursing behind me. *I needed to get out of here.* I took out my cell phone and dialed my girlfriend, Marisol.

Was she really a girlfriend? Since she hung all over me in the hallways at school, it was slightly more serious than previous relationships but how much more serious remained up for debate. It had been the same for the past several *girlfriends*.

"Hello?"

"Wanna go on a boat ride?" I asked.

"Sure," she purred. I climbed up the ladder and let the salty breeze cool me off as I waited.

"Hey, Sailor." I turned around as Marisol swung up onto the deck. She wore neon pink gym shorts with a matching bikini top. I waltzed over to her and eagerly pressed my lips against hers. She slid a perfectly manicured hand around my back. Her touch sent sparks of desire shooting through me.

I reluctantly parted from her and strutted to the control room of the boat. I slipped inside, fired it up, and slowly coaxed it away from the docks as soon as space opened up. Soon, we broke free from the crowds and were flying among the waves. She giggled when I let her sit on my lap and steer the boat. The old trawler had been in my family for years and years. It was rusty and rattled dangerously at high speeds. The old nets hadn't been used for any actual fishing in a while. The *Lazy River* wasn't pretty, but most other high schoolers didn't have their own boat, or if they did, they were rich and snotty about it.

"Love you," she flirted.

"Love you too," I said with as much emotion in my voice as I could come up with. *Dang it, this girl should have more friends telling her to stay away from me. I should break up with her soon.* Usually, my reputation kept the nice girls away from me. I leaned in for a kiss when a sudden bump along the side of the boat caught my attention. Marisol jumped. I unwound myself away from her and slowed to a stop, hoping I hadn't hit anything. I looked over the side and groaned.

"Great, these nets fell over," I muttered. Several old boxes of rotting fishing nets had broken loose from their ties and had fallen over the edge of the boat. Marisol raised an eyebrow.

"Can't you just leave them in the water?" she complained as I started climbing down the ladder on the side of the boat. I grinned back at her.

"That would be littering!" In truth, I didn't care. But if my dad ever found them missing and happened to be in a bad mood at the same time, I didn't want to be on the other end of his anger. I reached the bottom rung and hung on with one hand as I tried to grab one of the old nets with the other. I snagged a corner and pulled it back.

"Don't kill yourself," Marisol yelled out. *Wouldn't kill you to help me,* I thought. I finished pulling them to the surface and looked out at the water around us. We were close to the outcropping where I had set my mermaid trap.

"Hey, you mind if I check something while we're out here?" I asked, already steering the boat towards the cave.

"What are you checking?" I pulled the boat to a stop and climbed back down the ladder.

"I uh . . . kinda set a trap here. For mermaids." She burst out laughing.

"Seriously Tom, you're falling for that? I doubt the whole thing is real - it sounds totally made up!" I stepped onto the rock, holding my arms for balance as I walked to the opening.

"Just give me a second!" I snapped. She rolled her eyes and cocked her hip as I bent down to look into the opening. I grinned before pulling out my catch.

"Sure it's all fake?"

Behind me, Marisol began to scream.

AMY

I woke up every morning wishing I could sleep until humans forgot merfolk existed. Every day was the same - people who had previously rolled their eyes at Tom for being a drunk man-slut now clamored for his attention. Not only was he the first person to catch a mermaid – he had caught *two* of them. According to pictures and videos on TikTok, they didn't look any older than ten. Not that Tom or anyone else cared.

The day after his two-million-dollar reward processed, he showed up to school on a fancy new motorcycle - apparently the loudest one he could find at the dealership. He had a posse around his locker every day, begging for autographs or for advice on catching their own mermaids.

The thought of accidentally swimming into a hidden trap made me sick and grateful for my bathtub. What exactly had he designed to catch two merfolk? Even if we managed to get stuck here and there, we could usually figure out how to break free. What breed of thing had he created?

Surprisingly, the attention seemed to bother Cindy as well. Every mention of the new captures made her turn a slight shade of green. I thought she of all people would've been excited, but she just seemed to want to forget the whole thing had happened. Her fifteen minutes of fame must have had a sour aftertaste.

The only comfort during the day was watching the student teacher give Tom the hardest math problems to solve. He stared at the board with a blank look on his face, popping the cap on and off of the dry-erase marker. I imagined him to be a worm wriggling on a hook as he struggled. It gave me a small measure of satisfaction.

"Man, I dunno how to do this," he muttered.

"Looks like you need extra homework then," Mr. Johns smiled.

. . .

After school didn't end up being much better. Tom used his newfound popularity to host wild parties on his trawler. These parties lasted hours into the night and sometimes the morning. But of course - the one time I wished my parents would use their cop card and do something - they chose to ignore it.

"Let him celebrate. Maybe it'll encourage others to go out hunting for those things," my mom said over a cup of coffee.

Cindy wasn't having it either. She often spent the night since her dad was so busy dealing with mermaid stuff. We tried to do homework over the noise but often ended up staring out of my bedroom window at the parties we weren't invited to.

Tom took turns between making out with his slutty girlfriend and throwing back beers, screaming out into the night. Those beer cans usually made their way into the water.

"What an asshole," Cindy muttered. "You've got enough money to buy a trash can."

"My parents are cops. Why can't they arrest him for drinking right outside their window?" I complained.

"We should do something," Cindy said. My mouth twisted into a smirk.

"I know what might work."

CINDY

I don't know how she did it, but the next day when Tom opened his locker, mounds of seaweed littered beer cans and other garbage fell to the floor. His new posse screamed in disgust as the stench of rotted fish and mildew filled the hallway. Tom grimaced as he kicked the mess off his feet. Everyone except for Markus fled from the smell.

Amy lost it beside me. I had never seen her laugh so hard in her life. I wheezed beside her, wiping tears from my eyes. Tom's gaze flitted over to us, and his look of disgust quickly turned to anger.

"You think this is funny?" he shouted. I stopped laughing long enough to squeeze my thumb and index finger together.

"Just a little." He gritted his teeth, and all of a sudden, we were ten years old again on the dock for Amy's birthday party. He scooped up a handful of trash and threw it across the hallway. It splattered across my face and hair, and Amy stopped laughing.

"You son of a -" Another wave of garbage hit her in the face before she could finish her sentence. Markus grinned from the other end of his throw. I balled up my fists, rolling up my sleeves.

Five minutes later, the whole hallway was splattered with garbage, and we all sat in the principal's office.

The principal massaged the bridge of her nose, as she drummed her spindly fingers on her desk.

"Can you please explain to me why there is garbage all over my hallway?" she asked calmly.

"It's my fault," Amy admitted. "Tom was driving us nuts bragging about his mermaid capture, keeping us up at night with parties on his boat, so we decided to return the garbage they threw overboard back to him." She sighed.

"You didn't think to call in a noise complaint first?"

"This was funnier," I muttered. Tom called me a not-very-appropriate-for-school word under his breath. Markus sniggered. The Principal slammed her hands down on the desk.

"Okay. Since you and Amy seem to care *so much* about the environment - and since Tom and Markus don't seem to care about it *enough* - I think I know the appropriate punishment for all of you." She left her desk and returned with four huge black trash bags.

"By Monday, I want all four of these bags filled with garbage from the docks." Our mouths fell open.

"Are you serious?" Tom whined. She narrowed her eyes at him, shoving the bag at his chest.

"You have a boat, remember? It shouldn't be too hard to sail around and gather some trash. Who knows, maybe you'll find another mermaid while you're looking!" She glared around at each of us in turn. "Ladies? Any complaints?" We mutely shook our heads. She straightened up.

"Good. And you can also clean up your mess in the hallway before you leave. And I will be contacting your parents."

. . .

After the dismissal bell rang, the custodians handed us rags and brooms with looks of disdain before leaving us to our karma. We glared at each other as we worked in silence. I scrubbed the lockers until my knuckles bled. Amy had to take a break at one point to listen to her parents chew her out over the phone. I knew my dad would be too busy to care. Tom had probably had so many calls home that his dad no longer answered the phone. Markus looked paler than normal.

"What's the matter? Afraid daddy might take away your phone?" I smirked. Markus balled up his fists.

"Careful. The mermaids might smell you and come back to finish the job," he snarled. The color drained from my face. Amy held her broom like a baseball bat.

"Or maybe they'll come after you!" she hissed. Tom groaned.

"Can you guys just shut up and clean so we can get out of here? I had plans this weekend, you know! And now I have to spend it cleaning up garbage because of you two!" Tom complained.

"Maybe you should've kept the celebrating to a minimum!" I snapped.

"Shouldn't you be happy I'm getting rid of those things?" Tom retorted. I clamped my mouth shut. I wasn't about to explain how I couldn't watch the news anymore because every mention of mermaids sent my body into panic mode. Every party on the boat just reminded me of being dragged down below the surface.

"Maybe everybody doesn't want the constant reminder that those things are out there," Amy said. My best friend always had the uncanny ability to say just the right thing - it was like she could read my mind. Tom finally shut up, and we went back to scrubbing the hallway.

I wondered if my dad would even let me go on a boat to the open ocean knowing what was out there now. Then again, of all the boats to be stuck with, Tom's was probably the safest. Surely the mermaids had gotten the memo to stay away from him?

Or maybe they just knew who to go after for revenge.

AMY

We met Tom early Saturday morning to collect our garbage. Cindy oozed uneasiness as the dock rocked underneath us. Markus sent wave after wave of furious energy at me. The thought of him having to endure his merfolk-catching friend a whole extra day almost made me smile.

Tom was late. He showed up shirtless and yawning. Another man followed behind him.

"Who's that?" Cindy asked.

"My uncle. He's been down here visiting for a few days, helping me check traps and stuff. He volunteered to help us out today so we can get this over with faster," he said. The man stepped up and shook each of our hands. His belly drooped over his cargo shorts, and his beard had so many holes it reminded me of Swiss cheese.

"Name's Morris. Heard you three got my nephew here into some trouble," he said with a good-natured grin. *Some trouble*, I thought. If my parents weren't so worried about my mental health - they definitely would've killed me yesterday. I was surprised Markus' parents hadn't murdered him.

"Alright, let's get this over with." We climbed the ladder to the boat. It was a decently big boat - probably at least forty feet with enough room to have a bathroom, kitchen, and extra bedroom in the middle. Cindy swallowed as it rocked underneath us.

"Is this thing even safe?" she asked timidly.

"Course it is! She's a little rusty still - but what do you think I've done with all that money?" Tom gloated. He patted a box by the sink. "I got a water maker! No more filling up fresh water at the marina. Take as many showers as you want! We'll never have to stop to fill up again." He pointed up to a satellite on the roof. "And got satellite internet that'll stretch all the way to the Bermuda Triangle!" *Wow, water and wifi, life's two essentials*, I thought.

"What about food?" Cindy asked. He kicked open the mini-fridge.

"There's some beer in there if you haven't had breakfast." *We're going to get arrested*, I thought, rolling my eyes. Markus sighed and opened his black trash bag.

"Let's get this over with," he muttered.

The trawler chugged out to sea. Tom handed us long-handled fishing nets and we spent the next few hours scooping trash out of the ocean. There was actually less floating on the surface than I expected.

Then again, I knew a lot of it ended up on the ocean floor as well. And I would not dive down again to fill my bag up.

By the time noon rolled around, we were all sunburnt and exhausted. We retreated to the shade of the living room to take a break. The gentle rocking of the boat and the smell of salt water eased my troubled nerves, and I found myself yawning. Being stuck out at sea with Tom and Markus sucked, but it was the closest I had gotten to being in the ocean for weeks.

The others apparently felt the same. The yawns continued until we all passed out. However, my rest didn't last for very long. My eyes fluttered open as I heard footsteps. Markus' silhouette blocked out the light as he opened the living room door.

"What are you doing?" I hissed. He turned and motioned out to the water.

"I haven't had the chance to swim in actual water for weeks! And I know where the traps are out here. I'm taking advantage of the opportunity. You might want to do the same." I shook my head.

"You're crazy. It's broad daylight! What if someone sees you?" He shrugged.

"I'll be fine. I know how to not swim into a trap." *Those girls probably thought that too*, I thought as he shut the door.

I sighed and rolled back over, trying to fall back asleep. If the idiot wanted to get himself captured, that wasn't on me.

. . .

The boat was already chugging by the time we woke up a few hours later.

"Where's Markus?" Cindy yawned. I scanned the room but didn't see him. I ignored the bad feeling in my gut and shrugged.

"I don't know, bathroom I guess." That guess was declared wrong as the toilet flushed behind Tom, still shirtless and bedheaded. He burped and stretched, popping his back. Cindy rolled her eyes and pretended like she was throwing up. *Did he even wash his hands?* I wondered. The boat stopped churning.

"I'm going to check a trap while we're out this way!" Morris called out from the steering room. Tom gave him a thumbs up and strode towards the kitchen, throwing open all the cabinets. Morris slipped out and headed for the safety boat tied to the side of the trawler.

"Y'all hungry?" he asked. I munched on a stale protein bar. I had almost finished it by the time Tom realized Markus was gone.

"Hey, where's Markus?" he asked. At that moment, Morris ran back into the room, panting with his hands on his knees.

"You folks are gonna want to see this," he said.

. . .

We joined Morris on the rickety safety boat as he paddled it over to a large outcropping. He tied it off to a rock and motioned for us to get out. Slipping and sliding on the slick rocks, we followed him into a hole that opened up into a cave. Water dripped from the ceiling, echoing throughout the cavern in cheerful plops.

"Gotta warn you, Tom, this is going to be a bit of a shock," Morris said gruffly, taking off his battered baseball cap. Tom raised his eyebrow.

"What are you talking about?"

"You caught another one." We followed Morris around a boulder, and Cindy screamed. I held her as she staggered back into my arms, resisting the urge to scream myself.

Tom didn't scream. Instead, he curled his hands up into fists and stalked up to the figure writhing on the ground.

Markus lay on the rocks, half submerged in the water. Stuck halfway up his tail was some sort of contraption that looked like a circle that decided to grow fangs. Those fangs were embedded in his tail, drawing copious amounts of blood. Markus gasped for breath, his body clenched in pain.

"Guess he thought it was safe to go for a midday swim," Morris said, with no trace of sympathy in his voice. Cindy curled herself into my arms, crying and shaking as Tom stared down at his former best friend.

"You're one of those things?" he demanded. Markus shook his head.

"Tom I swear . . . I'm not dangerous . . . you don't need to do this."

"Yeah, I'm sure he decides to tell the truth now," Morris jeered. Tom swallowed.

"Tom . . . please. Don't do this," Markus begged. Tom looked up at Morris.

"Can you take care of this?" Tom asked coldly. Morris nodded. Tom strode past us in a huff as Morris walked over, carrying a length of rope. I tried to look away, but it was like passing a car accident. I had to watch.

In vain, Markus tried to drag himself back into the water, but Morris dragged him up onto land with a fistful of hair. Markus thrashed against his grip, but Morris pinned him down on his stomach and bound his arms behind his back before releasing the trap. Markus screamed as he phased back, his human knees gushing more blood than his tail had been. Morris tied what looked like an old bandanna around his mouth before kicking him once more in the ribs for good measure.

"Shut up." Markus' screams turned to whimpers as Morris picked his body off the ground and slung him over his shoulder like a sack of potatoes. He eyed us.

"Ladies first." I escorted Cindy back to the rickety boat as Morris stepped in behind us. We rode in silence. Part of me wanted to protest Markus' rough treatment, but no human in their right mind would ever protest the treatment of a merfolk. Who cares if the *dangerous* creatures are treated badly? Not me. Morris shoved Markus into an empty closet on the far side of the boat, sealing it shut with a padlock. Meanwhile, Tom sulked in the bedroom, anger radiating from underneath the door.

CINDY

"I want to go home," I sobbed, shaking as Amy tried in vain to comfort me.

"I'm sure we'll be home soon," she whispered. Morris handed me a bottle of water.

"I know it's upsetting, missy. He'll be taken care of soon." I drank the water, trying to force my lungs to breathe normally. *We've known him since we were little kids,* I thought. *He could've attacked us any time. His dad is a doctor for crying out loud! Have mermaids lived on land – pretending to be normal people – this whole time?* My blood ran cold.

Maybe it was just Markus' family that lived on land. But if they do it – who's to say how many more of them do it too? A fresh wave of tears fell down my cheeks. Until now, I had been telling myself that mermaids lived in the ocean.

Flashbacks of that woman trying to shoot me tore through my head. *If mermaids actually lived on land, there must be dozens more that want to kill me*, I thought. *Dozens more that know exactly how to blend in – to make me think I'm safe until I'm not.*

"Look on the bright side - I'm sure the whole trash thing will be forgiven now," Amy said through a forced smile. Tom burst out of his bedroom, eyes red.

"Let's go back to shore," he muttered, shoving past his uncle into the steering room. The boat whined and then went silent again. Tom swore, slamming down his fists.

"The damn boat won't start!" he shouted. My heart dropped further down. The boat made several more weird noises until it went silent again.

"Something's wrong with the engine. I'll have to call someone to come tow us in," he muttered.

"No - don't do that!" Morris protested. "If people find out you caught another one - we'll be swarmed with people wanting a piece of the pie. Let me try to fix it first. If I can't get it running by tomorrow night, then we can call someone." Tom sighed.

"What are they supposed to tell their parents?" he asked, waving his hand at us. Morris walked over to us, a big smile plastered on his face.

"Your parents would understand, right? Trash collection taking a little longer than we thought?" Something about his voice made the hair rise on my arms. Amy stiffened beside me but nodded.

"I'll text my parents." I wanted to point out that I was the aquarium owner's daughter - and that if anyone should be calling for a safe tow - it should be me. My dad would be so thrilled about the capture of another mermaid that he would forget all about me being forced to be near it.

The thought of that made me less anxious to rush home. I nodded.

"Just don't let it out of the closet."

MARKUS

Morris made a big mistake by leaving me in a closet. It didn't take me long to rummage around in the random piles of junk to find a pair of broken scissors. I sawed through the ropes binding my hands behind me and sighed in relief as they fell away.

My knees were a different story. They screamed in protest whenever I put weight on them - but I could still walk - and that was all that mattered. I had heard Tom and Morris shouting about engine problems - which bought me more time to escape.

I waited until the thin line of sunlight peeking from underneath the door dwindled to black. A quick push on the door confirmed it was locked. I gripped the broken scissors and started sawing at the handle. It would take longer, but it was quieter. I couldn't risk waking anyone up.

My mind flashed back to the only person on board who probably would hear the scissors scratching at the wood. I swallowed. *I should've listened to her. I've ruined everything. My parents are going to kill me.* Merfolk doctors were few and far between. They were crucial in emergencies - merfolk needed special care to avoid being discovered. Our bodies healed fast but reacted differently to common medications. With my dad gone - who else would help injured merfolk?

Even if I did make it back to shore - Tom would know what I was. He would send Arthur after my whole family. I had to make it back and escape to safety before they fixed the boat. Jobless and living in the ocean was one thing, but I would never forgive myself if my parents got hurt.

At least Tom didn't discover Amy too, I thought. It would be another kind of disaster if the humans figured out they could become like us too. As annoying as she was, it was more important to protect her than myself.

My sawing was interrupted as the door suddenly flung open. For a moment, I thought I had broken the lock, until I saw a thick figure standing in front of the door.

"Good evening," he drawled. I swallowed and backed up, holding my scissors like a sword.

"Stay away from me. Let me go, and I won't hurt you," I threatened. Morris laughed and took a step closer.

"I'm not going to let Tom turn you in," he said. My grip on the scissors faltered.

"Y-you're not?"

"No." He strode inside the closet and shut the door behind him. "I'm going to kill you before he gets the chance."

AMY

I wasn't sure if it was in real life or my imagination that I heard Markus crying. Merfolk didn't cry, after all.

Across the living room, Cindy tossed and turned on her bench, sleeping fitfully. No amount of comfort talk had worked - although I hadn't exactly been trying too hard. I had been too busy trying not to let myself panic.

You warned him, I kept telling myself. *He ignored your advice and look where he ended up! That's not your fault.*

Except it still felt like it was. The only reason humans knew about us was because of my stupid mistake. Didn't that mean that I was also responsible for Markus as well?

Even if I wasn't responsible - the scientists at the aquarium would still tear him apart. They would go after his entire family. The hospital would lose some of the only merfolk who worked there - and where would that leave the others?

You have to set him free.

I scoffed silently. If I got caught trying to set him free, then the others would know exactly what I was too. There was no such thing as a human who sympathized with merfolk. I could imagine the look on Cindy's face when she realized her best friend since childhood was another one of those *freaks*.

Nope. Not my job. Not worth the risk.

I told myself that for several more hours until I found myself tiptoeing out of the living room into the damp, night air. Thick, dark clouds swirled overhead, lightning flashing across the sky.

If I get caught, I can just pretend he was doing some weird brainwashing thing to me, I told myself. They'd believe it. That's what Arthur keeps saying mermaids can do anyway, right?

I reached the closet only to remember it was padlocked. I groaned and proceeded to scour the boat for something to break the lock with. I eventually found an old hammer and held my breath as I brought it down on the lock. Mercifully, it broke with one hit, and the door swung open. The metallic smell of blood hit me like a bomb.

Markus lay in a puddle of red on the ground. He stared up at me with panicked eyes, trying to shout through his gag.

"What did he do to you?" I demanded, yanking the gag down and getting to work on the knots. His ankles had been bound together as well - when had Morris done that? His knees looked like they had been through a meat grinder. Black bruises decorated his face. His nose was crooked.

"You need to get out here," he rasped.

"Yeah, you think?"

"No, you don't understand." He grabbed my arm and made me look him in the eye. "He's trying to kill me," he whispered. I furrowed my brow.

"Why would Morris want to kill you?" Something clicked behind me. I spun around to see Morris' silhouette framed in the deck lights. He clenched a pistol in his hands. He pointed it at me, sneering.

"Step aside." I slowly got to my feet and walked out of the closet. Morris kept the gun trained on me as he walked back over to Markus. He chuckled as Markus whimpered.

"How cute. You were trying to save it." I winced as he kicked Markus in the ribs. Markus cried out in pain and clutched his gut.

"Run," he begged. Morris stepped back out into the moonlight, glaring at me.

"Why were you trying to free it? Trying to get the reward money for yourself?" My head spun wildly, trying to make sense of the situation. *Why would he want to kill Markus?*

"What the hell is going on?" We turned our heads to see Tom standing in the doorframe of the living room, rubbing his eyes.

"He wants to kill Markus!" I shouted. Tom narrowed his gaze at his uncle. There wasn't much Morris could say to defend himself - seeing that he was pointing a gun at my chest.

"She was trying to set the creature free," Morris said coldly. "I was just preventing her from doing so." Never mind, there was a lot he could do to defend himself.

"He's lying!" I protested. "Look at him!" I pointed to Markus. Cindy stumbled out behind Tom, going pale at the situation before her. Tom's gaze flashed between the two of us. Something seemed to click in his eyes.

"Cindy. Go see if the boat will start," he said. She scampered off, and the boat rumbled to a start. Cindy walked back out, trembling. Tom shook his head, his eyes clouding over with tears.

"You sabotaged my engine you son of a -"

"Mind your language, son. Now put your hands up or I end it right now." Tom gritted his jaw and reluctantly walked over to me, his hands in the air. Cindy joined us. I could feel her fury radiating off of her. Morris leveled the gun at all of us, sweeping it back and forth.

"What's the point of killing him?" I asked. "That just means you lose your reward money."

"There are things going on here that you couldn't begin to understand!" Morris snapped. "Those creatures belong in a grave - not in a tank to be gawked at. Now, if we can all reach an understanding here - no humans need to get hurt."

"What the fuck are you talking about? *I* caught him. He's *mine* to do with as I see fit!" Tom snarled. "Put the fucking gun down."

"Tom, you need to listen to me. He's dangerous."

"Yeah, no shit. That's why he needs to be turned in." Morris and Tom glared at each other. *I don't understand,* I thought. *Why does Morris think merfolk are so dangerous they need to be killed?*

"Tom, please, listen to me. I know this doesn't make sense, but there are stories you don't know. Why do you think your grandfather had those traps?" Tom paled. "Please. Just let me get rid of him. Think of how much he's lied to you." Behind us, Markus whimpered. If I were in his shoes, I would rather choose death than being turned in, but he seemed reluctant to pick between the two.

"I don't care. He's my friend. I don't want him dead," Tom said. Markus' eyes widened. *Wow,* I thought. *Love your friend enough to not murder him, but still want to sell him off. I hope he does drown you.*

Morris scowled.

"Then I guess I have no choice then." He cocked the pistol. Cindy squeaked beside me.

"How are you going to explain the disappearance of three teenagers?" I demanded.

"Easy. I dump all of you overboard and blame your deaths on that thing in there. I managed to kill it, but only after it was too late." *Dang it, he had really thought ahead.*

"Those are my traps," Tom protested. "You don't know how to design them. You'll never catch another one without me." Morris scoffed.

"I've been designing mermaid traps since before you were born, son." *How could he possibly be designing traps since then? No one knew merfolk existed until a month ago, I thought.*

"Why don't you just throw us overboard? Let us take our chances?" Cindy begged.

"With your reputation, I don't think so. You'd make it back to shore, and we can't have conflicting stories." Morris turned towards me.

"One more chance. Change your mind now, and we can forget about this whole thing." Tom called his uncle some inappropriate words. Morris laughed and turned the gun on him.

"I guess I'll start with you first," he growled. Tom's eyes went wide as a figure bolted from the darkness of the closet. Markus screamed as he feebly tackled Morris. Blood dropped to the deck from his knees as he clawed at every surface of Morris he could reach. With a shout, Tom joined the charge, grappling for the gun. Cindy screamed as the gun popped, sending a stray bullet through the deck. Morris shoved Markus off of his back, swearing. Markus hit the ground hard and stopped moving.

I bolted to Markus' limp body and started dragging him towards the railing.

"Cindy, help me!" I shouted. She stared at me with wide eyes, frozen by the railing. "If we get rid of him, they won't have anything to fight over!" She stayed rooted to the deck. She shook her head, tears clouding her eyes.

"I can't," she whispered. Rage filled me.

"*He's* not the one who hurt you!" I shouted. Her jaw dropped. Had I ever yelled at her before? No, I hadn't, because nice gentle *chill* Amy Wilson never raised her voice at *anybody.* She hesitated a few moments more, then ran over to me. I ignored her fearful and disgusted expression as she grabbed one of his arms and helped me drag him.

Another gunshot rang out, making us both jump in surprise and drop him. I turned to see Morris toss Tom across the deck. Tom groaned and tried to drag himself away. Cindy stood frozen in shock, hands covering her mouth. Morris aimed the pistol. I clenched my fists and saw red. *How dare they,* I thought. *Murdering each other for the right to kidnap people. I'm sick of this.*

What happened next was a blur. I let out a scream and vaulted onto Morris' back, swiping the pistol out of his thick fingers like I had trained as a ninja for the past ten years. He swiveled, an astounded look on his face. Unlike Morris, I had qualms about killing people, so I grabbed the gun by the barrel and swung it like a baseball bat. Morris dodged the first swing, but he didn't dodge my leg swiping his own out from underneath him.

He hit the deck with a thud. He tried to grab my ankle only to be met with a swift kick. His yell didn't quite overpower the crunching sound, and he cradled his wrist to his chest. He yelled something at me, but I didn't hear it over the sound of blood rushing through my head. The thunder above us rumbled and broke, sending down sheets of rain. I stood over him, knowing I had him down. The gun shook in my hands. I wanted to pulverize the man into the deck until he was no more than a grease stain.

"Leave us alone!" I screamed. I brought the gun down on his head, and his eyes rolled back. Another strike had blood rolling out of the side of his temple. Another brought waves of the stuff splashing down on the deck. My arms froze up above my head and rain pelted down.

"Holy shit." I looked up and saw Tom and Cindy gawking. Tom slowly lifted his hands in the air. He smelled terrified out of his wits. I wrinkled my brow, wondering why he was still so scared if no one was chasing us with a gun. Then I caught a reflection of myself in the pool of blood I had created.

My eyes were gleaming solid blue - as were my markings. My ears had turned into merfolk ears - long and webbed. I reached up and felt them.

"Huh, that's never happened before," I whispered. The adrenaline pumping through my system promptly vanished, and I fainted.

. . .

"Okay, I put him in the closet," Tom said.

"What are we going to do?" Cindy asked.

"I don't know! We can't exactly call the police, can we?"

I must've made a noise because the talking stopped. I forced my eyes open and saw the ceiling of the living room. I looked over to see Cindy and Tom standing over another limp figure on the opposite couch.

Their hair was still dripping, so it couldn't have been that long since I fainted.

When I remembered what had just happened, I almost passed out again. I forced myself to stay conscious. How quickly could I make it to the door and into the water? Did Tom still have the gun? Did they give out any reward money for dead merfolk? Begging for freedom hadn't helped Markus much, but I wasn't above trying again. Cindy walked over and stood above me before I could say anything.

"You suck." I stared, unsure of how to respond. She stuck out her bottom lip and punched me hard in the shoulder. "I hate you so much. How could you not tell me? You're the worst!" She continued punching me as she yelled. I let her until she finally ran out of steam and walked back to the other couch to sit. She buried her head in her hands, shaking. Tom watched the display with one eyebrow raised. I stared at my best friend, equally confused.

"What's going on?" I asked, attempting to sit up, my head spinning in the process.

"That's a great question!" Tom snapped. "I would love to know what's going on!" He motioned towards me, his face twisted in anger. "Like . . . what the hell?" I blinked.

"Um . . . can you be more specific?"

"You're one of those freaks," he spat. "It's literally all over your face." I lifted my hands to my face, not realizing my markings were still showing. I automatically willed them away, making Cindy jump. Tom crossed his arms.

"You can't hide it now. Spill!" he demanded.

"What do you want me to say? You already know my secret!" I shot back. "What, you need me to admit it before you turn me in?"

"No one is turning anyone in!" Cindy snapped. I should've been immensely grateful for that statement, but all I could do was laugh.

"So when it's not *your* best friend, it's okay to turn them in?" I narrowed my eyes at Tom. "Oh wait, it doesn't matter," I hissed. Tom ignored my jab.

"Why didn't you let us die? Your species is supposed to be out drowning us, remember? Aren't you supposed to have freaky brainwashing powers?" Tom retorted.

"If that were true, Falcon, then why has Markus been your best friend for years? Why have I been Cindy's best friend for years? Look – if what Arthur said was true – you both would've been dead ages ago, along with a lot more people!"

"But then why has my dad said all that stuff about you guys?" Cindy asked.

"Because he's mad that his daughter almost died? Look - I am merfolk. Don't you think I would know what I'm capable of? How exactly would I mind-control anyone? You know damn well I can't sing to save my life - let alone convince someone to jump overboard." Cindy chuckled.

"Then why did you lie about it? Why did Markus?" Tom asked coldly.

"Why do you think we lied about it? Look what happened!" I hesitated. "Look, I know you guys must be freaked out right now. I would be too - if I were in your shoes. But merfolk aren't dangerous. It's all propaganda. Just because one of us is crazy enough to go on a killing spree doesn't mean the rest of us are like that. Besides - I wasn't the one who just tried to kill all of us out there. Sounds like your family did more than make up stories about mermaids when you were a kid, *Falcon*" Tom froze and clenched his fists.

"I should throw that bastard overboard," he seethed. "I-I knew my grandfather designed traps. But no one ever bothered to explain why." He plopped down on the floor, head in his hands. I stood up and walked over to Markus. I winced as I looked over his body. He was pale with dehydration. Angry red marks marred his wrists, cheeks, and ankles. His knees were still bleeding.

Morris must've done this, I thought. *He was trying to make it look like Markus died in a struggle before we got to shore.*

"He needs water on his skin. He's dehydrated." Cindy nodded. We walked to the sink and took turns soaking rags and laying them on his steaming skin. When he looked more or less like a soggy mummy, I sat down on the coffee table, wringing my fingers nervously.

"Should we uh . . . put him in the bathtub or something?" Tom asked. I shook my head. I wasn't even sure if he would phase with how bad his knees looked.

"Did you really think you couldn't tell me?" Cindy asked, sounding hurt. "I mean, even before all that stuff went down? We've been best friends for years. Didn't you think you could trust me?" I sighed.

"My parents don't even know."

"Okay - that's my next question. Your parents are definitely human. I've seen them swimming like a thousand times. Heck - I've even seen you swimming with them as a little kid. How on Earth are you like this now? Is being a mermaid like . . . an age thing?" *Yes, Tom, we go through metamorphosis like butterflies.*

"Um . . . yeah." Cindy rolled her eyes.

"She's lying," she accused.

"Guys, I can't talk about this. Some secrets aren't just mine to keep," I said. With that, they finally shut up. Tom rummaged around in the bathroom until he found some bandages, and the others helped me wrap up Markus' knees.

"Where is Morris?" I asked.

"We locked him in the closest outside," Tom said.

"Is he um . . . I didn't . . ."

"He's alive. But he'll wake up with a headache." A pause. "Probably a concussion. Nothing he doesn't deserve," Tom said bitterly. We all sat down again. I supposed I should've felt more guilty about hurting him so badly, but I couldn't bring myself to feel a shred of remorse.

"What are we going to do?" I asked.

"I vote we call the police," Cindy said. "We'll tell them exactly what happened and Morris will be locked away. No more problems."

"What about them?" Tom asked, motioning to me and Markus.

"We just bring them to my dad and they can explain that this whole mermaid thing is messed up! They can explain all the misunderstandings, and this whole thing will go back to normal!" I scoffed. Cindy pouted.

"You don't believe me?" she asked. I sighed.

"Cindy, it's not just your dad. It's the whole world. They've already bought the story. I doubt I or anyone else can change that now. Hell - Tom didn't even believe his best friend when he begged for help." Tom sighed and walked towards the door.

"Where are you going?" Cindy asked.

"I need some time to think." He disappeared. I started up after him.

"I have the keys to the ignition," Cindy said, taking them out and dangling them. "He's not going anywhere too far until he talks to us more." I sagged in relief again and sat back down. Cindy wrapped her arm around me.

"If it means anything, I wish I could've told you," I said.

"You've listened to me say so many terrible things about mermaids over these past few weeks. I'm so sorry." I shook my head.

"I can't blame you," I said. "Not after what you went through. I don't know why that one decided to go after you. I just hope you believe me - what I said." She nodded.

"I do. You're my best friend. You've saved my life twice now. I mean . . . you wouldn't do that if you were dangerous, right?" I saw myself beating Morris' head in with his gun. Blood staining the deck beneath my feet. I swallowed.

Right. Not dangerous at all.

Markus woke up hours later. He wearily blinked at us as Cindy recapped most of what happened. By the time she was done, he looked ready to kill both Tom and me. Mostly me.

"You're such an idiot," he seethed. "Do you even realize what you've revealed now?" I thought of the third secret I had yet to reveal – how I had changed from human to merfolk.

"They don't know about *that*," I muttered pointedly. "Unless you would like to reveal it now?" Markus paled and quickly shut his mouth.

"Hey man, don't yell at her. She saved our lives," Tom protested. Markus glared at him, all the years of acting melting away.

"Don't talk to me," he snapped. "You think you get bonus points for not letting your uncle kill me when you were going to turn me in anyway?"

"I'm not going to turn you in," Tom said quietly. "If I had known Arthur was lying this whole time I would've never gone looking for you guys."

"It doesn't matter. Morris saw Amy's eyes. He'll turn us in. And if he says that you two knew about us but didn't say anything - you'll both be in hot water. Not that I care."

"So, what do we do?" I asked. He snorted.

"I need to call my parents. They know a place where we can hide." Cindy handed back Markus' phone. He rose slowly and hobbled his way across the room until he reached the kitchen.

"Um, should you be walking?" I asked. He shot me a dirty look as the phone rang. He spoke in whispers as the rest of us exchanged glances.

"No need to lay into you like that," Cindy muttered. I shook my head.

"He's just upset. I'm fine." Cindy didn't look convinced. Neither was I. Markus finally came back over to us.

"Don't move your boat. My parents are coming."

. . .

A short time later, thumps on the deck sounded. We walked outside to see two very disgruntled parents with soggy backpacks. Markus ran up to them as much as he was able and threw his arms around them.

"We're so glad you're safe," his mom cried, pausing in her hug to glare at the rest of us. Tom wisely stayed back by the door, almost out of sight.

"Come on, we need to go." They started for the railing. I awkwardly followed them. They were just about to jump off when they noticed me trailing like a lost puppy.

"What do you think you're doing?" Dr. Mercer snapped. I froze.

"Um . . . coming with you?"

"You'll do no such thing. You've already caused enough trouble. You'll just bring it with you, and the rest of us need to stay safe," the mom said coldly.

"Mom, Morris saw her eyes too. He'll turn her in if Tom doesn't," Markus said quietly.

"That's her problem." With that, they vanished over the rail, leaving me in a cold puddle of fear. Cindy and Tom ran up beside me.

"Are you kidding me? They just left you? That's so not cool! Go follow them!" Cindy shouted. I mutely shook my head.

"It won't work. It never would've worked." I had already messed up enough things for them, why would they want to keep babysitting the Cursed? I turned and pushed past them, locking myself in the bathroom like a perfectly mature six-year-old. I sank to the cool floor, trying not to tremble. I should've known that they wouldn't let me tag along. I really was Cursed. This whole mess was my fault. I pushed that woman into the fountain. I revealed the species. I would just keep adding bodies to my list. I was no better than Tom. Maybe I should end up in a tank with his other victims.

I finally ventured out when I trusted myself not to break down in front of the others. Their concerned looks didn't make it any easier to hold it together. Tom attempted to apologize, but I cut him off.

"It wouldn't have worked out anyway. I told you - I'm different. So we need a different game plan."

"We can't just keep Morris locked in the closet forever. He'll wake up eventually," Cindy pointed out.

"What if I take him back to shore, hand him over to the cops, and tell them the truth? Markus and his family are gone, so it won't matter if the world knows about them. And then when we get to the Amy part - she's human as you and me. Morris must've hallucinated because of his head injury," Tom said. "They'll have to believe you because your parents are human." I nodded.

"It might work. I don't have another option. The ocean isn't safe enough to just wander with everyone setting traps and looking for us now. And I don't have any secret hidey-holes." I wondered where Markus and his parents were possibly going that was safe.

. . .

We made our way back to land where Tom called the police. I switched on my scared human acting and everyone and their mom bought it. The police went to arrest Morris. We gave final statements and were allowed to go. Cindy and Tom seemed frighteningly impressed with my slight of truth.

After my parents were done threatening to lock me in my room for the rest of time to keep me safe, I collapsed on the bed, allowing my body to tremble.

Lucky couldn't even begin to describe my situation, but I still felt far from blessed. Cindy knew. Tom fucking Falcon knew. At any point, he could decide he needed another million and rat me out.

I never should've dove off that dock, I thought miserably. Getting my foot stuck in that trap was the worst mistake of my life.

TOM

I stayed awake long after the police had gone. I stood by the dock, staring off into the distance at Amy's little beach house. *What was she doing right now?* I wondered.

Probably cursing my guts to kingdom come and back.

I blew through my lips, running my fingers through my hair. *What the hell just happened?* I thought. I thought mermaids were evil. That they drowned humans for fun. That they lived in the ocean and only came up to screw with us?

According to recent events, everything I thought I knew was wrong. They were liars – sure – but not dangerous ones. At least, not those two. Markus' dad was a doctor for crying out loud! If mermaids killed humans for sport, why would one go through all the effort of becoming a doctor?

Why was my uncle so adamant that they be killed?

Bile rose in my throat as I pictured Markus bleeding and crying on the floor. Harmless little Markus, who I was more than ready to exchange for more money I didn't know what to do with.

He must hate me, I thought. How had he held it together? I had been bragging about turning in those girls for weeks. I clutched my stomach. The girls. Had they been harmless too? Had I even paused to think about it before carting them to shore? Had I even really looked at them before accepting that check?

I swore into the night before turning the boat back on and speeding out into the darkness. Hours later, the remains of my traps lay in a pile on the deck.

Evil or not, I wasn't taking any more chances until I knew for sure what was going on. It was too late to apologize to Markus, but maybe I could still apologize to Amy.

Whatever the hell she was.

AMY

Monday came too soon. I convinced my parents no evil mermaids were going to come after me in the school building, and they finally let me go.

Cindy waved excitedly when she saw me in the hallway. I swallowed as she hugged me, halfheartedly patting her back. I had imagined telling her a thousand times, and my fantasies had always filled me with relief.

I did not feel filled with relief.

Tom strode up to his locker. His normal posse followed him, except for one person, who seemed to leave a gaping hole in the hallway.

"Hey, where's Markus?" Marisol asked Tom, hanging off his waist like a keychain. He shrugged before slamming his locker shut.

"Don't know." He spared me a glance before walking out of sight. My heart settled in my gut.

The day dragged on. I was used to pretending everything was fine, but news had spread of what had happened that weekend, and everyone felt the need to come up and talk to me about it. Even the Principal came by and told us not to worry about the garbage thing.

"Ohmygod, are you okay?"

"You're so brave."

"Those stupid mermaids just keep making your life harder and harder, huh?" I wanted to punch them and say that humans were the ones ruining everything.

Cindy did her best to keep the questioners away from us, but she couldn't be everywhere at once. After my millionth ambush of the day, I was tempted to call my parents and admit that they were right about me skipping school.

That time, it was Tom who rescued me. He pulled me down under a stairwell away from the crowds and bent down to look me in the eyes.

"How are you doing?" he asked. I clenched my fists.

"How do you think I'm doing?" I growled. He shrugged.

"I mean, you're not in a tank right now, so . . ." I punched him in the shoulder.

"Did you drag me over here to threaten me?" He put his hands up, wincing at my blow.

"No, no, of course not. I just . . . I just wanted to apologize. I wouldn't have been doing this the whole time if I had known . . . you know. Not all of you are evil like that." I blinked at him.

"Yeah, sure." I tried to push past him.

"I took down all my traps!" I paused and turned back around. My gut told me he wasn't lying.

"Why?" I asked.

"I told you. Until I can figure out a way to tell between the dangerous ones and the safe ones - I won't be doing any more hunting." I blinked in surprise.

"Well . . . good then." He nodded, staring down at his shoes.

"I'm sorry," he whispered. I nodded. I wasn't about to tell him it was okay, because it wasn't. But stopping now was better than nothing.

"Just . . . keep your mouth shut. Please." He nodded and the bell interrupted our little heart-to-heart. We started to walk to class, but questions still nagged at me.

"Hey - if you ever figure out why Morris wanted to . . . you know. Let me know." He nodded.

MORRIS

The cop stood behind me, guarding the door.

"You get one phone call. Better make it a good one," he said. I scowled as I sat down by the phone. It's not like my useless brother would have enough money to bail me out even if he was sober enough to hear his phone ring. I had no intention of going away for this. I pursed my lips as I considered one person who might be rich and desperate enough to hear me out. I drummed my fingers impatiently as the phone rang.

"Who is this?"

"Arthur, hello," I said. Arthur sucked in a breath from the other end as the guard raised an eyebrow.

"You better have a damn good reason for calling me after what you put my daughter through," Arthur growled.

"You won't be complaining by the time I'm done. I have information for you." My mind flashed back to the claw-like markings on that monster's face. I didn't know they could phase halfway like that. Her markings confirmed an ancient rumor my father had told me that I never wanted to believe.

"Well what is it?" he asked. I smirked.

"Amy Wilson. She's one of them." Arthur laughed on the other end.

"We already confirmed she's not. I've been watching her swim in the pool with my daughter since they were little kids."

"But not recently, correct?" He went silent. "I'm not sure when the last time you saw them swim together was - but I'd imagine at some point - something dramatic happened which she used as an excuse to not get into the water anymore - right? You haven't seen her swim in years." He stayed silent.

"And even though that dramatic event probably happened in the ocean - she milked it to include other places - pools, lakes - you name it. She won't set toe near any of them."

"I-if what you're implying is true - that means -" he stuttered.

"I know exactly what it means," I growled. "And I highly suggest you get her and figure it out before it happens to more people like *you*."

I hung up the phone.

TOM

I doodled on the side of my desk as I ignored Mr. Johns. For the first time, he seemed to be giving me a break with the difficult math problems.

I couldn't have focused if I tried. An actual mermaid was sitting behind me in class – a mermaid who had saved my sorry ass. A mermaid I had promised not to go after.

The reality of the situation made my head spin. All I had to do was stand up and out her – and I would have another million dollars. I could do it right now, in the middle of math class. Mr. Johns would call the police or the aquarium, and men would show up to drag her away and do . . . do whatever they did with mermaids.

The thought of her being dragged away made my stomach clench. I didn't understand how my uncle bought the whole story of mermaids being dangerous. He had tried to murder my best friend. Not just turn him in – *murder* him. Beat him to death. What psycho does that? Why did my uncle think mermaids were that dangerous?

I mean, Amy had looked pretty badass going after him the way she had. But that had been a life-or-death situation. She had saved all of our lives.

Guilt tore into me again. *I should've never opened that box of traps,* I thought. I never should have gotten involved in this. Promising not to catch any other mermaids was one thing . . . but it wasn't like I could go back in time and decide to not turn in those two girls.

"Any questions? Tom, why don't you come up and try to solve this problem?" Mr. Johns asked. *It was good while it lasted,* I thought. I started to get up, but the intercom buzzed on before I could.

"We need Amy Wilson and . . ." the announcer paused. ". . . and Tom Falcon to the front office please." The intercom buzzed off. My blood froze. Mr. Johns gave me a look as I slowly stood up from my desk. Amy followed me and closed the door behind us.

"Forget your lunch?" I joked. *After you barely survived last weekend? Not likely. This isn't a coincidence.*

I looked over at Amy. Her face was the same color as the floor. *Who would want to talk to us right now? The police? We already told them we were human. What else would they need to talk to us about?*

"Did you say anything?" she whispered. I shook my head.

"Of course not," I whispered. She narrowed her eyes at me but seemed convinced.

I briefly considered scooping Amy up in my arms and bolting for the door. No sooner had the thought crossed my mind, than a man stepped out of the office, smiled a fake Barbie smile, and placed a cold hand on my shoulder. He was thick as a wall and wore a suit that looked like it was made of iron.

"Right this way," he said. I forced myself to be chill as we were pushed towards an empty conference room. I couldn't help but notice that another suited man stood in front of the office door as if he was guarding it. *Are these cops?* I wondered. *Why aren't they in uniform?*

"Cuse' me, but do you know why we're here?" I asked. The man stayed silent. Two more suited men walked in from behind him. They had the same fake, Barbie smiles strapped on their faces.

"We just have to ask you two a few quick questions concerning last weekend," the one on the left said. Amy crossed her arms.

"I thought we had already answered everything?" she asked.

"We're just covering our tracks. We'll have you out of here real soon," Righty said. I nodded and channeled all my energy into being calm.

"Ask away," I said. Righty opened up a notepad and started writing.

"Tom, you said that Markus was the only mermaid you came into contact with – correct?" I nodded. "You sure? There were no other ones?" If mermaids did have special powers – Amy would be using them to kill me. I nodded.

"Pretty sure I would've noticed if there had been any more," I laughed. The irony of the statement burned through my veins. Some mermaid catcher I was – how long had I been best friends with Markus? How long had Cindy been best friends with Amy? Fool me once, shame on you. Fool me for ten years, lots of shame on me.

"And Amy, you were the one who knocked Morris out with the pistol?" She nodded silently. "Wow, first you beat that mermaid at the aquarium, and then Morris. You must be a superhero in disguise." She laughed awkwardly.

"I mean, my parents are cops. They taught me how to defend myself, so blame them I guess." The men nodded.

"Amy, do you swim a lot?" Lefty asked. *Oh no.* Amy plastered on a fake smile and shook her head.

"Not really. I-I was attacked by a shark when I was little. Water's not really my thing anymore," she said. More scribbling.

"Not even in the pool?" Righty asked.

"I actually have an allergy to the type of chlorine they put in pools to clean them – so no," she said. I wondered if that statement was a lie. Were mermaids allergic to chlorine? Righty closed his notepad.

"Alrighty, that about wraps up our questions. Amy, we're going to need you to come with us for a few moments," Lefty said. We froze.

"Oh? Why's that?" Amy asked. She was an incredible actor. If I were her – I would be shitting my pants.

"Just to follow up on a few things." Her eyes flitted over to me. *They're lying,* I thought.

"Um . . . okay. Where exactly?"

"Our office. It won't take but a few moments." *Their office? What kind of office?* I cleared my throat.

"Well, why don't I tag along? Your guys might have more questions for me too," I said.

"Just her," Righty said firmly. Amy swallowed.

"I'm not going anywhere without my parents knowing where I am and what you're doing," she said. "They've been really worried over this whole thing – I'm sure you understand." Lefty smiled.

"We've already contacted your parents. They permitted us to take you down there for a little while," he said sweetly. *Oh no.* I remained where I sat. Amy had stopped breathing.

"Come on," Lefty said, crooning to her like a dog. She remained rooted to her seat. Their smiles evaporated. Lefty came forward and grabbed her by the arm.

"Go back to class Tom," Righty muttered. He shoved me out the door back into the hallway as Amy was dragged towards the front door. I twisted around to give Amy one last frantic look as the two men pulled her through the double doors.

AMY

The men escorted me to their car – and by escorted I mean they half-dragged me. Their hands felt like chains on my forearms.

How badly will I get hurt if I jump out the window while they're driving? I wondered uneasily as the black car skidded out of the parking lot. I held my shaking hands in my lap, trying to still them as the suited men drove on. By the time I convinced myself that I could shatter the thick black glass with my elbow if I tried hard enough, we pulled into an empty parking lot beside a building that was a gigantic gray brick. Adrenaline coursed through me as they pulled me from the car. *They wouldn't be holding onto me if they just had more questions for me,* I thought.

I wanted to scream. I wanted to tear from their grip and run for the ocean, but my body refused to cooperate with me. I was too busy trying to figure out who the *fuck* had turned me in.

Was it Tom? Had he decided to be greedy anyway? Had Cindy? Tom had seemed just as worried and nervous in the conference room as I had been. Cindy had been extra nice to me lately. Had someone else seen me and ratted me out?

But I had already proved I was human the first time the cops questioned us. I was clearly the human daughter of human parents. There should've been no further doubt!

The man took an ID badge out of his pocket and held it to a grate on the ground. It beeped, and the door swung open, revealing a tunnel. They shoved me towards it. I climbed down the steel ladder and landed in a narrow hallway packed with doors. The whole place smelled like bleach.

What the hell is this place? I wondered. *This isn't Arthur's Aquarium.* The men grabbed my arms again and marched me forward until we came to a gray room that stank like stale water. I looked down to see the floor was just a grate over a pool of water. Fish darted below the surface. They finally let go of me and stood back by the door.

"Is this her?" a familiar voice asked. The men parted to let Arthur stand in the doorway. I could practically smell the rage radiating from behind his calm exterior. He was pissed. Very pissed. I tried to breathe.

"Hey, Mr. Johnson. What am I doing here? What's going on?" I tried to sound like a confused innocent high school girl.

"You should know perfectly well what you are doing here," he said coldly. I swallowed. *I should've run when I had the chance.*

"Well, I don't, so . . ." Arthur frowned, and for a moment, the heavy gaze in his eyes almost made him look genuinely sad. He reached for a switch on the wall.

A single gasp left my throat as the floor beneath me split apart under my feet. I fell to the side, desperately trying to grab the floor as it slid away from me.

I rolled off the edge and hit the water below me with a thud. I kicked frantically, trying to get out of the water before I phased, but it was too late. By the time I reached the surface again, the floor had closed back up, and my webbed hands weren't able to pry them apart. Arthur stood above me, glaring down at me.

I shied away from his glare, trembling.

"Please," I said. "This isn't what it looks like. I'm not dangerous - I promise. I saved your daughter!" He knelt, raking his eyes over my exposed body. I shrunk away from him. *Who did this to me? Who turned me in? Oh god, what is he going to do to me?* He smirked.

"I'm going to need to ask you a few questions."

PART TWO

"Man is the cruelest animal."
~ Friedrich Nietzsche

ADAM

Pinecones and gumballs stabbed my bare feet as I bolted through the woods. Dogs barked behind me as I desperately tried to hold onto the few possessions I had managed to grab before jumping out of my bedroom window. Shoes had not been one of them.

I had figured this was coming, but the shock still felt like someone had dumped icy water directly onto my central nervous system. I managed to get my book sealed inside the plastic sandwich bag and shoved it into my back pocket without tripping over roots or getting eaten by a slobbering German Shepherd.

Something whistled past my ear and plunked into a pine tree a foot away. *Or tranqed,* I thought.

111

I broke through the trees to see police cars dotting the road before the sand. I weaved between them, somehow dodging more tranq darts. I slid across the hood of one car and the cop swore after me as I chugged through the sand. If you had told my parents their son would be running from the police that night, they would've laughed. *Our son? What on Earth would our son have done to get in that much trouble?*

I told myself I would mourn my family later as I reached the choppy water. I clawed my way out towards the ocean as my body phased. I prayed I hadn't lost the book in the surf as I reached the dark depths, gills frantically filtering oxygen from the icy water.

I looked around me. Boats dotted the surface, no doubt already alerted to my presence. I wondered if one of them belonged to the family who reported me, or if they chose to gloat from the police cars that chased me. I was suddenly scared for an entirely different reason. My mad dash to freedom hardly mattered if I got caught in a trap two seconds later.

I wanted to take a moment to be mad, to scream at the water around me like it was the ocean's fault I was born this way. Instead, I cautiously inched my way across the bottom, watching for traps, until I reached the open ocean.

I swam for miles until my body went numb from exhaustion. I saw the sun peeking up from around the curve of the Earth right as I hit my head on a sand bank. I shook the silt out of my hair and peeked up above the surface to see an island hovering in the dawn. It looked like something out of Jurassic Park, saturated with ferns and thick trees covered in moss. Sand dunes rose from the ground. It smelled earthy and ancient. It was only a few yards away. If any humans happened to be gazing into the water - I would be easy viewing. *Nice going, Adam. Run from the police only to waltz onto a public beach a few hours later.*

My exhaustion made it hard to feel too bad. I clawed my way up to the beach and looked around. There was nothing around but dunes - which told me it probably wasn't a public beach. Humans destroyed most dunes forever ago, and these went as far as I could see. Some of them looked like they were eating the trees.

I crawled the rest of the way onto the sand and collapsed on the ground as my body phased back. I forced myself to stand up and start walking along the water. I felt in my pocket and almost cried out in relief when I felt that my book had made it. It was the most sacred thing I owned. Even if I wasn't free anymore, I couldn't bear leaving it behind.

Something crawling out of the dunes caught my eye, making me jump. I paused and watched as a sea turtle slowly crawled her way out of the dune and toward the water. She glanced at me and continued on her way. She seemed just as tired as I felt.

My eyelids drooped, and I walked up to the dune she just crawled out of. I found a crevice and snuggled down into the rough sand, falling asleep instantly.

CINDY

Tom burst back into the classroom with a bang. Literally - he threw the door open so hard it smacked against the wall with a loud pop that made half the class jump in surprise. He looked at me, eyes wide and red at the edges. I held my breath as I waited for Amy to follow him through the door, but he just stood there. Mr. Johns sighed.

"Are you going to sit down or just keep standing there?" Tom rolled his eyes and shuffled to his seat. As soon as the teacher had his back turned, I turned around.

What happened? Where is Amy? I mouthed. He shook his head and buried his head in his arms. My blood ran cold. As soon as the bell rang, we cornered each other in the hallway.

"You ratted her out didn't you?" he hissed.

"What the hell are you talking about? I didn't tell anybody, did you?"

"I didn't tell!" Tom's eyes shone as his chest rattled with every breath. I tried to steady my breathing and put my hands on his shoulders.

"Tom, what happened?"

"These weird guys were there. They were asking us a bunch of weird questions about last weekend. And then they took her." My heart dropped to my feet.

"What? How did they know? Where are they taking her?"

"I'm not sure. They just said they had questions for her."
Questions my ass, I thought.

"Okay, okay. If they're taking her anywhere - it's probably to my dad's place. If he has her - I'll just tell him what happened and that she's not dangerous and he'll let her go!" I said.

The look on Tom's face said he didn't believe me.

. . .

I raced back home only to sit at the kitchen table and tap my fingers for another three hours until my dad got back. I stood up as he came through the door and started blubbering before he stepped over the threshold.

"Dad - I know you guys have Amy - and listen - she's not like the others - she's not dangerous - we've been friends for years and -" He held up his hands.

"Baby, what are you talking about?" I paused.

"Amy. You guys have her."

"Honey, why would I have Amy? Wasn't she with you at school today?" I opened my mouth to retort but shut it. Even if the men had taken Amy to a different aquarium, he would surely know about it.

He had to be lying to me.

"N-nevermind." He raised his eyebrow and ruffled my hair like he used to do when I was a little kid.

"If she wasn't at school, she's probably just not feeling well. Can't hardly blame her after everything that's happened." I nodded, slowly backing away.

"Yeah. I'll call her." I hurried from the room, trying to breathe. My dad had my best friend, and he was lying about it. Why would he lie about it? Was he just trying to spare my feelings? Surely I would find out eventually when he put her on display in front of the whole world?

He hasn't hurt the other ones he's caught, I told myself. *He won't hurt Amy. He'll just study her. She'll still be safe.*

She had to be.

ADAM

I woke up starving. I shook the sand out of my hair and blinked in the harsh sunlight. Various insects buzzed around me. The wind whistled through whatever plants were growing on top of the dunes. I stood up and ventured further into the woods, hoping for a fruit tree of some kind. I knew I could technically stomach raw fish, but I wasn't quite that hungry. Giving in and eating that seemed like admitting defeat – like I'd been officially cast out of human society. If I could still get my hands on human food – there might still be hope. Right?

After what felt like hours of wandering through the dense vegetation, I concluded there were no fruit trees. The sun climbed further into the sky and the insect swarm around me got bigger. I eventually quit trying to shoo them away and let myself get eaten.

I was about to give up and head back to the beach where I could at least drink the salt water when I spotted it - an odd smear of white in the middle of the green. I snuck up closer and saw a dilapidated old cabin nestled in amongst the wild. It looked like it had been abandoned for a while. The porch was sagging and there were all kinds of old glass bottles and crates stacked around it. But more importantly, there was an overgrown garden off to the side. And that garden included an orange tree.

Like an idiot, I jumped through the foliage and sprinted for the tree. I tried to jump to reach the fruit, but the shortest branches were still out of my reach. I groaned in frustration and looked back to the pile of trash. I grabbed an old wooden crate out of the pile and lugged it over to the tree. I climbed on top, slightly worried it would collapse underneath me but too hungry to care much. I reached on my toes and finally snagged an orange. I laughed in relief as I started to peel it.

"You crushed my seedlings." I startled and fell off the crate, landing on my butt in the dirt. Orange still clutched in my grasp, I looked up to see an alien.

Okay, not quite an alien, but it may as well have been. The creature standing before me was an old white woman with wiry silver hair pulled back in a braid. Her t-shirt and shorts were smeared with dirt and the blood dripping from the dead raccoon slung over her shoulder. As I gawked at her, she rolled her eyes and pointed at the ruts I had created by dragging the crate. I could see several little bright green shoots trying to breathe over the dirt I had accidentally buried them in.

"Um . . . I'm sorry." She harrumphed and shook her head disapprovingly at me.

"Throw the orange peel in my compost pile once you're done." She pointed to the other side of the garden where a pile of moldy dirt sat mildewing in the hot sun.

"Um . . . yes ma'am." With that, she turned and marched over to the cabin. She plopped the raccoon down on an old stump and lifted a small hatchet from the ground. With an efficient thwack, she removed the raccoon's head from its body, skinned it, and removed the entrails like she was trimming fat from a chicken breast. I stared shamelessly as she chopped the raccoon into chicken strip-size pieces and gathered them together in her hands. She strode back inside, leaving me in the dirt with my uneaten orange.

After a few moments of her disappearing, my brain turned back on. I jumped to my feet and raced after her, throwing open the door.

"Wait!" I cried. "Don't call the police!" She turned, the raccoon strips still in her hands. The room was jam-packed with cluttered desks, a cluttered bed, and a desktop computer that looked like it was from dinosaur times. Small creatures I didn't want to know the names of clicked around in glass jars on shelves. The computer growled like the dinosaurs it probably used to live with.

"You're still here? Why would I call the police?" she snapped. I blinked. Then I looked down at my arms to make sure my markings were still showing. Yup – there they were – rather visible on my pale freckled skin.

"Um . . . can you see very well?" I asked. She rolled her eyes and plopped the raccoon strips in a small mini fridge on one of the cluttered desks.

"I can see well enough to butcher my own raccoon, can't I?" she retorted, adjusting her grimy glasses.

"Um . . . just checking."

"Sides. I can't call the police even if I wanted to. Don't got a phone. And we're about an hour away from law enforcement anyway." I raised my eyebrow.

"Where are we?" I asked. She rolled her eyes.

"Don't even know where you are." She went back to ignoring me, washing her hands in a rusty sink on the other side of the wall. How the old shack had running water or electricity, I didn't understand. I waited until she was done. When she saw I wasn't leaving, she sighed and sat down on the side of the bed.

"You know if I was out to hunt mermaids – you'd be in pretty bad shape right now," she said. I shrugged.

"Well considering you didn't shoot me for stealing your oranges, you're not out to hunt merfolk. Which is almost *more* confusing."

"Listen, if your species is more evolved and powerful than ours – then it's your right to do what you want. Nature always beats man. At least in the end, it does." She sighed wistfully. I looked over her messy desk and saw drawings of all sorts of creatures – sea turtles, insects, birds, crocodiles – you name it.

"I'm guessing you're a scientist?" She scoffed.

"Psh, a *scientist*. I'm one of the *best* environmentalists in the world! Not that people care anyway."

"What's your name?"

"Karen Bell."

"Wait – I've heard of you before! You're that crazy squatter who got the right to study sea turtles! You turned your whole island into a national park! Wait – that means I'm on . . ."

"Baldwin Island," she confirmed. *Oh wow, I'm trespassing on important ground,* I thought. My science teacher had lectured us on the history and ecology of the island for days last semester. It was only an hour's drive down the coast from my hometown. This place was famous. And protected.

But it was also limited. Only a certain number of humans could visit a day, and Karen was the only one allowed to live here because she was the famous scientist who protected it. I smiled. I might have just stumbled across a secluded gold mine.

"Wow. That's cool. Can I stay here?" I blurted. She raised her eyebrow. "Not here – like in this room – but like . . . around? I don't really have anywhere else to go. And . . . I'll replant your seedlings?" I offered meekly. I hadn't exactly had time to plan ahead while running from the cops. There was no way I could go back home. Everyone knew what I was now. The neighbors would fight over who got to turn me in.

I had no clue where other merfolk went to hide when they abandoned their lives on land. This protected wilderness area was probably my best bet until I figured out where to go and what to do next. She rolled her eyes.

"I'm not a babysitter."

"I don't need babysitting!" She raised her eyebrow and smirked.

"How old are you, twelve?"

"I'm fifteen! I'm a sophomore!" *Was* a sophomore. A few more weeks, and I would've been a junior. "I can catch fish for you?" She rolled her eyes.

"Don't let the park rangers see you. Stay out of my way. And don't steal all my oranges."

TOM

I knew there was bad news when Cindy refused to meet my eyes the next day at school. I yanked her to a more secluded area of the hallway, which made some people turn and stare.

"What happened?" She shook her head.

"He said he didn't know what I was talking about," she whispered. My blood ran cold. Why would he refuse to acknowledge there was another mermaid in his aquarium? Shouldn't he be off celebrating right now?

"If he doesn't have her then who does?" I demanded.

"I called every aquarium in a fifty-mile radius. None of them have anything." The bell rang and people started pushing past us to get to class.

"I don't know what to do," Cindy said, wiping her eyes. "Why are they hiding her? Why won't my dad tell me what's going on?"

The same question echoed through my head throughout the day. I walked around in more of an unfocused daze than normal. Mr. Johns seemed personally offended by it and made sure to mention it in front of the whole class as I attempted to solve an equation with at least five letters in it.

I kicked the sand as I walked to my empty house. Only the sight of Amy's parents sitting on the dock was enough to bring me out of it. I ran up to them, and they eyed me suspiciously.

"Hey," I said, trying to sound nonchalant. "Noticed Amy wasn't at school today. She sick or something?"

"Nope, she just went out of state to visit some family." They said it without making eye contact. The dad stared off into the ocean, tracing the edge of his glass. The mom pursed her lips together so hard they turned white.

"Oh yeah, what family?" I asked. The dad waved his hand.

"Her cousins." *Liars*, I thought. I knew neither of her parents had siblings. Amy had no cousins to visit. She had said so during a family tree project back in elementary school.

"Okay, just wondering." I turned without another word, my heart hammering in my chest. *They know exactly where she is - they just won't tell me. And they don't seem that worked up about it. Then again, they were cops. And what kind of cops let the kid next door stay with their drunk dad for years?* I shook my head and slammed the door as I walked inside.

Someone knows what's going on. And they won't tell. But why? The two I caught made national news. Reporters chased me for weeks.

Why would they keep Amy a secret?

ADAM

With Karen's blessing, I took up residence amongst the insects and whatever else called Baldwin home. I spent my days gathering oranges and replanting Karen's plants. I sometimes observed her as she came in and out, although we didn't talk very often. She preferred to keep to herself and her dead animals. The most noise I caught her making was when she stopped to shout profanities at the boats that came by. Sometimes, I left her piles of raw fish in her fridge as a thank you.

"I'm having an intern come and stay with me for a few weeks." I almost fell off the orange tree crate again. I made it safely back to solid ground and raised my eyebrow.

"An intern?"

"Yeah. Occasionally a high school student is crazy enough to come camp with the *squatter*," she quipped. "He'll be here tonight. So, stay hidden unless you want him attempting to call the police. Then we'll both be in trouble." I nodded.

. . .

I stumbled through the door, trying not to drop the slippery fish on the floor. I had to grab one with my teeth as it started to slip, and I shuddered at the slimy texture. After a few days of subsiding on just oranges, I had gotten hungry enough to stomach some raw fish. It tasted fine. The texture left more to be desired, especially the eyeballs. The eyeballs were gross. I told myself it was no different than eating sushi. Eating raw fish didn't make me any more of an animal than I had been before, but no matter how many times I told myself that, it still made me feel dirty.

I opened her mini fridge with my foot and started shoving fish in as I heard the door creak open. I spit the last one out of my mouth.

"I know, I know, intern is going to be here tonight, I'm leaving, I'm leaving." I turned around to see a skinny Hispanic teenager with a camping backpack bulkier than he was. He wore green cargo shorts and a green vest with enough pockets to make every girl in the world jealous. His jaw dangled. I could sense the acute fear and surprise from across the room. Outside, the shadow of a park ranger loomed through the window. I dropped the rest of the fish on the table and winced at the sound.

Good going, Adam. You are literally the worst at not getting captured.

I hadn't been bothering to hide my markings. What was the point when the only human around already knew what I was?

"Hey, is Karen in there? I need to talk to her!" the ranger shouted from outside. I waited for the kid to start screaming that he was trapped with a dangerous mermaid, but he seemed too shocked to make a noise. He was frozen like a possum, eyes wide and hands gripping the straps of his bookbag like a safety railing.

"Hello?" the ranger called. The kid's lips twitched the tiniest bit. I lunged across the room and slammed my hand over the teenager's mouth not a second too late. He froze up once again, hot and clammy in my hands. Mercifully, Karen started talking outside.

"I'm right here, Steve. What do you want? The kid get here okay?" "Yeah, he's fine. Just wanted to let you know there's been more complaints about your horse riding activities on the beach."

"Then tell people not to look and get off my island, you included! I have work to do." The ranger revved up his four-wheeler and spun away as Karen barged into her cabin. She rolled her eyes when she saw our awkward tango.

"I should've told you to leave too," she muttered. I unhanded the skinny kid, who immediately started wheezing and pointing at me.

"He . . . he . . . you know about him? He *lives* here?"

"He's more like an annoying pest who invites himself over sometimes. Who was *supposed* to be gone by nightfall," she hissed.

"It is definitely not nightfall yet!" I protested. "And I'm sorry, I'll leave. Please don't call the police." I pushed past the both of them and raced out into the dusk – sorry *nightfall* – and vanished into the water.

It took me a few days to work up the courage to go back up to the surface. I assumed Karen had talked the kid down because no extra boats showed up to catch me. Or maybe she just threw his phone in the ocean. Either way - I missed my oranges.

I spied on the cabin for a few moments to make sure it was vacant before venturing into the garden. I picked enough oranges to last me for the day and walked back towards the water before spying a pile of dried meat – raccoon probably – by the doorstep with a clumsy note attached to it.

Sorry for almost screaming at you. No hard feelings?

. . .

I found the skinny kid taking notes beside a sand dune.

"Um . . . hi," I said. He jumped up and swiveled around. It looked like the mosquitoes were attacking him twice as hard. I swallowed nervously. "The beef jerky was good."

"It was actually possum jerky," he said. "You know Karen doesn't stick with conventional meats." I laughed.

"Yeah, I gathered that."

"I'm sorry for freaking out the other day. Karen told me all about you and said you were cool . . . so . . . I hope you don't drown me." I snorted.

"We don't actually do that. And no hard feelings – I probably would've done the same thing if I were in your shoes."

"Haha, yeah." There were a few moments of awkward silence. Speaking with a human with my markings out felt like I was breaking a thousand rules. But I had barely talked to anyone for weeks - and I was desperate for conversation. He already knew exactly what I was – hiding my markings wouldn't change that.

"So, you're here for an internship thing?" At this, the teenager lit up like a Christmas tree.

"Oh yeah! I had to beg my parents for months before they would even let me sign up – and then I had to enter all these crazy contests and prove my worth – it was nuts! I'm super lucky to be here."

"What are you studying?"

"Well, several things, but mostly how sea turtles choose their nests."

"Oh, I saw one a week or so ago. It might've been laying eggs" Somehow, his face lit up even more.

"You saw her crawling out of the dunes?" I nodded. He all but grabbed my hand and dragged me down the beach. "Then she was laying! Can you show me? Please?" I led him down the beach and found the place where I had crashed that first night. The entire time, he sputtered facts about whatever he laid his eyes on.

Those wheat-like things growing in the dunes were sea oats, and they were *so important* to keeping the dunes anchored to the island. And the dunes on the island were *so important* because sea turtles needed tertiary dunes to nest in. And that plant over there would numb your teeth if you tried to eat it. And those birds . . . It all turned into mush in my head after a while. I got good grades in school but this kid was on another level of nerdiness. It was as if an encyclopedia had put on a vest and sprouted legs.

We finally came to the nest, and he frowned at my sleep indentation. When I admitted I had spent the night curled up there, he twitched like he was having an aneurysm. That earned me a lecture about how *delicate* the dunes were and how *careful* you had to be. He only relaxed when he uncovered the nest and saw that none of the eggs had been damaged by his newest ignorant merfolk friend.

We ended up hanging out until the sun went down. The boy - Emanuel, fifteen just like me - reminded me of my mom - full of curiosity and questions. I had always been afraid of humans finding out who I was or asking me questions I couldn't answer but answering Emanuel's questions felt strangely freeing.

For the first time in my life, I didn't have to lie to a human. He nodded as I talked, and I had the impression he was taking mental notes, committing everything I said to memory. I was apparently the most fascinating organism to study on the island, but I didn't mind. He believed me and talked to me like I was a normal person – not a dangerous creature worth a million dollars.

"Do you miss it?" he asked.

"Miss what?" Emanuel shrugged.

"Being a human. Or, pretending to be a human, I guess." I sighed.

"Yeah. I miss it a lot."

"But doesn't it feel better to be like . . . out? Like, to not have to lie to everyone all the time?" I snorted.

"I went from lying and hiding to just hiding." Emanuel blushed.

"Sorry, that was insensitive of me to ask." I shook my head.

"No. It's an honest question. I honestly do miss being a human. I miss my family, my friends. My church. My life was great before any of this happened. And the hard part is . . . I feel like if I ever did tell my family, they would've been cool with it. But I never got the chance to explain myself to them before I had to run." *I never had the chance to apologize.*

"Wait, your parents are human?"

"Yeah. My biological parents passed away in an accident when I was a little kid. We were super close friends with this family from church, and I had no other family to go to, so they adopted me. I think it was my nosy neighbors who called the police. They're the only other ones who could've noticed me sneaking out of the house and heading for the water at night. I literally had to run for it. I didn't even get to say bye." I sniffed and sighed.

"This is going to sound so stupid – but I was always the good kid back home. I held the priesthood at church. I had good grades. Never got in trouble. And now I'm homeless and trespassing on a National Park. I've never . . . been in trouble before." The memory played itself over again in my head.

I stood there frozen in front of my dad, my book in my hand, the window half open. If he told me to stay - I would have. I loved my parents. I was supposed to listen to them. *Thou shalt obey thy parents.* I hated lying to them. If being a good kid meant getting taken away, so be it.

But my dad hadn't told me to stay. He saw the fear on my face and mouthed *run.* I jumped through the window and made it fifty yards with the precious time my father had bought me.

Emanuel thoughtfully scribbled in the sand.

"Well, maybe you shouldn't think of it like you're a good or bad kid. Life is more complicated than that. I mean Corinthians talks about the letter of the law versus the spirit of the law. What?" he teased at my puzzled expression. "My parents are Catholic. I've read the Bible too."

"Sorry," I said sheepishly. "There aren't very many religious kids at my school."

"What religion are you?"

"Church of Jesus Christ of Latter-day Saints."

"So, Mormon?"

"We prefer not to be called that anymore. Too many negative stereotypes." Emanuel nodded.

"At least you're not a Baptist," he teased.

"My nosy neighbors are Baptist."

"Ah, that explains it." We both laughed.

"But seriously dude. I mean, I know humans are saying a bunch of bad things right now, but do you really think you're a bad person for running away? Do you really think that God would expect you to turn yourself in?" I pursed my lips. The laws said I had to be. And the church said to obey the laws of whatever land you lived in. Why would God say that if he hadn't meant it? Emanuel continued after a moment of silence.

"My dad usually has to work on Sundays. But sometimes, he would lie and say he was sick so he could get Sunday off and come to mass with us. Maybe that's a sin, but it's sinning for a good reason I think."

I found myself staring at the trawler out in the distance. Did God want sea turtles to die just because they got trapped in a net? Were those fishermen sinning? Sometimes, I wished God would be more specific with his laws. But I guess that wasn't the point. *Work out your own salvation with fear and trembling.* I found myself standing up.

"Where are you going?" Emanuel asked.

"I just need some time to think." I walked down the beach, shuffling my feet through the sand as I went. I pulled my book out of my pocket and fished it out of the plastic bag for the first time since running.

I sat down and thumbed through the pages. Thinking of reading filled me with guilt. Why should I be allowed to read my scriptures or pray if I was breaking the rules? I squeezed my eyes shut and bent my head.

"God if you're there, I could use a sign" *No, you're not supposed to ask for signs.* "Not a sign. I could use some . . . advice? Should I go home? Should I stay here? I just want to do the right thing. I don't want my parents to be worried about me. Please, tell me what to do."

The wind blew across the sand, ruffling the worn pages between my fingers. I quietly read the exposed pages before tucking the book back inside the plastic bag.

And whatsoever thing is good will bear good fruit.

My dad often teased me for being more religious than him, even though he was the bishop of our local congregation. I had figured being diligent would make up for lying all the time while crossing my fingers and hoping God wasn't always mad at me.

I had never considered a world where God wasn't mad at me until my father told me to run. To break the law. To get myself to safety.

I left the bag on the beach before diving into the waves and following the curve of the island down into the inky darkness. I headed right for the shrimp trawler Emanuel had been complaining about earlier. The nets were piled up on board, but several traps of a different kind hung in the water, glinting like needles in the moonlight.

I took a sharp shell and began to saw at the ropes, making sure to stay far away from the traps. When they broke, I swam up to the surface and with some careful maneuvering, climbed up the ladder to the deck. I left the traps in a tangled pile before diving overboard and heading to the next ship out in the distance.

If I was allowed to be free, so were the others. And it would be easier for other merfolk to be free if less humans were trying to catch them.

I hoped God would forgive me.

TOM

I knew my idea was terrible and poorly planned at best, but that didn't stop me from walking into Arthur's Aquarium at closing time. I barely needed to explain who I was to be allowed in without a ticket. I was responsible for their most famous exhibit, after all. Why wouldn't they let me in for free? The person working the front desk asked me how I was doing. I responded jovially, laughing and joking as I asked if it would be too much trouble to see behind the scenes of the mermaid exhibit. He escorted me down the dark hallway.

The burly man guarding the door let me through as one of the scientists started explaining how things worked. I didn't gather a word of it as I spotted the two girls.

They were held in separate cages – which made me mad enough to spit. I don't know why I was so surprised – they were immobilized in a tiny tank during the day anyway. At least that was what I had heard - I had never come to see them in person. I hadn't cared enough.

Each cage was big enough to hold a Great Dane. *Or an elementary schooler*, I thought bitterly. It occurred to me that I had no clue how old they were, or what their names were.

They were both huddled as far away from the door as they could be, burrowed into a thin blanket and their respective hospital gowns. One of them had cracked an eye open at my arrival but otherwise didn't move. Amy was nowhere to be seen.

The room had few other decorations. A stainless-steel gurney with straps rested off to the side – a tranq gun resting on top.

This might be a terrible idea, but it's worth it, I thought. The scientist jabbered away, motioning to other instruments in the room. He didn't notice as I quietly picked up the tranq gun and aimed at his leg. As soon as I pulled the trigger, he fell to the floor with hardly a sputter. *Jeez, what do they have in these darts?* The awake one jerked to attention.

"Where is Amy?" I demanded, diving for the cages and fumbling with the locks. They required keys. I swore. "Where are the keys?" I shouted. The girl wordlessly pointed at the scientist. I dragged him over and fished in his pockets until I felt them. I jammed it into the lock and yanked the door open before moving to the next one. The girl scrambled out and shoved me to the side as she crawled in after her sister and dragged her out.

"Who the hell are you?" she hissed as she attempted to wake her sister up. *Oh thank god they don't recognize me*, I thought. Convincing them to run away with me would be a lot harder if they knew I was the one who had turned them in to begin with.

Now that they were outside the cages, I could tell that the awake one was the older one – or at least the bigger one. The younger one's head lolled to the side as she struggled to blink and stand up. Their dark skin was pale and stretched tight over their cheeks. Their braids hung in tangles around their face. They did not smell good.

"What's wrong with her? Is she okay?" I demanded.

"She's just sedated. Who the hell are you?" the awake one hissed again. I hesitated. I doubted right then was the best time to tell the truth.

"Not important. Where is Amy? We need to get her out too."

"You're rescuing us?" She narrowed her eyes at me suspiciously. I rolled my eyes.

"What does it look like! Now please, tell me where Amy is, we need to get her too!"

"I don't know who you're talking about." The color drained from my face. My knees shook, and I had to balance myself on the wall to keep from falling. There were no other aquariums with mermaid exhibits.

"No," I muttered. "No, no, she has to be here! She's about this short, wavy dirty blonde hair, her markings look like this." I raked my fingers over the left side of my face. "You seriously haven't seen her?" I demanded, my voice shaking in desperation. If Amy wasn't here, then where the hell could she be? The girl slowly shook her head.

"We're the only ones here," she said. I swallowed. The scientist on the floor groaned, making us all jump. *Okay, time to improvise.*

"Okay. I need to get you two out of here. Let me help." I scooped up the younger mermaid in my arms and flung her over my shoulder. I peeked out in the hallway and saw the guard still standing at his post. I reached for my pistol only for the guard to suddenly drop to the floor. I turned around to see the older one holding the tranq gun. She trained her steely eyes on me.

"If you try anything funny, you're next," she threatened. I nodded.

"Let's go."

CINDY

It took three tries for whoever was calling me to wake me up from my crying-induced nap. I blearily blinked my eyes and tapped my phone screen until the buzzing stopped.

"What do you want?" I moaned, not bothering to check the caller ID.

"I need you to come down to my boat right now!" I winced at the loud voice.

"Tom, is that you? What the hell man?"

"NOW! It's important!" He hung up, leaving me mystified and my head pounding. I grabbed my jacket and stalked out onto the docks with my pajamas still on. I swore when I realized I had left my phone on my nightstand. When I arrived at the boat, all the lights were off. *If he's trying to play a joke on me*, I thought. I stalked up the ladder and pounded on the door.

"You better have a good reason for this, Falcon!" I shouted. The door whipped open, and I was dragged inside. The only light was coming from the grungy lamp without a shade in the corner. Tom had somehow gotten his fancy motorcycle through the door and had it shoved up against the far wall.

"Did anyone follow you?" Tom hissed, bloodshot eyes staring down at me. I shoved him away.

"Jeez, no. What the heck is going on? You're seriously freaking me out." I looked around the room and my hands flew to my mouth.

"Holy shit!" I squeaked.

"Cindy, this is Sam and Terri," Tom said, motioning to the two kids curled up on the far edge of the couch. The taller one stared daggers at me as the shorter one leaned heavily on her shoulder, eyes half shut. I recognized them from the constant barrage of pictures and videos from the news and social media.

I ran my fingers through my hair. "What were you *thinking?*" I hissed. Tom rolled his eyes.

"Look, you can yell at me for being stupid later – we have bigger problems on our hands. Amy wasn't there," Tom said. I swallowed.

"She wasn't? Are you sure?"

"We're sure. Never heard of her. Never seen her," Sam said. She watched me carefully out of the corner of her eye. Her face was framed in gentle, silvery blue swirls. Her dark eyes glittered with something deep that made me wonder how they ever contained her.

"Well, if she's not there, then where the heck is she? What exactly was your plan here? Why are they here?" I demanded. Tom sighed.

"I kinda . . . impulsively showed up to the aquarium at closing . . . pretended I wanted a backstage tour. I thought that I could get all three of them out and let them go before anyone caught me."

"That was literally as far ahead as you thought? Did you even know what you were walking into? How did you know this was going to work? Did you hide your face? Are there cops headed here right now?" Questions rolled off my tongue, unable to stop. "Why were they even willing to go with you? You were the one who turned them in in the first place!" I paused. "They know that, right?" I whispered. Sam rolled her eyes, answering my question.

"Yes, I told them," Tom said. I paced, resisting the urge to slam my head against the wall.

"Why didn't you come ask me for help! We could've worked together on this! What did you think was going to happen to you after all of this? You're going to get arrested! They're going to take them back to the lab!"

"I was going to give them the keys to the boat and let myself get arrested! It doesn't matter what happens to me! But we still need Amy. We can't just leave her!" Tom protested. The younger one, Terri, motioned haphazardly. Sam turned to look at her.

"Terri says that Tom's plan was ingenious. If he had tried to research how to break into the aquarium, he would've brought more attention to himself. Cops can look at your search history. Acting impulsively might've been the only reason we got out so easily." Terri went back to slumping on Sam's shoulder.

"Why isn't she talking?" I asked.

"She's nonverbal," Sam said. "She speaks ASL." *Mermaids can be mute?* I thought. Terri signed something else.

"Not deaf and not dumb either," Sam translated as Terri shot us a bird. I blinked in surprise. The tiny sleepy shell of a girl didn't exactly look old enough to know offensive gestures. Sam smacked her hand down.

"We have bigger problems to worry about. Tom's right. We can't risk leaving Amy behind if she's a Cursed." I furrowed my brow.

"A Cursed?"

"It's what they call merpeople who weren't born that way," Tom said. *How fitting*, I thought.

"How are we supposed to find her? When I ask my dad about her, he pretends he doesn't know anything."

"She must be in a different building or something. Arthur's keeping her a secret for whatever reason."

"And now that we've disappeared, I bet Arthur will up security wherever Amy is. Especially when they see you on the security tapes, Tom," Sam said. Tom groaned. Terri signed more.

"I can hack into his e-mail. I might be able to find something there," Sam translated. Tom and I exchanged a glance.

"Um . . . she knows how to hack into computers?" I asked Sam. Terri leaned forward and glared at me.

"My sister is incredibly gifted. Before we were taken, she was about to start taking high school classes," Sam said. We gawked at the skinny girl. "And you can talk to *her* if you have a question, not me," Sam added pointedly, eyes narrowing. I swallowed. Even without the mermaid thing - these kids were intense. How old were they?

"So, you're like . . . really smart," Tom summarized. Terri nodded.

"She is. She can hack an email no problem," Sam said. I nodded, hope building up in my chest.

"Okay, let's do that then! I'll go home and grab my laptop and . . ." I trailed off. "How much time do you think we have before the cops show up here? You guys need a place to hide." Tom nodded.

"We can just hide in the ocean," Sam said. "I promise we won't leave for real until we help you find your friend. If she's a Cursed, she's too valuable to be left behind." Tom shook his head.

"Hiding in the ocean would be suicide. There're a million boats out there – everything is laid with traps. The ocean is exactly where they'll be looking for you. And you can't stay on the boat, they'll look here too." Tom's eyes suddenly widened. He grinned at me. I narrowed my eyes.

"What?"

"I know where they won't look for us. Your house!" Tom said triumphantly. Sam made a choking noise.

"Are you crazy? You want to hide two mermaids under the roof of the man who's been holding them captive?" I hissed. Tom shrugged.

"Think about it. Where would Arthur never look? You said yourself he's barely ever there! And then Terri will have super easy access to your computer! Two birds with one stone!" I tried to come up with an argument, but my words died on my tongue. As crazy as it sounded, it might just work. Terri signed rapidly.

"She's asking if your boat has internet or any radios." Tom nodded. "Turn them off. Right now. They don't come on again unless she says so."

"Why?" I asked.

"You can track people through almost any technology nowadays," Sam translated. Tom rushed off to unplug stuff. Sam looked dangerously green.

"I'll go if Tom gives us his gun. So we can protect ourselves," she said. Tom shrugged and strolled over, handing Sam the gun out of the back of his pants.

"Tom, does she even know how to shoot that thing? She's like . . . ten!" I whispered under my breath.

"I can hear you; I'm thirteen, and I can shoot just fine," Sam said. *Mental note: merpeople can hear everything*, I thought, grinning sheepishly. Tom snorted.

"Yeah, no kidding." He glanced down at his watch. "We should go now before your dad gets home or the cops get here." I nodded. The girls stood up. For the first time, I noticed that they were wearing threadbare hospital gowns. Their hair was greasy and tangled, cheeks sunken in, eyes nervous and darting. Sam clenched the gun in one hand and what looked like a tranq gun in the other. Terri wobbled on her feet, balancing herself on Sam's shoulder. I offered my arm out as a support, but she refused to take it.

"They gave her sedatives whenever they put her on display to keep her calm. She's fine – just takes a while to wake back up," Sam said. I nodded and herded the group toward my car. Before we got there, Terri fished Tom's phone out of his pocket and chucked it in the ocean. I swallowed, grateful I had forgotten mine at the house.

We stole through the darkness towards my place. I counted my blessings that the docks weren't illuminated at night.

"Do you have any cameras?" Sam asked. I shook my head. We moved into the house and to my bedroom. I opened my closet and lamely gestured in. Random piles of clothes and swimsuits littered the floor. I gathered them up and shoved them out of the way the best I could. Tom helped me yank down some blankets and we constructed as fluffy of a nest as we could on the floor. We all sat down, breathing hard.

"Thank you," Sam said quietly, staring down at her feet. For the first time, I noticed little scars lacing her ankles. Tom sniffed.

"Don't thank us yet," he said gruffly. He sounded like he was going to keep talking but closed his mouth.

"Are you guys hungry? Or thirsty?" *Or okay?* It occurred to me for the first time that they might have injuries. How exactly had they been treated in the lab? I had never bothered to go see them. I had been too scared to go look at the same type of creatures that had tried to kill me.

"We're fine. I mean, hungry, thirsty, yes, but otherwise fine," Sam said.

"I'll grab some food." I jogged to the kitchen and grabbed an assortment of things I doubted my dad would miss. When I returned, the two girls immediately jerked to attention. Tom and I watched in fascination as they scarfed down everything they could get their hands on. I had never seen someone eat so fast in my life.

I realized with a pang that this was the first time in weeks that they must've had access to normal human food. Who knew what the scientists gave them in the aquarium? My mind strayed to how Amy was being treated. My eyes welled and I stubbornly blinked away the tears. I had way more hope than I had a few hours ago when I had been crying my eyeballs out. I had to keep it together.

. . .

The whole day at school, I waited for the cops to come bursting through the doors, guns drawn, demanding to know where the girls were. But nothing happened. Marisol stuck out her lower lip when she didn't see Tom, but that was about as dramatic as the day got.

On the way home, Tom's boat looked completely undisturbed. *Okay, something is wrong*, I thought. *Surely they've discovered the girls aren't there by now. Where are the reporters? Where are the search teams?*

Maybe they've already been found.

I raced inside and breathed a sigh of relief when I threw open the closet door to find them. They all huddled together, playing a game of Go Fish.

"You look like you've seen a ghost," Tom said.

"Why aren't you all over the news? No one cared that you were gone today! I haven't heard a single word about their escape!" I hissed. Terri smirked and held up my laptop. My dad's email account was open. I grabbed it and quickly scanned the screen.

Keep this quiet. No one can know. Find TF and the subjects.

Tom grinned. "If you check the aquarium website, it says the mermaid exhibit is undergoing renovations." I couldn't help but scoff. My dad would do anything to avoid admitting he slipped up or did something wrong - including letting his two most prized possessions out of his aquarium.

"That explains it then," I said. Terri signed.

"This is great. If no one knows - fewer people are looking for us," Sam translated.

"What about Amy? Do we know anything else about her?" I asked.

"There's no mention of her in his emails. He might be using a different computer account altogether or it might be encrypted somehow . . . I haven't figured it out yet," Sam translated. I sighed. *Be patient,* I chided myself. *She's like . . . eight years old.*

Amy doesn't have time for us to be patient.

Terri glared at me. "I'm going as fast as I can," Sam translated. I flushed, suddenly embarrassed. These girls had the same supernatural ability to read my mind like Amy had . . . wait.

"Do you have some freaky powers that let you read minds?" I demanded. Sam scoffed.

"Merfolk are empaths. We can very easily tell how others are feeling, especially if we're touching." *That makes sense. Amy had literally been reading me like a book my whole life.* I shivered. What other weird abilities had she hidden from me? "It also makes it easy to tell if someone is lying or not." How do these things have any privacy if they can feel and hear everything the other says? They must be the most honest species on the planet.

The thought of mermaids being honest made me laugh. How many years had Amy been lying to me?

"I know you're worried," Sam said. "But if anyone can figure out where she is - my sister can."

"So if your sister is so smart - what's your special thing?" Tom asked, going back to the game of Go Fish.

"Don't worry about it," Sam muttered, making another group.

"I have Monopoly too," I offered. We spent the rest of the night playing board games until my dad pulled in. Terri won every time, although I had the feeling that Sam lost on purpose. When they weren't being scarily smart or in tune with my emotions - they seemed like normal kids. They giggled at Tom's jokes and snapped at each other for typical sister things.

As I ate dinner with my dad that night, I analyzed him for any abnormal signs of stress or suspicion, but he seemed like everything was fine. He must've picked up lying tips from his *subjects*.

Tom pulled me aside after the girls fell asleep and handed me an unusually large wad of cash.

"Can you go to Walmart tomorrow and get some things for the girls?" he whispered.

"Where did you get this cash?" I whispered. He raised his eyebrow.

"I'm a millionaire, remember?"

"You didn't put it in the bank?"

"Not important! Can you get the girls some stuff?" The next day after school, I risked a trip to Walmart with Tom's list in hand. Terri had requested normal kid clothes - t-shirts and gym shorts. Sam had requested . . . a button-up shirt? What thirteen-year-old wears button-up shirts? There were also some hair products I had never heard of before. I searched in the ethnic hair care section and received several weird looks as I found them.

I checked out as quickly as I could and came home to find Tom sitting on a stool by Terri's head in the bathtub. Her long hair spilled out of the tub as she rested her tail against the wall, looking bored. I jumped in surprise, quickly averting my eyes.

"Did you get the stuff?" Tom asked. His fingers were in the middle of unbraiding Terri's long hair. Pieces of hair littered the floor. I nodded, dumping out the bag. Terri eagerly grabbed a bottle and started signing. *How do you sign with webbed fingers? I wondered.*

"Once you get the hair unbraided, we need to wash it and use that conditioner on it," Sam said. Tom sighed. He turned to me.

"This is taking forever," he whispered. Terri splashed him. I felt weird looking at her, but I couldn't help but stare. Her tail was long and graceful, a pretty powder blue that shimmered in the low light. Her curly markings spiraled down her body, and her skin seemed to have a silver undertone to it. Just like the brief glimpse of my attacker, I wouldn't have been able to tell if she was male or female if not for her long hair.

Although Tom seemed to be making it shorter rather than longer. As he untwisted the braids, extra lengths of hair fell to the floor. Her natural hair only went down to her shoulders.

"They added extensions to her hair to make her look more like a *real* mermaid," Sam said. I flushed in embarrassment.

"You guys don't have long hair?"

"You're a swimmer, right? Would you want long hair during swim season?" I self-consciously ran my fingers through my short blonde hair. During swim season, I never let it past my ears.

"Guess not," I admitted. *Is everything I learned about mermaids wrong?* As Tom finished unbraiding Terri's hair, Sam jumped in to help him wash it and braid it. My fingers were tired from just watching by the time she was done.

Sam traded places with her sister. Tom tag-teamed me in, leaving with Terri to go mess with my laptop. I tentatively sat down and followed

Sam's directions. Hers was at least easier - she hadn't had any extra hair braided in. *Why did they only add extra hair to Terri? I wondered.*

"They only put her on display," she answered for me. "They did all their tests on me in the back. I was never shown to the public." I swallowed.

"That's horrible," I muttered. She shrugged.

"It kept her safe. They kept her sedated. She never knew what was going on. It was better that way. She barely has anything to remember." *I guess that would be preferable, I thought. I could do without some of my memories.*

"I'm surprised you're doing as well as you are," I admitted. "Shouldn't you be like . . . drowning Tom right now?" She sighed.

"It doesn't do any good to dwell on the past. I mean, he's an idiot, don't get me wrong. But what matters now is finding your friend before they figure out what causes the Curse." *Serious little kid, okay then.* I finished unbraiding her hair, helped her wash it, and clumsily tried to braid it back. It didn't look the best by the time I was done, but Sam seemed satisfied enough with it.

"For a white girl, you didn't suck that bad." I laughed.

"I'm sure your mom could do a better job," I said. Sam tensed, and I immediately wished I hadn't said anything. Where were their parents?

"Our parents died in a car accident a few months ago. We were in the foster system with a human family when everything came out. We thought escaping would be best, but you can see where that landed us." I swallowed. Another family of merfolk that had lived on land like normal people. I was beginning to doubt that any of them were from the ocean.

"I'm so sorry." She shrugged.

"Don't be. I'm glad they're not here for this."

And so went the days. I went to school and pretended everything was fine and normal. I came home, played games with my closet refugees until my dad came home, and pretended to not seethe with rage as he pretended everything was fine.

Terri spent more time on the laptop, frowning more and more until my hope had dwindled to embers. I began to wonder how long we had to wait for her. Every passing day was another day those strange men were doing god-knows-what to Amy, and my patience was running thin. What were we supposed to do if Terri was never able to find her?

One night several weeks later – Terri finally grinned.

"Good news: I found her," Sam translated. "Bad news: I have no clue how we're going to get to her." My heart crashed back down as soon as it had risen.

Amy was in a building clear across town - miles away from the aquarium. Google Maps didn't have an address for it. From the outside - it looked abandoned - a gray cube covered in ivy. The real structure was underneath it - several feet of concrete with 24/7 armed guards and doors that would only unlock for an ID badge.

As Terri put it: we were screwed.

Tom paced the room, nearly pulling out his hair as we tried to brainstorm a plan.

"Terri, can you get us a copy of one of the ID badges?" I asked. She nodded.

"There's a guard at every single door," Sam said. "Even if we have a badge, they would see that we aren't the person in the picture. And no - there's no point in editing the picture because anyone with half a brain would realize that we aren't supposed to be there!" Sam retorted as Terri started signing. "We don't exactly look like guards or scientists." Tom paused in his pacing.

"We aren't supposed to be . . . but . . ." He turned to look at the girls. "If Cindy were to pretend that she caught you again . . . then we would have a valid reason to be there." He grinned triumphantly. Sam crossed her arms.

"And how would Cindy have caught me? And why would she bring me to this secret location instead of the aquarium? Or calling Arthur to come pick me up?" Sam pointed out. Tom's face fell and he groaned, running his fingers down his face.

"I don't know then, okay? What do you want to do - just storm the place and bust her out the old-fashioned way? They would just call the police and . . . wait." He jumped up, clapping his hands. "They can't call the police! Then they would have to explain what the place is. Their whole secret lab thing would be ruined. They're limited to the people they have inside - which - how many is that?" he asked Terri. She held up ten fingers.

"We can totally take ten!"

"With what? We have one gun, and one tranq gun. Are we . . . are we going to kill these people?" I whispered. *I don't think I can kill anyone.* Sam scoffed under her breath. I ignored her.

"If we can get our hands on another tranq gun - we hopefully don't have to use the gun at all," Tom said carefully. "This whole thing will be a lot less messy if we don't . . . hurt anyone." There was a moment of silence. Sam frowned as if she were dejected at missing a chance to shoot her former captors - which honestly - I probably would be too if I were in her shoes.

"So, our great wonderful plan is to show up, tranq all the guards, grab Amy, and go?" Sam asked. *We're all going to die,* I thought. *We don't want to kill them, but I doubt they'll have the same qualms about killing us. Maybe not the girls because they're valuable. But Tom and me?* I looked at Tom. *They'd definitely shoot Tom,* I thought.

"Wait, who exactly is going on this mission?" I asked.

"Me," Tom said. Sam laughed.

"You going by yourself would be a suicide mission. I'm the best shot. I'm going too," she said. Terri punched her hard in the arm, which Sam ignored.

"Tom, are you sure it's a good idea that you go? Amy probably thinks you're the one who turned her in. What if she won't come out with you? I need to go in. You can be the getaway driver or whatever," I said.

"So, you and Sam go in by yourselves? Like that's not a suicide mission," Tom muttered.

"She's right, though," Sam said. "Amy might not go with you. And if we get caught, you can take my sister to the ocean. There's no reason for all of us to get stuck." Terri punched her again until Sam turned, staring her down with her scary eyes. They battled silently for a moment until Terri sighed and crossed her arms. Sam turned back to us.

"So, is that the plan? When are we doing this?"

"Tonight," Tom said. "I'm tired of living in that damn closet."

EMANUEL

Karen slapped her hands down on the table.

"Would you like to explain to me why - for the past several weeks - every boat in a two-mile radius has reported their mermaid hunting traps being destroyed?" Adam continued to chew on his orange. The sun filtering in through the window hit his hair just right, making it match the peel almost exactly.

"Sounds like you have it figured out already," he mumbled. *So that's what you've been sneaking off to do at night,* I thought. Karen's eye twitched.

"They have you on camera. They know who you are." Adam waggled his finger at her.

"They know *what* I am. They don't know *who* because I've been wearing a mask to hide my face." Karen called him a rather colorful insult before stomping out the door. Adam went back to his orange.

"You realize you're asking to get caught, right? Especially now that word has spread?" I whispered. He shrugged.

"Oops."

"Dude." He rolled his eyes, rolling his shoulders.

"I have to do something," he whispered. "And besides - I only go at night when they're empty or people are asleep. I'm being safe about it. And I'm not hurting anyone. I would never hurt anyone." I sighed. *I just wanted to come out here and study sea turtles in peace for a month - not worry about impulsive mermaids.* Adam side-eyed me, and I blushed. There was no having private thoughts around an empath.

"I've been destroying the nets that aren't safe for sea turtles either," he said. My heart swelled with gratitude, and I cracked a smile.

"Actually, even the ones that fit regulation aren't that safe either."

"Whelp, then I'll start destroying those too." I stared at him, wondering at the sudden change. A few weeks ago, he had hugged his knees to his chest, wondering if he should've let himself be captured. Now he was playing Dread Pirate Roberts.

It was kinda impressive. I had never had a friend this cool before. I wished I could brag to my family. *I made a new friend on my camping trip, and guess what! Not only is he a mythical creature, but he's a badass vigilante too!* I chuckled to myself at the thought, which made Adam raise his eyebrow.

"Sorry," I said sheepishly, still not used to how he knew what I was feeling like he was some biotic mood ring. "Never mind me. That's like . . . super brave." Adam blushed and shrugged.

"Someone has to be," he whispered. We both jumped up as Karen came bursting back through the door, shutting it behind her, her face pale and taunt. Adam frowned, his eyes narrowing.

"What are you hiding?" he demanded. She sighed.

"No use lying to you creatures, is there?" she asked.

"Karen . . ." She blew through her lips and moved out of the way of the door.

"They got one. That shrimp trawler," she said. Adam's eyes widened.

"Adam, wait -" Adam ignored her and bolted out the door. Ignoring Karen's cries, I chased after him. Truth to be told - there was the trawler floating out in the distance. You could hear the men on board celebrating across the water. Silhouettes of nets and a lump on the ground stood blacked out against the sinking sun. I snagged his shirt just before he reached the water. He shoved me off.

"Take me with you!" I demanded. *What the hell are you thinking?* He paused.

"What?"

"I'm not letting you go by yourself. Take me for backup!" *You're an idiot.*

"Can you hold your breath for a long time?" he asked, raising an eyebrow.

"Yeah - wh -" He pulled me into the waves and shot out to sea. I scrambled to find something to hold on to as he phased. He wrapped my arms around his chest. I squeezed my eyes shut and held on for dear life, trying to keep my legs out of the way of his tail. I had been wanting to see Adam underwater for days but felt too awkward to ask. I never would've guessed it would happen like this.

We surfaced what felt like years later by the side of the boat. I gasped for breath as quietly as I could as Adam swam silently up to the boat.

"Stay here." I let go as he pulled himself up on the ladder. I couldn't help but gawk. His tail seemed to glow a pale blue in the moonlight - sleek and powerful. He hung awkwardly on the rungs for a moment before phasing and scaling it the rest of the way. I trod water as he disappeared over the railing, holding my breath, waiting.

This was a terrible idea, I thought. What was I thinking?

Adam's my friend. I've wanted to be an environmentalist for years. Helping him is just hitting two birds with one stone. Mermaids can count as an endangered species, right?

I yelped as a gunshot rang out. *Crap, Adam's in trouble.* Shouting sounded from the deck. I hauled myself up the ladder and peeked around the corner.

Two men guarded a small figure in a net. One held a pistol in the air. The figure in the net - who couldn't have been more than ten years old - trembled silently, tail flicking helplessly. Adam lay on the ground several feet away, clutching his stomach as another fisherman laughed, a phone in

160

his hand. I clutched my stomach in an effort to not throw up. *Did they shoot him?*

"Told you boys this would work. Now we've got two million dollars," he said. "Here's what's going to happen, Pretty Boy. You're going to stay there on the ground until we get to shore or I'll shoot your friend here." Adam glared but stayed still. No blood stained the deck. *Thank God,* I thought.

Sweat dripped from my brow as my heart hammered in my chest. How the hell was I supposed to save them both? I didn't even have a weapon!

I looked around for something to fight with - pocket knife - net handle - *anything* until my eyes landed on the wall, where an antique pirate's sword stood as decoration. *Better than nothing.* I grabbed it and stepped out into the light. The fishermen all swiveled to face me.

". . . Hey." *That's all you got? Good going, Emanuel. What's holding a rusty sword going to do?* The fisherman holding the gun scowled and pointed it at me - which was all the opportunity Adam needed. He jumped up and knocked the man's feet out from underneath him, sending him sprawling to the floor. The gun fell out of his hand and skittered across the deck. I lunged for it at the same time as the cameraman. He elbowed me in the ribs, knocking the wind out of me. I fell to my knees, wheezing, as he grabbed the gun and pointed it at my head.

"You one of those freaks too?" he shouted. I couldn't get enough air in my lungs to respond.

"Let him go." We turned to see that Adam had grabbed the rusty sword, glowering. The cameraman laughed. That turned out to be a big mistake.

I could barely keep track of what happened, but by the time Adam stopped moving, the cameraman had lost half his beard, a button on his shirt, and his gun - which flew into the water with a gentle pop.

"Now here's what's going to happen," Adam hissed. "You're going to jump overboard, and I am going to take my friends and go. And if I'm feeling nice, I won't drown you on my way out!" His voice had risen to a shout by the end. The man's knees trembled, as did my own.

"Okay, okay, just don't hurt me," the man pleaded as he walked slowly over to the railing, hands in the air. Adam turned to face the other two by the net.

"You guys want a haircut too? Move!" he shouted. They backed up and climbed awkwardly over the railing, hitting the water. As they disappeared, Adam deflated, dropping the sword and racing over to the boy stuck in the net.

"Are you okay?" I demanded, helping him untangle the boy.

"I didn't have my mask on," Adam whispered. "They're going to post that video and everyone will know. What are my parents going to do?"

"Are you seriously worried about that right now? You almost died!" We lifted the boy out of the net, and he phased back to human form, gasping for breath. He grabbed the sides of Adam's face, a bright smile breaking over his features.

"You saved me," he whispered. "Are you going to The Sanctuary too?" Adam and I exchanged a confused glance.

"The what?" Adam asked.

"*Should the humans chase you, sixty-seven sanctuaries towards the Sun and twenty-seven sanctuaries towards the cold will keep you safe.*" With that, he turned and dove off the side of the railing. *That was weird*, I thought. I turned back to Adam, who suddenly looked like a vampire had sucked his body dry. *But not as weird as that*, I thought.

"Since when do you know how to swordfight?" I demanded. *And since when are you scary?* I made a mental note to never make Adam mad. He shrugged.

"So my dad is like . . . second in the US for fencing. He teaches classes so I just kinda picked up on it." He hefted the sword in his hand. "I never officially competed because being merfolk gives me an unfair advantage." I blinked.

"Well, I'm glad you picked up on it. We'd both be dead otherwise," I muttered. Adam grabbed me in a hug, trembling.

"Thank you," he whispered. I hugged him back.

"Let's get back." We stood up. "And kick that phone in the water. He can't post it if it's underwater." Adam kicked it into the sea, and we dove overboard. Adam made sure to give the sailors a wide berth as he swam toward the island.

CINDY

My legs trembled like jelly.

"Calm down. You're freaking me out," Sam snapped. I took a deep breath.

"Yeah, sorry." *This ends a lot worse for her than it does me if this fails,* I thought. Yet, she looked too calm and poised for a thirteen-year-old girl about to break into a high-security lab.

"You ready for this?" I asked. Sam held Tom's gun by her side and cocked it before nodding. I hefted the tranq gun as I held the badge to the harmless-looking sewer grate in the dirt.

For a terrifying moment, nothing happened. Then, a sensor beeped, and the porthole swung open. The smell of bleach and stale water flowed out.

I dove in first, crawling down the ladder. I landed softly on the floor with Sam close behind me. I waited for guards to come rushing at us, but no one did. *Maybe everyone already went home for the night, and this will be easy peasy,* I thought.

"I smell her. Let's go," Sam said, pushing past me. I followed her down a long white hallway. The walls were marked with the occasional door. Our footsteps echoed. Sam paused by a door and took a deep breath before opening it.

"Amy?" I whispered. "Amy, are you in here?" The smell of blood made me wrinkle my nose. The room was empty save for a gurney you would find in an insane asylum. The straps and floor were covered with blood.

My heart dropped as Sam furrowed her brow. *There's no way that's Amy's blood,* I thought. But I knew from the look on Sam's face that it was. She had smelled her all the way from the porthole.

"She must be somewhere else," Sam whispered, turning towards the door. She jumped as a guard inserted himself into the doorway, a tranq gun pointed at us.

I instantly tore mine out of the back of my pants and pulled the trigger. He fell to the ground without a sound. I pocketed his gun before dragging his body inside the room. No sooner had we shut the door behind us than shouting sounded down the hallway. Sam finally had the common sense to look pale.

"Run." We sprinted down the hallway, twisting around a corner as shots rang out. I yelped, my heart hammering in my chest. I tried my best to look through the windows as we ran past them.

Sam suddenly skidded to a halt, turning towards a door. I nearly bowled her over.

"Get on the ground, now!" I turned to see three guards aiming their tranq guns at us. I pulled out mine and aimed it back at them.

"Sam, get behind me," I whispered.

"Is that Arthur's daughter?" one of the guards whispered.

"Yeah, it is. And if he finds out that you threatened me – you're gonna be in a lot of trouble!" I fibbed. Sam swore under her breath as three more guards came around the other corner. One of them snickered.

"Oh, look what we have here. Arthur's going to be very interested to find you here," the guard glowered at Sam. She bared her teeth.

I shoved Sam against the wall, covering her with my body as I shot at the guards. Four of them fell before my gun clicked uselessly. The rest inched closer.

"Stand down. We don't want to hurt either of you," another guard warned. I turned the gun around, holding it like a baseball bat like Amy had done.

"Don't you dare touch her," I warned. Behind me, Sam pulled out Tom's pistol and pointed it at the nearest guard. He laughed.

"You're not going to kill me." Sam cocked her head.

"You're right." She pulled the trigger, and the man screamed as his hand exploded in red. His tranq gun fell to the floor as he clutched what was left of his right hand to his chest. The other guards shouted as I lunged for his tranq gun.

"Your kneecaps are next," Sam threatened. She eyed the other guards, who wisely backed away. I quickly picked the rest of them off, my hands shaking.

"Oh my god, are you okay? That was badass." Sam was ignoring me, staring through a tiny window in a door. She pulled at the handle, but it refused to open. She walked over to one of the guards and pulled out another ID badge. She held it up to the door and it beeped before it swung open.

The room was empty except for a cage with a small figure inside. My heart sank.

"Oh no."

TOM

Terri fiddled with the radio as we sat in the Sonic parking lot. Cindy's car smelled like chlorine. I stared out the window, looking at the spot where Cindy and Sam had disappeared a few minutes ago.

"Rumors are circulating after several vandalisms last night off the coast of Baldwin Island. Everyone is speculating who or what is responsible for these attacks but everyone has pretty much come to the same conclusion: there's a dangerous mermaid out there who has decided to fight back. Even more boats are heading to the area tonight to catch this creature," the radio host blared. *Good for them,* I thought absentmindedly.

I checked my watch every ten seconds, tapping my foot until Terri punched me in the shoulder.

"Jeez kid, you hit hard," I yelped. She grinned, which made me ask for the millionth time how she was so calm and collected. Across the street, where Cindy and Sam had disappeared five minutes ago, was the riskiest thing I have ever done in my life. They had my gun just in case - but what if it ran out of bullets? What if they got cornered? If anything happened to them . . .

Terri punched me again and signed something I couldn't understand.

"I don't speak your weird hand language!" I snapped. She rolled her eyes and rummaged around the back until she found a notepad and pen.

It's called ASL stupid. And your stress is stressing me out.

I sighed, resisting the urge to beat my head against the window. *I should be in there with them,* I thought. I was seconds away from opening the car door and chasing after them when Terri pointed. I looked up and saw Cindy and Sam booking it across the road. I turned the car back on and backed out. Terri opened the car door, and they piled in.

"GO!" Cindy screamed. I floored it, heading to the ocean.

"What happened back there?" I shouted. "Is everyone okay?" I tried to look behind me, but Amy was blocked from view.

"She's fine, just drive," Sam gritted through her teeth. I drove as fast as I dared until we skidded onto the pier. I jumped out and raced to start up the boat as the others piled in.

"What am I doing?" I demanded as the boat started to pull out of the docks.

"Just GO!" Sam shouted, slamming the door shut behind her. I coaxed the old boat up to as fast as she could go and sped off into the night. I didn't let myself breathe until we crossed over into International waters and let the boat slow back down. The ride had been silent behind me.

I went into the spare bedroom where the others had gathered and immediately lost my breath once more.

"Oh my god," I whispered. Amy wasn't moving. *She's dead.* Cindy wiped away her tears.

"Help me!" she demanded tearfully. "Get me some rags!" I raced to the bathroom and pulled every towel I owned into my arms. I unloaded them on the side of the bed, and Cindy grabbed them and started trying to sop up the blood oozing from Amy's leg. *She's not dead. Dead people don't bleed like that.* Sam and Terri watched on, jaws slack. My brain sputtered, trying to figure out why Amy looked like this after only being held captive for a month. Shouldn't Sam and Terri have looked worse than she did? Why did she look like this?

It looked like someone had taken a chainsaw to her left leg. Almost a dozen thick red gashes sliced through her thighs and calf, perfectly spaced apart. Bruises covered her face and wrists. Her face was sunken in, her hair greasy and tangled. Her gray skin was pulled taunt across her bones, delicate and papery.

"What the hell happened to her?" I shouted, my voice squeaky with panic.

"You think I know? Just help me!" Cindy cried. I grabbed a towel and held it against Amy's leg. I never thought of myself as being squeamish about blood, but the sheer volume leaking through the towel made me dizzy.

"Sam, look in the bathroom and get me some bandages," Cindy said. "Do you have any rubbing alcohol?" she asked. I shook my head. "Regular alcohol?" I shook my head again. For the first time, I regretted throwing all my beer overboard.

"Our immune systems are strong. It's the blood loss I would worry about more than infection," Sam said. We continued to bandage her wounds in silence. Cindy found an old t-shirt that was big enough to replace the tattered hospital gown. Modesty went out the window as we stripped her and redressed her. It hardly mattered – if you had told me I was looking at the naked body of a teenage girl – I would've laughed. Her limp body rolled listlessly in my hands.

When there was nothing left to be done, we stood around the bed, hands covered in dried blood.

"Do you think she's going to be okay?" I asked. Sam hesitated and shrugged.

"If she's made it this far . . . hopefully. But she won't be swimming anytime soon. So, it looks like you won't just be dropping us off."

"I don't want to go back to land anyway," Cindy said, crossing her arms. "Not until I know Amy's going to be okay." I sighed.

"This vessel is not exactly meant for deep ocean adventures . . . it's a thousand years old and we can't breathe underwater." Sam smirked. Terri signed, and Sam rolled her eyes.

"What did she say?" I asked. Sam signed something back to Terri, who frowned and signed back, hands flashing like knives.

"What?" Cindy asked. Sam sighed.

"She thinks she knows where we can go to be safe," Sam said. She shot Terri a doubtful look.

"What place?" Cindy asked.

"We're not even sure if it exists, Terri," Sam muttered. Terri crossed her arms defiantly.

"What place?" I pressed.

"There's a place . . . a legend if you will . . . about a place merfolk can flee to safety. A place supposedly humans can't get to. Terri is suggesting we go there until Amy is healed up. And theoretically . . . we could hide there indefinitely too."

"What is this place?" Cindy asked.

"Our parents called it Atlantis," Sam said. "And no, it's not the literal Atlantis out of Greek myths, it's just called that because it's supposed to be a sanctuary."

"Then why not just call it The Sanctuary?" Cindy asked.

"Because Atlantis sounds cooler when you're telling a story to a five-year-old," Sam retorted.

"Well, where is it supposed to be?" I asked.

"*Should the humans chase you, sixty-seven sanctuaries towards the Sun and twenty-seven sanctuaries towards the cold will keep you safe,*" Sam recited.

"What the hell does that mean?" Cindy said. I rolled the words around in my head and grabbed a stray notepad.

"It's a code." I scribbled on the pad. "It's a code for coordinates. Sixty-seven degrees towards the Sun . . . which rises in the West. And Twenty-seven degrees towards the cold would be North. And those coordinates take us to . . . the edge of the Bermuda Triangle." I laughed and threw my hands up in the air.

"Guys. We are on a half-broken trawler. What part of 'this vessel is not meant for deep sea adventures' isn't sinking in? Ha – get it? *Sinking?* Because that's what will happen if I try to take this thing out much farther. My tank is only half full. Even if we could make it there – unless any of you have a couple hundred gallons of gas laying around, it's gonna be a one-way trip."

"Do you have any other bright ideas then? Any other secret islands we can hide on?" Sam said coolly. Cindy sighed.

"How long would it take us to get there?"

"In this thing? A few days."

"Doesn't look like we have much other choice," she said. "It's a little late to turn back now. People might be looking for us. We've got to try." I groaned and ran my fingers through my hair. We hadn't packed any extra supplies. We had very few clothes, and maybe some canned goods in the kitchen. I had my money stashed in an envelope in my nightstand, but I doubted there would be any Walmarts in the middle of the damn ocean.

"We're gonna drown," I muttered.

ADAM

I took my time swimming us to shore. My body ached from the rush of adrenaline, and Emanuel was heavier than he looked. I carried the rusty sword in my free hand. I figured it could prove useful.

After Emanuel staggered to shore, I hovered in the water for a few moments, pondering the boy's words and tracing the edge of the sword. A *place to escape? The Sanctuary?* I thought. I never knew such a place existed. I figured I would always be hiding amongst humans – in some form or another. Having a place to flee to felt surreal, like a bonus question that was too easy.

Shouting broke me out of my trance. The door to the cabin burst open, a police officer shoving a handcuffed Emanuel out in front of him. A small boat with blue and red flashing lights slowly chugged around the corner of the island and nestled itself on the shore – just yards from where I floated. The police officer jumped off the boat and walked up to his partner and Karen, who was very red in the face. She poked the newcomer in the chest.

"I'm sorry you're upset ma'am, but this kid matches the one in the Facebook Live video. He aided in helping another mermaid attack several humans. I have to take him in." My blood ran cold and pooled in the bottom of my tail. *It was a Facebook Live. Kicking it in the ocean did nothing. The world knew exactly who we were the second we got on that boat. The cops must've booked it here as soon as we raided the boat.*

I quickly swam around the boat and pulled myself up to shore. I ran through the trees, going around the long way until I came around to the back of Karen's cabin.

All things considered, Emanuel looked fairly calm, but I could feel the fear worming its way through his gut. I debated the wisdom of running out amid the police and rangers, sword swinging, and hesitated. I didn't want to get Emanuel in even more trouble. What did they even do with humans who conspired with merfolk? I knew merfolk didn't have any rights, but was it technically illegal to help us?

It was looking pretty illegal.

Emanuel turned towards the woods and caught my eye. He narrowed his gaze at me and mouthed, very deliberately. *Get me out of this.* I nodded and bolted back towards the water. *I can't believe I got him in this much trouble. How on earth was I supposed to fix this?* I dove in and using all my strength, shoved the police boat away from the shore. I bolted back to the cabin and right on cue, Karen looked up with a smirk.

"I do believe you haven't secured your boat properly, sirs." The pair of cops turned to the boat and took off after it, swearing, leaving Emanuel sitting in the dirt. I burst out of the woods and started sawing at the cuffs with the rusty sword.

"See what you've done now!" Karen cried. "You're getting your friend arrested!"

"I know, I know, I'm so sorry." I finally broke through the cuffs and hauled Emanuel to his feet. I looked him in the eyes. "I am so, so sorry, I never should've gotten you into this mess!" He took me by the shoulders, chains still swinging from his wrists.

"Get me out of here. I don't care where. But I can't go back, not after all of this. Take me with you!" he pleaded. I blinked in shock.

"Dude . . . are you sure? Why would you want to come with me?"

"Wherever you would take me would be less scary than facing my mom right now." He shifted his feet. "Please. I feel like the first time, I've made a difference. I can't go back to normal life where the most helpful thing I'll do is write a paper on sea turtle nests." He looked up at Karen with a sheepish smile. "No offense." She rolled her eyes.

"You might want to wrap up your little moment here. They're running back." I gripped his shoulders tighter.

"Are you sure?" I demanded. Emanuel nodded. My instincts told me he was sincere. The cops started to shout. I swallowed and dragged Emanuel behind me through the woods. The cops gave chase, making me flashback to that night several weeks ago. *I wonder what my parents would've said if someone told them their son would be running from the police twice in a month*, I thought.

We crashed into the water and paddled for the police boat. Emanuel pulled himself over the edge and dragged me aboard. I fumbled the key in the ignition and stalled the motor twice before it chugged to life. Emanuel cried out in relief as the boat slowly inched away from shore, leaving the police in the shallows.

Emanuel collapsed on one of the benches, breathing hard, eyes wide.

"Holy crap, I can't believe that worked!" he laughed. I grinned as I edged the boat to go faster. I hardly knew anything about boats, but it looked like a fast one. We cut through the water, passing by the trawler and its angry inhabitants on the way out into the darkness.

"So where are we going?" Emanuel asked. I thought back to the strange poem the merfolk had told me.

"A safe place."

TOM

I sat perched on the edge of an old chair beside my bed, where Amy lay sleeping. Cindy paced beside me.

"Cindy, go take a nap in the living room," I said. She stopped midstep to glare at me, but I met her gaze and refused to back down. Her nervous energy was driving me up the wall, and I knew it couldn't be good for Amy. Every time Amy jerked in her sleep, hope would fill up Cindy's face only to crash back down again when she didn't wake up.

"Please," I added, trying to sound nicer. "You haven't slept since yesterday. Take a break. I'll get you the second she wakes up." Her face softened, and she yawned.

"Promise?" I nodded, and she finally walked out, leaving me in the darkness. I turned my eyes back to Amy's limp figure.

I never knew how to act around sick people. One time - my elementary school had taken us on a field trip to visit a retirement home. I remembered hiding behind the legs of my teachers because the sagging skin and vacant stares of demented people in wheelchairs terrified me. They looked like ghouls and hags out of old fairy tales, and the ones who could smile and talk seemed even creepier. My teacher had tried explaining, *they're just old and have trouble getting around on their own. They have trouble remembering. They're just sick.*

Now the sick one was Amy, but instead of looking like a hag, she looked like a skeleton.

As much as the situation made me uncomfortable, I couldn't tear my eyes away from her. She tossed and flinched in her sleep, eyeballs darting under her eyelids. She sweated through the t-shirt, stopped, and then sweated through it again. I figured she would at least wake up to go pee or something, but she remained stuck as the hours passed. Occasionally, she would jerk her leg too hard and blood would start pushing against the bandages.

Days seemed to pass like that, but it was only hours. I sat in the chair, tapping my foot, staring at her like a creepy Prince Charming.

She laid still - stiller than she had been - and for a heart-dropping moment - I thought she had died. But as I peered closer, I felt the heat wafting off her skin. She was barely breathing, chest moving up and down in measured, delicate gasps, eyes squeezed shut. She was conscious.

I hovered over her, not sure what to do with a sick skeleton pretending to be asleep. I slunk back to my chair and fiddled my thumbs, feeling more and more like a creep as the minutes passed. I wondered if I should get the others - or if surrounding her with people would overwhelm her.

Movement caught my attention as I pondered my thumbs. I looked up and saw her sitting up, eyes wide and rimmed with red. Her head wobbled slightly on her neck as she balanced herself on her hands.

We stared at each other for several seconds before she grabbed the lamp on the nightstand and hurled it directly at my face.

I yelped and ducked - which was unnecessary because she missed me by a mile. The lamp clattered against the wall and the lightbulb shattered. I stared at its mangled wire body as Amy attempted to drag herself to the other side of the bed. She barely moved before her face contorted in pain and a scream screeched past her clenched teeth. Her face crumpled as she noticed her bandaged leg for the first time.

"Hey, calm down, it's okay," I whispered, holding my hands above my head. "I'm not going to hurt you. Stay still, you're really hurt." Her eyes remained glued to her bandaged leg until Cindy barged in, eyes wide.

"What the hell is going on? She woke up?" she demanded.

"She started throwing things and tried to walk." Cindy pushed me over and knelt in front of her friend.

"Hey, Bestie, it's me. You're okay," she crooned, reaching out a hand. Amy's crumpled face morphed into a snarl. She shied away from Cindy and grabbed the pillow, brandishing it like a shield, which looked more sad than funny.

"Don't fucking touch me," she spat. Cindy recoiled, mouth dropping open, as did mine. I had never heard Amy swear before - and it felt wrong. We had been at each other's throats since elementary school, but she had never spoken to me with so much hatred. Not even when she filled my locker up with literal garbage. Sam appeared in the doorway, rubbing her eyes. She surveyed the scene and put her hand to her temple.

"Give her some space," she stated quietly. Cindy and I backed up, leaving Amy in a trembling puddle on the bed.

"I don't think she recognizes us," I whispered. Sam nodded.

"She's very confused and very scared. I believe it would be best to leave her alone for a few hours until she wakes up more," Sam said.

"But she's my best friend, she should recognize me!" Cindy protested, eyes filling with tears.

"No, I think she's right," I said, trying to guide Cindy to the door. Cindy twisted around in my arms.

"I'm not just leaving her!"

"We can, and we will," I said firmly. Cindy did not calm down.

"This isn't fair!" she shouted. "I'm her best friend! She knows me. She knows I would never hurt her!"

"Your wild emotions are only hurting her worse," Sam snapped. "You're driving everyone nuts! We get it - you're her best friend - but she's hurt. This isn't about you." Cindy, finally stunned into silence, sat down on the couch, wiping her eyes.

A few hours later, I was voted to be the one to make first contact, which only upset Cindy more. I knocked lightly on the door before slowly opening it. Amy didn't look up from the bedspread, clutching the pillow to her chest instead of using it like a shield.

"Hey," I whispered. "Can I come in?" Her grip on the pillow tightened.

"Why am I here?" she demanded.

"I just want to talk. See how you're doing." I held my hands up. "I'll keep my distance, I promise." She clearly did not believe me. I sat down in the chair and tried my best to look relaxed, even though my heart was pounding out of my chest.

"Tom? Is that you?" she asked hesitantly, her voice still dry and raspy. I nodded. She quickly glanced at me only to glue her eyes back down to the bed.

"Why am I here?" she asked again. "I thought you two turned me in?"

"No, of course not. We rescued you. And the other two - Sam and Terri." I figured this would be the part where she started smiling and saying thank you - but she remained stone-faced.

"Why?" She spat the question like it tasted sour.

"Why? Like . . . why did we rescue you? Because . . . I felt bad? I wanted to fix it?" She scoffed.

"Why am I really here? Why is *she* here?" I blinked.

"Why is who here? Are you asking about Cindy? She's your best friend. She wanted to help rescue you too. Do you not believe me? Aren't you supposed to be able to tell if I'm lying?" Her grip on her pillow tightened.

"So, you're telling me I'm free? Safe and sound now? That you're not going to . . ." she trailed off. "If you're telling the truth then leave me alone," she spat. My protests died on my tongue. I slowly got up and left the room, shutting the door behind me.

"Yeah, so I told her that we rescued her, and she definitely doesn't believe us," I said.

"How could she not believe that we rescued her! I mean, what else would we be doing with her out in the middle of the godforsaken ocean?" Cindy snapped.

"They did something to mess with her head in the lab," Sam said. "She can't even look at us. Maybe we should all go in to try and talk to her in a little bit. She won't feel better sitting there in the dark forever."

. . .

A few hours later, we gathered around her bed in a cautious circle, inconvenient intervention style.

"We need to talk, and we figured it would be best if we were all here," I said.

"My name is Sam. This is my sister, Terri. Tom rescued us from Arthur's Aquarium. We're like you," Sam said.

"You are not like me. And I want Cindy out," Amy spat. The color drained from Cindy's face.

"Why?" I asked, trying to keep my voice calm.

"You know exactly why. And if you come near my other leg, I will kill all of you with it." Sam and I exchanged glances. Other leg?

"Okay. Cindy, can you please leave for a few minutes?" If looks could kill, I would've died on the spot. Only Sam's look was scarier, which is the only reason why she got up and left the room in a huff. She slammed the door behind her.

"Amy, why are you so upset with Cindy?" Sam asked. "She's not the one who turned you in." Amy scoffed but refused to answer. She curled in tighter. A flash of realization crossed over Sam's face.

"It was Cindy's dad who did this to you wasn't it? Hurt your leg?" Sam asked. "She smells like him. That's why you're upset." *Great, merfolk can have scent-induced PTSD*, I thought.

"Who else would it have been? I'm sure he did his fair share to you two," Amy muttered. Terri shook her head, which Amy didn't see because she still hadn't peeled her eyes off the bedspread.

"Amy . . . we barely saw Arthur in the aquarium. It was other scientists who worked with us. And we were treated . . . not great but not like . . . *that*." Amy's eyebrows bent in confusion.

"What did he do to you?" I asked. Amy's hands began to tremble on her pillow.

"What do you mean you don't know? He - he told me that everyone knew - that everyone was waiting on me. What do you mean you don't *know*?" Her voice rose to a shriek.

"Amy . . . no one knows what happened to you. As far as the rest of the world knows - you just disappeared. We think only your parents and well . . . us knew where you were." She shook her head.

"You're lying," she whispered.

"You literally know that we aren't," Sam said.

"No one knows what happened to me?" Her eyes flicked up to look at Sam. "Did you tell him? Did you tell her? Do they know about the . . ." Sam shook her head.

"No." She let out a shaky sigh of relief.

"Amy . . . why did Arthur cut your leg?" Sam asked. Amy let out a minuscule laugh.

"Because I wouldn't tell him either. And he got mad when I didn't talk."

. . .

We sat back in the living room in stunned silence. It took all of my energy to not punch the wall.

"He was torturing her!" I seethed.

"What are you talking about?" Cindy demanded. We had demanded more details, but Amy had shut back down and refused to give details. I could hardly blame her. We had left Amy alone to try to put all the pieces together, even though she could probably hear everything we were saying anyway.

"Think about it. Your dad saw you two hanging out all the time when we were kids - in the water. He knew Amy wasn't born a mermaid. He knew something must've happened to make her different - and they apparently couldn't figure it out the old-fashioned way with their tests and shit. She must have refused to tell him. And so he cut her to pieces to try to get her to spill how she was changed." My mind raced. What else had Arthur done in an attempt to get her to talk? Starved her? Beat her? She was lucky to be alive.

"Makes sense. Why else would he keep her a secret? If he told the world that he had a human-turned-merfolk but didn't know how that happened - it would create chaos. He didn't want to reveal her without having the answers first," Sam said.

"Guys, do you realize how ridiculous that sounds? I mean, obviously, my dad isn't the best person in the world, but torture? This is my dad we're talking about!"

"Cindy. She's more scared of you than Mr. Mermaid Catcher over there. Why else would she be?" Sam pointed out. Cindy's eyes filled with tears.

"Stop. Just stop. I need - I need some space." She turned on her heel and stormed out of the living room. Sam blew through her lips, massaging her temple. I plopped down on the couch, feeling a headache coming on.

This is bad. This is a thousand times worse than I thought it would be. Holy shit. I balled up my fists.

"Calm down. You two are giving me a headache," Sam muttered.

"How do we fix this?" I seethed.

"You don't. We just need to give her space and time to heal up. She needs to eat something. Get to Atlantis. And maybe before we get there - she'll calm down a bit," Sam said.

. . .

"Hey . . . you hungry? I hope you like peanut butter and jelly!" Amy risked a moment of eye contact to look disgusted at the slightly freezer burnt uncrustable sandwich I had found. I carefully put the plate on the bed beside her and backed away. She eyed the plate like it might jump-scare her. She had maneuvered herself into a sitting position on the side of the bed, legs hanging over the edge.

"Were you trying to go somewhere?" I asked.

"I need this stupid leg to heal up. How long have I been here? Arthur is probably already on his way here - and when he gets here - he's going to take me back and kill all of you. I need to be ready to run." I resisted the urge to scoff. The odds of Arthur wanting to kill us just because we had stolen his favorite science experiment seemed a little drastic. I was more afraid of ending up in the same jail as my uncle.

"I seriously doubt you're going to be running on that anytime soon. He uh . . . got you pretty good there. It's still bleeding - if you haven't noticed. Which reminds me." I pulled out a roll of gauze from my pocket.

"Have you been changing the bandages?" she asked.

"Not yet, but we probably should, considering they're red now." She held out her hand.

"I'll change them." I hesitated.

"Are you sure? You're probably still in a lot of pain."

"I wasn't asking." I tossed her the roll.

"Will you at least eat something? You're not going to heal if you don't eat anything."

"Gonna force feed me?" she muttered as she started unwrapping the bloody bandages. One could infer that it would not have been the first time she was force-fed.

"I mean no - but you're going to kick the bucket a lot sooner if you don't."

"Then why don't you just put me out of my misery?" I laughed on instinct and then debated if that was sarcasm or not.

"It was a joke, Idiot." I relaxed.

"Well good. But still. You need to eat." She winced as she threw the bloody bandages to the floor and inspected the gashes. She swallowed.

"I'll eat when I feel like it."

"How about we make a deal? If Arthur or anyone ever comes back to take you again, I'll kill you myself?" I offered. She scoffed.

"You're lying."

"I am. But please, Amy. None of us want to lose you. You've been through too much to go out like this. Besides, there would be no bigger middle finger to Arthur than living your best life outside of his control."

"Fine. I'll eat the damn sandwich."

Half an hour later, she threw up the damn sandwich. But she drank a can of broth about an hour later and didn't puke, so we counted it as a victory. She slowly started eating solid food and keeping it down. When she wasn't trying to eat, she was trying to sleep. Her record was a few hours before waking up with a start, sweating through her clothes.

No one asked her about her dreams.

AMY

Every morning, it took me several seconds to realize I wasn't in a cage. It took a few seconds more for the pain to register, and then a few more seconds for the conflicting emotions of everyone else to hit me like a punch to the gut.

Cindy was furious. Tom felt guilty. Sam and Terri were worried.

I knew I shouldn't hate Cindy back, but even the smell of her was enough to send a wave of nauseating memories through my head. After my last encounter with Naturals, I didn't trust the girls as far as I could throw them. That left me with Tom Falcon the mermaid catcher as my safest point of contact.

Whoopie.

Which is why I only made requests when he was in the room. I knew he felt guilty enough to do whatever I asked.

"I want to take a shower."

"You can't walk," Cindy said. "Plus, you can't get your leg wet."

"We can put the chair in the shower," Tom countered. "She can keep her injured one on the outside." Cindy sighed, irritation flashing off her in a hot flash.

"Well, how are we supposed to get her there if we can't touch her? Levitate her?" she snapped. Irritation flashed off Tom as well. I braced myself for a hit that never came.

"Amy, do you think you can drag yourself into that rocking chair so we can push you to the bathroom?" Tom asked gently. I eyed the chair, not at all sure if I could maneuver myself into it without falling to the floor but nodded anyway.

I slid myself to the edge of the bed, grimacing in pain as my leg moved. Tom held the chair still as I awkwardly let myself drop onto it. I wobbled dangerously for a moment before the chair stabilized. Tom dragged it to the bathroom and into the shower.

"Yell if you need help," he whispered. *As if I would yell for help.* I nodded anyway and waited for him to leave and shut the door.

I turned myself away from the mirror leaning against the wall and balanced my injured leg outside the shower curtain. I gingerly took off the dress-like t-shirt they had found for me and threw it on the sink.

I didn't flinch as the cold water hit me. I had been faced with much colder in captivity. But I shuddered and relaxed as the water turned warm, then hot. I couldn't remember the last time I had felt hot water touch my skin.

I sighed and leaned back as it washed over me, staining the tile brown and red. I reached for the all-purpose bottle of body wash, shampoo, and conditioner and went to work, rubbing my skin and hair raw. I tried to untangle my long hair with my fingers to no avail. It hung down to elbows - longer than I had ever had it.

I don't know how long I stayed in there or what felt better: the hot water or the alone time. The scientists had never left me alone. Even when I was in a room by myself - cameras or people were watching behind one-way mirrors, constantly staring, analyzing me. Even my rescuers were scared to take their eyes off me lest I fall over dead. A decently large part of me still wished I could fall over dead.

I finally turned the water off and pulled the curtain back. I turned and looked at myself in the mirror. I didn't recognize the person I saw.

She was pale to the point of translucent. The paper-thin skin was marked with angry red cuts and purple scars. The bruises had faded to an ugly, blotched yellow. Bones poked through her skin like knives. Her eyes were dark and hollow, wide and filled with fear. Someone paying less attention would see anger.

I jerked my gaze away, suddenly feeling nauseous. If that was really how I looked - no wonder everyone was so worried about me keeling over dead.

I look terrible. There's no way that's me, I thought, clutching my stomach.

But it is. They did this to you.

I didn't comprehend my wounds ever healing. I had never had to deal with a bruise or a cut for longer than a day. Arthur had gone Edward Scissorhands on me what – two days ago now? And my body showed no signs of getting better.

I'm never going to heal. I'm never going to grow my body back. Those scars will never fade. I'll be this ugly monster for the rest of my life.

I took a deep breath. *I can deal with being ugly as long as I can be free,* I thought. *As long as I never go back there.*

I shuffled the chair over to the closet - which as it turned out - did not have towels in it but a bunch of other random junk. I sighed and resigned to pulling the same clothes on as before something caught my eye. I rummaged through the boxes of random stuff until I yanked it free. I almost smiled at what I found.

A crutch.

Just one. I vaguely remembered the time Tom had broken his ankle in middle school and had hobbled around on crutches for a while. Heaven knew what happened to the other one, but it would do.

I took a deep breath and stood up on my good leg, balancing myself with the crutch. Even my good leg threatened to give out from underneath me - but it was a thousand times better than getting dragged around in a rocking chair. I took a few practice steps - holding back gasps of pain and sweating through my shirt in minutes. But I felt freer than I had in the days since my rescue.

I sat down in the chair to give myself a break and rummaged through the closet to see what else I could find. I came back with a rusty pair of scissors and almost smiled once more. I grabbed my tangled locks and began to cut.

. . .

I ignored the stares as I hobbled into the living room on my crutch. Tom lit up like a Christmas tree.

"You're walking! I forgot I had that thing!"

"You cut your hair," Cindy said.

"You have eyes," I muttered. She recoiled at my sharp tone at the same moment I wished I could bite back my reply. I was trying hard to not let my emotions control my responses to her. I knew in my head that it wasn't Cindy who had hurt me, but whenever I tried to look at her, her father's eyes looked back at me. She smelled like him. She was stewing in her anger and frustration like him.

"It looks good," Sam said. It definitely didn't look good, but I appreciated the compliment anyway.

"I could've helped you," Cindy offered. "I helped Sam with hers."

"Congratulations," I muttered. Silence settled back over the group. I hobbled over to one of the benches, almost losing my balance and face-planting several times. I breathed a sigh of relief as I made it, giving my screaming legs a break.

"Doesn't that hurt?" Sam asked. *Yes.*

"No," I said. She ignored the lie.

"Glad you're feeling better," Tom said. "We probably need to change the bandages again." I held out my hand and he tossed me the roll. I scooched back on the bench and gingerly lifted my leg. Everyone turned their heads as I unwrapped my leg, casting the dirty bandages aside.

"What exactly did they do to you?" Cindy blurted. The room seemed to suck in a breath. My grip on my bandages tightened.

"I'm sure she doesn't want to talk about it," Sam said quietly, but pointedly. Cindy opened her mouth to retort but wisely decided to shut it.

"You can stop acting like we're going to beat you every time we look at you," Cindy muttered. "We rescued you for God's sake. If we wanted to hurt you, we would've done it by now." The room stared at her in shock.

"Cindy!" Tom hissed.

"Well, it's true!" Cindy retorted. "This whole time she's been acting like we're the ones that hurt her! We're the ones who helped her! I've been her best friend her whole life!"

"You're right," I said, raising my head just high enough to glare at her. "It was just your *father* who did it." Cindy's mouth dropped open. I held my glare for a surprisingly long time before letting my gaze drop to the floor again.

"I'm not my father any more than Tom is a mermaid catcher anymore. You seem to be just fine with him!"

"Tom admitted his mistakes. You don't want to admit or believe your father did what he did," I snapped.

"I am not in denial!" Cindy shrieked.

"Yes, you are. I heard you. *My dad's not great, but torture? He would never.*" I snapped. Tears sprang into Cindy's eyes, and she stalked out of the room, slamming the door shut behind her, only for Terri to burst in and wave towards the outside. She signed something, which made Sam race out to the front with her. She smiled and pumped her hands up in the air.

"We did it! We found it!" Floating in the ocean, like a cover of a fantasy novel, was an ancient volcano smothered in luscious green vegetation. Waves crashed against its base, which was a thin strip of black sand. It towered into the sky, balancing on a little base no more than a few hundred yards. Tom joined them.

"Um, no we didn't. According to our coordinates, that is what we were aiming for," he said, pointing off to another island barely visible in the distance. "At least I think it is. My compass isn't doing the best job right now because, you know. *Bermuda Triangle.* But this is as close as I can get us with the amount of gas we have."

"Still. It's there," Sam translated for Terri. "Oh yeah. Um . . . can you dock your boat there? Or are we swimming?" Tom sucked in a breath.

"We can't swim," he pointed out, glancing back towards me. *Thanks for the reminder*, I thought, crossing my arms.

Once the boat was docked on the island, we carefully climbed the ladder down. Well - they climbed. I awkwardly hopped down with one leg - biting back screams of pain every time my bad leg was jostled. The black sand was warm and fine on the bottom of my feet. I wobbled, the sudden security of dry land way too still for my legs to figure out. I stumbled as soon as I took a step. I held my free hand out like I was attempting to balance on a beam to get back to my feet.

The island towered above us. Sorry - calling it an *island* was generous.

It was an extinct (hopefully) volcano. That was about it. Various tropical birds cawed and swooped above us, but other than that, the strip of sand seemed barren.

"I think you picked the worst possible island to maroon us on," Sam deadpanned, crossing her arms. Tom huffed, matching her glare.

"If you're so smart, why don't you mine us some gasoline so we can travel further?" he snapped.

"She wouldn't have to mine for any gasoline if you had planned this better," Cindy muttered. Tom's retort was cut off by a small pointed object whistling dangerously close to his head.

"DON'T MOVE." We swiveled around to see a lean figure poised several yards away. It wouldn't have occurred to me to be afraid of such a small figure, except for the glittering spear he was holding, and the viscous, angry gleam in his eyes. Beautiful thick blue markings framed his face on both sides, almost perfectly symmetrical. His bared teeth and translucent blue fins rising from his spine and arms took most of the attention.

He inched closer, more blades swinging from a loop on his cargo shorts as he kept his spear trained on us. We all held up our hands and froze.

"You humans are idiots for coming here, don't you think? You thought making them bring you here would get you a good bounty? You're on my turf now. *Get on your knees, humans!*" he screamed, eyes flashing. Cindy and Tom quickly dropped to their knees. The kid trained his glowing eyes on me. "You too," he hissed. I realized this kid didn't know what I was.

"Amy, show your markings," Sam whispered urgently. Swallowing the embarrassment, I let my marks fade into view. The kid snorted.

"A Cursed. Of course." He trained his eyes on Tom and Cindy, who were wisely avoiding his gaze.

"What do we have here? The mermaid catcher? And the aquarium owner's daughter? What kind of sick trick is this? *Don't move!*" he screeched suddenly, as Tom tried to open his mouth to speak. "I swear I'll kill you both!"

"Wait! Let us explain ourselves! We're not going to hurt you!" Cindy pleaded. The kid snorted and trained his spear on her instead.

"Like I've never heard that one before," he sneered. He scanned us until his gaze rested on Sam and Terri. "The only ones I want to hear from are them!" he said. Sam and Terri looked at each other. Sam cautiously stepped to the front.

"Terri can't speak," she said slowly. "You can put your spear down." The kid glared and lifted it higher.

"*Talk.*" Sam hurriedly explained the events over the past few weeks. The kid's spear slowly fell as she continued, mixed looks of shock and disbelief crossing his face. As she finished, he lifted his spear again. He trained his gaze on Terri.

"Is she telling the truth?" he demanded. "I'll know if you're lying to me." Terri rolled her eyes and nodded. The kid looked down at Tom and Cindy.

"Are they telling the truth?" he asked.

"Yes!" Cindy squeaked. Tom nodded, hesitantly looking up at him. The kid's eyes flashed between us several more times before he slowly lowered his spear.

"That's insane," he muttered.

"Tell us about it," Sam said, crossing her arms. "Can they stand up now?" The kid nodded curtly. Cindy and Tom slowly rose to their feet.

"Sorry we scared you," Tom said. The kid scoffed.

"Sure."

"What's your name? How long have you been here?" Sam asked.

"My name is Norman. I came here a few weeks ago." *How old are you?* I wondered.

"Why are you here?" Sam asked. "The Sanctuary is over that way." His gaze darkened once more.

"None of your business," he muttered. "Now come on. Let's get out of sight." We followed him around the curve of the beach. The volcano walls loomed above us like nightmarish skyscrapers. I used the rough stone wall as a railing to navigate over the sand.

Norman stopped at a beach just slightly wider than the one we had arrived on. Here, the volcano walls were pocked with holes and indents, creating dark caverns leading to who-knows-where. The pale remnants of a fire lay in front of one of the caves.

"This is where you've been living?" Tom asked. Norman scowled.

"I live underwater. I only come up when I want to cook something," he said. He plopped down by the fire and analyzed us with his dark eyes. "So, when are you leaving?" he asked. Everyone turned and looked at me. I recoiled from their gazes, wishing I could disappear.

"Well, our original plan was to drop the merfolk off and head back to shore, but Amy's leg isn't in very good shape yet," Tom said hesitantly. As if to prove his words, I slid down to the sand and allowed myself to stay there, trying not to gasp for breath. "She can't walk without the crutch," Tom continued. I wished I had the courage to glare at him, but I didn't, so I glared at the sand instead.

I could feel Norman's reproach even with his mouth shut. It oozed over the sand like tentacles trying to drag me under.

"So how long are you expecting me to let you stay here?" he asked.

"Enough time that it takes me to walk back to the boat," I spat. His glare deepened.

"Her leg needs time to heal," Sam said coldly. "I don't think it's asking too much to let a few of your own kind stay on your island for a few days." Norman laughed coldly.

"She's *not* my kind. You two, I'll give you a few days. But the Cursed can stay on the boat." I curled my hands up into fists and forced myself to look him in the eyes.

201

"Why don't you make me?" I spat. He glared back at me. The silence was so thick you could cut it with a knife. Tom held up his hands and strode between us as if that could cut the tension.

"How about the humans stay on the boat at night?" he suggested.

"Or we can throw this asshole in the volcano," Sam whispered under her breath. I held back a smile as Norman sighed.

"Fine."

We awkwardly sat on the beach until nightfall. The sisters went out to help Norman hunt and returned with several large fish between them. Tom went around pulling vines and other plants off the volcano wall to make a fire. We skewered the fish on sticks and soon the smell made our stomachs growl. We took turns picking off the cooked flesh.

"Is this all you eat here? Seafood?" Tom asked Norman.

"Considering that I am a *real* merfolk living in the ocean, yes, all I eat is seafood."

"Well, if you miss human food, we have some food on the boat. Like, pasta and canned stuff," Sam said. Norman stiffened.

"I *don't* miss human food." *Then why do you cook it?* I wondered. Norman turned his attention to me.

"Why didn't you help hunt, huh? Scared of the water?" I swallowed my bite of food slowly, equal parts confused and irritated at his question.

"Considering that I am a *real* merfolk living at sea, no, I am not afraid of water," I said coolly. Tom tried to disguise his laughter as coughing. Norman narrowed his eyes at me.

"Real merperson, sure."

"She got injured at the lab," Sam said quietly. "She can't walk yet, let alone phase. Give her a break."

"You're just lucky you managed to keep your mouth shut," Norman snapped back. "Otherwise our entire species would be even more screwed than it already is." I stiffened at his words. *Duh!* I wanted to shout. *That's why I didn't say anything.* Why was this guy being such an asshole?

"She's not lucky she kept her mouth shut," Tom said quietly. "She *chose* to keep her mouth shut. To *protect* all of you." Norman snorted.

"Again. She's lucky." He stood up and brushed the sand off his pants. "Goodnight." With that, he walked off into the darkness and dove back into the water, leaving all of us in shell-shocked silence.

"Who peed in his cereal?" Cindy muttered. Sam sighed.

"Who knows? But we're here now, and we're safe. That's all that matters," she said quietly, ignoring mine and the other human's gazes.

Yup. Perfectly safe and stuck with the one merfolk who has some sort of harsh vendetta against humans and Cursed, I thought. Well . . . that wasn't new actually. I was used to rude remarks from Naturals, and much worse from humans. I would settle for safe.

Sam and Terri chose to find a place to sleep underwater while I huddled up against the volcano wall.

"Are you sure you'll be okay here by yourself?" Tom asked. "You can always come back to the boat with us." I nodded. Tom and Cindy left for the boat, smelling of irritation, and I stretched out on the smooth sand. It was warm enough to be comfortable, and I fell asleep within moments.

. . .

I woke up to the sunrise peeking over the horizon. I allowed myself to sit against the volcano wall and watch as sunlight trickled over the curve of the Earth, painting everything in orange, red, and purple. For a moment, I could almost forget that my leg was torn to shreds and that my life was in shambles.

And then Norman surfaced, shot me a dirty look, and walked over to the fire, muttering unkind comments under his breath. I sighed.

So went the next few days. Tom and Cindy didn't dare venture onto the beach until the rest of us were up and moving. Well, everyone except me was moving. Whenever the others were preoccupied with fishing or cooking, I took my time to practice walking. My good leg was building up more muscle. They still felt tight - like someone had tied them into crude knots.

I desperately wanted to swim, but I dared not risk tearing the wounds open again after all the time it had taken them to heal this much. My bad leg still screamed in pain whenever I tried to move it. My skin ached for the sea, but at least dehydration wasn't killing me.

I knew everyone was waiting for me to get better before leaving. As soon as I could swim, Tom and Cindy would head for land and never return. I would never see my best friend again - not that we had been acting so friendly lately anyway. As much as the smell of humans brought back negative flashbacks, it made me nervous to be left alone with Naturals. So far, Sam and Terri have been nice to me. They were waiting for me to be ready to swim before they went to Atlantis, but what would happen after we got there? Would I even be allowed in Atlantis after all the trouble I had caused?

If it was up to Norman, I wouldn't. They would probably slice me into bits and feed me to the sharks. But even that was better than going back to shore.

At night, Tom attempted to cut the tension by singing songs and dancing around the fire. No one had yet to join him. After several minutes of painfully awkward attempts, he would sit back down, defeated. I didn't understand how his confidence could come back after such crushing defeats night after night.

On the fourth day, blue lights reflected on the water along with the usual orange, red, and purple. It took my brain too many precious seconds to realize that the flashing blue was attached to another boat.

Oh my god, it's a police boat.

I scrambled to my feet, my chest tight with panic. *They found me.* Tom and Cindy bolted down the beach, panting.

"We saw it too!" Tom said. "We need to get the others and get out of here!" I nodded. There was no way in hell I would let them take me back to shore. I couldn't bear being at Arthur's mercy again. I would kill myself first. I started hobbling for Tom's boat as he splashed around in the shallows, shouting into the water.

"Hey, wake up! Boat! Danger! Wake up!" Tom shouted at the frothing waves. I resisted the urge to roll my eyes as another figure popped up in the distance. I stopped and squinted. It looked like a tiny arm waving up from the depths.

Tom saw it too and squinted out to sea. The arm disappeared and reappeared several yards closer.

"Is that someone swimming to shore?" Cindy asked. Her question was answered by a skinny figure popping out of the waves, only feet away from Tom, who fell back into the water in surprise.

The figure phased and got to his feet, shaking salt water out of his red hair. His curly blue markings wound their way across his pale face, occasionally interrupting fields of freckles. He rested his hands on his knees, wheezing. He waved and something attached to his green joggers glinted in the light.

"Sup . . . guys." He stood up, wiping sweat off his brow. He motioned out to sea. "That's my boat . . . well it's not mine . . . we stole it . . . ran out of gas . . . human friend is stuck up there . . . help?" he gasped between breaths. Tom, Cindy, and I all exchanged confused glances.

For the first time, the kid's eyes seemed to focus on who he was standing in front of him. I could feel his panic building up in his chest.

"He's not a mermaid catcher anymore," I said, interrupting his thoughts. He raised an eyebrow.

"Um, are you sure?"

"I'm not hanging out with a bunch of merfolk in the middle of the Bermuda Triangle for kicks and giggles," Tom said. The kid sagged in relief.

"Oh cool. So . . . you guys feel like helping me?" Tom ran back to the boat to get a rope. The kid - who introduced himself as Adam and his human friend as Emanuel, waited patiently with us on the sand. He didn't seem bothered at all to be chatting with a human and a Cursed.

By the time Tom returned with the rope, Sam and Terri had surfaced and seemed equally bewildered by this cheery stranger. When he stood up to shake their hands, I finally made out what was strapped to his waist: a sword. *Of course*, I thought.

Sam and Terri agreed to help him pull the boat to shore after he assured them that the boat had no internet. They set off to sea and Norman was up by the time the boat was secured to shore.

Norman did not look happy to have more strangers on his beach.

He crossed his arms and glared at the dark-skinned teenager who clamored onto the sand. Dark wavy hair was stuck to his forehead with sweat, but he smiled through his exhaustion. Handcuffs dangled from his wrists.

"Do you guys have any water?" he croaked. Tom jogged back to his boat as they explained themselves. Norman regarded both of them suspiciously as they told their stories, and it made a small part of me glad that it wasn't just the human he didn't like.

"And I suppose you two want to squat here as well?" he gritted his teeth. To my surprise, Adam shook his head.

"Well, that wasn't our plan. We were headed to The Sanctuary. Are you guys going there too?" Adam asked. Sam nodded.

"Eventually. Once Amy heals up." Adam turned to look at my leg - currently covered up by a pair of Tom's cargo pants cinched to my waist with a piece of twine. I had graduated from wearing oversized shirts to a shirt *and* pants. I glared at him and protectively moved it away.

"What happened?" Emanuel asked.

"None of your damn business!" Norman snapped. Emanuel recoiled. *Oh sure, use me as an excuse to yell at the human kid,* I thought. I opened my mouth to spit something back out at Norman, but Tom interrupted me.

"She can tell you if she feels like it," he said quietly, glaring at Norman for me. Norman rolled his eyes, and Emanuel wisely shut his mouth, turning his gaze to his water bottle.

Tom told our side of the story, leaving out the grisly details. Emanuel's face grew paler as the story progressed.

"That's terrible," he whispered. "I had no clue things were that bad." Norman's hands tightened into fists.

"Of course you don't!" he snapped at Emanuel. "You shouldn't be allowed anywhere near us! And you certainly shouldn't be allowed anywhere near The Sanctuary." Norman stood to his feet and stalked off into the waves, disappearing from sight. Emanuel bit his lip. Sam rolled her eyes.

"Ignore him. He's a jerk. You're fine to be here with us," she said.

"Something terrible must've happened to him," Emanuel pondered aloud. "What's his backstory?" None of us answered.

"Haven't been brave enough to ask," Cindy said.

And just like that - eight refugees were taking up space on the island. I was shocked by how nice Emanuel and Adam were to me - to everyone. Neither one of them commented on my different markings, which almost made me want to jump in and explain it to them. Some twisted part of me figured they should know that they were supposed to treat me like dirt. I tried not to think about what that meant about my mental state.

As usual, Norman sat grumpily on the outskirts of the flame, looking like he wished he was anywhere else. Sam held Terri in her lap. I sat next to Tom, who poked the fire on occasion. Our newcomers sat beside him, looking equally as sullen. Until Adam decided to stand up.

"I think this is the most depressing campfire I've ever participated in!" he declared. We all stared as he started clapping a beat on his thighs.

"*What do we do with a drunken sailor, what do we do with a drunken sailor, what do we do with a drunken sailor, ear-ly in the morning?*" he sang, adding in some creative footwork. For the first few lines, all we did was stare. Then the biggest smile broke across Tom's face. He jumped to his feet and started singing and dancing right alongside the redhead.

"*Put in a longboat til he's sober, put him in a longboat til he's sober, put him a longboat til he's sober, ear-ly in the morning!*" They looped arms and spun each other in a circle, laughing and giggling like they were five years old.

Across the campfire, Sam suddenly burst into laughter, falling on her back in the sand. She howled, wiping tears from her eyes. Terri tried to look annoyed until she couldn't anymore and joined her sister on the ground. The two got up and started clapping to the beat.

I found myself starting to smile. I didn't have the energy to stand, but I joined in on the clapping, allowing a delicate smile to break my face. Tom looped his arm around Cindy's and pulled her into the spinning. Adam grabbed Emanuel, who was red with embarrassment but awkwardly tried to match Adam's footsteps.

"Shave his belly with a rusty razor, shave his belly with a rusty razor, shave his belly with a rusty razor, ear-ly in the morning!" Norman stubbornly refused to participate in the dance despite Sam's attempt to drag him to his feet, but I swore I saw a ghost of an amused smile pass over his face.

We went to bed that night with our feet sore, but a little happier.

. . .

The days passed slowly. Watching the three boys interact was the newest entertainment on the island. Emanuel was fascinated with everything and expressed that excitement by spouting off science facts until Norman was visibly fuming. Surprisingly, Sam seemed to enjoy following him around and giggling at his horrible science puns.

Adam was even more cheerful and upbeat than Tom was and seemed determined to sing his little sea shanties and dance around until everyone was smiling as much as he was. Tom was all for joining him –

much to everyone's annoyance. There were a few times they cajoled everyone into dancing with them, but you had to be careful not to impale yourself on Adam's sword which he kept strapped around his waist. Turns out it was equally useful for cutting wood and fishing as it was for swashbuckling.

As much as Norman hated the humans, he didn't seem shy about swimming around them. He usually walked around with fins out on his arms - which boggled my mind. I had only managed a partial transformation once - the night I smashed in Morris' head with his gun - and no matter how hard I tried - I could never replicate it. One could have said I was jealous.

Terri and Cindy seemed content to spend the days by themselves - listening to the radio. Terri said it was safe to listen to it as long as we didn't put out any messages ourselves. They both smelled like constant frustration - one I assumed from not being able to talk to anyone but their sister and the other because of me.

In another time, I told myself I would have sat down and tried to learn some ASL, but I spent most of my days trying to drown out everyone around me and focus on walking. My good leg and crutching arm were getting nice and strong. I mostly thanked the sand for that (seriously, have you ever tried using crutches in sand?) Sometimes - I could put weight on my bad leg without screaming. Every passing day where I wasn't magically healed made my heart drop a little lower. I knew merfolk wouldn't phase back and forth in the face of extreme injury - but I hadn't phased in over a week. I had never had an injury take longer than a few days to heal.

What if I never heal? What if I can never turn back? What's the point of being a freak of nature if I can't even do the freak of nature part anymore? If I can't turn back, does that mean I'm basically human again?

The thought of Arthur having accidentally destroyed his favorite science project made me smirk a little bit.

I let that thought fuel me as I crutched back to the others and let myself sit down. Off in the distance, Adam was demonstrating different swashbuckling moves to Sam. Emanuel had traced a chess board into the damp sand and was attempting to teach Tom how to play. If Emanuel was merfolk, he would've already caught on that Tom was about as interested in the game as the sand was. Norman watched from the shallows, basking in the sun, smirking at the situation.

"So I'm going to quiz you on all the pieces - what does the queen do?" Emanuel asked.

"Tell the king what to do," Tom quipped. I sniggered as Emanuel rolled his eyes.

"Norman, you want to play?" Norman responded with a particular hand gesture. Emanuel deflated and turned to give me a hopeful look. *Damn it,* I thought.

"Why do you have fins on your back?" Tom asked suddenly. All the merpeople except for me sucked in a breath as Norman went rigid. Without pausing to curse or make an offensive gesture, he disappeared into the ocean. Sam groaned, slapping her hand against her forehead.

"He's going to drown you in your sleep."

"What's the big deal? Why is that such a bad question?" Tom protested.

"I've honestly been wondering that too," Emanuel said sheepishly. *Me too,* I thought. The only other merfolk I had seen with fins had been Dr. Mercer.

"When a male has fins - it means he's *mated,*" Sam said, lowering her voice to a whisper. Tom furrowed his brows.

"Wait, what? What's mated?" I asked.

"Merpeople don't hit puberty the same way humans do," Sam said. "In fact, it's actually kind of the opposite. With humans, you guys usually get all these scheduled hormones that trigger puberty. With merfolk, there's no set schedule, and the hormones that trigger puberty in us are completely different. Well, I would assume they're different anyway."

"So, what triggers the hormones?" Emanuel asked. Sam dragged her toe through the sand.

"Coitus." I covered my mouth to keep from laughing.

"That's a joke, right?" Tom asked. Sam rolled her eyes.

"I know, I know, it sounds dumb, but that's how it works. Merfolk are empathic, which makes connecting with a romantic partner easy. Merfolk mate for life and once the feelings are strong enough and consummated . . . poof. Your body starts growing up so you can have kids and protect your family." *Are you serious?* I thought. *That's why I never got boobs? Or a period? Because I didn't have a hot merfolk to fall in love with? Why did Markus or his dad never feel the need to explain this to me?*

"So if you never find a mate . . . you just never hit puberty?" Tom asked. Sam nodded.

"Yup. If you ask me, it makes much more biological sense than the other way around. It saves energy and reduces unwanted pregnancies. Breasts don't develop until actual pregnancy and go away pretty quickly after breastfeeding because – you know – boobs aren't very water-dynamic when you're swimming.

"Plus, we have cool adaptations that help protect our mates. Men, as you have seen, grow fins on their backs – and in dangerous situations – those fins can inject poison that can paralyze someone for days. But it can only work on enemies – say for example he accidentally poked his mate. It wouldn't do anything. Family members are immune.

"Females develop the ability to cry – but we don't cry like humans do. Our tears are actually a build-up of what I believe are white blood cells and other healing agents that can speed up the healing process. Again, only works on family members. Not only are we incredibly emotionally in tune with each other, but our bodies literally evolve in real time to protect each other physically. It's pretty cool." *I have healing powers?* I thought. *That's why I don't cry when I'm upset? Why can't I use them on myself?*

"That is pretty cool," Emanuel said.

"But wait, that means Norman . . . he has a mate? Where is she?" Tom asked. Sam shrugged.

"Judging by his attitude . . . gone. Dead. Captured. Something terrible must have happened. Which is why you don't ask people about their fins!" she snapped, kicking sand at him. Tom wiped it off his pants.

"But wait, he said he's only fifteen. That means he's . . . you know . . . not a . . ." A blush rode up Tom's face, and the sand on his shorts suddenly became a lot more interesting. Sam rolled her eyes.

"It's normal for merfolk to find their mates when they're young," she said.

"But he's just a kid!" Tom protested. I squawked out a laugh.

"Please, you're one to talk. Didn't you sleep with like, half the girls at our school by sophomore year?" Tom's face grew redder. Emanuel suddenly saw some firewood on the beach he had to collect for drying, radiating second-hand embarrassment as he went.

TOM

Norman didn't surface again until later that night, and we all made sure to avoid him. I didn't understand why he hung out with us so much if he hated us. Maybe he was just keeping an eye on us to make sure we didn't do anything sketchy on his precious island.

No one tried to sing or dance during dinner that night. Cindy and Terri didn't even show up - which wasn't a total surprise. They tended to keep to themselves on the boat.

I watched Amy out of the corner of my eye as I ate. Thankfully, she seemed to be eating more and more every day - and keeping it down. She was starting to look more like a person instead of a skeleton. Small miracles.

"Guys, come quick!" We all jerked to attention as Cindy came running down the beach, waving her arms. She skidded to a halt, motioning wildly to the boat. "Terri - she found something - it's important - come on!" she shouted. We all exchanged concerned glances but dropped our food to follow. We all crammed in the living room around the radio, Terri's hands folded tightly in front of her.

"What was your reaction to finding out about all of this?" the radio host asked.

"I think we were all shocked. Amy had been best friends with my daughter for years." My hands clenched as Arthur's voice oozed through the radio, smug and full of fake sympathy.

"She was such a trustworthy kid. Always got good grades. Never got in trouble." Amy went stiff at the sound of her mom's voice. My heart dropped. *This cannot be good.*

"That seems to be the trend we see with these creatures. Everyone is surprised when they reveal their true selves," the host said.

"These creatures are extremely manipulative. You could think of them almost as people who have multiple personalities - they've mastered the art of having this 'human' personality. And no one ever suspects until it's too late," Arthur said.

"Are you saying that Amy was a danger to the humans around her?" the host asked.

"Oh absolutely. She was extremely violent and aggressive towards all members of our staff. We had to make sure everyone was stocked with sedatives just in case. We had to restrain her. We even have to do that with the mermaids in the regular aquarium – as anyone who visits can see. These two are extremely lucky that they were not harmed. My daughter was not so lucky," Arthur said. Amy clenched her fists, gritting her teeth.

"I'm not the one who tried to kill her," she muttered under her breath.

"Are these creatures dangerous by nature?" the host asked.

"Behind every myth is a grain of truth. These creatures don't think in terms of good and evil like we do. They aren't human in the same way tigers aren't human. It's in their nature. And they evolved very well to do their job. This is why it is so imperative that we catch them before they hurt more people," Arthur explained.

"This must be incredibly hard for you two. She was your only daughter, after all. It took you years to be able to adopt her." Amy's jaw dropped. *So that's their story now,* I thought. *She's adopted. Arthur must have revealed that Amy was a mermaid – but not that she was born human. He's saying she was adopted so no one thinks it's weird she has human parents. Why are her parents going along with this? Is he threatening them?*

"We loved her," the mom sobbed. "It's just so hard to believe."

"If there is any human-ness left in her, she would realize that she needs to turn herself in. Before she hurts anyone else," her father said gruffly. Amy's jaw snapped shut again, her eyes wide with shock. *Amy is harmless,* I thought. *How could they possibly think she was dangerous? Why are they buying this shit?*

"May I remind our listeners that the reward for her capture - alive - is five million dollars. If she is returned dead, there will be no reward given." Amy swayed slightly, and for a moment, I thought she might pass out.

Five million dollars? What would someone do with that much money? I thought, my guts twisting.

"Turn this off," Cindy whispered. *Arthur must be in so much of a panic over his favorite experiment and daughter going missing that he's finally coming clean about some things,* I thought. *He admitted Amy was a mermaid, but what else was he still hiding? Does anyone know Sam and Terri are gone? Does anyone know we rescued them?* Norman let out a long whistle.

"Whelp, if I never saw anyone get disowned before today . . ." Sam lifted a pillow to chuck it at his head, but not before Amy stood up and spoke in an eerily calm voice.

"Shut up." Norman scoffed.

"Excuse me?" She turned to face him, teeth bared. Her markings melted into view, like vines growing on a wall.

"I told you to shut up, asshole," she repeated. Norman held his hand over his heart in mock hurt.

"Bless your heart, you can't think of a better insult? Can I give you some pointers?" Amy cut him off by marching over and punching him in the face. He sprawled over the end of the coffee table and landed ungracefully on the ground. I let out a very inappropriate laugh as Norman scrambled to his feet. It was the first time I had seen Amy touch anyone willingly since her rescue. She waited patiently before swinging again, but this time Norman was able to dodge it.

"What the hell?" he demanded.

"Didn't you hear? I'm dangerous and violent. It's only a matter of time until I kill everyone around me, so I might as well start with you, you son of a bitch!" she seethed, swinging again. Norman dodged but clenched his fists. His fins grew from his arms and back.

"You really want to fight? Why don't we take this out in the water like real merpeople? Oh, wait, you forgot how to swim when you were stuck in the lab!" They both reached for each other. Sam grabbed Norman and held him back as Cindy unwisely inserted herself between them, trying to shove them apart. I debated the wisdom of grabbing Amy. I didn't exactly want a black eye either and unlike Norman, I didn't exactly deserve one.

"Get off me!" Norman shouted, struggling against Sam's grip.

"You all are acting like kids!" Cindy shouted. *We are kids*, I thought.

"She's crazy!" Norman shouted. Amy laughed.

"Of course I'm crazy! I'm crazy and violent and dangerous and evil. Even my parents think so! And since I can't make myself go back to the lab, I guess I'll just off myself instead before I hurt anyone else!" she screamed. She spun on her heel and stumbled out of the room.

"Tom, go after her!" Cindy shouted, still helping Sam hold Norman back. I raced out the door and saw her limping on the shore. She disappeared into the darkness of a cave. I took my time walking towards her, not sure what I would say when I got there and feeling like it had to be a good idea to give her some space. Then again, maybe she shouldn't be given space given she had just threatened to kill herself.

She had curled herself up in a ball in the far corner of the cave. She didn't turn to look at me as I ducked inside and leaned against the opposite wall. We sat in silence for a few moments.

"I'm sorry," she finally said. I shrugged.

"I mean . . . I've been wanting to punch that asshole this whole time." I hoped for a laugh, but she just curled tighter into her ball.

"They're right about me. I am dangerous. I'm a liar. No one can trust me. I end up hurting everyone around me."

"Amy, that's not true."

"Yes, it is," she said, her voice wavering. "If I wasn't like this, you and Cindy would be safe on the shore. Merpeople would have never been revealed to the world. Everyone would be safe."

"If it wasn't for you, Cindy would be dead with a bullet in her brain. And Markus would be in that same lab as Sam and Terri. And jeez, you only lied about who you were because you *had* to! If anyone thinks you're a terrible person for that, then they don't get it. Sometimes you *have* to lie."

"My parents hate me. Humans all over the world hate me. Cindy can barely stand to be around me. Heck . . . even other merfolk hate me. This is all my fault." She started to tremble. I ran my fingers through my hair.

"If we want to get technical, this is all my fault," I said. "I mean, sure, you revealed the species, but I'm the one who figured out how to catch them. If I hadn't done that . . . Markus would be safe. Sam and Terri would be safe. You, Cindy, everyone."

"You're different. You made up for all of that. You rescued us. I can't make up for what I did. I can't go back in time and not push that woman in the fountain. I ruined it for everyone."

"Well . . . what if we figured out a way for you to fix it?" She snorted. I shrugged.

"Look, I don't know how you or I or anyone would fix it. We're all in a big mess right now. But I do know this." I scooched closer. "You are one of the bravest people I've ever met. I sure as hell wouldn't have saved someone I hated from getting shot. You're a good, brave person, Amy. And if your parents can't see that anymore because of some lies that asshole cooked up – then they never really knew you to begin with." She glanced at me through her trembling fingers before looking back down at the ground.

"You're not lying."

"I know better than to lie to an empath," I said. She chuckled.

"You're allowed to look at me, you know," I said. She bit her lip and shook her head.

"No. I'm not. I wasn't allowed to make eye contact. If I did they . . . they hit me." My blood boiled as she trailed off.

"I've had enough of people staring at me," she said bitterly. "Especially when I'm not allowed to look at them back. I'm just sick of all of this. Everyone has been lying to me. *Your legs will be healed soon. You're safe now.*"

"You don't feel safe?" I asked.

"Arthur is going to stop at nothing to get me back," she whispered. "He just put millions of dollars on my head. I'm shocked he hasn't found us already. And when he gets me back . . ." She buried her head in her hands, trembling. "Who knows how much worse it will be." I stopped myself from wrapping my arms around her at the last second.

"I'd die before I let him take you away again," I vowed, the words coming out a little more fiercely than I imagined.

"I want to believe you but . . ."

"Then believe me when I do it," I said. "I promise. I'll keep all of you safe, come hell or high water." She snorted.

"That's cheesy."

"It's true. I promise, Amy. Hell or high water. He's not taking you away from me again," I whispered. She peeked back up at me and tentatively reached out her hand. I was confused for a moment until I realized what she was asking. I gently placed my hand in hers and she held it tight.

I let it tremble in mine for the rest of the night.

CINDY

Norman never apologized to Amy, despite multiple threats from all the other islanders. He stalked back off to whatever hole he lived in in the ocean and rarely showed his face.

Amy did the same thing, although she seemed just fine with hanging around Tom instead of her best friend. Every time I saw the two of them together, my heart cracked a little more. I knew she was hurting, but she was still acting like I was the one who had turned the knife on her in the lab.

At least I never kidnapped anyone, I thought bitterly. Being around Tom, Adam, and Emanuel hurt too much - reminded me of all the joy I wasn't feeling - so I started avoiding them. I found myself counting down the hypothetical days until we could return to shore, which only made me feel worse.

The tension among all of us felt thick enough to cut with a knife. Amy refused to let anyone near her despite her obvious pain and difficulty moving. Norman was constantly brooding, watching all of us to make sure we didn't destroy his precious island. Tom was becoming more and more restless as well. I noticed him whispering with Terri more often.

That night at dinner, he dropped news I was secretly ecstatic to hear.

"If you guys are okay with it, we'll leave for shore tomorrow," he said, face crackling in the heat of the flames. Amy deflated and Norman smirked into the flames.

"Terri risked the use of the laptop to track down Norman's parents. She scrambled the signal so they shouldn't be able to find us. I'm going to rescue his parents and bring them back here," he said calmly, poking the fire. "Then - we'll take you all to the Sanctuary." Norman got to his feet, face pale.

"How did you find out about my parents!" he shouted, clenching his hands into fists.

"Like I said - Terri did some research for me. They're being held at an aquarium about a ten-minute drive inland from Baldwin Island." Norman stood speechless. "So, is everyone good with that?" Tom asked, scanning the group.

"Why the fuck do you want to rescue my parents?" Norman demanded. Tom narrowed his eyes at him, holding up several fingers.

"One, I care about helping merfolk, even though their son is a piece of work. Two, it's not like I can go back to my normal life anyway. I'm probably a wanted man at this point. Three, if I get caught, I end up in jail, not an aquarium," he explained.

"You're going to do this by yourself? Do you have a plan?" Sam asked. "I mean, you've been lucky so far, but at this point, they probably have drills practicing for you."

"I'll help!" Adam raised his hand like he was in kindergarten. "I can be your bodyguard."

"If you're going, I'm coming with you," Emanuel said. I suspected he mostly said this because he didn't want to be left alone with the rest of us. Tom shrugged.

"Up to you guys. But if we get caught, Emanuel and I are going to jail and Adam's going to join Norman's parents." They both nodded.

"I can't let you guys go alone," Adam said quietly.

"Well, you aren't going without me either!" Norman sputtered. "They're my parents! What makes you think they'll even go with you? They know who you are!" he accused Tom. He nodded.

"Fair enough." I sighed.

"Well, sign me up too," I said. My relationship with my best friend clearly wasn't healing. There didn't seem like much of a point in me staying on the island any longer. It wasn't like I could go to Atlantis with them once Amy's leg healed.

"Might as well. I . . . I should probably go home anyway. One last shebang before my dad kills me." Amy ducked her head away from me. *She doesn't even care that I'm leaving,* I thought. Tom looked at the remaining merfolk.

"Will you guys be okay while we're gone?" he asked, his gaze lingering on Amy. She hesitated, then nodded.

"If we're not back in four days, assume we've been caught. Go to The Sanctuary without us," Tom said. Sam nodded, gripping her sister's hand.

"We leave at dawn."

EMANUEL

Tom gathered us together in the living room that night and told us the plan.

"We'll wait until they close. We'll pick the lock to the back door and sneak in. There will probably be a guard or guards, but Norman can use his fins to take them out!" Tom looked particularly excited about that part of the plan. I wondered briefly where Tom had learned to pick locks.

"We'll find Norman's parents, break them out, bring them out to the car that we steal, drive away, hop back on the boat, and be out of here. Oh - and I've got to fill up on gas at a marina too."

"You're assuming the aquarium won't have an alarm system. What are we supposed to do if the cops show up?" I asked.

"I know how to disable alarm systems," Tom said. *He can disable alarm systems too? What had this guy done in his spare time before he started catching merfolk?*

"What if they're injured?" Cindy asked. At this, Norman paled visibly.

"We'll get them back here as soon as possible so we can fix them up," he said grimly. "But I doubt they'll be worse off than Amy."

"You don't think anyone will recognize your boat when we pull up?" Adam asked.

"There won't be anyone to recognize it where I'm docking."

True to his word, after he filled the boat with gas, Tom docked at the most decrepit-looking dock I had ever seen. Parts of it lay submerged underwater, and the whole thing wobbled precariously as we stepped out onto it. I almost screamed in surprise as Norman grabbed my arm to keep from falling off the edge. He just as quickly let go of it, refusing to meet my gaze. His skin was clammy enough for me to wipe the sweat off with my t-shirt.

We followed Tom up the beach and towards the city lights.

"How far away are we?" I whispered.

"As far away as it takes to steal a car," Tom whispered back. "Wait here. I'll flash the lights when I return." With that, he bounded off into the darkness, leaving the four of us alone. Cindy plopped down on the sand and stared down at her hands. Adam practiced swiping with his sword, and Norman paced.

Norman reminded me of my little brother, who whenever he got scared, would lash out with bitter words and fists. I figured Norman had to be terrified - of what condition his parents might be in and what would happen to him if things went wrong. I crossed myself and prayed that things would go as planned. He was an asshole, sure, but no one deserved to be locked away against their will.

Fifteen minutes later, an old white van crawled to a stop and flashed her lights. We trudged up through the sand and piled in. Adam and Norman wrinkled their noses.

"You had to find the one creepy van owned by a pothead?" Norman grumbled, holding his nose.

"Would you have rather me stolen it from someone who wasn't zonked out and noticed it go missing?" We rode on in silence. My heart pounded faster and faster in my chest. Helping Adam rescue the kid in the net was a spur-of-the-moment brave thing. Somehow, planning out a brave thing made it harder. I didn't want to think about what would happen if we got caught. My mom would be the least of my worries.

The aquarium shone in the darkness. They had erected a huge sign pointing to the mermaid exhibit and surrounded it with LED flashing lights. Norman scowled in the darkness.

"Are you guys ready for this? You can always stay in the car," Tom whispered tersely. We all nodded. Tom slid out a gun, previously hidden in the back of his pants and loaded it with a handful of bullets from his pocket. I wondered if that was the same gun Morris had tried to shoot him with.

"If any of you are in trouble, scream." With that, we slid outside and stole for the doors. Tom bent down by the lock and worked his magic. It popped open and mercifully, no alarms went off.

"You guys go find his parents. I'll search the place for any guards. Cindy, will you keep watch by the door and shout if anyone pulls up?" She nodded. Tom ran off down a hallway, and Norman started following the signs pointing toward the mermaid exhibit.

I looked up at the security cameras we passed them, wondering how clearly they would be able to see us when they watched it the next morning. Not that it mattered if we escaped.

Fish and other creatures ignored us as we traveled down the twisting hallways. Blue light shimmered on the walls and carpet, painting the illusion that we were all underwater.

Adam hesitated before entering the mermaid exhibit. The entrance was closed.

"Do you think there's an alarm on those?" Adam whispered. Norman squared his shoulders and kicked the door open. They swung wide with no sounds, revealing an empty tank.

"Where are they?" Adam whispered. The tank loomed empty before us. There wasn't so much as a speck of algae on the inside.

"Tom said the sisters were kept in cages in the back at night. Are there any doors?" I asked. We searched the room and found a door hidden in the wall. Norman pushed past us and ripped it open, disappearing down a white hallway. He returned in a moment with haunted eyes.

"They aren't there," he whispered. "Nothing is back there. It's completely empty." I swallowed. Norman threw his fists against the side of the tank. "No!" he seethed. "They're supposed to be here!"

"Too bad, so sad." We all whirled around to see another teenager - a human one wearing a puffy security guard jacket. His hands were spread out on either side of the door frame, boxing us in.

"Who do you think you are?" Adam asked, raising a skeptical eyebrow. The guy smirked.

"Norman hasn't told you who I am?" If there was one thing I could never picture Norman doing - it was freezing. But yet, the devil-may-care irritable merman's eyes were wide and unblinking. His face had drained of color. I narrowed my eyes at the human's security uniform and noticed it had a nametag: Jason.

"What are you doing here?" Norman whispered. I threw Adam a look. *Who is this Jason guy? And why does Norman look more scared than I do?* Adam shot me back an equally confused look.

"Not all alarms make noise," Jason laughed. "The police will be here any minute. I'm just so lucky you came during my shift."

"Where are his parents?" Adam demanded, sword flashing dangerously in the light.

"They were transferred earlier today," Jason said with a smirk. "You're too late." Norman's face lost the rest of its color. Jason cracked his knuckles.

"Now how about the two mermaids stay where they are, or things get messy," he threatened. Adam snorted.

"Yeah. We'll stay right here," he said sarcastically. Jason smirked and unearthed a tranquilizer gun from the back of his belt. At this, Adam took an uneasy step back. I stood in front of him. My legs were shaking, but it would be better for me to get caught than the other two.

"I got this," I squeaked. Jason snorted and aimed the gun. I forced my trembling legs to move and flung myself at him, screaming. He fired as I tackled him, but he was thick as a wall. He merely stumbled backward a few feet, dropping the gun. He grabbed me by the arms and threw me to the side. Adam lunged for the fallen gun as I crashed against the wall. Black dots peppered my vision as I scrambled to my feet. Adam had secured the gun in his hands, but Jason now had Norman trapped in his grasp. One hand was clamped over his mouth while the other pinned his arms to his side. Norman struggled for a few moments before going stiff. His panicked gaze turned on us.

"Let go of him!" Adam shouted, aiming the gun. He clicked the trigger, but nothing happened. He stared down at the gun in shock. Jason smirked.

"It never worked." Adam grabbed it by the nozzle and swung it like a bat.

"I bet it'll work like this," he threatened.

"And risk me hurting your little friend?" Jason shot back. He turned to look at me. "Switch sides now and I'll split the reward money with you." I shook my head, nauseated. Norman squeezed his eyes shut. His arms began to tremble.

"Fat chance." We were at an impasse. I desperately prayed for Tom or someone else with an actual weapon to show up and give us the upper hand. But the thing was - we shouldn't have needed an upper hand. This was the point where Norman should be screaming swear words and doing everything in his power to break out of Jason's grip. But he wasn't doing anything. He just stood there, trembling. He was poisonous for crying out loud! He was our secret weapon! This battle should already be over! What was going on?

I tried to get Norman to look at me, to understand what was going on with my eyes, but he wouldn't meet my gaze. Adam began to take a step forward, but Jason jerked Norman to the side, making him squeak.

"Take another step, and I'll snap his neck!" He tightened his grip and Norman whimpered in his grasp. I took my chance.

"Norman, I know you're scared of this guy, but you're stronger than him." Jason laughed.

"Don't tell me he's manipulated you too," he said, directing his gaze towards me. He removed his hand from Norman's mouth, instead using it to squish his cheeks like an old grandma would do.

"Their words can be quite alluring, you know. They make you do things you don't want to do. He's probably controlling you right now! Don't let him fool you too!" At this, a familiar flash of anger passed over Norman's eyes.

"If you believe that, you're lying to yourself," Adam retorted. "Merfolk can't control anyone but themselves." This statement seemed to infuriate Jason.

"Don't tell me what they can or can't do!" he roared. "He's the dangerous one, not me! Now let us through or he gets it!" Adam and I stared at each other, unsure of what to do. Would Jason actually hurt him? Suddenly, in the silence, Norman found his words. His voice came out small and cracked.

"I never did *anything* to you." Jason screamed as Norman's fins erupted from his back and arms, needles piercing through his torso and out his back. Jason's body went slack before collapsing to the floor, sliding off the poisonous needles with a sickening noise. Once on the floor, his body slowly stiffened, face contorted with his mouth open and eyes wide.

At that particular moment, Tom burst into the room. Police sirens sounded in the distance.

"We've been set up, they're not here - whoa - what happened?" I grabbed Norman's hand, as he was still standing there, frozen in shock, staring at the damage behind him.

"Yeah, we noticed. Come on, we have to go." I literally dragged Norman behind me as we raced from the building.

CINDY

I never had a chance to scream at the cop cars. A burly figure came up behind me and grabbed me before I heard a thing. Tom should've picked a merfolk to guard the door.

I kicked and attempted to scream through his meaty hand but he held me fast and shoved me to the ground. I clammed up as a cold nozzle was pressed against my back.

"Move and you're dead," he snarled. "Where are the others?"

"At your mom's house," I growled.

"We'll find them. The cops are on their way." I swore inwardly and prayed the others would get Norman's parents out safely. I was planning on staying anyway, so it hardly mattered if I was caught, but the others? If Tom was arrested, there would be no one to rescue the rest of them.

The nozzle was yanked away from my back as shouting sounded down the hallway. Tom, Adam, and Emanuel dragging Norman like a limp doll burst into the foyer. The gun popped and Norman screamed. For a terrifying moment, I thought he had been shot, but Norman swung his finned arm at the guard's face. The needles sank into his flesh and the guard collapsed to the ground. Tom yanked me to my feet and dragged me out the door as flashing police lights bathed us in blue and red. I grit my teeth.

"Go! I'll distract them!" I shouted. Praying the cops could see I was human, I ran right to the middle of their group, screaming and thrashing my arms. I was immediately tackled and held to the ground. Cold metal cuffs clenched around my wrists, and I tilted my head just enough to see Tom and the others piling into the van. Tom gave me one last despairing look.

"GO!" I screamed. "GO NOW!" The door slid shut and the van screeched across the asphalt. The remaining cops not holding me down shot after the van, but it got onto the main road safely and disappeared into the darkness. One of the cops spoke into their radio.

"We need backup. Got Tom Falcon and other fugitives fleeing in a white Toyota van, heading down South." The cop looked at me and tsked.

"Cindy Johnson. Your father is going to be very happy to see you."

EMANUEL

We rode back in silence, except for Tom, who was swearing and punching the steering wheel at random intervals.

"Tom, it's okay. You didn't know," I said hollowly. He wiped his eyes.

"Norman, I'm so sorry," he whispered. Norman curled up in a ball in the back of the van and ignored him. He stared off into space, eyes wide and unblinking. Adam and I exchanged concerned glances. *What's wrong with him?* I mouthed. Adam shrugged helplessly.

We ditched the van by the beach and sped away on the boat before the police caught up to us. The ride was equally as quiet. Cindy left a looming gap. *She was going to stay anyway,* I told myself. *Better her than us.* Somehow, thinking that only made me feel worse.

As soon as we arrived, Norman bolted to the beach, leaving Amy staring at us.

"What happened?" she asked. Tom ran his fingers through his hair and began to explain. I tugged Adam over to the beach and pointed out to sea. Norman was curled up in the middle of a sandbank, head buried between his knees, his body shaking. Adam and I glanced at each other.

"We need to talk to him," I said. He raised his eyebrow at me.

"He hates us," he whispered. I glared at him.

"He's crying!" I hissed. Adam rolled his eyes.

"But he hates us!" he protested.

"I can hear you," Norman mumbled. We both winced. I gave Adam one more glare, and he reluctantly followed me out on the sandbar. Norman didn't lift his head as we sat down on either side of him.

"Hey, buddy. You . . . okay?" Adam asked awkwardly. I shot him a look. *Are you the dumbest person on the planet? He is obviously not okay!*

"Do you want to talk about it?" I asked gently. At this, Norman lifted his head and stared out at the water. I took his movement as a yes.

"Who was that guy?" I asked. Norman white-knuckled his knees and swallowed.

"Promise you two won't judge me?" he whispered. Adam and I shared another surprised look.

"Of course not," Adam said. Norman swallowed.

"He . . . he was my ex-boyfriend." Adam's jaw hit the sand and my eyes widened in shock.

Merpeople can be gay?

Of course they can be gay you idiot! I scolded myself. *They're people too, and if people can be gay, so can they!*

Wait, does that mean there are transgender merpeople too?

Focus.

This confession reduced Norman to another bout of trembling. He buried his head in his knees. Very carefully, I placed a hand on his shoulder and was surprised when he didn't stab me in retaliation. He leaned further into my touch, trembling more violently. Adam nodded to himself.

"Was he your mate? The one who gave you your fins?" Norman nodded silently. We both winced on his behalf. Suddenly, Norman's behavior made total sense. His burning hatred of humans. His utter refusal to talk about how he got here or his partner. His utter terror at seeing him.

No wonder he had been afraid to use his fins on his ex. The whole point of fins was to protect your partner, not hurt them. It was a feat in itself that it had even worked.

"Did he know? That you were merfolk?" I asked. Norman shook his head.

"Not until after the reward was put out. He figured it out somehow," Norman said.

"He was the one who tried to turn you in?" Adam asked. "That's why you ran?" Norman lifted his head off my chest.

"My parents and I were supposed to flee to go to the Sanctuary. I didn't want to leave without telling him goodbye because I was an idiot and thought he loved me. I thought he would understand. But when I showed up, he was with his dad and police dogs. I barely escaped." I swallowed, tears springing into my eyes.

"I'm so sorry." Norman sniffed and held his arms.

"I didn't know if my parents made it to The Sanctuary or if they were captured. I was too scared to go there because they would find out and they would never forgive me."

"Forgive you for what?" Adam asked. Norman opened and closed his mouth several times to get the next few words out.

"He - he wasn't out of the closet yet. And my parents hate humans. So, we kept our relationship a secret. But he -" Norman choked on his words and had to take several deep breaths to continue. "He - he made me do things I didn't want to. I wanted help, but I was afraid to tell my parents because I knew they would be upset. So, I didn't tell anybody, and it just kept getting worse until . . ." He motioned towards his fin. "Until it was too late." Adam and I shared a shocked expression. *Oh my god.*

Adam covered his hand with his mouth as I debated hugging the sobbing merman. Touching him seemed even more risky than it did before. I didn't want to make him uncomfortable. A few tears of my own escaped as I squeezed his shoulder, trying to whisper comforting words. All the while, Norman blurted out more sorrows.

"Finding your mate is permanent in merfolk culture - especially to my parents. Bad things happen to those who don't make it work - or do it with anyone who's not merfolk. I couldn't let my parents know what happened, so I didn't swim around them for weeks. And if they ever find out, they're going to kill me. They always told me to stay away from humans, and they were right." Adam placed his hand on Norman's shoulder.

"You didn't *let* him do anything," he said fiercely. "He was the one who made you do things you didn't want to do. This isn't your fault. They won't - or shouldn't - be mad at you for any of this!"

"Besides, you won in the end. You stabbed him! You poisoned him! Doesn't that mean that the mate thing or whatever is canceled?" I asked. Norman quieted.

"You can't cancel a mate. Or have different ones. It's permanent," he mumbled. I scoffed.

"Apparently not. You're telling me no mermaid couple has ever gotten divorced?" I asked. "There's no way you're the only one. How else could you have poisoned him?"

"Yeah! I mean, you probably won't grow a different fin, but it would only make sense that you could have more than one if you can get rid of the first one! Which you did! That was incredible! That's like . . . the bravest thing I've ever seen!" Norman cracked a smile and rubbed his eyes.

"You're safe now," I promised. "You know for sure that you can protect yourself now, no matter who it is." Norman nodded. His trembling finally ceased. He took a deep breath.

"I'm sorry," he said. "I've been a huge asshole to everyone."

"Don't apologize," I said. "You've been carrying this on your own for way too long."

"Can this stay between us?" Norman whispered. "I don't want the others to know what my ex did." We both nodded.

"Of course, this stays between us."

"Thanks."

"If he dares show his face around us again, I'll drown him myself," Adam vowed. Norman laughed.

"How long will he be paralyzed?" I asked.

"A few days."

"I hope it hurts." Norman giggled. He placed his hands over both of ours.

"Thanks, guys." I grinned back.

"Hey, through hell or high water, right?" Norman chuckled.

"Through hell or high water."

. . .

That night, as I tried to find a spot on deck to sleep on, Norman slowly walked up.

"Mind if I sleep next to you?" he asked quietly. I blinked in surprise but nodded.

"Sure." We found a spot near the corner of the boat. As night descended, I felt Norman roll over to face me.

"I apologized to Tom. And Amy. For you know . . . being such an asshole," he whispered. I chuckled.

"Not Norman apologizing," I teased. He whacked me in the chest as he flushed in embarrassment.

"My parents are wrong." I raised an eyebrow.

"About what?" Warm hands clasped themselves around mine. I almost jumped out of my skin. They were surprisingly soft, not clammy like before. I had to force myself to concentrate on the words coming out of his mouth.

"Not all humans are bad. There's at least . . . three good ones out there." I chuckled. He squeezed my hands. My heart jumped.

"You feel so much different than him," he whispered. "Besides, if you or anyone else here wanted to do something . . . you would've done it already. You're so nice. And cheerful. It's annoying. But brave."

"Hey, don't think like that. I would never hurt you." I squeezed his hands back. "Do you think your parents would really be that upset if they found out you dated a human? I mean . . . you're already gay." I flushed, suddenly worried I had insulted him.

"Not that being gay is bad but like . . . usually that's what people get upset about," I stammered.

"Merfolk don't really care about gender," Norman said. "We're mer*folk*, not mer*men* or mer*maids*. They wouldn't care who I date as long as they have a tail."

"Well, when we find your parents and explain the situation, I'm sure they'll understand. And if they don't, it's their problem, not yours," I said. Norman giggled. It was a delightful noise - to hear him laugh like that. I don't think I had heard him laugh once before that day.

"Thank you, Emanuel."

"No need to thank me." Norman yawned and rolled back over, his back facing the ocean. I missed how his hands felt in mine.

CINDY

My father was surprisingly calm when he saw me. In fact, he ran up to me and threw his arms around me, sobbing. I stood stiff in his arms, wanting to scream and confront him, but he was sobbing so hard it made it hard for me to tear myself away and be mad.

When we finally sat down away from prying eyes, I let him have it.

"You lied to me," I spat. He furrowed his brows. "Don't give me that," I said, my sympathetic mood from earlier wearing off. "I asked you where Amy was when she first disappeared, and you lied straight to my face." He sighed.

"Honey, she was dangerous. I was just trying to protect you." I crossed my arms.

"When we rescued her, she was almost dead. She said *you* did it to her because she refused to tell you how she changed. Which is another thing you lied about. When are you planning on telling the world that she changed from human to merfolk? Oh wait, you're not because you're not smart enough to figure it out." A vein on his forehead twitched.

"I never hurt her. She did it to herself in a violent fit. One of many violent fits." My vitriol died on my tongue. I knew he was lying, but part of me still wanted to believe him. This was my father, the man who raised me after my mom died. How could my father be such a terrible person?

He looked tired as if he hadn't slept in weeks. His eyes were swollen and red.

"So, what, am I grounded or something?"

"You need help, Cindy. That creature has messed with your head, and I intend to make it right."

. . .

And now I was here.

The office was tiny as if the designers wanted to make sure the inhabitants would be allowed no personal space. The door was locked, just like every door in the mental hospital.

The words on my file displayed a new term my psychologist coined: mermaid mania. I would've rather been arrested.

"How did it feel to discover that your friend was a mermaid?" I wanted to correct her and say that they called themselves merfolk, but I didn't. I didn't say anything. I hadn't said anything since I was forcibly admitted three days ago. I knew that whatever I said - she would twist it around and make it seem like merfolk were the dangerous ones - and not the humans.

I was still so mad at my best friend it didn't feel like it would take a lot for a psychologist to reroute my brain into thinking our whole adventure was another series of me being brainwashed.

She sat patiently with her legs crossed, tapping her pencil on the corner of her clipboard. More than ever, I wished I could smell emotions on other people as I pressed my back into the hard metal chair. The cold seeped up through my paper gown, making the soles of my sock feet and my buttchecks numb. Even though my father told them I wasn't suicidal - just delusional - they took away anything that could be used as a weapon.

"Cindy, we aren't going to get anywhere if you don't talk to me," she said with a delicate smile that oozed pity. It doesn't take merfolk to divine the hidden meaning. *You'll never get out of this asylum if you don't talk to me. Do you want to spend the rest of your life locked in this tiny room by yourself?*

I wished therapists were paid based on how well their treatments worked instead of by the session. I would make sure this lady never made a dime off of me.

"Cindy, please?"

"I already told my dad what happened. You won't believe me either. So you can go ahead and leave."

"I believe all my patients. Just because things happen in your head doesn't mean they aren't real." I snorted.

"You ever hear about that story where several normal people checked themselves into an asylum to see if the workers could tell the difference between normal people and crazy people? Spoiler alert - they couldn't."

"Well, how am I supposed to tell if you're not crazy if you won't tell me your side of the story?" It made me angry that she had a point.

"Because I already know which version of the story you believe. And you're not going to convince me that I imagined the whole thing or that the merfolk got in my head."

"If you're so sure you're right, then why are you so scared that I'll convince you otherwise?" I clenched my fists tighter. She raised her eyebrow just a smidge.

"It must've been really scary when you were kidnapped." I paused because no one had ever referred to my encounter with the first merfolk as a kidnapping - just an attempted murder. That incident at the fountain took all the attention. "And then to learn that your best friend was part of her same species must've been just as scary." I nodded, so shocked my defenses momentarily lowered.

"Yeah. It was."

"Did you feel frustrated when no one believed you when you said you were kidnapped by a mermaid?"

"I thought I was going crazy."

"And you didn't want to tell me what happened because you thought I would do the same thing? Not believe you?"

"Yeah. And I already know what you think about merfolk."

"You must've known back then that no one would believe you when you started claiming a mermaid kidnapped you, but you still spoke up then. Why? What's different now?" The memory made my chest ache.

"I didn't trust just anyone. I trusted Amy." Both of her eyebrows went up.

"You told her first? I didn't know that." A pause. "What did she say?"

"She told me I was crazy. She had to."

"I bet it still hurt though. You trusted her - but she couldn't trust you." I squeezed my eyes shut, trapping the heat behind them. I would not cry in front of this stranger.

"Why are you trying to protect her when she doesn't trust you?" It was a genuine question. One I'd asked myself but was too scared to answer out loud.

Because she was still my best friend.

I clenched my fists and climbed out of my chair, kicking it across the room.

"Get out. I'm done. You're not going to get in my head."

. . .

I lay awake in my room at night, wrestling with my brain until I had a headache. The therapist hadn't force-fed merfolk are dangerous ideology down my throat like I thought she would. Instead, she'd exposed all of the doubts I had been hiding about my friendship with Amy and made me think about them for the first time.

My last glance at Amy flashed through my brain on a loop. We never even said goodbye.

Were we ever friends? Or was I just part of her elaborate scheme to look like a normal person? Did she ever really like me? Did she miss me?

I imagined her glaring at me, tears finally leaking through my eyes. *She hates me*, I thought, crying silently into the darkness. And I deserve to be hated. I didn't believe her when she told us what my dad did to her. What kind of a friend was I? At least she had a reason not to trust me before. I had no reason to distrust her. I was just mad at her for not making me the special exception for her secret.

My door opened, spilling fluorescent light inside. I sat up, furious at being caught in my exposed feelings.

"Get out of my room!" I shout, chucking my pillow across the room at the other white wall.

Something hit me in the back. I turned around, startled to see the pair of shorts and T-shirt I wore when I was brought here in a lump on my bed. I looked up to see my therapist standing in the doorway, pale as a ghost and clenching her car keys in her hands.

"We need to leave. Now." Five minutes later, I clutched the car seat as she weaved through traffic, my brain struggling to keep up. She white-knuckled the steering wheel as she drove.

"I'm so sorry," she rasped as she weaved through traffic.

"What the hell is going on?" I demanded.

"Your father. He came to me to ask about your progress but got upset when I told him you still weren't convinced mermaids were evil." My blood ran cold.

"How upset?" I asked.

"He was shouting and told me he was going to put you on medicine to make you more . . . compliant." We stopped at a red light. She turned to me.

"I need you not to lie to me right now, okay?" I nodded. "Your friend. Amy. She isn't dangerous, is she?" I shook my head no.

"She was born a human," I blurted. "That's why my dad is so desperate to get her back. We rescued her before he could figure out how she changed." I slapped my hands over my mouth, shocked I had just let such an important secret loose. The therapist's face drained of color. The light turned green, and someone had to honk at her for her to drive forward.

"So Arthur's been lying to everyone. And he expected me to gaslight you into thinking you were crazy this whole time," she whispered. I nodded.

"Yeah, that about sums it up."

"We have to tell someone." I tried not to laugh.

"Who on Earth would believe us?" She turned abruptly, smashing me into the door.

"I know someone who might listen."

AMY

This time when Tom called us all to gather around the radio, he grinned like he just solved the final riddle to get past a sphinx. At first, the sound coming through was grainy, like it was recorded in someone's pocket.

"How is my daughter doing?" I inadvertently clenched my teeth at Arthur's voice again.

"She's doing quite well, but there's still progress to be made." That voice I didn't recognize, but it sounded calm and melodious.

"Does she see how she's been tricked and taken advantage of?" A pause.

"Well, that's not what we're focusing on at the moment. She's currently working through the trauma she experienced before this little trip into the -" A bang sounded, like someone slamming their hands down on a table.

"I'm not paying you to talk about before! You're supposed to be convincing her everything that fool mermaid said was a lie! That she's been brainwashed." The other voice came out shakier.

"Sir, I understand how worried you must be about your daughter. But therapy can take a long time, and she has several things she needs to work through. To try to rush her along and force-feed her a message she's not ready to hear will only make things worse."

"If you can't make her believe it - then I'll take her to someone who will give her medicine to believe it."

"Sir, there is not a medication for that! You must be patient."

"If you can't undo the brainwashing, then you'll have to brainwash her back to normal!" There was another pregnant pause. My body felt like it was one inch away from crossing the finish line. A grin to match Tom's crawled its way across my face. *Arthur's about to dig himself into a spectacular hole.* My hands gripped the edge of my seat and my lungs tightened as I held my breath.

"If what she is saying is false - I shouldn't have to brainwash her at all." The woman's voice was threateningly calm and logical. "Is what she said really false? All of it?"

"I will be finding her a different therapist in the morning." The recording ended. I could only assume the woman in the recording was Cindy's therapist. *Arthur sent her to a mental hospital,* I seethed.

"Margaret, can you explain what happened after this interaction with Mr. Johnson?" the host asked.

"I got Cindy and drove us here. I had suspected something odd was going on for several days, so I started recording our meetings. When Arthur said what he said, I knew Cindy wasn't a victim of mermaid mania as her father claimed. I knew I had to get her somewhere safe and tell the truth."

"Why do you feel the need to tell the truth?"

"Because if mermaids aren't dangerous, they don't deserve to be treated as such. Humans who support them shouldn't be assumed to be controlled or brainwashed."

"Cindy, according to your father, Amy Wilson used her powers to manipulate you and Tom Falcon into rescuing her. She then made you and several others come back to shore to attempt to rescue even more mermaids to be released into the ocean. What is your side of the story?" My best friend's voice flowed out of the speakers.

"My father has been lying. First of all, I never knew Amy Wilson had been captured. No one did - because my father kept it a secret and lied about it. It was Tom who asked me to help rescue her after he had rescued the two other girls my father had kidnapped." She paused. "Their names are Sam and Terri, by the way. They have names. And they're cool kids. But you didn't know that - because when they were rescued, my father covered it up and said the building was under renovation.

"When we rescued Amy, she was in really bad shape. It was obvious she had been tortured physically and emotionally. She didn't recognize anyone and had severe cuts all down her left leg. I chose to come back to shore to help Tom rescue more captured merfolk, but I was caught while the rest made it back out. My father then forced me to attend therapy in a mental hospital."

"Your story sounds incredible. But why wouldn't your father be honest about all of this? About the girls being rescued, not telling the world about Amy? Why would he keep her a secret?" the host asked. There was a moment of silence. I swallowed, sweat running down my back. Norman glared at the radio as if daring her to say more. *Here it is*, I thought. *All my secrets are about to be spilled to the whole world. Everyone will know.*

"That . . . that is Amy's secret to share. Not mine."

Holy shit.

Sam and Terri both looked like they won the lottery. Adam and Emanuel shared similar expressions, while Norman's jaw dangled. Tom covered his mouth with his hands, shaking his leg.

"Holy crap," Sam giggled. "That was dramatic."

"And awesome," Adam laughed. "I hope everyone hears it." Tom shook his head in disbelief and side-eyed me. I swallowed, not sure whether to feel relieved that she didn't spill all my secrets or nervous about what she did spill.

"Everyone knows now. Maybe things will start to change," Emanuel said hopefully.

"Amy telling her side of the story would change things a lot. Imagine how mad Arthur would be if you told your secret after you escaped," Tom joked. My hands clenched into fists.

"I'm not telling anything," I snapped, eyeing the other merfolk in the room. "Come on guys, back me up. That's a terrible idea." The boys exchanged glances.

"I mean . . . it would cause an entertaining amount of chaos if you did. It would make you worthless. I mean . . . not *worthless* but you know . . . worth *less* than you are now," Norman offered. "The only reason the reward on your head is so high is because Arthur doesn't know how you changed." I resisted the urge to punch him in the jaw again.

"But what good would it do?" Tom asked. "She tells, the humans freak out, then what? That doesn't necessarily lead to anyone's freedom."

"Are we really working towards freedom? I thought your thing here was to rescue as many merfolk as possible and call it good? They're never going to free us for real," Norman said.

"I'm not revealing anything either way," I muttered. "But at least people know Arthur's a liar now."

Later that night, I gingerly eased myself onto the deck and stared out to sea. I tucked my hands into Cindy's flannel shirt she left behind and let my hands tremble into it. I rested my head on the steel railing and let out a slow breath.

I'm a terrible person. I should've told her goodbye.

She had given up so much to help me. She had literally carried me out of that cage in her arms, and all I had been was an asshole to her. I drove her away. What if I never saw her again? I never deserved to be her friend.

If I ever did tell my side of the story, the first thing I would do is apologize.

EMANUEL

Life continued - slightly quieter than before without Cindy. Norman no longer spit acid at everyone who tried to talk to him. Adam kept practicing his swashbuckling. No one was in a hurry to go to the Sanctuary. How well Amy or Norman would be received was up for debate, and Sam and Terri didn't want to leave their new friends. There weren't any other merfolk to rescue at the moment, so Tom was content to stay as well. And I had time to explore the island.

All my life, people had made fun of me for being a nerd, which I was to be fair. But what people didn't see was how I trained myself to be ready for any adventure that might further my nerdy interests. What good was a marine biologist who couldn't swim? So, I taught myself how to swim. Then I taught myself how to hold my breath for minutes at a time. I taught myself to keep my eyes open underwater (that part was the worst). So, I was a nerd, but I was a cool nerd.

Which is why I was able to dive into the ocean and sink to a comfortable depth and hover there, gazing at the life around me. Ferns and other underwater plants grew along the rock walls. Schools of small fish darted in and out between the fronds.

I grinned as one particularly large one Bluefin swam towards me, brushing over my belly. Off in the distance appeared a small Sandbar shark - maybe about three feet long, a baby. He swam towards me, mouth slightly ajar. *Hello friend*, I thought. I held out my hand, prepared to push his nose up and away from me. Sharks were one of nature's most misunderstood creatures. Way more humans killed sharks than the other way around. All it took to keep them from eating you was a gentle nose boop.

Suddenly, a much larger and longer thing darted out in front of me. I gasped, letting some of my oxygen bubbles escape. For a moment, my brain didn't process what was now shielding me from the shark, which had now hastily darted out of the way and was headed in the opposite direction. The figure slowly came into focus, and I had to clamp my mouth shut to stop myself from choking on the salt water.

Norman had wrapped himself around me, his back towards the shark. The spikes in his fin extended out at least a foot, glinting in the sun. His webbed hands held onto my shoulders as he glared at the shark. For the first time, I realized merfolk's eyes didn't actually glow blue. There was simply a bright blue membrane covering their regular human eyeball -

like a frog's second eyelid. He was close enough that I could see his pupils beneath the waterproof shield sparkling in the light. His tail brushed against my feet, and it was rougher than I expected it to be. It felt more like a snake tail than a fishtail. The rest of his human skin looked like it had been dip-dyed in methylene blue and sprinkled with glitter. I wouldn't have recognized him save for the dark brown wavy hair floating like reeds above his head.

Norman was in no equitable terms . . . beautiful. Stunning. Something I would have stared at for hours had he let me. He hadn't been shy about phasing back and forth in front of us, but I had never felt comfortable looking at him directly.

As he realized I was staring at him with an open mouth, he pushed away from me. I clamped my mouth shut again and gave a tentative wave. He shot me the middle finger as best as one could with webbed hands. I grinned and shot him one back. *Wait, is Norman afraid of sharks?*

"That shark wasn't going to hurt me!" I shouted, bubbles dancing from my lips. He furrowed his brow, shaking his head. He pointed to his mouth. *Mouth the words. I can't see through your bubbles.*

That shark wasn't going to hurt me, I mouthed.

Fine, die then.

I shot him the middle finger back as he grinned. I pointed back up to the surface and swam up, gasping for breath. He followed me, a smirk on his face.

"Imagine having to hold your breath underwater." I splashed him.

"Curse me then," I challenged.

"A nerd like you? You'd never make it. I need to go get dinner."

"Can I watch?" I asked hopefully.

"Sure, loser." He dove back under the surface, and I hurried after him. I watched from a respectful distance as he nestled himself in a cloud of reeds, barely visible. For the first time, I noticed that the markings on his face almost matched the curls of the seaweed. *Wait, doesn't he need his spear?* I thought.

That answer turned out to be a solid no as he lashed out with his webbed hand, snatching a fish right out of the water. It struggled for a moment before he sank his teeth into its neck, releasing a little cloud of blood as it went limp. *Gross,* I thought. *But cool.*

He repeated the process several more times before swimming back up to the surface. I followed, gasping for breath as I surfaced.

"This whole time . . . I thought you used your spear to hunt . . ." I gasped, walking back up onto the shore. He chuckled, phasing and gathering the slippery fish in his hands.

"Nope. It's easier to do it by hand. That spear was for humans."

"You put in all the time and effort to make a spear just in case humans showed up?" He shook his head.

"I just found it here." *Wait, why would there be a random spear lying around here?* I wondered. We walked down the beach to the others gathered around the fire pit. Norman tensed as Terri ran up to us, sweating, eyes wide. She signed something. Norman and I glanced at each other. The color drained from Sam's face.

"Are you sure?" she whispered. Terri nodded, grabbing her sister and practically dragging her towards the boat. The rest of us followed, trading mystified glances.

This time, it wasn't the radio we gathered around. Terri had opened the laptop to a YouTube video.

"Why are we risking the internet right now?" Tom asked. Terri shook her head and signed more frantically. Sam turned to face us.

"You might want to sit down," she said. Dread twisted in my gut. The merfolk traded glances, worry sinking in. We all sat down and watched the laptop in silence. Terri pressed play.

Cindy, along with a crowd of protestors, swarmed the steps of her father's aquarium. Spectators watched from the sidelines, recording the drama with their phones. Police sirens wailed in the background. The protestors held signs.

Free the merfolk!

Arthur has been lying to you!

Merfolk aren't dangerous!

"Free the merfolk, free the merfolk!" the protestors chanted. Cindy took the cake up at the very front with her unique sign. She had covered it with glitter so it sparkled obnoxiously at the cameras. But what was more striking was her face paint.

She had painted blue markings on the right side of her face, a mirror image of Amy's. She glared at the onlookers fiercely, holding her sign high above her head.

merPEOPLE

Police lined up in front of the steps, hidden behind body shields, hands on their guns. They shouted at the protestors as police cars pulled up behind them, lights blazing. One cop shouted through a bullhorn.

"STAND DOWN. YOU ARE UNDER ARREST." The protestors only chanted louder. A smile stretched across my face. There were maybe a dozen people in the crowd - but that was twelve more people than I had previously thought supported merfolk. This was awesome! Why was Terri so upset?

More cops ran from the cars, guns drawn.

"STAND DOWN. THIS IS NOT A SANCTIONED PROTEST." They motioned to each other and a small sphere was tossed in the center of the protestors. Cindy batted it out of the air with her sign - sending it back to the line of police - where it exploded in a cloud of gas. The line broke in confusion, and Cindy smirked.

Then her chest exploded in red.

Screams erupted as several people fell to the concrete steps. Cindy hovered for a minute before collapsing. The clip ended and turned back to a news reporter.

"Three people were shot by police at the riot last night. Two are in the hospital, and they are expected to recover. Cindy Johnson died on the scene. The policeman that shot her claimed they thought she was a mermaid and were acting in the best interest of the other humans in the vicinity." The screen went black.

"Oh my God," Adam whispered. *This can't be real.* I covered my mouth.

"Those bastards!" Norman seethed, jumping to his feet. "They did this on purpose! They killed her on purpose!" Amy limped out the doorway on her crutch and slammed it behind her. Tom buried his head in his hands. I curled my arms around Adam, and he melted into me, trembling. Norman shouted at the laptop until he lost his voice, falling to his knees and shaking. Sam and Terri held hands, their eyes closed.

In the distance, Amy screamed.

AMY

She's dead.

She's dead.

She's *dead.*

I didn't remember if I just thought the words in my head or screamed them every time I slammed my fists against the volcano. I remembered wanting to be able to cry.

She had painted her markings to look just like mine. A Cursed.

My markings killed her.

I stayed there until a figure walked up and grabbed my hands in theirs. I was so blind with rage that I let them hold my bloody knuckles without protest.

I never said goodbye.

The figure rubbed my back as I collapsed, wishing I could sink into the sand and disappear forever. I wanted to swim back to the mainland and claw her blood out of the asphalt until she was alive again.

She couldn't be gone. She was just here.

"Shh, it's okay, I'm right here," Tom whispered. I sobbed without tears. Tom scooped me off the ground and carried me until I landed on a soft surface. He stroked my hair until my body was too tired to grieve.

If I had just been a better friend – if I had forgiven her – she wouldn't have left. She would still be here. She would still be alive.

This was all my fault.

TOM

I left Amy in the bedroom by herself. The others had already fallen asleep in a pile in the living room. I took a blanket out to the deck and picked a spot, too tired to care.

If Cindy was here, I would've teased her for getting killed on her third death threat. And she would've laughed and said *the third time's a charm.*

But she wasn't here. She would never be here again.

I wiped my eyes.

If I ever found the cop that killed her . . . no. I could deal with my anger later. Being angry would only upset the empaths more. I had to be strong for them. For Amy.

. . .

I rubbed my face as the sunrise woke me up, thinking what I was seeing was gunk in my eyes at first. But after getting the sleep out, the four figures were still there, and one looked very familiar.

"Markus? Is that you?" I asked groggily. The figure on the far right nodded, although he avoided eye contact when he did so.

"Your presence is required at The Sanctuary," the tall one in the middle said. Sam slunk up behind me, protectively shielding Terri behind her.

"Tom, who are these people?" The figures straightened their backs.

"We are messengers from The Sanctuary. We have been keeping an eye on your little party here, and in light of recent events, it is time we have a chat."

"Sam, watch over our guests. I'll go grab the others," I said. I got to my feet and hurried to my bedroom door. I knocked before entering. Amy lay on her side, staring at the wall. *This is horrible timing*, I thought. I walked over to her and risked putting a hand on her shoulder.

"There are some other merfolk here to talk to us. From the Sanctuary." She nodded.

"I know. I heard them talking. What do they want?" I shrugged. She sat up and followed me out. By the time we walked back on the deck, the others had joined. Emanuel casually stood in front of Norman, who had retracted his fins and looked paler than normal. Adam let his hand rest on the handle of his sword.

"What do you guys want?" Adam asked. Markus cleared his throat.

"My dad wants to talk to you guys. We will lead you to the Sanctuary if you follow us in your boat." We all exchanged glances. Currently, it was seven against three if it came down to a fight, but who knew how many more would come if Markus and his friends didn't return?

"Lead the way," I muttered. Markus and his posse nodded before diving overboard. I powered up the boat and started following their wake towards the island in the distance.

. . .

The others stood by me. Amy was quiet, her face a stone. I wanted to ask her how she was doing, but I doubted it would be wise to ask.

"What the heck is this about?" Adam hissed. "Why do they want to talk to us?"

"Shut up and listen!" Norman snapped. "I'm the one who has the most experience with traditional merfolk here - so listen. Those guys have apparently been spying on us this whole time - which is super creepy but because we're still alive - it means they didn't think we were a threat. Be nice," he demanded.

"You're telling *us* to be nice?" Adam retorted. Norman glared at him.

"This sounds scary," Emanuel said. "What if we just like . . . not go?"

"We have no clue how many merfolk are there. I'm assuming we are vastly outnumbered. So, unless Adam can swordfight everyone on that island, we need to see what they want. Merfolk do not like outsiders. And if they know about . . ." he paused, swallowing. "If they know about what's going on and want to talk to us . . . we need to go." We all nodded again. I followed the tails in the water as they led us to the island floating in the distance. It was a good thing too - as soon as I started up the boat again - the compass started doing weird things.

"Don't worry," Emanuel said. "It's just because of the weird amount of magnetite in the volcanic rock around here."

"Nerd," Norman muttered.

The Sanctuary slowly grew larger and larger. It was definitely fancier than our island. It too looked like a volcano - but this one had much more pretty green stuff growing on the outside of it. It loomed out of the ocean like a skyscraper - and twice as thick as one.

If my gut hadn't felt heavy enough to drag me down to the bottom of the ocean, I would've been enamored with it. The others seemed to have the same feelings as they stared.

Markus and his buddies anchored the boat and motioned for us to come down. As we stepped down onto the black sand, Norman grabbed my arm.

"One more thing. I do not have fins." I raised my eyebrow.

"Why does that matter?" Norman gripped my shoulders and yanked me down to his eye level.

"I. Do not. Have. Fins. Got it?" he growled. I swallowed and nodded.

Markus led our group into a literal hole in the wall. We walked in pitch-black darkness for what felt like forever until the tunnel spit us out into the center of the volcano. Emanuel gasped.

Inside the cavern were dozens of merfolk. Most wore what looked like the remnants of their human clothes. Some looked like they had dove into the ocean right after work - torn ties and sports jackets dotting the crowd. Others wore nothing but a skirt of plants tied around their waist. Most of them clustered in families. The only way to tell them apart from a crowd of lost refugees were the blue markings on their skin.

The inside of the volcano had somehow been completely hollowed out. Small caves and indentions marked the walls. Birds swooped in and out between them. Carvings of merfolk decorated the smoother spots.

In the very center was a pool of some of the clearest water I had ever seen. It descended into eerie darkness as if it were a portal to another world.

This place is insane, I thought. *No wonder they picked it as a Sanctuary. No one would ever guess anything was here.*

As we walked, the merfolk whispered and pointed. Emanuel was too busy gawking at the nature to notice. Adam, Sam, and Terri offered tentative waves. Norman looked like he wanted to dive into the pool and hide.

As usual, Amy kept her eyes trained towards the ground. I was used to getting dirty looks from merfolk, but she seemed to be getting her fair share. I resisted the urge to put my arm around her shoulder and instead glared at everyone giving her a dirty look. *Yeah, that's right empaths, read my feelings. I'll rip your scales off if you say one mean thing to her.*

Markus stopped as a tall figure pushed their way through the crowd. I remembered his father very well from our last interaction. He frowned at me as he slammed a tall staff down onto the sand. It was massive and looked like it had been carved out of bone. I swallowed as I wondered what giant sea monster had to die to make that staff. The crowds instantly went silent.

"Come with me," he said, leading the way into another dark cave. We sat around a stone slab of a table. Dr. Mercer sat at the head and stared down at the rest of us. We had been assigned seats, and I couldn't help but feel like the assignments were laced with privilege.

Emanuel and I sat at the very back, followed by Amy and Norman. Adam, Sam, and Terri were closest to the front and looked extremely uncomfortable. Every time I wiggled my butt on the stone floor, trying to get comfortable, the other merfolk guarding the room shot me dirty looks and exasperated glances with each other.

Dr. Mercer stood up and cleared his throat. Amy and the others started to stand up but he held his hand out.

"Please, remain seated." Norman clenched his fists. "I am the Protector of The Sanctuary. It is my job to keep everyone here safe. And your little group has been causing quite a stir on the surface, I hear. Care to share your side of the story?" Sam raised her hand like she was still in school and began to explain. The others listened with rapture as she summarized the events over the past month in calm, delicate detail. Even Cindy's death.

"And those were your friend's last words, so to speak? It is confirmed she is dead?" Amy sucked in a breath but simply nodded at the table.

"It doesn't surprise me that the humans have mobilized their police force. It's not the first time they've done such a thing to suppress a minority," Dr. Mercer said darkly.

"That's why Cindy spoke up," I said. "She knows that if people tell the truth, the other humans will know they have sides to pick from." Dr. Mercer nodded.

"I believe such a course of action would be advisable. I have given this matter much thought, and based on your story, we will go forward with my decision. Amy will tell the world our secret, that she was born a human. In doing so, she will expose Arthur, provide validity to Cindy's final words, and prove that merfolk are inherently persons. The humans will be forced to reconsider their decision to take away our rights."

Amy's fingers screeched across the stone as she balled up her fists.

"*Our* secret?" she gritted through clenched teeth. I leaned back as she sat up and stared directly at Dr. Mercer. "Growing up, I only ever remember you telling me that this was *my* secret," she hissed, motioning to her body. The rest of us exchanged glances around the table. Terri didn't bother to hide her smirk. Dr. Mercer stiffened.

"Contrary to your feelings, this isn't about you. This is about -"

"Oh, believe me, I know what it's about. You can treat me like shit for my whole life and shame me for something that wasn't even my fault and threaten me with everything in the kitchen sink if I dare breathe a word to *anyone*, but the second it's convenient for you, it's *our* secret and it's *my* responsibility to share it with the entire fucking human world?" Amy was on top of the table, her voice a shrill shriek by the end. Her chest rose up and down rapidly, her ears red. Dr. Mercer stared at her in shock, and Norman giggled very loudly.

"You're damn right it's not about me. It's about your best interest," she seethed.

Dr. Mercer slammed his hand down on the table. "It's about *our* best interest! We are in a war now, Sweetheart. People are *dying*. Individuals don't matter in a war."

"Unless they're useful, right?" she sneered.

"Sorry man, I gotta agree. You're totally trying to Katniss Everdeen her, and you don't look cute doing it," Norman said, voice dripping with fake sympathy.

"I will not have a divorcee speak at my table," Dr. Mercer spat. The jaws of all the other merpeople around the table hit the floor as Emanuel covered his mouth. Norman's face drained of color.

"How do you even know? He doesn't have his fins out!" I blurted. Sam rolled her eyes as Adam got to his feet and called Dr. Mercer a very unchristian word.

"Don't you dare insult my friend!" Amy growled.

"You have no idea what he's been through!" Emanuel shouted, sounding close to tears.

"Real merfolk make it work. Or they don't fall for people that they can't work with," Dr. Mercer said coldly. Adam's hand closed around the handle of his cutlass. Emanuel stood beside Amy, hands clenched. Terri laughed silently as Sam's eyes flitted around nervously.

"As for the rest of you, you are all being selfish! Our kind is in a war, and we have a weapon that could crumble most of humans' prejudice!" Dr. Mercer shouted.

"That doesn't freaking matter! It's her secret! She's not your soldier! If she wants to tell her secret - then she tells it. If not - end of story!" I argued.

"You obviously don't care about personhood enough to give it to treat members of your own species with respect," Sam said coldly. "If you thought of her as a person – if you respected her - you would give her a choice."

"You're the one who doesn't deserve to be counted as a person," Norman seethed. "Don't forget about when you abandoned her the first time." Dr. Mercer took a deep breath.

"Then it appears there's only one way to settle this. We will commence in a -"

"Oh don't tell me you have some BS ancient fighting ritual!" Amy retorted. "That would be just like you, wouldn't it? Fight the girl who can't walk without a cane? How's this for a fight?" Amy lifted her crutch and sent it hurtling at Dr. Mercer's face. It clipped his cheek and sent him stumbling backward.

"Screw you and your traditions! I'll tell my secrets if and whenever I damn well please! And if you know what's good for you, you'll stay far away from our island and my friends." Amy turned and hobbled towards the door. The others wisely parted for her. She paused by the opening and turned to face Dr. Mercer one more time.

"People like you make me ashamed to be merfolk," she whispered. "If I was still human, I wouldn't want to free us either." She continued out, and the rest of us followed in silence. Emanuel draped his arm around Norman and glared at the others as he escorted him out. Adam kept his sword out and Terri left them behind with her favorite word in sign language.

. . .

We gathered in steamy silence in the boat's living room. Adam and Emanuel fiercely held Norman's hands, whose face was still drained of color.

"No offense. But your species kinda sucks," I said.

"They do," Norman said. I couldn't help but smirk.

"What, I didn't quite hear you?" Norman rolled his eyes, and Emanuel shot me the bird on his behalf.

"What's up with the whole fin thing?" Amy asked.

"When merpeople mate - they mate for life. *Always*," Norman said sarcastically. "The failures are . . . not treated well. I tried to hide it, but I guess they could smell it on me." *Merfolk can tell if someone's mated by smell? These people get weirder and weirder by the day.*

"They don't know it can be reversed," Adam said defensively. "If they knew."

"What happened to her?" Amy asked. Norman swallowed.

"He assaulted me. And then I poisoned his ass," Norman said through a broken smile. *Damn.* Norman was super annoying, but the thought of anyone laying a finger on him made my blood boil. Why he had been so scared and defensive for the longest time suddenly made perfect sense.

"And they would shame you for *that?*" I whispered. Sam and Terri nodded.

"They don't just throw shade. Norman, you need to stay far away from that island," Sam said warningly.

"Why? What would they do to him?" I asked. Sam started to answer but Norman shook his head.

"Don't say it," he warned. "They don't need to know." Sam closed her mouth.

"They think since we're empaths, we wouldn't end up with people who would treat us badly. But the best liars are the ones who don't admit to themselves they're lying. I'm really sorry, Norman," Sam translated for Terri.

"It's over," Norman said. "And it's pretty damn useful to be poisonous." Adam and Emanuel squeezed his hands.

"The whole thing doesn't science," Sam said bitterly. We all turned to look at her.

"What doesn't science?"

"Mating. We were told that when we fall in love for the first time amongst other things - males grow their fins and females get the ability to cry. And we're told that those abilities only work for your family. Like - you can only use your fin to defend your partner - not against them. But we know that's not true. Norman did it. So that whole story is a lie. You mean to tell me that if my sister was in mortal danger, I wouldn't be able to cry to help her?" The merfolk exchanged glances.

"I mean . . . makes sense," Adam said. "Maybe those stories became gospel because that was what happened normally? I mean, how many times would you have the opportunity to use healing tears for someone who isn't your family? Statistically speaking . . . it's not very likely."

"Scientifically speaking, the chemicals in your body that make the healing tears or venom don't know who you're using it on. So it's going to work no matter what. Chemicals aren't sentient," Sam murmured. Norman nodded to himself.

"And I'm sorry they're trying to use you, Amy," Sam said. "I see their point, but it's your life and it's your secret. You're the only one who can tell that story. No one would believe it if a Natural said it." Amy sighed.

"I just want to go home," she said. I resisted the urge to reach out and grab her hand.

"It's your choice," Adam said. "And we won't fault you for whatever your decision is. We'll keep doing what we can to save people. But it's not our job to save the world."

. . .

Everyone chose to go walk around and blow off steam. I followed Sam and found her sitting on the sand, kicking her feet in the tide. I sat down next to her.

"Does that feel weird?" I asked. She stared at me out of the corner of my eye.

"Does what feel weird?"

"Having your human feet be in the water . . . like wet but not . . . you know." I made a motion like a tail swimming in water. She rolled her eyes.

"You know we still take showers in human form, right? Like . . . I know what water feels like on my regular human skin?"

"How do you not phase?" She sat up straight.

"Well - I've wondered about that a lot actually - like how exactly our bodies know the difference between - say shower water versus ocean water - so I did a test when I was little to see if it was the salt. I rigged up a

281

saltwater shower to see if that would cause the transformation - but it didn't. And besides - there are merfolk that live in lakes anyway - so the salt thing doesn't make sense. So, then I tried different quantities of water - but the only thing that seems to trigger it was being totally submerged in water for at least three seconds. If you get out before then - you won't change. Which is convenient - because it wouldn't be very nice to change whenever it rained or . . ." she trailed off as she noticed my smirk. "What?" she demanded.

"You love science, Sam." She paled.

"No, I don't."

"Yes, you do. That's your thing. The only reason you don't talk about it is because of your sister and Amy." She sighed and crossed her arms.

"I'm not supposed to like science. You saw what happened."

"For someone who's not supposed to like science, you were surprisingly okay after being a science experiment. And you didn't crack a smile until Emanuel started making all those horrible science puns."

"Why are you bringing this up?" she muttered. "It doesn't matter."

"Because it's bothering you. And you're never going to talk about it on your own."

"If the others found out what really happened in that lab - they would never forgive me," she whispered.

"I'm not merfolk," I said. "Try me." She clenched her fists.

"When we got there - I told them I would let them do whatever they wanted to me if they would leave my sister alone. That's why she was the only one ever on display. She was never brought into the lab. She thought I was protecting her - which I was - but I also did it because I was curious. I wanted to see what they could find out. I cooperated. I answered their questions. I lied about the more important things, but I never once fought them." Her hands began to tremble.

"There I was - doing whatever they wanted while Amy never gave an inch. I was a coward. I told myself it was for my sister, but it was . . . it was really for me. And the sick thing is . . . I miss it," she whispered. "They were figuring out so many things. Things I've always wondered about but never had the answers to. And now, I'll never find out." I let her tremble in silence for a few moments.

"I'm sorry," I finally said.

"Sorry for what? Rescuing us? Getting involved in this hot mess?"

"No, of course not. I'm sorry you miss it. I'm sorry that's the only way you could learn about yourself. It's not fair." I tried to catch my breath. "But I don't ever want you to hear you blame yourself for being stuck in there. That's my fault. Your cooperating with them is the only reason you and your sister didn't end up like Amy. Even if your motives were different - you kept your sister safe, you hear me?" She nodded. I stood up and held out my hand.

"Come with me." She followed me back to the boat, where I knelt below my bed and pulled out an old book bag.

"I kinda took off after school one day and never went back, so I still have my stuff." I rummaged around in the bag and pulled out a dusty textbook. I pulled a candy wrapper off of the cover and handed it to her. Her mouth fell open, and she nearly dropped it.

Essentials of Biology: Ninth Edition.

"You'll probably understand way more of that than I ever did. It's yours now. Just maybe don't let Amy see you reading it. She is not a fan of science, after all." She held it to her chest, eyes welling up with a new set of tears.

"Thank you," she whispered. I smiled and offered a hug, which she accepted.

"I hope you'll be able to figure out the answers to all your questions one day," I whispered. "You can study in peace once we get off of this godforsaken island."

EMANUEL

We all glared when Markus came up to the boat a few hours later.

"So, there's been more discussion-" he started.

"You can take your discussion and shove it up your-" Norman muttered under his breath.

"- and my dad says he understands Amy's decision. He's . . . still mad . . . but he understands. If you want to go back to your island, I can take you back tomorrow morning," Markus continued. Tom nodded.

"Fine." Markus left, leaving us alone with hours to kill.

The carvings on the wall kept flashing through my head. We had been walking too quickly for me to get a good look at them, and I desperately wanted to go back. Who knew how many ancient carvings decorated the volcano? What stories did they tell?

Adam had left with the girls to go hunting, leaving me with Norman, who was uncharacteristically quiet. I nudged him. Maybe it would help him feel better if I distracted him. And Markus had already said they weren't going to hold a grudge – so going back inside should be fine – right?

"Want to do something fun?"

. . .

"This doesn't sound like fun, and you're a dumbass." I grinned as we peered up the volcano walls. The sunlight was dwindling rapidly, and most of the merfolk had disappeared into the center pool. Approximately twenty meters up the rough surface stood a smooth wall - covered by vines and a decent amount of bird poop. I could see the faintest hint of carvings sticking out on the left side.

I finished tying the safety rope around my waist and made sure my flashlight was tucked securely in my pocket. Norman shook his head at me.

"Seriously, you're a dumbass if you think you can make it up there. What if you fall?"

"That's what the rope is for." I stepped up to the wall and found a handhold easily, lifting myself. Among my various other nerd skills, rock climbing ended up becoming part of my training. What kind of environmentalist doesn't know how to rock climb?

As I crawled up the wall, I tied off the rope to my handholds - ensuring that if I did fall - I would only fall a few feet. Norman watched me impatiently from below, crossing his arms. I grinned to myself. Better to have him exasperated than upset.

I gripped the last ledge and pulled myself over the top, wheezing, arms shaking.

"I'm not dead!" I shouted over the edge. Norman didn't respond. He probably couldn't hear me from up here. Oh well.

I staggered to my feet and got out the flashlight. The volcano wall towered another fifty feet above me - the ledge only a few meters wide. The ground was slick with moss, but the wall itself seemed relatively dry.

I started scanning with the light, ducking under the vines. A wide grin broke over my face.

A huge mural was carved into the black rock - spanning at least five meters. On the left was a ship, half buried in water, sailors fallen in the water screaming and reaching for help. A merfolk stood off in the distance, what was clearly the Protector's staff held high in their hand. Others were diving in the water and dragging the victims to the island. One merfolk held a knife to their arm as they knelt over a child. The blood dripped down on the child's limp body. I paled. *Oops, I think that's one of the secrets I'm not supposed to know.* The next panel over - the child - a Cursed now - swam with the rest - his smile still showing through the stone.

I walked up to the Protector and gently pulled the algae off of their face. I felt the faded chiseled markings and felt my stomach drop to my feet.

I white-knuckled my flashlight as I heard footsteps behind me. I turned around to see Markus and two other very large individuals glowering behind me, ropes in their hands.

"You're not supposed to be up here."

"You lied to us," I said coldly.

They dragged me kicking and screaming down the cliff.

AMY

After Norman and Emanuel disappeared, I decided to go on an adventure of my own. Being stuck in the living room just reminded me of the YouTube video. I supposed a part of me was grateful Dr. Mercer had picked today to start fires. It was easier to be angry at him than grieve.

I climbed down the ladder as the sun began to set, shuffling through the sand. I rounded the island until I was sure that no one was around me. I didn't need anyone making fun of me. I leaned the crutch against the wall and took a deep breath as I tried to put weight on my bad leg.

It still hurt like a bitch. But I was too upset to care.

I gritted my teeth as I forced myself to walk on it. It wobbled like a gummy worm with every step, but it wasn't collapsing, which I considered great news.

I walked in circles until my body was soaked in sweat. I finally let myself lean against the wall, gasping for breath. The cool rock felt like AC against my burning skin.

I frowned, lifting my head as I heard voices coming from Tom's boat.

"Grab him. We've already got the others. We just need Amy."

"Are we sure this is a good idea? If we go through with this - we'll have no leverage over her."

"Merfolk don't bluff. Now go get him. If Amy knows what's good for her - she'll cooperate. It's not only humans who know how to torture." My blood ran cold. I stayed rooted to the spot as I heard something being dragged through the sand. Once all was quiet, I moved as quickly as I could to the boat and reached under Tom's pillow in the bedroom. My hand closed around cold metal.

I had already knocked one murderer unconscious with it - maybe I could knock out a few more.

TOM

For the second night in a row, I was awoken surrounded by mysterious figures. I groaned, throwing my arm over my eyes. *Are you kidding me? Can't a man get a good night's sleep?*

"Have y'all ever heard of knocking? What time -" They interrupted me by yanking me off the bed by my feet. I hit the floor hard and wheezed as one of them squashed my face against the floorboards. Another one roughly bound my arms behind my back and hauled me to my feet. The third walked close enough for me to see the plaque on his teeth. I was no longer sleepy. My heart thudded in my ears. *We should've left when we had the chance*, I thought.

"Where's Amy?" he seethed. I laughed.

"Don't you mean where's Waldo?" He slapped me. I spit on him. They dragged me off the boat and through the tunnel. Torches burned bright around the center pool. Several merfolk families watched the display from the center pool. Across the way, three others wrestled with a screaming Emanuel, who was hollering obscenities like Norman usually did. On the opposite side, two others guarded Sam, Terri, and Adam at spearpoint. They knelt quietly in the sand, their fingers interlaced behind their heads.

I was dragged over to Emanuel and thrown to the ground beside him.

"What the hell is going on?" I hissed.

"They're liars!" Emanuel seethed. The others walked off, leaving us with Markus, also holding a spear.

"Hey buddy, want to tell me what the hell I did this time?" I asked. He refused to look at me. I glanced across at the others to see Adam's eyes light up with rage. I followed his gaze and saw the others dragging Norman's limp body to a pole in the sand. Emanuel stopped fighting his ropes long enough to watch as they strung Norman up on the pole so he was hanging by his wrists. His head lolled around listlessly, his eyes half open, gills flaring open and shut in vain.

"What are you doing with him?" I demanded.

"For the crime of breaking off a mating, he must be Removed," Markus said.

"Removed?" Emanuel asked. "What the hell do you mean *Removed?*" One of the merfolk guarding him unsheathed a giant knife, experimentally holding it against the back of Norman's neck, right at the tip of his fin. My mouth went dry.

"You're going to cut his fin off?" I snarled. Markus looked down at me, fiddling with his fingers and looking down at the ground. *How on Earth was I ever friends with you?* I thought. Emanuel spat swear words and started thrashing against the ropes once more.

"You're all monsters!" Emanuel seethed behind me, vibrating with rage. "Let him go, asshole!" Markus swallowed.

"You must understand. This isn't my decision. This is how things are. Divorcees cannot be trusted. They must be Removed so everyone else knows what they have done."

"I thought this whole fight was about changing *how things are*," I said coldly. "You know this isn't right. You're about to chop a body part off of a *kid*."

"It is how things are done here. For him to keep it would bring further shame upon him. You've seen the damage it has caused. He has avoided this island for weeks because of it. Mating is an extremely sacred act. You can't just break it without consequences."

"There are always exceptions! Not all relationships work!" Emanuel screamed. "His love life has nothing to do with you!"

"It is dishonorable ‑"

"His ex assaulted him," Emanuel said coldly. "And then turned him and his parents in. And Norman used his fin to protect himself. That doesn't count as an exception to you?" Markus' face drained of color. He stumbled backward.

"That's . . . that's . . ." he sputtered.

"Impossible?" Emanuel sneered. "Can't you tell if we're lying?" Markus turned away with his jaw hanging open. *Great load of help that did*, I thought.

"We can't let this happen," Emanuel whispered, eyes glinting with tears. "Where the hell is Amy? She can still get out of this." *Could she? The poor girl's best friend was just murdered, and she still can't walk!* I looked across the sand where the others were being held. Sam looked calm and collected as usual. She held eye contact with me and nodded very subtly.

"Amy can't help you. And you won't be uncomfortable for much longer," Markus muttered. Emanuel and I gawked at each other. *Won't be uncomfortable for much longer is definitely code for killing us*, I thought. And the only reason they haven't done it yet is because they're still trying to find Amy. They were pulling a Morris on us.

I was really fucking tired of people trying to kill me for not cooperating.

Please don't come back here, I prayed. *Please stay wherever the hell you snuck off to - just don't come back here.*

Footsteps shuffled through the sand, and I saw Dr. Mercer walking by us, the staff in his hand. He stopped behind his son.

"Where is she?" he asked calmly. I slumped in relief. They wouldn't keep asking me if they had found her.

"Up your asscrack." He kicked me in the head, hard enough to make my ears ring. He looked at Emanuel as I tried to blink my vision back.

"Your turn. Where is she?" he snarled. Emanuel clenched his jaw, bracing himself for a hit as a familiar voice rang out across the cavern.

"Guessing you never won hide and seek as a kid." *No.* Dr. Mercer turned around as Amy emerged out of one of the dark tunnels, almost collapsing every time she put weight on her bad leg to take a step. She was minus one cane but plus my gun from the boat. She clutched it in her hands, her knuckles white.

"Let them go. Now. All of them," she demanded.

"No." She clicked off the safety. Dr. Mercer laughed.

"You won't shoot your own kind." Amy's eyes fixed on him like a cat stalking a mouse.

"You have made it abundantly clear that I am not your *kind*. Now let my friends go." Beside me, Markus had turned even paler.

"Dad, is this worth it?" he whispered. One of the guards around Norman stepped closer, grabbing him by the throat and holding a knife to his fin. Emanuel screamed behind me, spitting swear words and spraying sand. Adam tried to get to his feet only to have a spear pressed against his throat.

"Last chance," Amy said.

"Do it," Dr. Mercer said. I sucked in a breath. "One way or another you will learn that tradition is-"

Amy pulled the trigger. The merfolk with the knife fell into the sea as a spray of red splashed across Norman's face. Emanuel stopped struggling. I struck out my leg and brought Markus down to his knees. I slammed him to the ground, dragging Emanuel with me as I kicked his spear away from him.

Across the beach, Adam ripped free from his captor and tore his sword loose. Screaming, he slashed across their captors' chests, spraying blood over the white sand. Sam took off, dragging Terri behind her. Adam turned and faced Dr. Mercer, his eyes gleaming, sword dripping blood.

Emanuel maneuvered the spear and cut free from his bonds. He left me still tied as he bolted towards Norman. The other guards had wisely backed away and fell away as Emanuel pushed his way past them. He threw his arms around his friend, shouting through his tears.

"Are you okay? Let me see it - did they get you?" Norman hung silently as Emanuel checked his fin and untied him.

Meanwhile, Amy kept her eyes and gun trained on Dr. Mercer, who watched the ensuing chaos with the same shocked expression his son wore. I kept Markus pinned to the ground with my knees against his shoulders. I managed to maneuver the spear into my own hands and cut myself free. As Markus struggled beneath me, I pressed the spear against his throat.

"Don't move!" I hissed. He struggled weakly against me.

"You won't hurt me! You don't believe in hurting merfolk anymore, remember?" I pressed the blade deeper into his throat.

"I might make an exception," I muttered. Amy stalked slowly toward Dr. Mercer.

"Don't just stand there, get her!" he shouted at the remaining guards. They eyed the rest of us warily. Emanuel hauled Norman onto the beach, still limp.

"Do it, Amy," Sam shouted, holding Terri protectively in her arms. Amy shifted her weight.

"Get the fuck out of here. And leave the stick behind. You don't deserve to be a leader over anybody." Dr. Mercer scoffed.

"You have no right to challenge me for leadership of this island!" He screamed as the gun cracked. He dropped his staff to the ground as he clutched his left elbow, blood dripping to the ground.

"I don't want your stupid staff, but as far as I'm concerned, anyone else would be a better leader than you. Leave or the rest of you die." I knew I was bluffing when I threatened to slash Markus' throat, but judging by Mercer's face, Amy wasn't bluffing. And considering everyone else had brought spears to a gunfight - there wasn't much of a fight left to be had.

"You're going to regret this," he spat.

"I'm sure I will. Now go before I change my mind," Amy said calmly. I slowly stood up and Markus scrambled to his feet. He ran over to his dad and let him lean on him for support. The other guards reluctantly dropped their weapons and coaxed their ex-leader back into the center pool. They disappeared below the surface.

We waited in silence for what felt like an hour before we all dared to move again. We all rushed Amy, who was still frozen with her gun aimed at the sea.

"Are you okay?" Adam asked, sheathing his sword and scanning her over. I gently plucked the pistol from her hands.

"Amy? Talk to us. Are you okay?" She swayed.

"I don't feel . . ." And in typical Amy Wilson fashion after performing a dramatic event - fainted flat on her face.

AMY

I woke up to a random kid staring down at me. He leaned closer and sniffed me before yelling out, "She's awake!" in a volume that made my ears ring. I groaned and clutched my head as more people swarmed me. I found Tom in the chaos, who offered me a hand. I took it, pulling myself into a sitting position.

"What the hell happened?" I muttered. My friends exchanged concerned glances and looked over to the corner. I swiveled to see that we were all gathered in a dark cave. Adam stood protectively in the entrance, sword drawn. Emanuel sat on the opposite side, Norman curled up in his lap, eyes wide open, body stiff. I could smell the fury radiating off Emanuel as he cradled Norman in his lap, lips pinched and eyes red. My stomach flip-flopped as memories came back to me.

"She's gonna throw up!" the random kid warned. The crowd evacuated as I turned on my side and vomited what little was in my stomach. Tom rubbed my back and scooched me away from my pile of sick.

"Is everyone safe?" I rasped.

"Yes," Adam said, grip tightening on his sword. I swallowed, grimacing from the taste. Fragments of memories hit me, making me clutch my stomach once more. Norman hanging helplessly. Adam with a blade to his throat. Tom and Emanuel bound. A gun in my hand.

I killed someone.

"They lied," Emanuel said from across the cave. Norman shifted in Emanuel's arms, swallowing.

"Growing up, my parents always told me that merfolk attacked ships that got too close to protect themselves. That wasn't the case," Norman said.

"We rescued the victims instead of letting them drown. We would bring them back to shore and Curse them if they wanted to stay. The Protector was the one who kept an eye out for ships and decided whether it was safe to help or not," the kid explained.

"The other merfolk would vote for who should be Protector, but due to the nature of their job, they have traditionally been Cursed," Emanuel finished. "I guess they figured the Cursed would be the best ones to decide what humans were worth trying to save." I blinked, not quite processing. *We weren't murderers? We never drowned humans? The legends were wrong?*

"How do you know all of this?" I whispered.

"I saw it carved on the wall I climbed up to. And he helped fill in the gaps," he said, motioning to the kid, who beamed proudly. For the first time, I noticed he was holding the staff.

"And who are you?" I asked the kid.

"My name is Caspian. I grew up here. My parents taught me our true history." Caspian walked forward and handed me the staff. "This is yours." I shied away from it.

"Hold on - you just said that I have to be voted in to have that thing apparently - not just steal it. So - no it's not."

"You were voted in," Tom said. "As the last Cursed - it should belong to you anyway." My mouth went dry.

"I was *what?*"

NORMAN

I was on Amy-duty when she woke up again. After the initial news break, she requested another nap in the actual bed. She had been out for hours. She blinked up at me slowly. I flashed her a shit-eating grin.

"Good morning, Protector." She groaned and rolled back over, throwing a pillow over her face.

"I'm Protector of shit." I chuckled.

"Seriously though, are you okay?" She stilled.

"No." Her hands trembled. I gently lifted the pillow off her face.

"You saved my ass. And Tom and Emanuel's ass. Hell - you saved everyone's ass. You did what you had to do, okay? If those bastards hadn't come after us first - none of this would've happened. This is their fault, okay?" She sat up. I offered my hand and after a second of hesitation, she took it. It felt much nicer than her punching me in the face.

"And for the record, it isn't your fault Cindy's dead either." She instantly stiffened.

"I don't have time to worry about that right now. I have to figure out what to do with that stupid thing." She glanced towards the staff leaning in the corner. I stood up and walked over to it. I hefted it in my hand and placed it next to Amy.

"I mean you need a cane to walk anyways, so this is an upgrade." She scoffed.

"Doesn't exactly have a nice handhold for me."

"At least you're not the leader of some stupid insane cult now. You're the leader of a group of people who genuinely *thought* that cult was their actual heritage, which is objectively better." She rolled her eyes.

"Why would they even vote me in? Everyone hates Cursed."

"I guess there are more people who have problems with merfolk culture than we thought. Or people who thought you would suck less than Mercer."

"What if they don't believe it? That their history is all messed up?"

"Oh trust me - they believe it. That Caspian kid? Turns out he's one of the descendants of the last original Protector. When the rest of merfolk decided that acclimating into human society was safer - his family and a few others stayed behind. Guess they didn't want to abandon their home. It's the ones who came to shore who invented this whole new narrative that humans are evil - to keep their babies safe. Loyal to only their own. *Extremely* loyal to their own." For the millionth time that day, I felt the fins on my arms just to make sure they were still there. Amy caught the movement and frowned.

"Are you okay?"

"In one piece." There was no way I was about to admit how much I had trembled in Emanuel's arms after the incident. Adam was a great friend too, but I knew from Emanuel's rage that he would do anything to keep me safe. Plus, he smelled good. Not that he needed to know that.

Amy fiddled with her fingers. We stood in silence for a moment.

"The rest of the island is waiting for you to talk to them. And I don't think they'll take you very seriously if you don't even show your markings," I said. Amy snorted.

"It's not like they'll like me any better. I'm Cursed whether I show them or not. I should give this stupid thing to that kid."

"He would tell you it belongs to you. Look, I know merfolk can be assholes. But they're only assholes because they're scared. We've been scared for a long time because of stories that were never true. Now that we know the truth, maybe a Cursed telling them what to do is exactly what we need." She smirked.

"I thought the goal was to rescue people and try not to get killed?" I rolled my eyes and crossed my arms.

"I mean . . . being free would be cool."

"It would be. But how am I supposed to protect merfolk if I hate being one of them?" I blinked at the surprising amount of candor. I leaned the staff against the wall and sat beside her.

"Let me see them," I said. She raised her eyebrow.

"Why?"

"Please?" A look of shock passed over her face and the markings faded into view. I raised my hands.

"May I?" She nodded. I very gently held her face in my hands, tracing over her jagged marks with my thumbs.

"There's a lot of history that we have forgotten," I said. "And I can't begin to apologize for how we've treated you. You should have been honored. There should be *more* of you. It was fear that broke us." I pulled away.

"What you do or say is your decision. But you are the most fearless person I have met in a long time. You are *true* merfolk. Tom may be great at rescuing people, but Cindy started a rebellion for you. And if you wanted to - you could be the one to save us. *All* of us."

AMY

I hobbled out onto the beach, using the Protector's staff as a cane. The refugees milled around the pool, some on land and some in water. All chatter and movement stopped as I stepped into the light. I took a deep breath, willing my heart to not fall out of my chest. My posse fanned out behind me, Adam staying close with his sword drawn. I hadn't seen him put that thing down in the past 24 hours. Had he even slept? *Focus.*

Caspian waved enthusiastically from the crowd. A man who looked like his father pulled him back down - and for the first time I noticed that they were the only ones not wearing human clothes. They smiled encouragingly at me.

"Um . . . hi," I said. The crowd did not say hello back.

"Get on with it," Tom muttered behind me.

306

"Hi!" I said louder. "My name is Amy Wilson."

"We know," someone deadpanned from the crowd. I grit my teeth.

"Fine, then I will skip to the point. As Protector - it is my formal . . . decree? Whatever you want to call it . . . . I'm going to tell my secret to the humans and get us our rights back." The crowd exploded.

"You can't! That's too dangerous!"

"That was *his* plan! Now that he's gone - you're just going to do the same thing?"

"This would have all been for nothing!" I slammed the staff on the ground, and the crowd immediately went silent.

"You are all scared. And I get that. Believe me, I get it. But you have all forgotten where you come from. You used to save humans. You used to honor the Cursed ones."

"It got too dangerous!" someone in the crowd hissed.

"It's also apparently too dangerous to go back and rescue your own kind!" I retorted. "You've all been hiding here while we have been trying to save *your* friends and family!" The heckler went silent.

"Look. I understand that we are all scared. I spent my whole life being scared. I lied to my friends and family for years to keep all of us safe. But the lying didn't work. The humans still found out, and they reacted badly just like we thought they would. And hiding here on this island for the rest of our lives isn't going to work either. The humans will find this place eventually, and you'll have to find another place to hide."

"So, what exactly do you propose?"

"How many of you want to be free again?" I asked. The crowd whispered and exchanged glances. I slammed the staff down on the sand again.

"You all want to be considered animals for the rest of your life? You're totally fine with being shot on-site or kidnapped and not being able to do a damn thing about it because you don't have a single fucking right? You'd rather be merfolk than *people*? Come on, how many of you want to be free again?" I shouted. Slowly, the hands began to rise.

"So, here's how we do that. Cindy already put everything in motion. We need to tell our side of the story. That means being honest." I turned back to my friends.

"Tom, Norman, Adam, and Emanuel will continue to rescue those stuck on land." I eyed the crowd. "I know it's dangerous. I know it's scary. But this is the price we have to pay if we want to be free again. Do you want your children to grow up in a world like you did? Where you have to spend your entire life lying and hiding? Where your parents lied to *you*?"

"I agree with her," someone said quietly. The whispers got louder. Someone's family flashed me a thumbs-up.

"I still don't trust humans," a woman murmured. I turned my gaze on her.

"You don't have to trust any human who doesn't deserve it. But Tom and Emanuel? If you can't bring yourself to trust them, you can get off my island right now. And if any of you dare to give Norman any flack, I will personally cut out your tongue and make you eat it. That practice is *gone*, done. For *everyone*. You got me?" The woman nodded nervously. Another one spoke up.

"You said we were going to tell our side of the story. What exactly do you plan on being honest about?"

NORMAN

"Hii. Whoo - my friends back home are going to be so psyched to see this. My name is Norman Davis. I was a sophomore at Greenbrier High School before I was outed and had to escape. I'm a Natural merperson as you can see by my markings. Gosh, I feel like I'm on an awkward first date . . . um . . . I don't know? I'm a normal person? I like to watch terrible movies on Netflix and make fun of them . . . I've got a shitty ex-boyfriend. Oh - I'm gay - Tom was shocked when he learned merfolk could be gay! So that's a thing. Um . . . yeah if y'all could stop kidnapping us and locking us in cages that would be cool. I'm loving the island life, but it would be cool to see my friends again. You losers must be super bored without me."

EMANUEL

"Okay, the story of how I got out here is crazy. So, like - I got this super cool opportunity to go study at this island no one has ever heard of and ended up following this crazy pirate merfolk out to sea because I realized everything about them wasn't true at all - and now I'm here with them and it's super cool. I'm kinda the environmentalist out of all of us - I love science obviously - and let me tell you - almost none of the crap that humans have said about merfolk ever adds up if you think about it for more than a second. Like - the original sirens had wings – they were bird people - not fish people. Why would fish be able to sing? Also - if merfolk could sing and bewitch humans - why wouldn't they do that to escape the labs? Seriously, if they could mind-control people - none of this would have ever happened! Also - why would someone who swims a lot want long hair? It's *so* hard to brush out!"

SAM

"Many of you already know who I am, but never learned my name because Arthur's tech people scoured the internet to erase my existence. My name is Sam Miller. I am thirteen years old. If I had not been kidnapped, I would've started a full-time college schedule. I wanted to study biology and become a marine biologist myself - which I realize sounds ironic after having been a science experiment myself. I can assure you - if I had been one of the scientists experimenting with my body - I could've figured out a lot more. And I fully intend to fulfill my dreams once we are made free again."

ADAM

"I hate being on camera honestly, so I'm sorry if I stutter through this whole thing. My name is Adam Harris. I'm from the Georgia coast. Most of you have heard of the merfolk kid vandalizing boats and destroying traps – that's me. Despite popular rumors, I have never actually killed anyone, and I never will. It wasn't my goal to hurt any humans, just to destroy the traps they use to hurt my friends, which I will not apologize for. I love humans, don't get me wrong. I was adopted - both of my parents and my brother are humans - and I love them to death. But humans don't have the right to kidnap my friends and sell them. And I will do everything in my power to protect my kind and humans alike."

TERRI

I can't speak, but I am scary-smart, so you better hide your servers because as soon as I figure out how, I'm hacking all of your files and releasing them to the world so everyone can see how we were really treated. My name is Terri.

TOM

"Everyone already knows who I am. Some of you think I'm a traitor, a hero, an asshole, and I'm probably a little bit of all of that. I've learned firsthand how horrible merpeople are treated by humans, and I feel terrible about the role I played in turning in Sam and Terri. I was greedy. It's my goal to keep rescuing captured merpeople and setting them free or die trying. No one deserves to be treated like they have been. Except Arthur maybe."

AMY

"Cindy said this was my secret to spill, and I have decided that it is time that I speak up and set the record straight.

"Arthur kept me a secret for a very specific reason. You see - most merfolk are born the way they are. I was not. I was born a human, from human parents. I was not adopted - my mom complained about giving birth to me enough times for me to know that for sure. Later on in my life, through ways I will not yet explain, I was turned into what I am today - merfolk. That is why my markings are different. In our culture - I am referred to as a Cursed.

"Arthur knew I was born a human. He knew that if he revealed to the world that being a merfolk was contagious in some way - it would cause panic. So, he kept my capture a secret. While trapped in his lab, he and other scientists performed tests to try to figure out why I became this way, but they never figured it out. When their tests didn't work, they resorted to physical and mental torture.

"The night I was rescued by my friends, Arthur had strapped me down to a table and cut into my leg with a scalpel to get me to spill how I had changed. When I passed out, they locked me in a cage and left me there without so much as a Band-Aid. I fear that if I had not been rescued that night, I would have died.

"I know this must be hard for everyone to believe. If I were in your shoes, I probably wouldn't believe it either. But I am begging you to listen to me. Merfolk are not dangerous creatures. Most of us live our lives as normal as possible, regular members of your communities you would never think twice about. We do not have special powers that allow us to control humans. All we want is to have the same rights and freedoms we had before so we can be safe. When people like Arthur are allowed to kidnap us and treat us like animals - you are allowing innocent people to be hurt and killed.

"I will be the first to admit that I spent most of my life lying to my friends and family, but I am done lying. I am merfolk. I am not dangerous. I deserve to be treated with respect. And I hope that you realize that before anyone else gets hurt. Less than a week ago, my best friend died trying to tell the truth. I am not going to let her die in vain.

"And to Arthur, who I'm sure will be watching this: I'll make you a deal. The moment we are freed, I will tell you personally how I was Cursed. Until then, we will continue to rescue our brothers and sisters.

We will continue to protect ourselves. We are not just merfolk, we are mer*people*. And we will fight to win back our freedom, through hell or high water."

I posted the video.

PART THREE

"Love is a willingness to sacrifice."

~ Michael Novak

AMY

Shrieking startled me awake. I jumped to my feet (okay, maybe jumping was an exaggeration), ready to fight only to see Emanuel crying tears of laughter at Norman.

"Dude . . . it's just an eel! You like . . . live in the ocean. How are you scared of *eels?*"

"You live on land, how are you scared of spiders?" Norman shouted, face red with rage. "It scared me, okay?" I spied the offending creature swimming the shallows of the center pool. Adam sat up from his bed on the sand, rubbing his eyes as the two boys continued arguing. He smirked as he walked to the edge of the water and gently scooped the eel out of the water before chucking it at Emanuel. Emanuel's laughter turned to screams as he flung it back towards Norman, who added some curse words to the mix of noise.

By the time they were done screaming and laughing, most of the cavern was awake and grumpy about it. Tom sat up beside me, rubbing the sleep out of his eyes.

"I'm going to kick their asses," he muttered.

"Don't be mad. Now we know that Norman and Emanuel are scared of eels. We can use that knowledge to our advantage." Tom groaned, rubbing his back. He had started camping out on the sand with the rest of us once the other refugees had learned there was a bed on his boat. There was a line of people who wanted a chance to sleep on an actual mattress for a night, which Tom couldn't exactly argue with. The sand was not treating him kindly.

Now that everyone was up, people begrudgingly started going about their day. There wasn't much to do other than hunt for food, eat said food, and try not to panic while we figured out our next move.

"Am I the only one who's noticed that Norman and Emanuel snuggle a lot?" Tom muttered, brushing the sand off his legs.

"Merfolk are cuddly by nature. It helps them regulate their emotions. And it's not just those two, Adam cuddles with them too," I said. Tom raised a skeptical eyebrow.

"Yeah, okay. Because you're super cuddly." I kicked some sand at him.

"I have held your hand on multiple occasions."

"Ooh, let's get married then."

"You wish." Our conversation was interrupted as Adam walked over to us, grinning. I sighed.

"It's too early for this." He unsheathed one of his swords. Yeah, he had *two* of them now. After we had posted our videos, he insisted everyone on the island learn how to defend themselves against potential attacks. We were safe for now, but the humans could still find us.

Terri had spent the last few days explaining the risks of using the satellite internet in the midst of using said internet to convince Adam's and Emanuel's old science friend to let them crash on their island once more.

Based on Emanuel's stories, Terri was convinced she could use Karen's old computer to gather beneficial information – which was code for hacking to figure out where kidnapped merfolk were being taken. After several rounds of spicy emails, Karen had relented. Sam and Terri were due to leave the island in a matter of days – which meant Terri had to teach us how to use the laptop without leading the enemies to our direct location.

She could do this magical technology thing that would bounce something called an IP address around the world whenever it was turned on so we couldn't be tracked. But the more often we used it - the more time we gave our enemies to figure out the puzzle. And once the puzzle was solved - they would know exactly where we were.

We had to risk it to post our videos to YouTube. She had created a special channel for us - which was quickly shut down - but they had already been copied and shared a thousand times. Our faces were all over YouTube, TikTok, Instagram, you name it. We were famous.

Comments on the videos mostly ranged from inappropriate questions to conspiracy theories.

mermaids aint real. the govnm is skamming u

How do you guys go to the bathroom?

Tell us where your hiding

Looks fake smh

It remained to be seen how many of those shares and likes were from people who believed us.

Now that she and Sam were leaving, the laptop would be in our control, which meant we had to know how to do the magical IP address thing. They would keep in communication from the mainland using Karen's computer on Baldwin Island - which meant we would have to risk using the internet more and more to receive communications. Hence - why Adam insisted we all become fellow swashbucklers.

He had recruited some of the merfolk to dive down and collect whatever materials could be fashioned into weapons - hence his second sword - which he had carved out of a bone. Sea creatures generally left us alone in the water, but the thought of finding bones of a creature that big made me a little glad I couldn't phase yet.

Norman had added the brilliant idea to dip the weapons in poison. That way - all you had to do was give someone the equivalent of a paper cut to dispatch them. Let me tell you - squeezing poison out of the mated merfolk was not a job that looked comfortable for either party.

I limped over to a wide strip of beach and took a deep breath, trying to prepare myself. Merfolk were supposed to have faster reflexes and better eyesight than humans - which I technically had. But my bad leg and general Cursedness made using those skills more difficult. I couldn't run if cornered, couldn't even bend my left knee, so Adam focused on teaching me to dodge literal bullets and throw them if needed.

Our stolen tranq gun had long run out of actual darts - but Adam solved that by making fake ones out of bits of bone - which sounded cool until one hit you.

I dodged the first three he shot at me and blocked the fourth with my crutch. The fifth hit me in the thigh, drawing a swipe of blood. I winced in pain and across the beach, Tom clenched his wrists. He was all for us learning how to defend ourselves, but he thought shooting darts at the disabled girl was a bit much. Adam had coolly explained to him with his scary Adam face that I was the most valuable one on the island and that he was not going to go easy on me just because my leg hurt.

And he was right - but that didn't make training any more enjoyable. I endured for another half hour before Adam decided to give me a break. He motioned for Tom to join him as I limped down the beach and towards the boat. Merfolk turned to stop and stare at me as I did so. Most of them smiled and waved or nodded their heads in respect. It made me want to throw up.

As I approached the boat, I heard the radio blaring like normal. Based on recent news, Arthur was ruined. After it was confirmed that he no longer had the girls in captivity - the humans boycotted his aquarium, saying they refused to support a man who had lied to them. Letting three merfolk escape from your aquarium was bad enough. Trying to cover it up was ten times worse. Even the new Mermaid Catcher Association had banned Arthur from having any more merfolk in his custody.

The thought of him in so much pain would've made me smile if his daughter hadn't been my best friend.

I couldn't spend time grieving. There was too much to do. The best I could do was finish her battle and wear my markings. If she was brave enough to have them - then so I was I.

I was also doing much better at eye contact. The jolt of fear that I would be hit whenever daring to look at someone's face was beginning to fade away. I think having the Protector's staff helped. People usually looked at that before they looked at my face, which gave me a moment to steel myself and remind myself that I could hit back now.

Now all that was left to do was win our freedom back. I was still working on that part.

Days after our initial posting, the President came out with his new announcement. Any human caught helping merfolk was a felon. Merfolk were the property of the newly established Mermaid Catcher Association – or MCA. And they could use whatever means necessary to catch us.

We had told the truth and the government responded by making us and any human who helped us illegal. It felt like taking a step forward only to get knocked to the floor.

We were at war.

Posting videos was a start. The boys wanted to keep rescuing people. Terri acting as communications on land would help accomplish both of those tasks. Tom had told me a surprising secret about Sam that just might give us an advantage. Learning some self-defense would help in emergencies. Beyond that - I had no clue what to do next.

The fancy staff didn't help.

SAM

Terri and I packed what few possessions we owned, including my textbook, which was encased in about a dozen plastic bags. We had volunteered to swim so the boys could use the boat for rescue missions. It would take days, and the thought of being exposed in the open ocean again made me nervous - but it had to be done.

Terri punched me in the arm, and I looked up to see Amy standing in the doorway, arms crossed.

"I need to talk to you," she said. I motioned for Terri to go on without me and set my bag down. Amy waited for Terri to leave and closed the door behind her.

"I know you want to figure out the science of the Curse," she said. I paled. I opened my mouth to attempt to lie about it - but she silenced me with a wave of her hand.

"Tom told me everything. And while I don't . . . *understand* . . . I don't have to. If you can figure it out before those assholes on land . . . then you should do it. I've already talked with Karen about it. She's on board, but she told me to warn you that genetics and organismal physiology aren't her thing." I blinked, furrowing my brow.

"You hate that," I said. Amy nodded.

"Yeah, I do. I never want to learn another fact about my body ever again. But you do. Others probably do. And you deserve to. You're literally the smartest kid here. If anyone can figure it out - it's you." I danced in place, opening my arms to hug her, but she shied away. I put them back down, smiling sheepishly.

"I won't disappoint you," I said.

"I don't want to hear another word about it. But good luck. Stay safe out there."

EMANUEL

We stood on the shore as the girls disappeared below the surface. It was more emotional than I thought it would be. Tom wiped his eyes several times, and Amy chewed her bottom lip like it was taffy.

Terri had painstakingly shown all of us how to operate the laptop safely - at least as safely as possible. They could use Karen's computer to communicate back to us - so it wasn't like we couldn't talk to them - but still. Being separated by such a long distance felt dangerous.

"They'll be okay," Adam said. *I hope so*, I thought. Norman leaned his head on my shoulder, our spat from that morning already forgotten. Even though I knew merfolk were cuddly by nature, I blushed and tried desperately to smush my embarrassing thoughts.

Amy and Tom turned to go back inside the volcano as the rest of us sat on the sand, letting the tide tickle our toes.

"You boys excited to keep playing pirates?" Adam asked with a grin. *Definitely not, but I'm going to have to be,* I thought. With how famous we were, I wasn't sure how we were supposed to sneak into any place on land to rescue anyone.

"We might need disguises," I mused. "Adam, you still need shoes." Norman scoffed.

"You two might need disguises with your red hair and . . . what are you, Mexican? Everyone is going to think every brown person they see is you." I opened my mouth to retort, but it was true. Even growing up in a diverse town (diverse for Georgia anyway), my white friends had constantly mistaken me for the other Hispanic kids in our grade.

"It's okay. Norman can pretend he's a lost child and can sneak into places that way," I teased. Norman's face turned red as he shoved me. Adam frowned and squinted out at the ocean.

"You little fucker!" Norman squeaked.

"*Little* fucker? I'm like . . . a foot taller than you."

"You are six inches taller than me at best you little . . ." Adam interrupted us by standing up, shielding his eyes as he looked out to sea.

"Do you guys see that?" I strained my eyes and saw a small current making its way towards us. A figure popped up from the surface. I assumed he was another merfolk from the Sanctuary until I saw the cuts on his face and body. He collapsed to the sand, gasping for breath as he phased. We ran over as he rushed to explain himself.

"Please, you have to help my friend! They have him!" We half-carried him to the center pool, trying to listen to his babble as he caused a scene. "You don't understand. Since you posted those videos - things have gone crazy. People are still hunting for us, but they're not turning us in. They don't trust aquariums anymore. - They're keeping us captive on their boats and charging people admission to see us - like little personal zoos. They're making bank. I barely got out. My friend is still back there. You have to go back for him!" he begged.

Tom looked at all of us.

"We're going to need to borrow some hoodies."

A few borrowed hoodies later, we boarded the small police boat Adam had originally stolen (now filled with more gas from Tom's boat) and headed out to sea. We figured this boat was a lot less conspicuous and famous compared to the *Lazy River*. We left the injured merfolk behind, promising to return with his friend. Beside me, Norman vibrated with excitement. Or nerves. I couldn't tell which one.

"We'll be okay. This is far less risky than our other rescue," I said, putting a hand on his shoulder. *If they dare lay a finger on them, I'll tear it off*, I thought. He rolled his eyes.

"Psh, I know." He still vibrated. Across the boat, Adam practiced with his sword. Tom drove the boat as fast as he could, and we pulled back into civilization much faster than we normally did. We docked far away from the other ones and pulled our borrowed hoods up as we prowled the docks.

According to the merfolk's instructions, we had to knock on the hull of the boat five times and pay a hefty fee. We found a rusty broken broken-looking thing I was surprised was still floating, and Tom knocked accordingly. A moment later, a disgruntled-looking man burst from the cabin, smoke trailing from his cigarette. He took his time stepping down the ladder and surveyed us carefully.

"Five hundred. Each." Tom fished the cash out of his pocket and shoved it into the guy's hands. He grinned and motioned us to follow him. He didn't recognize us. We followed him to the cabin and walked down to the engine room. I wiped the sweat off my brow as the humidity hit us like a wall.

"Not the most comfortable viewing place but can't have the MCA poking their noses around where they don't belong," the man laughed. Beside me, Adam and Norman flinched at the smell at the same time I did. It stank of rotting fish and stale water.

We rounded a corner, and I gasped. The captured merfolk was tied to the ceiling by his wrists – much like how Norman had been strung up to be Removed. The bottom part of his tail lay submerged in a kiddy pool of brown water. He gasped for breath, his ribs looking like they might tear through his skin at any moment.

As he saw us, he struggled weakly against the ropes, soft pleading sounds muffled by the gag tied around his face.

"Now unlike those aquariums, this here exhibit is interactive. You can pet him," the man laughed. "But you only got five minutes. Then it's another five hundred." Norman sucked in his breath beside me. The man

333

looked at me and gestured towards the merfolk. "Go ahead, pet him. Those scales don't feel like you would think." *I know exactly what their scales feel like!* I wanted to scream. *Because I got* permission *to touch them!*

Tom, ever the actor, strode up and ran his hand over the merfolk's hip. The merfolk made a weak effort to push himself away.

"Wow, those do feel different. You got any more of them?" Tom asked.

"Used to – but it escaped. Had to up security to keep this one. You wouldn't believe how much money I've made. A few more months and I'll be set for life. Might even get a bigger boat." Tom smiled and removed his hood. The man frowned. Adam whipped out his sword and held it against the man's throat, letting his markings slither into view.

"Keep talking if you want to lose your head." Norman stood point, his fins out and ready as I ran up to Tom. Tom turned back to the merfolk and knelt to look into his eyes.

"Hey, I know you're scared, but we're here to help, okay? Do you understand?" The merfolk nodded, eyes open wide.

"I'm going to take your gag off, okay?" Tom gently reached around and cut the gag free. The merfolk gasped for breath, flexing his jaw as it fell to the ground.

"Emanuel, cut the rope around his wrists while I hold his body up. I'm going to hold you up for a minute so you don't fall, okay?" The merfolk nodded. I took out my new poison-infused pocket knife and started sawing through the swollen rope. The merfolk cried out in pain as it broke, his body collapsing into Tom's arms. *How long have they been tied up like that?* I wondered. Tom rubbed his back as he gently lowered him to the ground.

"He doesn't look healthy enough to phase," Norman said. "We'll have to carry him like that until we can get him to water." Tom scooped the merfolk off the ground and turned to face the jailor.

"Give me one good reason why I shouldn't string you up by your ankles and let you drown in that dirty water," Tom asked coolly. The man's face went pale. Tom cracked a smile.

"Adam, destroy this man's boat. I want it sinking by the time we sail away."

The boat wasn't quite sinking, but the jailor probably wouldn't be catching anything by the time we chugged away. On the small boat, there was nothing we could do except cover the merfolk's tail with our wet hoodies.

Still – it was better than what he had been in. The merfolk shuddered, holding the wet cloth around his body. His wrists and mouth had been rubbed raw by the ropes and gag. Norman held his hand as Adam massaged the sore muscles in the merfolk's arms.

"What's your name?" I asked.

"Kole," he said hoarsely. "I had heard stories of you guys. I wasn't sure if they were true. Thank you." I smiled and offered him my hand to hold. He took it with his free one, sighing.

"My friend – Christian – did he make it?" I nodded.

"He did. You're both safe now." I looked up at Norman, who smiled. My heart thudded with adrenaline. Adam had a satisfied grin on his face, and Norman's tense shoulders were soft. We rescued another merfolk without incident. We were all still safe. No harm, no foul. *One down, a million more to go,* I thought.

AMY

I paced the entire time Tom and the boys were gone. It was completely irrational for me to want to go with them considering the state I was in. At this point, my leg had had weeks to heal and was still functioning as a gummy worm at best. It probably wasn't going to get any better - which meant running or fighting was out of the picture. No matter how many bullets I could dodge, there would be no rescue missions for me.

That meant I was all alone on this island full of strange Naturals who all looked up to me as their leader and literal Protector. Great.

I hadn't realized how much I used the others as a security blanket until they were all gone. I wasn't especially friendly with the boys or girls, but I knew they would do anything to protect me. Tom was the closest thing I had to a real friend - which still made me want to laugh. If you had told ten-year-old me that her future bestie would be the annoying twerp from next door, she would've rolled her eyes and probably gagged.

He was less annoying than he used to be. Tom had given up his newfound popularity to fight in a war he didn't have to. No human had a really good reason to fight with us - but there he was - just like Emanuel.

When I wasn't worrying about my friends, I tried to figure out how to get the humans to believe that we were harmless. We had told our truth. What else was there to say? We couldn't make anyone believe us.

No new ideas came for the two days Tom and the boys were gone. My heart nearly collapsed in relief when the boat appeared in the distance and all four of them landed safely. Part of me wanted to throw my arms around Tom, but I blushed and thought about how awkward that would be. Instead, I watched as the other three carried a limp figure to the center pool. The other merfolk cried out in relief and tackled his friend in a rib-crushing hug.

"He's a little more beat up, but he'll be fine," Tom said. "Those bastards had him strung up by the wrists. Turned him into a petting zoo. Guy was charging five hundred bucks for five minutes." I shook my head.

"That's horrible." Tom stuck by my side as the boys attended to their most recent rescues.

"How was it?" I asked. He shrugged.

"Fine. Norman didn't freak out. No one else saw us. You know, you would think that every fisherman in the world would be on the lookout for four mysterious teenage boys by now."

"Humans are dumb," I said. Tom gasped, putting his hand over his heart. I raised my eyebrow at him. "You especially." He stuck his tongue out at me, and I cracked a smile.

"How were things here?" he asked. I shrugged.

"Fine." *Stressful.*

"Don't lie to me." *Damn it.*

"I was worried about you four," I admitted. "And everyone keeps staring at me like I have all the answers. But I don't know what I'm doing. I feel like a sitting duck." He found my hand and walked me to our corner of the beach.

"Well, let's be sitting ducks together for a while." I soaked in the comforting warmth from his hand, letting his calm soothe my frazzled nerves. *Emotional regulation*, I thought. *Emotional regulation is nice.*

SAM

I didn't know how, but Karen was waiting on the shore with her arms crossed as soon as we surfaced. I tried to look as professional as possible and failed immediately as I stumbled - my legs shaky after days of being a tail.

She harrumphed and turned around without sparing us a second glance.

"You have any idea how much I'm putting myself at risk for helping you guys? I'm already on thin ice after the police found out that Emanuel kid was helping out Mr. Pirate." We followed her up to her cabin. Terri signed and Karen raised her eyebrow.

"I don't speak that language, kid."

"She says thank you," I said. "And that if you were nicer you would have more friends." She blinked once and then grinned.

"I like that one. You got a sense of humor too? Or are you too serious?" I straightened up.

"I have a mission. Not sure if being funny is going to help me with it or not."

"Yeah, I heard all about your mission. You know genetics isn't my thing, right?"

"That's okay. It's my thing." I pulled out Tom's textbook from my soggy bookbag, relieved to see it was still intact. She frowned as she looked at the cover.

"Thing's outdated. You'll need a new one. And wifi, probably." She sat down at a desk overflowing with papers and tried in vain to clear a space. I helped Terri unpack her bag. She watched us with a quizzical look in her eyes as we signed back and forth. Terri skipped out the door and vanished into the woods.

"She just wants to explore," I said. "She'll stay out of your way. And so will I." She leaned back in her chair.

"You know, I can't help you if I don't know what causes this so-called Curse." I narrowed my eyes at her.

"Why do you even want to help?" I asked.

"Wow, trusting this one is," she smirked. I didn't smile back.

"I'm a scientist, kid. I'm curious. And I like other humans just about as much as you do. They think they're little gods – that they can just do whatever they want to the planet and never face any consequences. I know I'm not a god. I'm just a speck on this planet, but it sure is fun to stir up some trouble every once in a while." The gleam in her eyes felt unstable to me. I could feel her chaotic energy from across the beach. *This woman is nuts*, I thought.

"I don't need help," I muttered. "I just need supplies." She nodded.

"As you wish."

EMANUEL

Norman sidled up beside me as I stared off into space, watching Adam practice his swashbuckling on the beach. Amy and Tom sat with their feet in the center pool. *Those two have been spending a lot of time together,* I thought. *Then again, with her best friend gone, he was the one she knew the best.*

"Relieved you survived your second rescue mission?" I asked. Norman rolled his eyes and shoved me, but secretly, I was very relieved. I knew there was no logical way his ex would've been miles and miles away up the coast, kidnapping random merfolk, but my brain wasn't satisfied until we were back to safety. If I ever saw that asshole again . . .

"Yes, very relieved. Enjoying the view?" Norman asked.

"I mean, yeah, it's beautiful out here." He grabbed my jaw and tilted my head so I was focused on Adam. His sword flashed in the sinking sun. Sweat gleamed on his fair skin. I could practically hear him panting as he swiped his glowing red hair out of his eyes.

"That view." I blushed. Norman chuckled. "There's no shame in admiring a hot redhead with a sword." My heart almost fell out of my chest.

"Why would I be staring at Adam like that?" I sputtered.

"Because you're gay." My face turned bright red.

"I'm not gay!" Norman rolled his eyes.

"You definitely are."

"What, you're telling me that you can *feel* sexuality now too?"

"No, but I can *feel* sexual frustration and embarrassment. And you sir - are the stereotypical closeted kid who thinks his best friend is hot. I mean, he is hot though, so at least you have good taste." I grabbed my chest. Part of me was embarrassed beyond belief, but also relieved Norman hadn't noticed who I actually caught myself staring at more often than not.

"That is so not true," I protested. "I *don't* have a crush on Adam."

"I *didn't* say you have a crush on him. I'm just saying redheads in general are hot. Come on, we're friends. You can't stay in the closet surrounded by empaths." I crossed my arms and stared down at the ground.

"You don't have to rub it in my face, asshole. It's hard enough to be the weird nerdy kid. I didn't want to be the gay weird nerdy kid," I muttered. Norman softened the tiniest bit.

"Let me guess. Your parents would disown you? You're that type of closeted?" I sighed.

"Well at this point, I'm not sure if they would disown me for being gay or running away from home to aid the enemy." Norman laughed.

"Maybe if you're lucky you'll get to do both before we're all arrested or shot." I snorted.

"I'd rather focus on the not getting arrested or shot part."

"What's the joy of not getting shot if you have no one to make out with when you get home?"

"Well, if you see any gay bars out here, let me know so I can get on that." Norman pouted.

"What's wrong with me?" he whined. I smirked, praying he wouldn't notice my heart pounding against my ribs. I could handle running away from home and living on a desert island in the middle of nowhere to fight a civil rights battle for a mythical species.

But I could absolutely not handle my feelings for the stupid fluffy brown-haired merfolk beside me. I could tackle being gay once we were all safe.

"I told you. You're an asshole." He pouted more.

"But I'm a cute asshole." I rolled my eyes.

"I'm gonna go check the laptop for news." He followed me into the living room as I pulled out the laptop and started typing away. Norman toyed with his split ends beside me.

"So . . . are redheads actually your type or . . ." I went pale as I read Terri's latest message

"Go get Adam. He's going to want to see this."

Terri had forwarded us several links to news reports.

Video from a student's phone showed men decked out in body armor stalking a line of students in a hallway at Putnam High School. MCA was spelled out in large white letters across their chests. The students were pinned up against the lockers, kneeling with their fingers laced behind their heads. Monstrous-looking dogs sniffed each one.

"This is fuckin' crazy, man," the recorder of the video said. One dog went nuts barking and pawing at one particular student. The officers grabbed the kid and yanked him out of the line.

"Hey man, I'm not one of those things - ahhh!" The student screamed as one of the officers brought down a taser on his chest. He convulsed for several seconds until he went still on the floor. The student next to him jumped out of line, tackling the MCA officer.

"Get away from my friend!" he screamed. He convulsed as he was hit with the taser, slumping to the ground as the other kids started to panic. The dog tore loose from its handler and lunged at another student, tackling him to the ground, and clamping onto his ankle. The student screamed as his markings melted into view.

"According to multiple sources, the MCA is now taking anonymous tips. They have received several for various schools all across the country. They use sniffing dogs to search for mermaids, but as you can see from this video, humans are occasionally injured in the process. Several have been severely injured."

The next video showed footage of shouting parents, furious that the schools would let armed MCA officials into schools. Another showed teachers screaming and blocking doors as MCA officials tried to ram their way into classrooms.

Adam clenched his fists. *This is escalating quickly*, I thought.

"I think we just figured out our next rescue mission."

SAM

Terri was having an excellent time causing chaos.

The first thing she did was steal all of Arthur's research, including footage from security cameras in his secret lab. I told her to wait to post the footage until reactions from the initial videos cooled down. In the meantime, I combed through Arthur's research, looking for any clues he might have missed in his experiments.

The desktop dinged with a new message, interrupting my mission. Terri shoved me out of the way.

What's going on? I asked.

The boys want me to hack into the MCA and figure out where they're getting their tips from, she signed. *Can I steal this for the next few hours?*

I sat outside, letting the tide tickle my feet as the sun descended around the curve of the Earth. To my surprise, Karen sat down next to me, her dirty trousers rolled up past her ankles.

"Know why the tide looks green like that?" she asked.

"Biofluorescent dinoflagellates," I answered automatically. She nodded approvingly.

"Any progress?" I sighed, shaking my head. My eyes were numb from reading DNA sequences for hours, and I had hit the same roadblock Arthur had. The exact same DNA sequences were tacked onto the ends of all 23 pairs of chromosomes. Not a letter of difference between mine and Amy's.

I knew letters being the same didn't necessarily mean identical phenotypes - our different markings proved that already. There could be epigenetic tags affecting us, but those were usually caused by environmental factors. And it still didn't explain how the DNA got there in the first place.

"You know, I could help you figure this out. *If* I knew what caused it."

"I'm not supposed to tell. That's Amy's secret. She promised to tell once we're free."

"And I'm not trying to talk you into betraying your friend. I'm just trying to help." I breathed through my lips. *She's going to kill me. But I need help.*

I explained how Cursing worked. Karen listened thoughtfully as I rambled, picking flecks of dirt off of her boots.

"So, you're saying the same strand of DNA causes the same changes in a person - almost sounds like a virus." I laughed.

"Viruses make people sick, not turn them into mythical beings," I muttered. "Besides, viruses change and evolve constantly. Not every single strain of a virus is identical."

"Would a virus that powerful need to evolve and change?" I shrugged. I didn't know a lot about viruses, but from what I did know, it seemed improbable. Viruses evolved quickly and only infected certain areas of a body before getting wiped out by the body's immune system or killing it. They certainly didn't help people . . . which our DNA technically did. It was an evolutionary advantage to not be able to drown.

But . . . how else would the DNA get into cells? There's got to be some sort of vector that carries it, I thought.

A virus.

I got up, racing back to the computer.

"Move Terri, I might be onto something." She held up her hand, pointing at the screen.

Surprise, surprise, she signed. *The MCA isn't receiving tips. They're raiding schools at random. I just sent the boys the list of where they're going next.*

"Jeez, okay. Move." She rolled her eyes as I sat down, eager to pick up where I left off. I groaned as another message interrupted me. Terri's eyes narrowed as she read it. All thoughts of viruses left me as the words burned themselves into my brain. The message was from a Mr. Duncan.

Our boat will reach your Sanctuary tomorrow morning. We come in peace. We need to talk to Amy Wilson. Pass the message on.

TOM

A long yacht showed up on the horizon right at five in the morning as promised. Instead of going to the Sanctuary, it docked at the old island, white flags waving in the wind as they waited for us to come to them. Amy was sweating as I started up the boat.

"This doesn't feel good. How the hell do they know where we are? Why aren't they attacking us?" she muttered.

"If they were going to attack us, why would they tell us they were coming?" I asked. Amy blew through her lips.

"Maybe it's a distraction."

"They still didn't have to tell us they were coming." Amy's eye twitched.

"We don't have to do this," I said. "We can ghost them. You're the Protector. You decide." She shook her head.

"We need to see what they want. But if things go south . . ." She trailed off, but I knew what she meant. My gun was tucked in the back of my shorts.

I maneuvered the stolen police cruiser to their boat. The boys had taken the other boat to their rescue mission last night, leaving us without our best fighters, but I refused to worry about that. Adam had been teaching us how to fight, and I still had some bullets left in my gun. I could protect us. I could protect Amy. I *had* to protect Amy.

We landed and stepped onto the black sand. I very pointedly rested my hand on my pistol as a heavy-set man in a suit not made for the weather stood waiting for us, his hands folded over his belly.

"Amy Wilson. Tom Falcon. Thank you for meeting me here. My name is Mr. Duncan." He extended a hand, which neither of us took. *Duncan, why does that sound familiar?* I wondered.

"How the hell did you know where to find us?" Amy demanded.

"My team figured out where you were days ago. You did make it difficult though." Amy paled. *If this guy's team was able to find us, how far behind is the MCA?* I thought.

"But never mind that. We have more important things to discuss. You two have caused quite a stir up on land," he said, smiling. "And I want to help. I'm assuming you've heard of the court case going around?" Amy and I exchanged glances.

"I see. Well, to make the story short, the MCA took a dear friend of mine's adopted daughter. This dear friend is an incredibly successful lawyer, and she has decided to sue the United States to get her daughter back." Amy laughed.

"I mean, that's great, but that's never going to work. The law says that the MCA automatically has the power to do what they will with all merfolk and the humans that support them."

"Ah - but all laws are final until someone decides to challenge them. Of course - they already lost the case at the district level, but they've appealed to the next level. Depending on how that goes, the next step is the Supreme Court." My mind flashed back to all the famous court cases I had been forced to memorize for history class. I didn't remember much from school, but I remember that getting a case to the Supreme Court was super rare. Winning them and changing precedent was even rarer. Exactly how rich and powerful was this woman to hire lawyers to challenge the whole damn government?

"Where do we come into this?" I asked.

"By the time this case gets to the top, everyone and their grandma is going to know about it. And those judges are swayed by public opinion. If the whole country is on your side by then - they'll declare the whole situation unconstitutional - which means the MCA will have zero power over merfolk. You will have your freedom back. I am offering you my help in convincing the general public that your kind is safe.

"I have a boat stocked with food, medicine, things I'm sure your refugees need. It can be here tomorrow. Also - I have a present for you,

Amy. May I run to grab it?" Amy nodded. He jogged back to his boat and returned with a much nicer crutch than the one I had shoved in my bathroom all those years ago.

"It's called a forearm crutch. Should be much nicer walking with that one. Not as hard on the armpits." Amy tentatively took it and let the old one fall to the ground.

"What's in it for you?" Amy asked, narrowing her eyes at him. I had the same question. True, Emanuel and I had decided to give up everything to fight this battle – but these were our friends. What could be motivating this guy to take such a risk?

"I am the owner of a large biotech company. We figure out cures for diseases. And to put it frankly . . ." He looked over Amy like she was a rack of ribs. "Your kind is a biological gold mine. The ability to shift between forms? Whatever is in your DNA that makes you special might have the ability to find cures and vaccines for thousands of other diseases." *There it is*, I thought. *At least he's being honest about it.* Amy's grip tightened on her cane.

"So, what I'm hearing is that you're no different than Arthur," she hissed.

"Of course not. Unlike Arthur, I know that forcing people to do things doesn't yield the best results. I will simply offer the opportunity to help if anyone so desires. I don't need to dissect people against their will to accomplish my goals." Amy scoffed.

"I do care about your kind," he continued. "I don't think it's right that any species be treated as yours has been. There are more ethical regulations for field mice."

"You can keep your crutch and shove it up your -" I grabbed her arm.

"Would you excuse us for a minute," I said sheepishly, dragging her away. The look in her eyes said she wished the volcano was still active so she could throw me into it.

"Amy, I know the science thing makes you uncomfortable, but listen to what he's saying. He wants to help us. He has supplies. He has resources. He's on our side here."

"I don't trust him," she said coolly.

"Is he lying?" I asked. She pursed her lips. "Exactly. Just hear him out, okay?" I pleaded. She crossed her arms, her jaw set.

"Having an ulterior motive doesn't automatically make him bad. Him studying your kind after you're free is something we can worry about later," I said. "You have my word. He lays a finger on you - I'll drown him myself."

"Fine. But if he puts us in danger, it's on you," she muttered. I stepped back, stung by her words.

"Really, we're going to play a blame game here?" I snapped. She rolled her eyes as she limped back over to Mr. Duncan.

"And how exactly do we convince the general public?" she demanded. "We've tried telling our side of the story. It doesn't seem that public opinion has changed that much."

"Which is a great start, but we also have to make humans doubt the sincerity of the MCA. Which - shouldn't be that hard. Not only are parents and teachers upset that they're raiding schools now - but look at this." He pulled a newspaper clipping out of his pocket and handed it to me. My blood ran cold as I recognized the man on the front page. It ran even colder as the headline registered in my head.

"Your uncle Morris is the President of the MCA," Mr. Duncan confirmed. "And I have a team of investigators digging into his past to figure out exactly how that happened." The newspaper crumpled in my hands.

"I thought he was in jail?"

"He apparently convinced some important people to let him out. And according to your family history, Morris has a lot more to do with merfolk than you probably ever realized." I flashed back to that night he had tried to shoot me.

I've been designing traps since before you were born.

At the time, the statement hadn't seemed that important compared to getting shot. But how could Morris have been designing traps before they were revealed to the world? I knew my family believed in mermaids . . . but lots of people had before. That didn't mean they knew what merfolk actually were.

Unless he did. He knew enough about them to think they should all be dead.

I swallowed. "If Morris is President of the MCA, then he doesn't care about capturing merfolk. He cares about killing them." *He could use his*

356

officers to wipe them off the planet. And no one would bat an eye. My stomach twisted. Amy looked green beside me.

"I've got connections with powerful people. They're investigating your uncle's past as we speak. They're making sure the MCA can't track your location. I am prepared to do whatever I need to do to help." I glanced at Amy, who looked slightly less furious.

"The boat with food and supplies will be here tomorrow?" she asked. Mr. Duncan nodded. We weren't technically going hungry, but the thought of eating something other than fish made my stomach growl.

"You're also going to provide Sam with all the scientific equipment she needs to conduct her research," Amy said. He raised an eyebrow.

"The little girl you rescued? Her research?"

"*And* if I find out you're lying to me, I'll drown you," Amy finished. I held back a smirk. *Bold words for someone who can't phase yet.*

He extended a hand, and this time we shook it. "It's a deal."

"Your name sounds familiar. Have we met before?" I asked.

"You might have known my daughter at school. Her name is Marisol."

ADAM

Riverside High School. Thursday morning. Eight AM. The same morning the mystery boat was supposed to show up.

I debated staying behind, but Amy would have none of it. She practically kicked us onto the boat, insisting they would be fine. I knew she was lying, but reluctantly left. Tom waved from the shore. He obviously wanted to go, but there was no way he was going to leave Amy alone with Mystery Boat.

This one was going to be tricky. The school lay twenty miles inland - at least a half-hour drive. We would have to steal a car, drive there, sneak into the school, sneak however many merfolk out, and make it back to the ocean without being caught.

And none of us had a driver's license.

But Norman, for some reason, knew how to hotwire a car. I debated asking him how he had acquired this skill as the trawler chugged to shore but decided I would rather not know. We dispatched Norman to steal a car, and he returned an hour later with a minivan (you're less likely to get pulled over in a minivan, right?). Norman took the wheel and swore many times as he struggled to maneuver through the early morning traffic.

We stopped at a Walmart, where Emanuel hopped out to get us some book bags, clothes, and shoes for me. We had given our borrowed hoodies back and figured we needed our own for the future. Clothes were scarce on an island in the middle of nowhere, and my green cargo shorts and white t-shirt were beginning to disintegrate. I shoved my swords into the bookbag as Norman nervously munched on a 100 Grand bar.

"Did you seriously steal candy? We're on a mission here!" I snapped. Emanuel shrugged, his mouth full of a Payday bar.

"We haven't had candy in weeks! Don't come at me!" he protested. "And I didn't steal it - Tom's rich, remember? I paid for it all."

"And why a Payday bar of all things? You had hundreds of candy bars to choose from in there, and you chose a *Payday?*" Norman smirked.

"He likes nuts, leave him alone." Emanuel choked, and Norman nearly crashed the car as Emanuel threw the rest of the candy bar at the windshield. *Oh Lord, we are going to die.*

"Would you two stop being children for five seconds?" I hissed.

"Did you have to say that?" Emanuel sputtered.

"Calm down, you two, we're here." The car screeched to a halt in an enormous parking lot. I whispered one last prayer as we hopped out of the car, blending in perfectly with our hoods up and bookbags hunched over our shoulders. We followed the crowds through the front entrance.

Norman and Emanuel stood by the office doors as I slunk into the office. The secretary ignored me until I leaned over the counter. She furrowed her brows.

"Can I help you, kid? Late bell hasn't rung yet." I took a leap of faith.

"The MCA is going to be here in half an hour. My friends and I can quietly get everyone out to safety before then if you let us." I let my markings melt into view. Her mouth fell open. She looked out the window, where Emanuel and Norman nodded subtly at her. She floundered for a minute, sweat beading on her forehead.

"A-are you sure?" she asked.

"I promise. No one gets hurt. No one will know we were here." She hesitated and then nodded.

"I'll tell the teachers. We want to keep all of our kids safe." I raced out the door to my friends and we melted into the hallway.

The air was thick with the smell of hormones and stress. I did not miss high school.

"Find them as quickly as possible and meet back up by the front bathroom in ten minutes. The teachers are going to help us out," I whispered. We split up. I took a long hallway that smelled like formaldehyde, purposely bumping into as many people as I could, trying to sniff out any hints of salt. I found nothing.

I moved on to the next hallway as the warning bell rang. I picked up the pace as more students filtered into their homeroom classes. One kid milled outside his social studies class, scrolling on his phone. I wrapped my arm over his shoulders and steered him out into the main hallway, forcing him to look at me. He paled as I did so.

"Oh my god," he whispered. "What the hell are *you* doing here?"

"Getting you and the other merfolk out before the MCA gets here in twenty minutes. Are there any more of you?" I demanded. He swallowed and nodded.

"My brother. I - I need to call my parents. They're at work."

"Hurry. Where's your brother? I'll go get him."

"He's at the elementary school next door. Are they going there too?" I swore under my breath.

"I don't know, but we are now." I shoved the kid up towards the bathrooms and found Norman in the crowds.

"Go to the elementary school. There's a kid there." Norman swore.

"I hate kids!" he complained.

"You're the shortest." I pushed past him as he flipped me the bird and raced through the rest of the hallways as the morning announcements started blaring over the intercom.

"Students, please stand for the pledge of allegiance . . ." I peeked my head into the classrooms, praying I wasn't missing anyone. "Now for a moment of silence. Teachers, please check your emails."

Sweat poured down my back as I turned down the last hallway.

"Hey, you there. Where's your hall pass?" I spun around to see a hefty gym teacher stalking towards me, holding another kid by his shoulder. He shoved the kid towards me and leaned down to whisper in my ear.

"He's the last one. Get out of here." The teacher vanished, and the kid trembled under my grip as I steered him toward the bathroom.

Emanuel and the other kid breathed a sigh of relief as I walked in.

"Just these two?" he asked.

"Norman is getting a kid out of the elementary school," I said. "We need to go." I turned out of the bathroom only to skitter back. An MCA officer with a growling dog stood right by the office doors. More oozed out into the hallway, tranq guns clanking against their chests. I pushed the others into the farthest stall.

"We're too late – they showed up early." The kids paled.

"What do we do? How many of them are there?" Emanuel asked.

"At least twenty. They're all over the hallway – all armed. And they have dogs." One kid wobbled dangerously on his feet. I steadied him.

"Passing out isn't going to help us, kid. Did you call your parents?" he nodded.

"They're leaving work now and heading to the ocean. How are we going to get past all the boats looking for us?"

"We have a boat. We won't need to swim past anything," I said.

"W-what about my brother?"

NORMAN

I hate kids, I hate kids, I hate kids. And I am not *that short!*

There was no bothering to disguise myself as I burst through the elementary school doors. Teachers and students stopped in their tracks to stare at me. I sighed.

"THE MCA IS GOING TO BE HERE ANY MINUTE. IF THERE ARE ANY MERFOLK IN THIS BUILDING - THEY NEED TO COME HERE RIGHT NOW IF THEY DON'T WANT TO DIE!" I shouted. The hallway remained silent for a moment before the kids started screaming. Teachers dragged their kids into classrooms before slamming the doors shut, leaving me with a half-empty hallway. I groaned, running my fingers through my hair.

"You're too late." I turned to see an MCA officer standing behind me, a taser flickering in his hands. The screams got louder. I grinned as my fins grew from my arms.

"That's what you think." Kids stopped and gawked as he attacked, swiping at me with the taser. I slid down between his legs, stabbing him with my poisonous needles. He went down with a crash. I leaped up, ready for more, but he seemed to be the only one so far. *That must mean all the others are at the high school already,* I thought.

I shouted a word that was definitely not appropriate for an elementary school and ran through the hallways.

"Any merfolk, please, come here, I'm trying to help you!" I shouted. I nearly tripped over a small child who stepped in my path, blue curls staining his face. I grabbed his shoulders as he trembled in my grasp.

"My brother is in high school," he whimpered. I nodded.

"We've got him already. Listen to me very carefully buddy, are there any more of you?" He shook his head. I scooped him up and pushed my way through the crowd and out the front doors. I stopped dead in my tracks at the commotion going on in front of the high school.

I let out another inappropriate word as I bolted for the chaos.

EMANUEL

All four of us huddled in the last bathroom stall as shouting sounded from the hallway. My heart pounded in my ears as I considered how much it would hurt to get eaten by a snarling dog.

"All students against the wall! Heads down, hands above your heads, now!" We stayed silent as the other students shuffled through the halls. *Maybe the dogs won't smell us if we're all hiding in here*, I thought.

Adam blew through his lips.

"This might get messy."

"I'll go distract them," I said. "And you guys can run for the doors. Before Adam could tell me it was a bad idea, I bolted out into the hallway. Teachers and students turned to stare as I skidded out right in front of an MCA officer.

"Oooh, I'm a mermaid, come get me!" I turned and booked it down the hallway as officers and dogs gave chase.

I hit the ground hard as something flew over me. As I rolled to a stop, I reached up to discover a net had been thrown over me.

"Seriously?" MCA officers surrounded me, aiming their tasers and tranq guns at me.

"He's not one of them! It's that Mexican kid!"

"That's rude, how do you know I'm not Puerto Rican?" They hauled me to my feet just in time for me to see Adam and the others making a break for it. They stopped abruptly at the wall of officers blocking the front door.

The crowds gasped as Adam unsheathed his swords from his book bag, letting it fall to the floor. He transformed into scary Adam in a moment, ears pressed flat against his head as his eyes shone with rage.

"Let us through!" he snarled, spinning his blades. A distant shout broke the silence, and the line of guards broke as another figure pushed past them. Norman landed in the middle of the hallway, a kindergartener clinging to his back.

"You said they were coming at eight!" Norman shouted.

"They came early!" Adam retorted. I took the distraction as an opportunity to swipe the ankles of the MCA officers with my poison-infused pocketknife. They all fell to the ground, and I balled up the net as I bolted back down the hallway.

Students screamed as Adam lunged after the guards holding the door, swords flashing. Norman set down the kid and circled all three of the rescues as MCA officers surrounded them, tasers sparking.

I tackled the closest MCA officer to me, wrapping the net around his face as I poked him with the knife. He went down. Norman grew his fins and started swiping. I screamed as a taser hit me, sending me twitching to the ground. My vision flickered in and out as the smell of burnt flesh filled the hallway.

I forced myself to get up as Adam's body flew across the hallway. It crashed into a trophy display case - where the glass shattered and rained down. He scrambled to his feet, now missing a sword as he raced back into the fight.

The MCA officer that had tased me suddenly fell to the ground, one of Norman's needles poking through his chest. Norman dragged me across the hallway. We had dispatched about half of the guards, but the rest were fighting like hell.

"GO!" Adam screamed as he lured the remaining guards further and further from the entrance. How he managed to swordfight ten grown men with tasers and tranq guns, I would never understand and didn't have time to.

I grabbed the hands of the two merfolk and pulled them towards the doors. Norman scooped up the little one - piggyback style - but ran back to help Adam.

"Shit, shit, shit, shit!" he screamed, the kindergartener holding on for dear life as he joined the fray. A few more moments later the rest of the MCA officers lay paralyzed on the ground. Adam gasped for breath, leaning against the shattered display case, sweat pouring from his brow.

"That was not quick and quiet!" one of the office ladies hissed at him. He groaned as he stumbled over to me.

"Let's get the heck out of here," he croaked. Norman faced the hallway one last time.

"Come with us now or forever hold your peace!" he shouted. No one moved. He bowed and raced out the door with us.

Cheering sounded behind us.

AMY

As promised, a huge yacht arrived the next morning, filled to the brim with food and other supplies. The refugees all but stormed it, clamoring for the best stuff.

I nearly wept as I held a loaf of bread in my hands and sank my teeth into it. Mr. Duncan watched in awe as we gorged ourselves. He had changed out of his ridiculous suit and now sported a pair of khaki shorts with an awful Hawaiian shirt. The fact that he wanted to use merfolk to further his scientific research still filled me with rage, but the taste of fresh bread almost made me want to forgive him.

The boys arrived in time to join the feast, five new refugees in tow. A weight lifted off my shoulder I hadn't been aware I was carrying.

Merfolk sat and ate, full of smiles. They welcomed the new refugees with open arms. No one gave the humans suspicious looks. The atmosphere was light and cheery for the first time in what felt like forever. That is - until a pink figure wove from between the boxes of supplies. My bread became crumbs in my hands as Marisol strode right up to Tom and smashed her shiny pink lips against his. Someone in the crowd whistled until she pulled away, her stupid smile bright enough to see across the island. Tom's eyes were wide.

"Um . . . hi? What are you doing here?" he asked. *You're not going to tell her off for almost chewing your face off?* I screamed inside my head.

"Duh, I'm here helping." She went in for another kiss, but Tom stumbled backward. She pouted, putting her perfectly manicured nails on her hips.

"What's your problem? We were dating before all this happened, remember?" she whined.

Heat of a new kind flooded my face as I grit my teeth. I wanted nothing more than to crutch over there and kick her overboard. *That stupid fisherman is mine. You can't just waltz in here and rub your makeup all over his face.*

Out of the corner of my eye, I saw Norman look back and forth between me and Tom. He sniggered. *I'll throw you overboard next,* I thought, clenching my fists.

"Yeah, we were but . . ." Tom trailed off, looking over at me. "You know, a lot of things happened. I just assumed . . ." She backed away, blushing.

"Oh." The silence grew painful. I finally cleared my throat, knocking Tom out of his trance.

"Oh, Marisol, this is Amy. I think you guys might have known each other at school?" Marisol turned to look at me and smiled.

"Hi! Wow . . . you look a lot different," she said, gazing up and down. I bit my lip instead of cussing her out. *What, shocked I don't have boobs anymore? Do I look too much like a boy to you? Are my markings too weird for you? Are my scars too ugly?*

"Good to see you," I muttered.

"I'm really happy I can be here to help," she said cheerfully. "My dad told me what he was doing and swore me to secrecy about all of it. I think it's really cool what you've started, Amy." *Damn it, why is she so nice?*

I nodded, and we lapsed back into awkward silence. Mr. Duncan walked up to his daughter and gently steered her away.

"Why don't you let them eat, honey? I'm sure they'll show you around later." I gladly took the opportunity to flee with my bread, finding a secluded spot to munch in peace, my head spinning with emotions. To my chagrin, Tom chased after her. *Boys are the worst,* I thought.

Adam joined me a few moments later, looking as exhausted as my brain felt.

"You look tired," I said.

"Thanks," he muttered, stabbing his sword in the sand as he plopped down next to me. "Next time, I want to take Tom with us and leave Norman here." I sniggered. He quickly flushed in embarrassment.

"I'm mostly kidding. Norman's a great fighter. I was just hoping to get out of there quietly and quickly. Norman is not quiet or quick."

"Well, you got out safely. That's what matters." He blew through his lips.

"I'm nervous Amy. There are way more raids than we could ever dream of helping. You should've seen the officers up close. And they can just barge into the schools whenever they want. The teachers and students were terrified." He hunched his shoulders. "People are going to get hurt - humans and merfolk alike." *Just wait until he finds out who's in charge of the MCA*, I thought. I decided to keep that knowledge to myself for now.

"You can't save everyone," I said. "There's only so much we can do. But we're about to get a lot more help." I briefly explained Mr. Duncan's deal, leaving out the part about Morris.

"And you trust this guy?" he asked. "I'm surprised."

"I don't . . . distrust him. He wasn't lying. And he does have an ulterior motive. But it's a motive I can live with for now," I muttered. More footsteps sounded in the sand. I looked up to see Norman escorting Marisol, a cheesy grin plastered across his face.

"Amy! There you are. I was just telling Marisol that you would be *so* excited to give her a tour of The Sanctuary," Norman grinned. *I'm going to kill you*, I thought. Marisol grinned, dumb as she was pretty, as I clamored to my feet. I hobbled along in the sand, pushing myself to go faster than she was. This cane was easier to walk with compared to the old one. And no sloppy ex of my friend was going to show me up - even if it was just walking on the beach.

And then I tripped, further proving the universe hated me. Marisol reached out to help steady me, but I jerked my arm back.

"Don't touch me!" I snapped, steadying myself on the volcano wall. She shied away.

"Sorry - just habit," she said sheepishly. "Tom had told me not to . . . do that." *Tom told her to keep her hands away from me? Is that why he chased after her - to brief her about how to handle me? How many other people did he tell that to?* I wondered. I wasn't sure if that made me feel better or worse about my situation. On one hand - it was thoughtful. On the other hand - what kind of person has to give disclaimers about interacting with their friends?

I buried my salty comments as I showed her around the inside of the volcano. I wasn't sure how to give her a tour. Look, there are some rocks! Our real history is engraved on those rocks up there. That's the pole where Norman was almost Removed. That's the ocean I can't swim in. Any questions?

The whole time, she was sickeningly nice. She waved at the little merfolk kids, who giggled and waved back. *How did someone so genuinely nice end up with a douchebag like Tom?* I wondered. *And if Tom is such a douchebag, why am I so upset at the idea of her dating him?*

When we had looked through all the possible rocks, I dropped her off by the yacht, where she thanked me profusely.

"I really appreciate it. And - I wanted to apologize for earlier. I didn't know you and Tom were dating now." My body went rigid. "I mean

- he's right - I should've asked first before going at him like that. But you know how physical of a guy he is." I shook my head, my face turning red.

"Tom and I are *not* dating," I said, my heart palpitating. "Th - that's not a thing. Merfolk and humans do *not* date. That's *not* a thing, especially him like . . . ew . . . gross." Sweat dripped between my shoulder blades.

"Oh . . . sorry . . . I could've sworn . . ." I prayed for an asteroid to fall out of the sky and kill me where I stood. Anything would've been better than having this conversation. Did *everyone* think Tom and I had a thing for each other? Was it because we held hands? The boys held hands - and no one thought they had a thing for each other!

Except Tom.

I concentrated very hard to stay on my feet as Marisol watched me with a quizzical look on her face. I tried to say more words to convince her that I definitely did not have a thing for her gross handsy ex but ended up pushing past her without another sound. I limped back over to where Norman was lounging in the shallows and chucked my cane at him. He laughed.

"You seem upset."

"You're an asshole!" I hissed, yanking my cane back before he could throw it back at me. "Do you just like to cause trouble for fun?" He grinned, stretching out on the sand like the Cheshire cat.

"Aw, don't be upset. I've got to cause some drama to keep our minds off of our impending dooms." I smirked and leaned down by his head. *Let's see if Tom's theory has any merit.*

"Do something like that again and I'll tell Emanuel you have a crush on him." He immediately flipped over, eyes wide.

"I-I do not!" he sputtered, cheeks blossoming red.

"Uh, huh, tell that to your face." I walked away, leaving the flustered merfolk a sputtering mess as I searched for Tom. I found him on his boat, unboxing and organizing supplies.

"They even brought us toothpaste. We can brush our teeth now," he said, hugging the bottles to his chest.

"Yeah, you really need to." He stuck his middle finger up at me as he rummaged.

"There's also medical supplies in here. Maybe some of it can help you with your leg." I sank next to him. After weeks without a real shower, he almost smelled like merfolk. Nice and salty. *Stop smelling him, that's weird.*

"Yeah, I don't know. I think my leg is just dead at this point."

"You think you could phase if you tried?" he asked. I shrugged.

"Not super keen to try." He tsked, shaking his head.

"You know, you can't phase, can't keep any secrets. You're pretty bad at being a mermaid." I punched him in the arm.

"You're pretty bad at being a mermaid catcher." He laughed.

"It's all a part of my big scheme to become a trillionaire. I'm just going to sell off the whole island." I laughed.

As we fell asleep in our usual spot in the sand, I couldn't help but wonder what it would be like to have a life here. Growing up, I had always assumed I would die a single, old, crazy cat lady with some mundane, average job. No self-respecting merfolk would ever want to marry a Cursed. But things were changing. My life now was anything but loveless and boring. I didn't know if any merfolk would want to marry me, but they tolerated me enough to be their leader. At the very least, I would die with some dramatic things on my rap sheet.

I looked over at Tom while he slept, his mouth open as a string of drool oozed to the ground. I laughed silently and reached out for his hand.

Merfolk are just cuddly. It helps us regulate our emotions, I thought. Just like Norman and Emanuel - just friends - nothing more. I do not have a crush on Tom Falcon. Merfolk and humans don't fall in love.

SAM

By the time the others had updated us on the Mystery Boat situation, I was vibrating with excitement. I stood on the shore, impatiently tapping my foot as Mr. Duncan's fancy boat appeared in the distance.

It docked, and men appeared, carrying down boxes of supplies I had requested. I tried to be as quiet as possible (it was the middle of the night), but Karen was already awake. She shoved her glasses up her crooked nose and helped bring them inside, muttering about all the trash. I opened one and squealed in delight.

"My centrifuge," I murmured, running my fingers over the stainless-steel curves. I hefted it out of the box and set it on the messy desk.

"Do you have everything you need?" I turned to see Mr. Duncan, looking rather tired and rumpled in his Hawaiian shirt.

"I think so." He nodded, gazing over me like I was an oddity in a display case. I was familiar with the sensation. I crossed my arms.

"Do you need something?" He flushed and shook his head.

"Sorry, I don't mean to be impolite. It's just . . . Amy told me what you were trying to accomplish here, and well . . . I'm both impressed and intimidated." It was my turn to flush. Terri was usually the one getting complimented for her smarts. She had been allowed to show off her skills, while I had been forced to temper mine. *Biology, really? Why not physics or astronomy? Those never put anyone in danger.*

"Thank you, sir." He offered his hand to shake, and I took it.

"If you need anything else, let me know. I've heard other scientists are working on the same thing. I would rather you figure it out first." I nodded solemnly, the pressure building on my shoulders.

I immediately started unpacking boxes, pulling out micropipettes, dyes, needles, even a microscope. Karen watched tiredly from her bed.

"This can't wait until tomorrow?" I wrapped a piece of medical tape around my forearm and started pumping my hand.

"I can go outside if you want me to." She winced on my behalf as I inserted a needle into the crook of my elbow and started collecting vials of blood.

"Jesus kid, let me help you." She knelt by my arm and held the test tubes in place, replacing them as they grew full. Once I had several filled up, I removed the needle and slapped a Band-Aid over the wound. I placed the tubes in a rack and started filling up the smaller vials that would fit into the centrifuge.

"What are you doing with your blood, kid?"

"I'm going to centrifuge it. If there's a virus in my blood, I'll be able to find it." I turned on the machine and waited impatiently as it spun. Fifteen minutes later, I removed a vial and carefully spilled the top layer of liquid onto a microscope slide. I applied dye and pulled the microscope between my legs as I started analyzing the sample. Karen leaned over my shoulder.

"Well, what do you see?" I sighed.

"Nothing. Which could mean nothing - a lot of viruses are too small to see under a regular microscope. But I can't exactly ask them to bring me an electron microscope. Those things are huge." I drummed my fingers on the floor.

"Is there any way to grow more of it? Make more copies?" she asked.

"Well, that's the thing. Viruses only replicate inside cells. They insert themselves and take over the cell's organelles to make more copies of themselves. They typically then burst open and all the copies go off to infect other cells. But with us - there seems to be no sign of initial infection. Virus DNA doesn't attach itself to the host's DNA - it just floats around separately in the cytoplasm."

"I don't understand half of what you just said - but it sounds like you need to study Wilson's blood." I paused and turned to her.

"Or another Cursed's blood," I mused. She frowned.

"I don't want to Curse you!" I said hurriedly. "But . . . could I Curse a sample of your blood?" She harrumphed.

"Fine Dr. Frankenstein." I spared her the needle and carefully pricked her finger instead, squeezing it enough to fill a small vial. I dyed my blood sample with a fluorescent dye before mixing the two. From Amy's story, the change had happened within 24 hours - and that was after the Curse had spread into every cell in her body. With such a small sample, surely it would take a shorter amount of time.

I waited an hour just to be safe before testing the sample. I frowned at what I found.

The Curse hadn't spread. The fluorescent dye was barely illuminated under the black light.

"I'm going to need more blood samples," I whispered.

TOM

Mr. Duncan's boat continued to show up every week, bringing more food and supplies. With every visit, he brought more risk of being tracked by the MCA and news from the shore - along with his daughter. Which, if I wasn't hallucinating, made Amy vibrate with rage.

Hatred of the MCA was spreading quickly. The rate at which they were surveying schools had escalated. Several businesses had even been attacked. We barely saw the boys before they took off again on another rescue mission - whether it was defending another school or rescuing merfolk from personal zoos. They were running themselves ragged but would hear none of it when Amy or I tried to convince them to take a break, Adam especially. Dark bags stained the skin under his eyes, and his ears seemed permanently stuck in their mer-form. He claimed it helped him fight better.

As far as good news went - more humans seemed to be on our side. Videos of human protestors painted with Cursed markings swarmed the internet. They were everywhere - aquariums, schools, the White House. Occasionally, the police would shut them down, but there were so many of them that it was impossible to arrest everyone involved.

Other merfolk had turned to YouTube and TikTok, making their truth videos. Hashtags like #FreeTheMerfolk and #ComingOutOfTheSea had been trending for weeks, but it still wasn't enough. The case of Merfolk vs. MCA as people were starting to call it - failed at the circuit level, so we were all waiting on our toes to see if it would be accepted by the Supreme Court.

Meanwhile, tensions rose at the Sanctuary as merfolk waited for things to change. Amy spent lots of her time pacing. More petty fights broke out amongst the refugees. And Mr. Duncan contacted us more and more for updates, fishing for any extra information we could give about Morris.

Terri messaged early one morning, offering a secret weapon she had been holding onto for a while. She had hacked into Arthur's security cameras from the lab and stolen hours and hours of video footage. Footage that showed how Amy had been treated at the lab. She had offered to post it after debating how much it would offend Amy.

It had indeed offended Amy, who flatly declined, despite my protests.

"Look, I know you don't want anyone to see you like that but think about it. When the humans see how cruel the scientists were to you, surely it'll change some minds," I said. She stared out at the ocean, arms crossed.

"Tom, I said no. Drop it," she snapped. I sighed, throwing my hands up in the air and walking away. I knew she had been through untold trauma, but my patience was wearing thin. She stressed all the time about what else could be done to convince people, but wouldn't go for this one thing? I blew through my lips, pausing, knowing she could probably feel my anger across the beach.

Fine, let her feel my anger. She's not the only one here who's allowed to be mad. This is my fight too, I thought bitterly. *Why couldn't she trust me for once? Haven't I shown that I'm not the same asshole I was before?*

My thoughts were interrupted by a familiar sight on the horizon. I sighed, turning back to Amy.

"He's here!" I called out.

"I'm not blind," she shouted back, limping up the beach.

"No, you're just stubborn," I muttered. She paused, eyes narrowed.

"I'm not deaf either."

"Good!" I shouted back. We stood next to each other in silence, our arms crossed as we waited for the yacht to dock. We joined Mr. Duncan in the cabin as he lifted a heavy box onto the table.

"We searched Morris' house." He dumped out its contents. Envelopes went flying.

"You brought us old letters?" Amy asked. I opened an envelope and pulled out a newspaper clipping. *Young girl drowns - riptide to blame?* I grabbed another. *Toddler falls from boat and drowns.* My lunch churned in my stomach.

"Why would my uncle have a bunch of clippings about kids drowning?" I asked.

"Turn it over," Mr. Duncan said. I turned the clipping over. In bright red Sharpie, someone had scribbled the words *FOR OLIVER.*

"Do they all say that? Who is Oliver?" Amy asked.

"That's what we were wondering. My team did some more digging into Morris' past." He laid down a photograph on the table. It showed a tan teenage girl with blonde hair grinning at the camera. She sat on the edge of a dock, her tangled curls blowing in the wind as she laughed at whoever was taking the picture. My blood ran cold.

"Is that . . ." I whispered.

"The merfolk who tried to kill Cindy, yes. According to the back of the picture - her real name was Amanda Flowers." Mr. Duncan handed me another photo. Amy grabbed my arm, our spat forgotten.

The picture was yellow with age and stained with salt water, but clear as day, my uncle was sitting next to Amanda on my boat.

And they were kissing.

My jaw dropped. The thought of my uncle possessing enough heart in his body to kiss someone made me want to laugh. The image of him kissing the species he claimed to hate . . . my stomach churned. *Did he know?* I wondered. *There's no way he knew. He would never date merfolk.*

"Whoa," Amy said. "That is unexpected."

"Morris never mentioned having a girlfriend when he was younger?" I shook my head.

"It gets weirder. We're not sure how long they were involved, but a few months after that picture was taken, Amanda disappeared from the area." He reached inside his bag for another picture, but hesitated, shoving it back down. "I won't show you that one - it's too sad." He sighed. "Not long after her disappearance, police got a call about a domestic disturbance in a trailer park. By the time they got there - all they found was a baby with I quote, *strange blue markings on his body*. Emergency responders at the time thought they were caused by broken blood vessels."

"What happened to the baby?" I had a sinking suspicion I already knew the answer.

"The baby was found dead. He was shot in the head." Amy turned a pale shade of green. My grip on her hand tightened. "A few months after the baby was found dead, Morris got his first letter in the mail."

Oh my god.

"Humans can't get merfolk pregnant," Amy whispered. "We're different species."

"Oh, yes they can. We had forensics double-check the remains. It was definitely his baby. And we can assume he had tried to kill Amanda too. Forensics found her blood all over the trailer. Police assumed the killer had dragged her body somewhere else to dispose of - but they never found it."

"So, Morris got Amanda pregnant. She had the baby in secret. Morris found out - I'm assuming found out what she really was. Freaked out. Killed the baby . . . thought he killed her. But she survived and escaped," Amy whispered.

"That's sure what it's looking like."

"And went on a murder spree for revenge. For Oliver. That must have been their baby's name," I whispered. "She became the very monster he thought she was."

She couldn't even let Cindy go, I thought. She couldn't stand the thought of one of her victims escaping. No wonder Morris thought merfolk were evil. She had pinned the death of every person she drowned on him for years. That was enough to drive anyone crazy.

"It all makes sense," I murmured.

"What exactly do we do with this information?" Amy asked.

"I'm glad you asked. The trial is coming up soon. We need to show the world how twisted the MCA is - so we're going to reveal Morris' true intentions. Even if people don't think merfolk deserve freedom, they're going to be pissed to find out the leader of the MCA wants to murder instead of study them. We'll have an Arthur situation all over again."

"Won't that just make merfolk look bad though? I mean . . . Amanda was the stereotype that convinced Arthur all of them were evil," I said.

"Before Amanda did any of that - Morris shot a baby in the head. I think that's what the public is going to focus on," Amy muttered. The world still seemed to spin under my feet. *Humans can get merfolk pregnant. I could get Amy pregnant.* I blushed, quickly banishing the thought from my head. *Stop it, Tom. There is no way in hell she would ever let you get her pregnant.*

"Exactly," Mr. Duncan said. "We need to reveal Morris' true character, and with this, we have proof."

"So, what, we're going to make another YouTube video?" Amy asked.

"I was thinking something a little more . . . dramatic. Something to make the Supreme Court Judges think." I blinked.

"Wait, so . . ."

"The Supreme Court agreed to hear the case. They're publishing their final decision in the next few weeks."

AMY

The next several weeks passed by agonizingly slow as we waited for the next stage of our plan. The air was still slightly tense between Tom and I since our last argument.

I didn't know how else to explain my aversion to publishing the lab footage. I had been trying my best to bury those memories. If the whole world saw those videos, other people would ask questions and make comments just like how they had after Cindy's attempted murder by the fountain. I would never be able to escape. No one should be able to see what happened to me, and if Tom didn't want to understand that, it was on him, not me.

Meanwhile, I was trying to understand how the hell Morris fell for a merfolk. The thought of him getting her pregnant made my stomach roll. I was sure Sam would be fascinated by such a situation. The baby had obviously been merfolk - did that mean merfolk was some sort of a dominant gene? Was there any such thing as a half-merfolk? Why were merfolk so adamant that falling in love with humans wasn't a thing when it was?

On the day of Mr. Ducan's dramatic surprise, Tom and I took turns washing our clothes in the sink, trying to look halfway decent. I wrinkled my nose as a copious amount of brown stuff oozed out of my shirt and pants. At least the viewers wouldn't be able to smell us through the cameras.

"Nervous?" Tom asked.

"Duh." He grinned and playfully nudged me.

"Don't be. You'll do great." Mr. Duncan had used his connections to set up a live news interview. How the reporter or news station wasn't going to get in trouble for talking to us boggled my mind - but I guess they were willing to risk it to get good views.

"Yeah, I love the idea of being on camera with a million strangers staring at me," I muttered.

"You won't be able to see them staring at you." Tom stripped off his t-shirt and dunked it in the dirty sink water. I forced myself not to turn and look at him. *He can get you pregnant, remember?* my brain teased. I death-gripped my soggy tank top. I pulled on a bulky t-shirt and tried my best to smooth it out as Tom pulled on a dry t-shirt.

"Ooh, look at those shoulders," he teased. I hid my flush by rolling my eyes as I looked at myself in the mirror. I wasn't exactly what one would call a beauty. You had to concentrate to tell I was even a girl with my flat chest and short choppy hair. *At least you don't look like a skeleton anymore*, I thought, admiring the sinewy muscles in my arms. Walking with a crutch for months *does* give you nice shoulders.

"You two ready to head out?" Mr. Duncan asked, poking his head in the bathroom. We nodded and followed him. The yacht carried us into the open ocean, where another boat awaited us. Mr. Duncan had sworn up and down the news station was neutral - but the look on the reporter's face, once we stepped onto their fancy boat, made me think otherwise.

Her jaw fell open as she saw us. Flustered, she rushed to get us seated and set up with microphones hidden in our clothes. Cameras and lights were set up around us, making me feel like a specimen on a microscope slide. I guess we technically were.

"Don't be nervous," Marisol whispered before ducking out of view with her father.

"We're live in five . . . four . . ." I cleared my throat. Tom squeezed my hand one last time.

"Good evening, America! Tonight, we have a very unique opportunity to speak with the leaders of the Mermaid Rebellion, Amy Wilson and Tom Falcon. How are you two, tonight?" *Leaders of the Mermaid Rebellion, is that what they're calling us?* I thought. Tom grinned, leaning back in his seat.

"It's merfolk," he said. "Mermaids or mermen isn't a term they use. They say merfolk or merpeople." I bit back a smirk as the reporter blushed.

"Oh, my apologies. Well, let's just go right into the questions, shall we? Tom, you used to be one of the humans capturing merpeople and turning them in. What made you switch to their side?"

"When this all started, I believed that merfolk were dangerous and needed to be turned in - as Arthur had stated. Because of Amy here, I realized that was a lie." The reporter turned to me.

"Amy, what did you do that was so significant that Tom no longer believed you were dangerous?"

"I saved his life." I explained the story of what had happened that night on the *Lazy River*.

"Wow, that's incredible. So, if merpeople aren't all dangerous like humans have believed, what is your kind like?" I hesitated. *Be nice.*

"Honestly, there's not a lot of differences. Just like how humans can be racist, sexist, homophobic . . . merfolk can be the same. Many of them are prejudiced against humans - which is understandable - but still. But they're very loyal. They'll do anything to protect their families and each other."

"You talk about merpeople like you're not one of them. Why is that?"

"I wasn't born this way. That makes me an outsider. Many merfolk still think of me as just human, even though historically, Cursed were honored." I explained the story of the giant mural on the volcano wall - detailing how merfolk had saved drowning children.

"That is quite different from what humans have been told about your kind. Why do you think Arthur and the MCA have been so dead-set on painting you in this other light?"

"Greed," Tom said. "And there's something about the leader of the MCA that people don't know yet." I gripped the edge of my seat. *Here it is.* Tom leaned forward, passing the picture of Morris and Amanda to the reporter. A cameraman zoomed in on it.

Tom explained the creepy letters and the unsolved crime from thirty years ago, right down to the grisly details. The reporter's face got paler and paler as he did so. I couldn't help but smile. *Suck on that, Morris.*

"That is news indeed."

"As far as Arthur goes," I paused, the words stuck in my throat. "What he said is . . . almost understandable. The only merfolk he knew was the one who tried to kill his daughter. And if some new strange creature had tried to kill my daughter - I would do everything in my power to hunt it down too. But he was still wrong in his assumptions."

"How did you react to the loss of your friend?" I tensed. A faint whine sounded in my ears.

"I miss her every day." Across the boat, Marisol and her dad suddenly got to their feet, looking towards the sky. Mr. Duncan squinted as Marisol's jaw fell open.

"She was murdered," Tom said flatly. "Plain and simple. Whoever shot her deserves to be in prison."

"GET DOWN!" Mr. Duncan shouted. The whining turned into chopping. The air cracked above us. The reporter fell to the ground, blood leaking out from underneath her. Mr. Duncan joined her as the air exploded in pops.

Marisol yanked both of us from our chairs and shoved us underneath the benches, squeezing in beside us. Screams joined the sounds of shattering glass. I squeezed my eyes shut. *We've been set up*, I thought. *No, there's no way. Not if they're shooting at Mr. Duncan and the reporter . . . oh god . . . please don't let them be dead.*

Black figures dropped from the sky, clutching rifles to their chests. Real rifles, not just tranq guns.

Marisol screamed as one of them dragged her from underneath the bench. Tom was next, but they left me alone. Tom swore and struggled as they held him still, multiple guns pointed at his chest. I wiggled out of my hiding spot, ready to curb-stomp those assholes to dust with my cane.

"Let them go!" I shouted. The boat went silent. One figure turned to face me, and my blood went cold.

"I thought I would find you here." Tom screamed, lunging against his captor's grasp. I stood my ground.

"I take it you saw us on TV." Morris scowled. "It's too late," I said. "Your stupid scheme is finished. Everyone knows your intentions now." He smirked, his lips exposing his yellow teeth.

"I know. But if you want to buy your friends on land and at your precious Sanctuary sometime, you'll come with me." I forgot to breathe. Morris laughed.

"Oh, you're wondering how I know about your secret hiding place? We've known about it for weeks. There's a certain helicopter with some pretty nifty tech on it that'll blow that volcano back to hell on standby." *Oh my god.*

"If that's true, why haven't you killed us yet?" I demanded.

"Oh, believe me, I've been trying to convince everyone your kind is better off dead. But *you* are too important to die," Morris said. "So, I made the military a deal. I get you back, then I get to do what I want with the rest of you." I stopped breathing.

In an instant, I was trapped in my old memories. I was tied down to a table, screaming through a gag. Gloved hands poked and cut whatever they wanted. Cold eyes stared at me, merciless and hollow.

The scientists wanted me back. And they had bartered the lives of every other merfolk in the Sanctuary to get me.

My knees trembled. I couldn't go back. I couldn't. But what would happen if I refused? Morris would kill my friends, take me anyway, and then go blow everyone else up before they knew what was going on.

But if I could get him to leave Tom and Marisol alive . . . they could go back to the Sanctuary and warn everyone. Maybe even have time to evacuate.

As for me . . . it didn't matter. My life wasn't worth everyone else's.

"You let them go first. On their boat," I said, motioning to Tom and Marisol.

"Amy, don't you fucking dare!" Tom screamed.

His past words echoed through my head. *I'll never let them take you again. Through hell or high water.*

I refused to make eye contact with him. If I did - I would lose my nerve. *I'm so sorry,* I thought. *I have to.*

"Deal," Morris said. I closed my eyes as the men dragged Tom and Marisol to the railing.

"Tom, I'll be okay. Make Adam the new Protector. I'll be back soon," I whispered.

I stared Morris in the face, refusing to break eye contact. He snapped his fingers and someone grabbed me from behind, chucking my cane overboard. He dragged me towards a ladder hanging in the air and held me as we were whisked up into the air.

EMANUEL

My body ached with exhaustion as we ran from yet another group of angry sailors. Our ambush hadn't been planned. We had been trying to go home when we noticed a frenzied group pulling up a struggling figure out of the ocean. Adam had crashed the party, and Norman and I had no choice but to follow.

I held onto Norman's back as he cut through the water, reaching the boat and pulling us both up. I squeezed his hand one last time before we jumped into the fray. It had become my good luck charm. Besides, if either of us ever didn't make it back, I wanted to remember what his hand felt like in mine. Which wasn't gay. At all.

We pushed through the sailors. I frantically sawed through the net as Norman flashed his poisonous fins, forcing the humans to back away.

The figure inside - no older than ten (seriously, where were this kid's parents?) screamed. Someone yanked me back, holding me against his chest. Adam pulled the kid out of the net and shoved him into Norman's arms. Norman dove overboard as the sailor ripped a gun from the back of his pants and pointed it at Adam.

"You're gonna wish you were never born, freak." Adam reached for his sword as the gun popped. He fumbled his sword and stumbled to the deck. He didn't get up.

I screamed as blood started leaking out from underneath his torso. The man holding me laughed as I struggled against his grasp. The sailor holstered his gun as he walked up to Adam, turning him over with his foot.

Adam wheezed for breath as he feebly pressed his fingers against his abdomen, face paler than normal. The fisherman laughed.

No, I thought, tears gathering in my eyes. *Get up, Adam.*

"Someone should've got you a long time ago. Think we'll get a reward for a dead one?" he laughed. Adam winced as he turned his head towards the sailor's ankle.

"Tis but a flesh wound." He sank his teeth into the man's ankle. The sailor screamed as he jumped into the air, hopping on one foot as he cradled his ankle. Adam forced himself off the ground and grabbed one of his swords with his free hand. He stumbled to the hopping sailor, pushing him over the railing and into the ocean with the butt of the sword.

I took advantage of my captor's distraction to stomp his foot. He yelped, and I sank my teeth into his arm. He let go of me, and I raced over to Adam as he fell back to the deck. I ripped off my shirt and tied it around his stomach - tying it as tight as I could.

I lifted him off the ground and jumped over the railing, praying Norman was still down there. We hit the water with a thud, sinking instantly. Adam's body was heavy as rocks in my arm. I held my breath, waiting for him to phase, but he remained in human form, weakly kicking his legs. *Shit, his* legs.

With panic, I realized he couldn't breathe, and swam for the surface. He gasped for breath, shivering as he held onto me.

"Norman!" I screamed. "Someone, help!" Norman swam up beside us, still clutching the kid in his arms. The color drained from his face. He shoved the kid at me as he grabbed Adam.

"Hold on to me and hold your breath!" I grabbed the end of his tail as he pulled all three of us underwater, swimming frantically for the boat.

We pulled Adam up the ladder, and I rushed to try to make him comfortable as Norman started the boat.

"Just hold on buddy, we'll get you help once we get back, there are medical supplies on the boat, NORMAN HURRY!" I screamed. Adam grabbed my hand.

"It's fine, I'm fine," he whispered. *At least he can talk*, I thought. I squeezed his hand, smoothing his hair out of his face.

"It's okay, just keep talking to me, okay? You'll be okay."

"Tis just a flesh wound," he repeated, his hand trembling.

We arrived back at the island in chaos. Tom stood on the helm of his boat, pointing and screaming as merfolk dove into open water. Families scrambled to locate their children. Others gathered up all the weapons they could carry.

Norman and I carried Adam to the boat. Tom turned to us, chest heaving.

"Good, you three are back. I need you to . . ." His eyes went wide as he saw Adam. "What the hell happened?" he shouted.

"He got shot!" I said. "What's going on here?" Tom swore and dragged us to the cabin, where he started rummaging through the medical supplies.

"They took her. They took her. And they're coming here with a bomb."

"I'm sorry, *what?*" Norman demanded.

"Can you breathe?" Tom demanded. "Can you talk? Where does it hurt?" Adam nodded, pointing to his stomach. Tom ripped off the shirt, revealing the wound. "The bullet is still in there. I need to get it out." Adam paled more.

"You're an idiot," Tom said.

"I didn't get shot on purpose," Adam wheezed.

"Do you know how to remove bullets?" I asked.

"Yeah. You grab it with the tweezers and pull it out!" Tom snapped. "Hold him down. He can't move while I do this." I bit my lip as

400

I grabbed Adam's right wrist, pinning him to the ground. Norman grabbed the other. Adam squeezed his eyes shut as Tom went in with a pair of tweezers.

I shook as Adam's screams filled the cabin. He struggled weakly against my grip, sweat pouring down his face. Tom finally came up with a small metal bullet clutched in the tweezers.

"Got it!" Adam shivered on the ground as we wrapped his stomach in clean bandages. We transferred him to a bench and wrapped him in blankets. He promptly passed out.

"Is he going to survive?" I asked, the tears finally falling down my cheeks.

"We better fucking hope so. We have to go." Tom sprinted off, looking over the edge of the boat.

"Norman, go make sure everyone is out of the cave. We need to move."

"What the hell is going on?" Norman demanded. "Who took who? Who's headed here with a bomb?" Tom trembled against the boat railing, tears plopping softly to the deck.

"Morris took her. Amy. He took my Amy."

AMY

I had never been very religious, but I found myself praying in silence over the helicopter ride, listening for the sound of any other aircraft headed towards my island. Several guns remained pointed at me until we touched back down.

I was forced to march out, hobbling dangerously on my bad leg, with my hands up in the air. I held back my despair as I saw what building we had landed in front of. The fountain was still running. A familiar pink stain marred the concrete. The first protest flashed through my head.

"I thought merfolk weren't allowed to be here anymore," I said.

"What Arthur doesn't know won't hurt him." A cold nozzle against my back forced me to walk through the infamous double doors of Arthur's Aquarium. The inside was unrecognizable.

Children, teenagers, and adults all stared at me from the display tanks as we walked through the hallways. Some beat their hands against the glass or made rude gestures, but most floated listlessly, eyes hollow. Ribs pushed through skin. Scales dull and lifeless.

"This is what happened to all the freaks you and your band of pirates couldn't save," Morris said.

Oh my god, he's going to put me in a tank. I panicked, my legs pushing against the floor. The guards forced me forward. *What happens if they dump me in and I can't phase? How am I supposed to swim with one leg? I haven't gone swimming with human legs in years! I'll drown! How ironic.*

The guards pulled me to a stop in front of an empty display. I gasped as I recognized a figure lying on the floor, across the hall - the only one still in human form. They had tied him to the wall. Blood stained the carpet underneath him.

"Mr. Johns?" I whispered. My old student teacher from math class turned his head towards me, wincing and straining as he did so, and attempted to smile.

"If you can't phase, you'll end up next to him," Morris said. *Why can't he phase?* I thought.

"Or you could skip the water part and just put me there now," I muttered. Morris ignored me as the guards yanked me up a ladder and opened a hole in the lid. I squeezed my eyes shut and took a deep breath as they shoved me into the water.

I sank like a stone, my skin numb from the cold. I gasped in shock, losing most of my oxygen as my back hit the bottom of the tank. My legs started to tingle.

Oh no, no, no, no. I dug my fingers into the sand, bracing myself for the pain.

Ow, ow, ow, ow. It *hurt.*

I arched my back, my vision blurring at the edges as my legs burned. I let out a scream, losing the rest of my oxygen as my lower body convulsed. It went on for what felt like hours. *I'm going to drown before my body finishes changing,* I thought weakly. *This is so lame.*

I cried out in relief as sweet oxygen hit my veins. My gills frantically flared open and closed. I risked opening my eyes and saw my tail floating in the water. I gave an experimental flick, surprised when it obeyed my command.

It worked. I had phased. It *hurt,* but it had worked. I was still merfolk.

I curved it, surprised at how easy it was to move. The left side of my tail looked like it had warped in a 3D printer, but it didn't ache the same way my human leg did.

I turned my attention to the assholes outside the glass and did the only thing I could - flip them off. Morris grinned, raking his eyes over my body. I ignored my instinct to hide, swimming up to my full height. My tail was nothing to be ashamed of. Morris wasn't worth hiding from.

"Enjoy your stay. I'm sure your science buddies will be thrilled to see you again," he said. He took out his phone and held it up to his ear as he disappeared around the corner.

I sank to the bottom of the tank, wondering how long it would take the scientists to show up and start cutting me open again. Maybe they would start nice like last time and try interrogating me a few days before the torture started.

I turned to Mr. Johns, who smiled sadly. He said something, but he was too far away for me to hear him through the glass. *Do they know what Morris is doing?* I wondered. Do they know the Sanctuary is about to be destroyed? Is the government going to let Morris kill the rest of these merfolk too?

This is bad, I thought. *This is beyond bad.* How did we miss this many people? We should've been doing more. They had attacked *my own* high school.

Mr. Johns pushed himself into a sitting position against the wall, his legs dragging lifelessly. I had a sickening feeling I knew why he couldn't phase.

I'm so sorry, I mouthed. To my surprise, he grinned and held his finger to his lips. He reached into his pants and pulled out a walkie-talkie.

SAM

Karen and I sat on the ground of her cabin, surrounded by Petri dishes, and packs of blood falling out of the mini-fridge.

We had spent days testing various blood samples. With all of them - the same mysterious phenomenon had happened - the Curse didn't work. Except for one.

I nearly screamed with excitement as the sample stared back at me - the human blood glowing with the fluorescent indicator.

After days of work, we had finally managed to Curse a test tube.

"I don't understand, what's so different about this one sample?" Karen asked. I racked my brain as I turned the blood bag over in my hands. It had come from an eight-year-old boy with type B blood.

What could be different? Why would the Curse only work with this type of blood? According to the records my sister had stolen, Amy wasn't type B . . . but she had been ten years old.

"Karen, did any other donations come from kids?" I asked. We searched through the samples.

"A few, why?" I paced.

"Are there any other type Bs? Or Os?" She fished through the cooler and pulled one out. I grabbed for it and quickly set up another test tube, pricking my finger for what felt like the millionth time.

"What's your theory here, kid?"

"My blood type is B. And so far, it's only worked on a kid with type B blood. What if the blood types have to match? What if the merfolk blood can only infect you if you have the same blood type?"

"What about the age though?" she asked.

"That mural in the cave didn't show us rescuing people from ships, they showed us rescuing kids. What if . . . what if it only works on kids?" We held our breath as we watched the blood pool together in the tube. It began to shine.

"Oh my god. You were right!" Karen said, her eyes wide. "It only works on children. Children who have the same blood type as the merfolk." I vibrated with excitement, jumping up and down.

"Okay, but we still don't know how the DNA gets from cell to cell." I paced, drumming my fingers together. I took my blood sample and spilled it onto an agar dish, shoving it under the microscope. The glowing

DNA glared back at me. I carefully added a drop of human type B blood and watched.

I held my breath as one of my cells turned on its human neighbor. It stalked towards it and promptly engulfed it. The human cell struggled as it was pierced, and I gasped as a tiny section of glowing DNA was inserted into its nucleus. It stopped struggling and was immediately spat back out. Now glowing with the new DNA, it turned on another human cell, repeating the cycle over again.

"That's what I've been missing," I whispered. "It doesn't have a virus capsule. It doesn't *need* a virus capsule to replicate itself. It makes our cells the capsule." I stepped away from the microscope, jumping up and down. "Oh my god. We're not a different species. We're humans. We're just humans that got sick," I whispered.

"Um . . . Sam?" I spin around to see Karen staring out the grimy window.

"Do you understand what this means!" I shouted. "It means they can't treat us like animals. Genetically speaking, we are humans!" She waved at me, dropping under the window. I could sense the cold fear wash over her from across the room.

"Get down!" I blinked in confusion as the window shattered and bullets burst into the walls. She crawled over and dragged me down to my knees before one hit me. I covered the back of my neck as the smell of burning metal filled my nostrils.

The door burst inwards, and I didn't have time to scream as a bag was shoved over my head. Strong hands dragged me through the woods.

Karen screamed obscenities in the background as the hands tied my wrists and ankles together.

I was shoved into the back of what I could only assume was a boat based on the metal clang my body made. Another body was shoved down next to me, and the floor started rumbling. I could smell Karen but not my sister and that was when the panic set in.

"Terri! Where the hell is she? What did you do to her?" I screamed, thrashing against the ropes. Karen tried to talk but it came out muffled.

After what felt like hours, my body refused to struggle any longer, and I lay there stunned. Why had we been taken? If they just wanted money – there was no need to kidnap Karen as well – so it wasn't that. They must have figured out what we were researching. The odds of being kidnapped the same night as our big breakthrough was too much of a coincidence. But how had they known what we were doing?

My heart sank as I realized our research was most likely gone. Vanished. Destroyed by whatever humans realized we were getting too close to prove that merfolk should be treated as people.

The despair crushed me, making me gasp for breath. Karen wriggled over to me and attempted to hold my bound hands. She was trying to be calm for me, but I could feel her fury and fear.

I smelled the mainland as the boat rumbled to a stop. Strong hands jerked me to my feet, and when I tried to ask for my sister, someone punched the air out of my lungs. By the time I had enough oxygen to speak again, we were shoved into the back of a van. We rolled around the back as it raced through traffic.

It wasn't long before the van came to an unwilling stop, inertia slamming our bodies against the seats. More gunshots rang out, paired with shouting. The car rocked as the back was thrown open.

"They're both in here."

"Are they injured?"

"Doesn't look like it." Another body joined us in the back as the doors slammed shut again. I heard the body walking towards me and glared even though they couldn't see my face.

"Don't you dare touch me!" I seethed. To my surprise, they stopped. "What are you doing with us? Who are you? Where is my sister?" I demanded. They didn't respond.

Karen and I were separated once the van stopped. They cut my bonds loose and took the bag off my head but didn't let go of my arms as I was marched through what looked like the hallway of a boring office building. The air smelled like paper and polished wood. The two people holding me didn't smell like the original kidnappers.

"Where am I?" I asked again. No one punched me in the stomach that time. Instead, they opened a door and finally let go of my arms. I stumbled into a conference room with at least half a dozen strangers lining a dark oak table. The door closed behind me with a loud bang. One of the people at the table, an older woman in a white lab coat, stood up and nodded at the two men.

"Thank you. You may go now." They nodded and exited, but not before one grabbed my shoulder and whispered, "I'm sorry for your loss." They vanished before I could ask what they were sorry for. My heart raced with panic, wondering what I had lost.

I stared at the people sitting at the table and suddenly felt very dirty and sweaty. The strangers were all polished to a shine - wearing either a lab coat or a suit. They looked at me like I was a test answer key. I stood up straighter, my chin in the air.

"Who are you? Why have you brought me here?" The standing woman bowed her head.

"My name is Kirsten. I am - was - one of the scientists working for Arthur," she says. I automatically stiffened. She waved a hand over to the other people in coats. "These others were part of my team. We never worked with you or your sister but with Amy. After news of Arthur's lies came forward, we quit and started working with Mr. Duncan."

She held out her hand, and I reached out and grabbed it. I could feel her guilt and bitter determination to make things right. She was telling the truth. She motioned towards the other people.

"These others . . . are the lawyers working on the Merfolk vs. MCA case." I sucked in my cheeks and wished even more that I looked presentable. They stared at me through narrow eyes, hands folded primly on top of the table. I took an involuntary step back, my knees wobbly.

"Why . . . why am I here?" I ask.

"You and Karen figured it out," she said simply. I furrowed my brow. Our research was currently lying on the floor of Karen's cabin - probably shot to pieces.

"How do you know -"

"That cabin was bugged. We've been spying on you for a while. A lot of people have. That's how we knew to intervene tonight."

"Intervene?"

"Yes. The MCA was watching you as well. When they saw that you had scientific evidence to prove merpeople could be considered . . . well . . . people, they took action. So, we took action back." That explained the second round of gunshots. And the first.

"Wait . . . but all of our research . . . is it?" Kirsten nodded. She took a file folder out of her messenger bag and slid it over to me. My heart soared in relief as I recognized the papers. They had saved it after all. It wasn't lost.

"Oh, thank god," I said, hugging the papers to my chest. "You know what this means, right?" Kirsten nodded.

"With your permission, we can use those papers as official evidence in the Supreme Court case." I nodded, gladly shoving the papers back towards her.

I'm sorry for your loss. Wait, what had the man been sorry for? Nothing was lost, all the evidence was right here.

"Is Karen okay? Where is my sister?" I asked. This time, Kirsten hesitated. She looked down at the table, and then at her team.

"Karen is fine. She's being patched up now." I blinked. I could smell the dread oozing from across the room. My heart started to sink back down.

"And my sister?" I whispered.

"Well . . . when the MCA raided your cabin . . . your sister got between them. "We tried to revive her but . . . she didn't make it."

EMANUEL

Our Sanctuary was no more. Tom had told the merfolk to scatter. Morris couldn't bomb the whole ocean, but they stubbornly refused to swim out from underneath the boat as it chugged deeper into the open ocean.

I stood by the helm next to Tom and Marisol as she held back tears. They had been forced to leave her bleeding father behind in their rush to escape.

"What are we going to do?" she whispered. Tom shook his head.

"We need to get Amy back," he snarled. *But how?* I thought. *We no longer have a base of operations. We have no clue where Morris took her. And according to Morris' track record - Amy's probably already dead.* But I didn't dare say that.

"Have you heard anything from Terri?" Tom asked. I checked the laptop for the millionth time and shook my head. Yet another great omen - communication with the mainland had vanished. Terri - who usually responded in minutes - hadn't responded in hours. I ignored the pit of despair growing in my gut. Somehow, telling myself *at least you tried* didn't seem to make me feel better.

We're all going to die, I thought. *And no one is going to be freed. This was all for nothing.*

"We need to protest one last time," Marisol said suddenly. "And this one needs to pack a punch. It needs to really mean something. This may be our last chance before . . ." *Before we all die*, I finished. Tom slammed his hands down on the railing.

"I don't care about protesting!" he shouted. "I care about getting Amy back! How is a protest supposed to help us get her back?"

"A protest is going to help convince the country that she deserves to be free!" Marisol shot back. "What's the point of her being with you if she isn't free?" Tom's mouth snapped shut.

"Where would we even protest?" I asked.

"Go ask Adam. He's Protector. It should be his choice," Marisol said.

"He's still sleeping," I said. *At least he's alive*, I thought.

"Let's stop here for the night until we decide," Marisol said, walking back towards the cabin, leaving me with Tom. I tentatively put an arm around his shoulders.

"I'm sorry," I whispered. He shook underneath me. Amy and I had never been super close, but the thought of her all alone with her worst nightmare made me nauseous. I couldn't even imagine if it had been Adam or Norman in her place. I would be swimming back to the mainland.

"We'll get her back," I said.

"I know where we need to protest." We turned around to see Adam standing with Norman and Marisol, supporting himself with the Protector's staff.

"You should be resting," I protested. Adam ignored me.

"Arthur's Aquarium. I just have a feeling." Norman's jaw fell open.

"You just want us to die," he accused.

"Are you not brave enough to stand where she stood?" Adam asked coolly. Norman wisely shut up.

"Why there?" Tom asked.

"I know it seems questionable. But I feel it's only right that this ends where it started. Protesting there will be powerful. And besides, it's closed. No one should be there. It'll be easy to get to." Tom crossed his arms.

"You sure?" he asked.

"I'm sure," Adam said. "If we get there early in the morning, we should have a few hours before the Court publishes their decision." Tom nodded slowly.

"We'll head to shore then." Adam nodded, leaning heavily on the staff.

"I'm going to go lay back down." He hobbled off back to the cabin, Norman following him.

"I'll set course," Marisol said, leaving me with Tom, who sighed heavily, tangling his fingers in his hair.

"Hey, look at it this way. Maybe we'll all get killed and we won't have to worry about whether or not they free us," I joked. He laughed.

"Well, you've got some time to make sure your life is in order before you bite the dust." I laughed. There were so many things I had wanted to accomplish with my life before dying, but only one was remotely possible with the time we had. Tom side-eyed me, and I blushed.

"Norman's a good guy. Why are you so afraid?" I looked down at the floor. *Was it that obvious?*

"Humans and merfolk aren't supposed to fall in love," I whispered.

"Yeah . . . they're not." Tom and I made eye contact and burst out laughing. This whole mess could be traced back to Morris falling for Amanda. The whole damn island knew Tom and Amy were basically married. *But now they might never have the opportunity to tell each other,* I thought. The possibility was enough to bring tears to my eyes. *What's worse? Confessing my feelings only to die a few hours later? Or regretting it if we survive?* One look at Tom was enough to answer my question.

I found Norman sitting in the dark, alone in the bedroom.

"Whatcha doing?" I asked, trying not to let my voice squeak.

"Contemplating all the things I wanted to accomplish before I die," Norman said, staring at the ceiling. He turned his big brown eyes at me, and I subconsciously bit my lower lip. I forced myself to chuckle and sat down next to him.

"I was doing the same thing. Want to contemplate together?" Norman sighed.

"Did I ever tell you I wanted to be an astronaut when I was a kid?" he asked. I snorted.

"Not Norman wanting to be in a career that involves science. What a nerd," I teased. He rolled his eyes and shoved me.

"Being an astronaut is way cooler than being an environmental whatever. What, did you want to live in a shack on some random island too?"

"No! I wanted to live in a normal house. Have a family. Some kids." I forced another laugh. "And now I'm going to die without ever having kissed a guy. That's so depressing." Norman shifted and toyed with his hands.

"Yeah, that's pretty lame." *Come on, tell him you like him, you wimp!* Norman straightened and then slumped again, avoiding my eyes. "You know . . . I can take care of one of those problems for you." I froze, my confession stuck in my throat. Norman rambled on, his voice growing more and more high-pitched. "I mean – if you want. Just trying to do you a favor so you don't die like . . . a total lip virgin." I swallowed. I turned towards him and noticed despite the darkness that Norman's face was bright red. He snuck a glance at me, and I immediately averted my eyes.

"I . . . don't really know how to kiss a guy," I admitted softly. A few seconds ticked by, and Norman's hands found mine.

"I can . . . teach you." His voice was no longer mocking, but soft. Our eyes met again. His grip on my hand tightened as we searched each other for true intentions. *Is this offer real? Or has my secret crush been unreciprocated this whole time? If it's just for mercy – is it worth it?*

"Do you want to teach me how to kiss, Norman?" My voice came out huskier than I meant it to, and Norman's eyes dilated. I squeezed his hands, hoping he could feel my emotions. *Please, yes, kiss me, but only if you want to.* He leaned over and softly planted his lips on mine.

I melted into his touch, my hands rising to his face. He was gentle and slow, and my whole body filled with warmth and the aching desire for more. I had been dampening my feelings for Norman for weeks, and my gay desires in general for years – and this kiss was opening up a floodgate. Even though I had no idea how to kiss, I scooched closer and let out a little sigh as Norman's fingers tangled themselves in my hair. I felt him smile against me, and we both lost ourselves. The kisses got deeper and more frantic, our hands braver in exploring. Norman opened his mouth and the moan he made when I experimentally slid my tongue in was enough to grab him in my arms and bring us down to the mattress.

Then his tongue was in my mouth and my fingers were in his hair, and I really needed the Supreme Court to vote us free tomorrow because there was no way I could live out the rest of my life without this boy's kisses. Norman giggled against me and unraveled in my arms, holding onto me like a safety railing. I rolled over so I was leaning over the top of him, panting.

"Is this okay?" I whispered. He grabbed the front of my shirt and yanked me down towards him, sighing as I let my body weight crush him into the mattress. He stayed down until my lips discovered his neck, and then he flipped us over, hands exploring my chest as his legs tightened around my waist. I cradled his face in my hands, and even though I wasn't an empath, I could feel Norman's broken heart starting to heal.

By the time we were too tired to continue, we couldn't separate our hands as we lay on the mattress.

"So . . . not half bad for a baby gay, right?" I teased. And for the first time, Norman was too flustered to make a snappy remark.

TOM

We made it to shore by the time the sun was peeking over the horizon, and dozens of merfolk followed us as we started the walk to Arthur's aquarium.

Adam led the way despite our many protests. He had stopped bleeding but still winced as he leaned on the Protector's staff. His swords hung off of his belt loops, flashing dangerously in the sun.

Cars came screeching to a halt as we crossed over the main road. Phones came out of windows as people pointed. Others yelled and made rude gestures.

"Why are there so many cars out this early in the morning?" Marisol asked. When we turned the corner to the aquarium, I quickly saw why.

The steps were already filled with people. Most of them were merfolk in varying conditions of disarray. Some sat on the steps, soaking wet. Humans raced around, shouting. Amid the chaos, the aquarium doors stood busted open, humans carrying other merfolk out in their arms. I recognized one.

"Is that the math teacher?" Marisol asked. We stared as the humans carrying him gently set him down on the grass. They looked no older than Adam or Emanuel, and they all had the mark of the Cursed painted on their faces.

Other spectators had surrounded the building, filming and watching in awe. Our crowd watched, equally as confused.

"What the hell? Why are there so many merfolk here? I thought Arthur was banned from keeping any more of us?" Norman demanded. Among the sea of bodies, I saw several that weren't being attended to. Their rifles had been stripped away, leaving them in their black body MCA armor.

There's no way.

I raced to the front steps, grabbing a random high schooler.

"What the hell is going on?" Everywhere I looked, merfolk were being lifted out of display tanks and helped to the ground. The high schooler ignored me. I ran through the hallways and almost ran past her. I skidded to a halt, my jaw hitting the carpet.

Amy slammed her webbed hands against the glass, her tail flicking angrily in the water. Her blue eyes glowed - her dirty blonde hair floating in a halo in the light. Despite the chaos, my body found time to blush. She was gorgeous. Not in the dainty, pretty way - the fierce scary way.

"Get me the fuck out of here!" she shouted through the glass. I sprinted up the staircase beside the tank and threw open the lid. I reached into the water and pulled her out. She was heavier than she looked.

She flopped out onto the lid, gills flaring. Tears flowed down my cheeks.

"I'm so glad you're safe -" She cut me off as she hunched over, grabbing my t-shirt. Her fist tightened as she groaned, her whole body going tense. Sweat beaded on her forehead as she phased, and she collapsed on my chest, panting.

"That . . . fucking . . . hurts," she gasped. I wrapped my arms around her, crushing her.

"I'm so glad you're safe," I sobbed.

"Don't count your chickens before they hatch," she muttered. I let go and helped her to her feet, which proved difficult. Her bad leg wobbled dangerously as she made her way down the stairs. "Don't suppose you brought a cane for me?" she wheezed, nearly falling to her knees at the bottom. I helped her up, letting her lean on my shoulder as we walked back outside. The crowd cheered at our arrival. Adam laughed in relief, raising the staff high into the air.

"Through hell or high water!" he shouted.

AMY

I allowed myself to laugh in relief after I found my balance. Tom grabbed me in another rib-shattering hug. I pushed him away as gently as I could, holding his face. *He's still alive*, I thought. *He's safe.*

"Can you two stop making out and explain what the hell is going on?" Norman shouted.

"It's a long story. Morris made this the MCA's base of operations. He's been keeping all the captured merfolk here. Luckily, he didn't plan on our high school fighting back after he took their favorite math teacher." I motioned to where Mr. Johns lay in the grass, surrounded by a protective ring of his students. "When he was captured, they didn't catch his walkie-talkie, and he was able to radio for help. What are you guys doing here? Is the Sanctuary safe?"

"We fled. Marisol and Adam decided that we needed to do one last protest before the Court decision. Adam picked here. Something about this ending where it started."

"I told you I had a feeling!" Adam shouted, standing on top of the fountain. My eyes zeroed in on his stomach.

"Did he get hurt?" I demanded.

"He got shot - but he's fine. Listen - where is Morris? Where are all the MCA people?"

"Haven't seen any more. The high schoolers made pretty quick work of all the guards that were here. And I haven't seen Morris since yesterday." I grinned as Tom held my hand and stood beside me. The doors closed behind us - all the merfolk free once more. The high schoolers had formed protective rings around the most injured while the rest had stood to join the ones from the Sanctuary.

All together, we lined up in front of the building. Adam stood on the edge of the fountain, the Protector's staff held high in his hand, one of his swords in the other, the look in his eyes fierce enough to stop a lion in its tracks.

No sooner had he settled into place than a black and white figure pushed their way through the gathering crowd.

"Move!" the figure shouted, breaking free. "That's my brother!" Adam dropped his sword as the figure scooped him up in a hug and spun him around, tears pouring from his face.

"Ethan?" Adam sputtered. The figure laughed and nodded.

"I just got home!" Tom and I exchanged a confused glance.

"Is that a Mormon?" he whispered.

"I don't understand, what are you doing here?" Adam demanded.

"We heard what was happening on the radio on the way home from the airport. I told them to bring me straight here. No way was I gonna miss this," he grinned.

"But . . . have you even been released yet? Isn't this . . . you know . . . definitely not in the white handbook?" The missionary shrugged.

"What are they gonna do, send me home? I've been praying for you and your friends, brother. I am here with you, through hell or high water." Adam covered his mouth with his hands, and I knew he would be crying if he could.

"I didn't . . . I didn't know what you thought about me," he whispered.

"There were certain things I couldn't do or say as a missionary. But as far as I'm concerned, I am home, and helping you and your friends is my new mission. If my brother is not free, then I am not free."

"I don't want you to get hurt," Adam said, uncertainty creeping into his voice. "This is dangerous."

"Do not fear, brother. God is with us." With that, the missionary picked up Adam's sword and stood beside him. Adam unsheathed his other sword, and they crossed the blades. I couldn't help but smile at the odd duo. Tom squeezed my hand, and I looked up to see even more people walking up from the crowd. They stood beside Adam and Ethan, slowly fanning out around the building in a protective circle. Some of them carried signs - others swords or protective shields. Several of them passed around boxes of tranq guns. Some of them were families. Some of them were people I knew from school. Many of them had painted their faces.

They kept flowing in until the merfolk were surrounded by a wall several humans thick. The air pulsed with energy. I tucked a tranq gun in my pants as Tom was handed a sign.

News trucks pulled up in the distance, reporters spilling out. Cameras scanned the crowd, broadcasting us to the world. The crowd began to chant.

"Free the merfolk, free the merfolk, free the merfolk." Tom and I lifted our sign high above our heads, joining the cry.

*Mer*PEOPLE.

Other cars pulled up behind the newscasters. Their doors opened and dogs leaped out, running right for us, snarling and frothing. Norman let go of my hand and pushed his way through the crowd, fins out.

The cries for freedom turned to screams as the dogs attacked - humans and merfolk alike. Ethan and Adam broke their stance and went on defense, using themselves as shields. Norman used his arms like pinwheels, a dog going down with every swipe of his poisonous fins.

The men in the trucks weren't far behind. They hid behind large shields and padded armor, guns just barely poking out. One of those guns popped, and the crowd dissolved into chaos.

I looked at Tom one last time, memorizing the curve of his face.

"Go," I said. "I'll be fine."

"I'll come back for you," he said, tears filling his eyes. I nodded, my words stuck in my throat as he let go of my hands and rushed into the crowd.

I stayed still as I unholstered my tranq gun and started picking off MCA members. There were dozens of them, and even more dogs, but we still vastly outnumbered them. If we could get rid of them quickly, maybe we would be okay.

My world lurched to the side as a warm body collided with me, knocking the tranq gun out of my hand. I lifted my arm not a second too late as teeth lunged for my throat, paws scrabbling at my legs. I ignored the burning of sharp teeth sinking into my arm as I tried to reach my fallen gun with my other hand.

The dog was knocked to the side by my fallen sign. I gasped for breath as a stranger grabbed my gun and shot the dog for me.

"Thank you," I gasped as I scrambled back to my feet. The stranger didn't stay to chat as they shoved the gun into my chest and ran off, hitting more dogs with the sign. I winced as blood dripped down my arm. I switched the gun to my nondominant hand and kept picking off bodies. My heart pounded in my ears, all of my senses on high alert as I worked to keep myself alive.

Off in the distance, Norman screamed like a maniac as he stabbed people and dogs left and right. Emanuel's nose was gushing blood. Adam radiated rage. Ethan was on the ground. Tom was nowhere to be seen.

I buried the panic in my chest and hobbled forward, trying to get a better vantage point. The air was thick with blood and chaos. I picked off an MCA officer just before they shot Norman in the head. Rage filled me, giving me new energy as I searched the crowd.

We cannot die here, not after all we've been through.

The tide started to shift. More dogs and unconscious bodies littered the ground than attacked us. Ambulances sounded in the distance. I picked off another MCA officer who had unwisely gone after Mr. Johns and his ring of protective students.

"LEAVE US ALONE!" I screamed. Cop cars joined the din, screeching to a halt beside the news vans and ambulances. They poured out, waving their hands over their heads.

"PUT DOWN YOUR WEAPONS, IT'S OVER!" one of them shouted. It wasn't clear who exactly they were shouting at. I made eye contact with one of them, keeping my gun aimed at them. A familiar stranger spilled out of his passenger seat. I let my aim falter.

"Mr. Duncan?" *He's alive?* He sprinted to me, beet red in the face, his arm in a sling.

"Amy, tell them to stop, it's over," he panted.

"What? What's over?" I demanded.

"They voted. It's over. You're free . . ." The rest of his words faded into the background as I processed the first two.

You're free.

"We're free?" I echoed, grabbing him by the shoulders. There was no way. It had to be a trick – something to get us to stop fighting so we could all be caught. "Are you sure?" He nodded frantically. My heart dared to soar through my chest. For the first time, my fingers trembled out of joy.

We're free.

It worked.

We saved everyone.

The cops behind Mr. Duncan jumped on top of their cars, shouting the news into bullhorns.

"STAND DOWN. PUT DOWN YOUR WEAPONS." I left Mr. Duncan, racing to find Norman in the crowd. He startled as I grabbed him, nearly stabbing me with his fins.

"You're the loudest one here," I said. "Tell everyone to stop." He raised his eyebrow.

"Why on Earth would I -"

"Just do it!" He cupped his hands around his mouth and screamed.

"EVERYONE STOP!" People paused throwing punches to look for the source of the noise. The chaos slowly died down, attention on the cop with the bullhorn.

"As of 7:04, the Supreme Court reached a decision. They have declared the capture of any merperson to be unconstitutional!" The cop shouted. The crowd stayed silent. All around us, hands went to mouths, uncertain glances exchanged. Suspicious whispers raced through the crowd. The ground rocked under my feet.

What made them change their minds?

"It's true!" someone shrieked, holding up their phone in the air. "We're free!" The crowd dissolved into screams of joy. Norman himself grabbed me in a hug before racing off into the crowd. I wobbled on my legs as I watched the celebrations. I wanted to collapse to the ground in relief, but my body felt frozen in shock.

We did it. We actually did it.

A smile slowly broke over my face. *I have to find Tom.* I pushed my way through the crowd, trying to find him amid all the happy tears and celebrations.

They were interrupted as a series of gunshots rang out.

I instinctively dropped to the ground as the crowd went silent again. As everyone looked around for the source of the shots, I finally smelled Tom in the crowd. I stood up and turned around, only for my heart to drop to my feet.

Morris had Tom by the hair, a gun held to the back of his head.

"Amy. How good to see you again," he smiled. The crowd parted around us. *Oh no, not him, anyone but him.* I clenched my fists.

"It's over, Morris," I whispered. "We're free. There's not a damn thing you can do about it."

"And you were *free* before the world knew what you were. I don't care what the Supreme Court says. You're all monsters."

"Morris, I'm sorry your girlfriend didn't tell you what she was. She was scared. She was following rules she shouldn't have had to follow. But she wasn't dangerous until you killed her baby. *You* made her the monster she was." Morris' eyes glinted with tears.

"Don't tell me what I did or didn't do!" he growled, jostling Tom.

"Say the word, Amy," Adam hissed, appearing out of the crowd, swords flashing as he stepped closer to Morris. Morris dug the gun deeper into the back of Tom's head.

"Here's what's going to happen. Everyone is going to take five big steps back and put their weapons down, or your little boyfriend is going to die," Morris shouted. I dropped my tranq gun and hobbled five steps back. Adam reluctantly did the same. The cops kept their guns drawn.

"This isn't going to end well for you sir. Drop the gun," one of the cops threatened.

"This isn't going to end well for Tom if you don't back off," Morris barked. The cops slowly backed away, whispering into radios by their shoulders.

"Now, I want Wilson on her knees. Hands behind your head," Morris said.

"Let him go first," I snarled. Morris shoved Tom forward but kept the gun trained on his back. I grit my teeth as I slowly got down on my knees, my bad leg screaming in protest. Morris smirked before aiming the gun at me.

"Now, you're going to do one more thing for me before I kill you," he whispered. "You're going to admit that you've been a monster the whole time. That you've manipulated my nephew. That your whole species is dangerous. That without you – Tom and all of your other friends would've been safe and sound."

Seriously, I get my freedom back only to have to spend my final moment lying? What kind of a sick power trip is this guy on?

"Her lying to you isn't going to make you feel better. Like it or not, it's your fault Amanda murdered all those kids," Tom retorted, lifting his head off the ground and reaching for me. I winced as Morris placed a foot on his nephew's back, aiming the gun at him once more. Behind him, Adam had slowly started creeping up again, a sword in his grasp. Morris hadn't noticed. Adam nodded at me.

Keep him busy.

"Fine. I am dangerous," I said. "I hurt my friends, my family, those closest to me. I lied to them for years."

"Keep going!" Morris hissed.

"I-I manipulated Tom into doing things for me. He never wanted to help me in the first place - I made him. I made lots of people help me." Morris took his foot off Tom's back and took a step closer to me.

"And?"

"And . . . I'm the reason my best friend died." I had to force the words out of my mouth. Morris smirked and aimed the gun at my head.

"Doesn't it feel nice to be honest? Now you can die with peace of conscience." Tom's eyes went wide. Adam raised his sword.

"Killing me won't change the past," I said, staring Morris right in the eyes. "But by all means - knock yourself out."

"NO!" Tom screamed. A gunshot sounded but from the wrong direction.

I looked to the side to see a skinny shell of a man in the crowd holding a pistol. I would recognize that smell anywhere. It was the same smell that had given me endless nightmares and made me lose my best friend. The air rose on my arms as we made eye contact. His eyes were sunken in, his face gaunt and pale.

I'm sorry, Arthur mouthed, lifting the gun. Morris cursed and aimed back at him. People screamed and dove out of the way as gunshots popped. I held my hands over my head. Out of the corner of my eye, I saw Arthur drop to the ground. Morris bellowed as blood leached from his side. Adam lunged forward with the sword. Morris screamed as the tip of the sword appeared where his heart should have been.

The world went silent as Morris collapsed to the ground, eyes wide and glassy. Adam stood behind him, the blood splatter almost matching his freckles. Tom scrambled to his feet and grabbed me, running his hands over my face.

"Oh my god, are you okay?" I could only nod as I watched Morris spasm on the ground in front of me. Tom turned around, holding me behind him.

"Burn in hell," he hissed. Blood trickled down Morris' mouth. He lifted his gun one last time. Tom staggered against me as it popped.

Time slowed down as Tom slid to the ground, holding his chest. I hovered over him, pressing my shaking hands against the hole in his chest as he struggled to breathe.

No.

Blood gushed through my fingers as I pressed them against the wound, the world swaying around me. *It's too much blood, it's too much blood.* Tom's face grew pale.

"Amy," he croaked.

"No, no, no, you're going to be okay, just stay with me," I pleaded. He smiled, holding his bloody hand against my face.

"You're free now." I shook my head.

"Not without you, no, no, no, Tom stay with me," I begged. He smiled, tears in his eyes. His hand fell from my face.

"Tom, no." I leaned my head on his chest, my body wracked with sobs. "Tom, don't go, please, I can't do this without you." His skin grew cold.

"I love you," he whispered. Tears slipped past my eyes.

"I love you too." His hand fell away from my hair. More tears pushed past my eyes, and with every tear, my body grew heavier. My vision grew dark. The colors and sounds sounded farther and farther away.

"Move, paramedics coming through!"

"Amy, can you hear me?"

"She's crying. Like . . . *crying* crying." My head swam. My body went limp, and everything faded to black.

EMANUEL

"All right, all finished. Just keep this on and you'll be good as new in a few weeks."

"What if I need to blow my nose?" I asked. The nurse smiled and patted me on the shoulder.

"Try not to. It'll hurt."

"Em?" I turned to see Norman peeking around the door.

"I'll leave you two," the nurse said, brushing past him. He quickly entered the room, holding onto his arms. I instinctively held out my hand and he took it, sitting on the stool beside my bed.

"You look like you've seen a ghost," I said.

"People keep staring at me. It's weird," he muttered. He scanned my face. "How are you feeling?"

"It's just a broken nose, Em. I'll be fine," I promised. He smiled and looked down. We both noticed that we were holding hands and averted our eyes. I swallowed, feeling my stomach twist with a different bunch of nerves.

We were both alive, and there was no going back to undo the previous night's make-out session. What do you do when you live your last day only to realize you have more to live? *Change the subject.*

"Have you seen Adam yet?" I asked. He shook his head.

"He's with Ethan and his parents, waiting for him to wake up. I didn't want to disturb them." I nodded.

"Ethan will be okay, right?"

"Yeah, the bullet just grazed him. He'll be fine."

"What about Wilson? Is she awake yet?"

AMY

The smell of bleach made me force my eyes open. Everything was blurry - no - just whitewashed. Something tickled my nose, and when I tried to lift my hand to scratch it - my whole body screamed in protest.

Did I die? I forced my hand up and felt my face. The tickler was a nose tube. I sat up and looked around the room. Blue curtains framed my bed. Machines beeped around me. Another tube went up into my arm.

For a heart-stopping moment, I thought I was back at the lab. But then I remembered what had happened. My heart dropped for a different reason.

Tom.

I ripped the tube and IV out of my arm. The machines beeped angrily as I hauled myself over the edge of my bed, sprawling gracelessly to the floor. I groaned as I fought to get my legs to cooperate with me, but they felt like lead. I hauled myself up by the railing as a nurse burst through the curtain, eyes wide.

"Ms. Wilson, please, lay back down." She reached for me. I shied away, grabbing for my cane that wasn't there.

"Don't touch me!" I shouted. She stopped, eyes wide. I tried to figure out how to push my way past her on my legs which barely worked as another figure burst through the curtain.

"Amy! You're awake!" Norman gently pushed the nurse out of the way and held his hand out to me. My grip on the railing shook.

"Where is he?" I whispered.

"He's fine, Amy, I promise. He's in surgery right now. They're removing the bullet - but he's going to be just fine." I collapsed in relief.

"He's alive?" I whispered. Norman nodded.

"Why don't you sit?" he suggested gently. I let him touch me and ease me back down onto the edge of the bed. The nurse watched awkwardly until Norman shot her a dirty look. I wrapped my arms around myself, feeling naked in the paper-thin hospital gown. Every blink felt like swimming through concrete.

"How are you feeling?" Norman asked. I struggled to remember what happened - but all I could think of was red blossoming across Tom's chest.

"What happened?" I asked. *He was bleeding out. His skin went cold. How is he going to be okay?* Norman took a deep breath.

"Do you want the long answer or the short answer?"

"The long one." Norman sighed.

"Well, we're free." I vaguely remembered a cop screaming that message into a bullhorn and my heart soaring out of my chest. Norman didn't seem to remember the moment too fondly.

"You don't seem too thrilled about being free," I said. Norman chuckled.

"I – I just wish there was a better reason," he whispered. He shook his head. "Anyways, the cops told us we were free, but Morris attacked you and Tom. He made you admit that you were dangerous. Adam stabbed him in the chest. Morris shot Tom. You cried." *Is that why my body felt like I had been hit by a truck?* Norman paused in his explanation to wiggle his eyebrows. I flushed red.

"We never did *that*," I protested weakly.

"I know. I'm just teasing you. There's apparently a lot about mating and merfolk we don't understand," he said, turning gloomy again.

"Anyways, Tom is in surgery. So is Ethan – he got grazed by a bullet. Emanuel broke his nose, but he'll be fine. Adam is a mess, but he's still alive. Sam . . ." Norman trailed off for a moment. "Sam's alive," he finally said. "But . . . we lost Terri." My mind spun as it tried to process the new information. Sam and Terri were on Baldwin Island with Karen, not at the rebellion. How could they have been hurt?

"Sam figured it out," Norman said. "She figured out what causes the Curse. The MCA had been spying on them, so when they realized what she had done, they raided the cabin to destroy her research. And they shot Terri before Duncan's crew rescued them." My mouth went dry.

I had never known the little girl especially well, but she had been the glue for our entire operation. Without her, we would have never been able to rescue anyone.

And now she was gone.

I swallowed. Poor Sam. Tom is never going to forgive himself when he hears about this.

"Wait . . . why would the MCA care about Sam's research?" I asked. "Why would they want to destroy it?"

"That's what saved us," Norman said. "The thing that changes us isn't technically blood . . . it's a virus, inside our blood." I blinked, suddenly very aware of the veins and arteries under my skin. Norman scoffed. "We were never a different species. We were just humans who got sick. The only difference between you and me was that I was infected at conception. You were infected at ten years old." I shrugged.

"So?"

"So? The only reason the Supreme Court voted us free is because we're genetically human – not because they actually thought we deserved freedom. They're just scared of what would happen to them if they ever got infected," Norman said bitterly. I laughed.

"Yeah, because getting Cursed is something that happens super often. It's not like merfolk are going around Cursing humans on purpose," I said.

"It doesn't matter. They set us free because they had to – not because they wanted to. We're still freaks of nature to them," he muttered.

I surprised myself by reaching out to hold his hand. It felt like acid was radiating from his skin.

"Hey. We're free. If humans still think we're freaks – that's on them," I said.

"I don't want to be thought of as a human who got sick," Norman whispered. "I just want to be merfolk. That's it." At the moment, I didn't care why I was free. If having some crazy virus meant I had equal rights again – then so be it.

But Norman and the other Naturals had spent their whole lives believing they were a different species – a different species with its own culture rules and history. Boiling all of that down to a virus made the whole thing seem . . . pointless.

"It'll be okay," I whispered. "We're still merfolk. How we got this way doesn't change that." The look in his eyes said he didn't believe me.

A few hours later, I was allowed to go visit Tom. I shuffled through the cold hallway, praying my gown wouldn't tear as I crutched along. Nurses and doctors turned to stare at me. TVs blared from all angles, showing footage of the rebellion.

A nurse opened the door to Tom's room, and my heart collapsed with relief. He smiled up at me from his bed, his chest covered in white bandages. I closed the door behind me and let my hands shake.

"I thought I lost you," I whispered.

"Not yet," he whispered. I all but ran to his bedside and threw my arms around him, ignoring his wheeze of pain as I crushed him in my arms. The achiness from my bones seemed to melt away at our touch.

"I can't breathe," Tom gasped. I hastily pulled away, settling for just holding his hand as he caught his breath. He looked down at our entwined fingers and smirked.

"I knew it. I knew you were secretly in love with me this whole time," he teased. I rolled my eyes.

"I thought merfolk had to have sex to be mated?" he asked. "Is there stuff we did on that island that I forgot about?" I flushed scarlet and shook my head.

"Definitely not. There's apparently a lot about mating and merfolk that we don't understand yet," I said, echoing Norman's words from earlier. I slowly explained the events of the last few hours to Tom.

"You're . . . you're just *sick?* That's it? That's all it was the *whole* time, just a virus?" he demanded. I nodded.

"So, what, they just argued that because it's a sickness, hunting you guys down and discriminating against you is a HIPAA violation now?" I cracked a smile, Norman's cynical words from earlier playing through my head. *They're only doing this to save their skin. They don't want to be treated like us if they ever get infected.*

"It's illegal to discriminate against people with certain illnesses or disabilities," I said. Tom looked me up and down.

"You don't look sick."

"I don't feel sick," I said. "But at this point – I don't care what they call it as long as we have our rights back."

SAM

I sat in a folding chair by the nurse's station as they went about patching up my friends. I saw Amy shuffling to Tom's room, but she hadn't noticed me.

My body felt as numb as the chair. I kept waiting for Terri to sign something for me to translate or make a rude gesture to the nurse who kept giving me strange looks, but she was gone. I hadn't protected her, and now she was gone.

I curled up my knees to my chest, half-listening to the blaring TVs. They kept referencing my accomplishments over and over again, but the praise felt empty. Who cared if I had figured out a way to prove that merfolk had equal rights to humans if my baby sister wasn't here?

I could hear Norman complaining about how he wasn't sick, he was just merfolk, from across the ward. At this point, I didn't care if I was sick or not. I just wanted to turn back the clock and save my sister before it was too late.

Footsteps sounded in front of me, and I looked up to see a familiar ugly Hawaiian shirt.

Mr. Duncan smiled weakly down at me, his arm in a sling. I waited for him to apologize for my sister's death or some other half-assed pleasantry.

"We need to talk." He pulled me into an empty room and shut the door behind us. He was breathing hard as if he had run all the way here. Stress radiated from his troubled eyes. I instantly tensed.

"What's wrong?" Even as I asked the question, I wasn't sure if I could handle anything else going wrong. I wanted to curl up in a ball at the bottom of the ocean and bury myself.

"Have you been listening to the news?" he asked. I shook my head.

"Things are not good. Don't get me wrong – some humans are happy that your species is free. Many others are not." I shrugged. Why did I care? Let the humans be upset. There was nothing they could do about it.

"Tell them to cry a river," I muttered. Mr. Duncan deflated.

"Humans are demanding that there be precautions taken to make sure that no humans become Cursed."

"Seems pretty simple. Tell them not to let their children stab themselves with vials of merfolk blood."

"They want a vaccine. A cure." The ground wavered underneath me. I looked up, forgetting to breathe. Norman's paranoia suddenly made perfect sense.

"They want a vaccine?" I repeated. Mr. Duncan nodded.

"And since you discovered the virus to begin with . . . I think you would be the best person to . . ." His words faded away as I clenched my fists. The humans wanted a vaccine – just to be sure that they could never become one of us on accident. They didn't want their children to become one of those *freaks*.

My head spun as I thought of the repercussions. Vaccines had wiped out entire viruses before – made them extinct. Would a vaccine wipe out our entire species? Or would it do the opposite? Would a vaccine only make the merfolk virus mutate and grow stronger until nothing could stop it? How soon would they start demanding an actual cure for those already infected? How long until the government made the vaccine mandatory?

"Sam, are you listening?" Mr. Duncan asked.

"You want me to make a vaccine for my *species*?" I demanded, my hands shaking.

"I want you to be able to give people a choice," Mr. Duncan said. "Can't you agree that no one should have to go through this if they don't want to?" I thought of Amy, who for the most part, had seemed to hate being a merfolk. If she could take a shot to reverse the virus, would she do it?

"What if people want to be like this?" I asked. "We aren't just sick . . . we're an entire culture. We have incredible abilities that no humans could ever dream of!"

"Look, I'm not asking you to make a decision right now. But scientists all over the world are about to jump on this – studying every aspect of your species. If you work for me, I'll make sure that you and your kind stay protected. Treated fairly."

"Work for you?"

"I want you to work for my biotech company. If you do, I'll pay for your college – every cent. I'll get you whatever supplies you need. You can study whatever you want – I'll fund it. I'm just asking you to consider . . . one day . . . a vaccine. A cure."

The possibility of unlimited funding almost made me forget about my sister. Mr. Duncan was giving me an opportunity I had scarcely dared to dream of. I could figure out everything – how mating worked. How the viral DNA forced our cells to morph. How we were empathic.

All at the cost of thinking about creating a vaccine.

"No other merfolk get involved unless they strictly volunteer. No bribes. No prizes," I said. Mr. Duncan nodded.

"Deal." He extended his hand. My breath caught in my throat. I had known from the moment he showed up that he had an alternative motive. It hadn't mattered back then – we were desperate for help.

He looked so innocent. Like a concerned father who just wanted to help, just wanted to keep everyone safe.

I felt no malice as I took his hand, but I couldn't shake the feeling that he wanted me to make the vaccine more than he was letting on. But I would make sure he couldn't go back on his word. I would read every word of whatever paperwork he wanted me to sign – and at the first red flag – I would leave. He wasn't going to force me to study anything I didn't want to. And he wasn't going to force me to make a vaccine.

Still, shaking his hand felt like Eve taking an innocent bite of apple. *I'm smarter than Eve*, I told myself. *I won't let him take advantage of me.*

"Deal," I whispered.